FOUNDER

DEAD HOLLOW TRILOGY (BOOK TWO)

JUDY K. WALKER

Cover design by Robin Ludwig Design Inc. http://www.gobookcoverdesign.com/

ISBN: 978-1-946720-02-3

1
___

"She shouldn't have called you."

He could barely make out his wife's face in the dark car. She didn't reply, but he heard her sigh as she adjusted her hands on the steering wheel, emerging from one sharp turn to enter another that veered in the opposite direction. His body swayed slightly with the car. The world was gray in their headlights—asphalt and trees, subdued double lines that should be yellow. Or maybe it was him, the grayness. Sometimes he lost his colors. Not completely, but just enough to notice their absence.

"I was fine," he continued, rubbing his sore hand, but she didn't respond. "I am *fine*."

Finally, she glanced in his direction, before her eyes returned to the mountain road. "No, you're not."

Her voice was sad. Why was her voice always sad lately? "What do you want me to do?" he asked. "And don't say, go to that place."

"What place?" she asked, now with a spark of anger. "Prison? Or the morgue? Because that's where you're gonna end up. That's where you're headed now. Is that what you want? To leave me a widow?"

"No! Of course not. But he was—"

"He was what? Tell me. Tell me what he was doing that made you swing a chair at the back of the man's head."

He felt a grinding frustration inside, one that went beyond his worn teeth into his very bones. "I wasn't drunk."

She laughed, short and harsh. "I know you weren't. That's what scares me."

He struggled to get the thoughts, the words, to line up in his head. He'd been so careful about what he said lately, but he had to tell her. She had to know. And yet, as he spoke, the anger built in him again.

No, not anger—fear.

"He was going to hurt you," he said, and he heard the same grinding in his voice that he felt in his bones.

She glanced toward him. "What do you mean?"

"I could hear him, wanting to hurt you."

His wife sounded as though she didn't have enough air to speak, forcing the words out from the bottom of her lungs. "How did you hear him? Who was he talking to?"

He paused. "He wasn't talking out loud. But I heard him. I heard the things he wanted to do to you, in my mind."

"Jesus," she whispered.

She didn't believe him. She loved him, but she didn't believe him. That's why he had to protect her.

"I can't do this anymore," she said, still barely above a whisper. "It'd be one thing if it were just us, but I have to think about—"

"I won't leave you."

She glanced over, and he thought he saw tears shining, reflecting the light from the console. "I don't want you to. But I'll be safe with Iris while you're gone. And it won't be long, just until we can get your medication right again. I promise."

"It's real! I swear to God, this is real!"

"Sweetheart, I know you think it is." She paused, and the car slowed as she approached the Dead Hollow curve.

"It is real!" he exploded, raising his arms toward the heavens. "I have to stop him! If I'm not here, he will rape you and kill you and—"

In that moment, he saw her face turn toward him, her beautiful face. He saw it in the headlights of an oncoming vehicle as it rounded the turn, on the wrong side of the center lane.

"Charlotte—"

But did he actually speak her name? Did he hear it, before her eyes grew wide and she jerked the wheel? Before the car pitched and the sound of brakes—theirs and the other vehicle's—ripped through the air? Did he hear himself say her name before she screamed?

Their brakes dragged and clawed at the road, but the car struck the guardrail anyway, whipping his head but barely slowing them down. The front tires left the asphalt, his stomach lurched, and they were airborne. Then it all became a jumble of sound and sensation: tree limbs snapping, glass and metal breaking, the impact of the ground, of his head against the side window, of a tree, and then a second one, and then suddenly realizing that they'd stopped even though the sounds kept ringing in his ears.

The driver's side was mashed against a tree trunk, but somehow the headlight on his side still sent a weak beam through the forest, visible through the space that used to be the windshield. His head itched. He reached up to scratch his temple, but scratching hurt, and his hand came away sticky.

"Charlotte?" He still wasn't certain if he was speaking out loud. There was something wrong with his hearing. That must be why he didn't hear her answer. He could make out her shape next to him, head back and immobile, but he couldn't reach her.

Seat belt. *His fingers fumbled with the release, and he could feel the noises of fear and frustration emanating from his chest and tearing through his throat. He felt but couldn't hear the click as the buckle came free. The shoulder strap got hung up around his head, and his body shook with exasperation as he tore it loose.*

"Charlotte."

Her name was on his lips—he could feel it there—whether he heard it or not. He leaned across the gap between the bucket seats until he could feel her breath on his face. It didn't smell right, and it came out heavy and uneven. She was in pain. Her face was a pale blur, with patches interrupted by darkness, and he was afraid to touch her without seeing where and how she was hurt.

Dome light. *The roof had buckled some toward the windshield, but was mostly where it belonged overhead. It hurt to lift his arm, and he couldn't find the little switch for the light. He tried to open his door, but it stuck until he gave it a mighty push with both legs.*

Miraculously, the light came on. And he saw what he feared most in the world. Her pallor, the dark blood staining her face and shining wet below her chest. And something else. A kind of shimmering... She's dying.

"No!" He stepped backwards from the car, clutching at the door as his legs buckled. From his knees, he turned and looked behind them, up over the bank in the direction of the road. There was a glow there. Headlights? And a figure silhouetted against them.

"Help me! Please, help me!" he screamed. The figure turned, hesitated. "If you leave, I will find you! I swear to God, I will!"

His throat felt so raw, surely the person must have heard him, but the figure disappeared. Moments later, the light left as well. A sob rocked his chest before he climbed back in the car.

"Charlotte, sweetie," he said, leaning toward her. Her eyes swung in his direction, but they didn't look right. Different sizes or too big or something. He tried not to think about it. "I'm going to get you out of here."

"No," she said, before burping a trail of blood from her mouth.

His chest seized. She was right. He couldn't move her. But he had to save her. How could he save her? What could he do? He looked over his shoulder, into the forest. Into the places where his father had dwelled. The place where he had died. And that's when he heard it—his father's whisper. He couldn't make out words, just an echoing whisper like the hiss of a snake, telling him what to do. If he could remember the language. If he could interpret the signs. He turned to his wife.

"No," she said. Except he was watching her, and her lips never moved. But her voice was clear in his mind.

No, Virgil.

As his ears strained for more words, from his dying wife or dead father, he began to distinguish other sounds. Like the screaming coming from the back seat. How had he not noticed the shrill noise before?

He got out and tried to open the back passenger door, but it wouldn't budge, not even when he levered one booted foot against the rear of the car. He climbed back in the car, wedged his broad shoulders between the bucket seats and peered through.

The boy looked fine, unharmed in his little denim overalls and still strapped into the child's seat Virgil kept thinking he'd outgrown, his chubby face screaming with terror. Good thing he'd listened to Charlotte...

And that's when he heard the voice again—his father's voice—and although there were still no distinct words, the voice carried intention. Instruction. *There was still a way to save his wife. If he were willing.*

He reached for the child—

2

"Adam! Adam, wake up!" Iris's voice was firm as she grabbed him.

Adam jerked into consciousness, unsure of where or when he was, of whose hands were on his arm. He scrambled backwards, slamming into something and feeling it in his ribs. *The headboard.* The headboard of the bed in his old bedroom at Iris's.

Iris stood next to the bed, hands up in a sign of surrender, easing closer. "It's okay, kiddo. It's just me. You're okay."

Adam nodded, but his heart was pounding, and his stomach—

He lurched to the other side of the bed and vomited in the trashcan he kept there. Heaved, anyway, but he didn't have much to show for it. Remnants of a bowl of cereal? He'd forgotten to eat lunch.

Please, let me be done. Adam hung over the mattress, gripping the sides of the trashcan, waiting long enough to be sure and for his breathing to even out. He closed his eyes and rolled over onto his back, clutching an arm to his chest before he could stop himself.

"Those ribs still bothering you?" Iris asked, and he felt a cool, damp washcloth come to rest on his forehead.

"Thanks," Adam said. "A little."

He didn't like to remind his grandmother of the lingering pain, a souvenir of a particularly bad day nearly two weeks ago when JJ had performed CPR on him a few hours after he'd suffered a beating at Otto Nicholson's hands. He heard Iris sigh, and his fingers fumbled over mattress and through air until they found her hand. Her skin felt slightly loose, sliding over the knuckles and finger bones, and he had to restrain the urge to squeeze too hard, just to keep her there. He lay there for a minute or two, breathing and holding her hand, then released her and peeled the washcloth from his head. It took a conscious effort not to groan when he sat up. *That sound is a force of habit, not a reflection of how you actually feel.* He almost smiled at the lie.

"Did you have the dream again?" Iris asked.

Dream. Yeah, that's what it was. "Yes," he said.

"I heard you screaming from downstairs," she said.

Iris was a master at hiding her emotions—neither tone nor expression changed—but she couldn't control everything. In the weeks since he'd returned to Cold Springs, the wrinkles on her face were a little deeper. Her white blonde hair reflected more white than blonde and appeared brittle, its natural wave reduced to the occasional unruly bump. It was as though Iris were drying out inside. Had he done this to her?

"I'm sorry." He grabbed the trashcan and pushed off the bed too fast, becoming light-headed as he stepped past her to the bathroom. After dumping and rinsing the vomit, he brushed his teeth quickly, avoiding his reflection in the mirror. Adam could feel his jeans hang loosely on his hips, and he didn't really care to see the rest.

Iris waited outside the door, ready to interrogate him. He pretended not to notice, keeping a hand on the rail as he descended the stairs slowly, trying to look casual.

Iris followed. "Is that why you're not sleeping at night?"

Adam headed toward the kitchen. "What do you mean?"

"I mean, you sit in a chair in the living room at night and just stare at the windows, as if you're avoiding lying down."

Adam opened the refrigerator. He didn't want food—he seemed to have lost his sense of taste lately—but he knew he needed it. "What are you doing up at night?"

"I'm old. I'm not supposed to sleep. But you, you're barely thirty and the only time you ever sleep is napping, usually in the afternoon."

He looked at her, unsure if he'd ever heard Iris admit to being old. "I'm fine," he lied. "It's just habit, from spending so many years bartending. I can't remember the last time I slept normal hours. It takes some getting used to."

Adam turned back to the refrigerator and found a ham sandwich in cellophane from a convenience store. That would do. He unwrapped the plastic and took a bite. The taste seemed a little off, but everything tasted funny lately. He gave it a sniff. It was probably fine.

"When did you get that?" Iris asked, fiddling with her purse where it sat on the counter.

Adam shrugged and took another bite. "Couple of days ago, maybe."

Her eyes widened before turning her attention back to digging in her bag. "Then throw it away! I doubt if it was worth eating the day they put it out. I swear, they're lucky—"

"You look nice," Adam said, still chewing but wanting to head off her rant. Iris was wearing a pair of gray slacks and a matching, thin sweater with a geometric pattern. "Why are you dressed up?"

Iris avoided his eyes, finally pulling her keys free with a metallic jangle. Adam finished his sandwich at the counter while she puttered around, rinsing a teacup and putting it in the dish drainer. When he crumpled the plastic in his hands, she still hadn't spoken, so he did. "Are you going to see Harlan?"

"No," she said. "Do you need a ride somewhere?"

Adam glanced at the kitchen clock. "Crap, yes. Thanks for the reminder. I'm supposed to meet the tow truck guy to finally get my car. Let me grab my jacket."

IRIS WAS RIGHT; Adam wasn't sleeping, not since he'd left the hospital, and he was exhausted. He stared out the window at the world blurring by. This was the route the car had followed in his dream (*and in my life*). Adam tried to ignore a persistent overlay of the landscape at night by concentrating on the fuzzy brightness of the late afternoon sky (although it hurt his eyes) and on the details it illuminated, details that were absent in the darkness of his dreams. The deciduous trees were now nearly naked. The rest of the leaves had fallen over the past weeks, except for a few brown stragglers (the multi-fingered oak leaves seemed particularly tenacious) that would hang on until their replacements pushed them out in the spring.

A bleached field fell away on the left, and soon the road was flanked by leaf-strewn, forested banks on either side. The land rose and fell haphazardly. A dry creek bed emerged from the crease between two slopes on the right, then continued parallel to the road. Remnants of a rusted plow peeked from the leaves in a low spot next to the creek. Adam wondered how long it had been there, who had left it behind.

"Harlan wants to speak with you," Iris said.

"I know." Adam picked at a spot of something (*paint?*) on the window with his fingernail, but it held fast. "Do you blame him?"

Her hands gripped the wheel more tightly, but she didn't look at him. "Who?" she asked.

"Harlan."

"For what?"

"For me doing what I did."

"Why?" she asked. "I could just as easily blame JJ for what you got up to."

"No, you couldn't," he said. "You couldn't blame her for the *how*, for the... the way I opened my mind to Rachel."

"You mean the way you almost died," she said, finally glancing at him.

He waited, but she didn't say any more. She didn't have to. He knew she blamed Harlan; he just wanted to see if she'd admit it. There'd been a distance between the couple over the past week or so since Adam had gotten out of the hospital. Harlan had called a few times from his neighbor Jim's phone, but he'd never been to Iris's house, and so far as Adam knew, Iris had never been to Harlan's. At least, if she had, she'd never stayed the night.

Iris made the turn onto JJ's road, the turn Adam had missed in his own car. And there was the hatchback, sitting with half its front end in the ditch. Iris drove past the car and pulled over, but left hers in Drive, engine idling.

"What time's the tow truck guy supposed to be here?" she asked.

"Soon. I don't mind waiting in my car," Adam said, but made no move toward the door. "Tell me. When you screw things up with Harlan enough that he finally lets you push him away, who will you blame for that? Me?"

He watched his grandmother's pale face flush. She was either speechless, or taking a deep breath before tearing into him. He risked a grin, the way he couldn't remember grinning since he'd left the hospital. It felt good, like the warmth spread from his face throughout his body. Iris shook her head, and slowly her lips curled in a smile.

"You think you're so damned smart," she said.

Adam threw a hand over his mouth in mock horror at her uncharacteristic choice of even mild profanity. "Iris, language."

The phrase (Harlan's response the first time Iris unexpectedly discovered Adam in his kitchen) struck a chord. Iris plucked a scarf from between the seats and threw it at Adam's head. He laughed, and once he'd untangled the fabric, leaned over and gave her a quick kiss on the cheek.

"Oh, stop it," she said, but when Adam pulled away to leave, she held his arm. "Wait. You're right; I might visit Harlan later. But right now... I'm going to see *him*."

"Who?" Adam asked, even though he knew.

Iris seemed as reluctant to say his father's name as Adam was. "His lawyer asked me to. Do you want to come with me?" she asked.

"No," Adam said, careful not to raise his voice in the enclosed space. It wasn't so long ago (*ten days? twelve?*), lying in a hospital bed, that he'd asked her about seeing the man. How had he built up so much anger in such a short period of time?

"Are you sure? I can wait with you and we can go together, if you want to see Virgil."

A sound like a laugh's bitter cousin escaped Adam as he shoved the door open. "Remember, I've seen him already. And he almost killed me."

3

─────

Deputy Luther Beck figured the only thing worse than dealing with a lawyer was dealing with two lawyers over some hours-old coffee. And the only thing worse than that, without multiplying the number of lawyers, was dealing with said lawyers about Virgil Rutledge.

They should've seen the backside of Virgil by now. He definitely shouldn't still be in their jail, which wasn't much more than a glorified holding area. The county facility, larger and appropriate for longer-term detainment, was in Plattsville. But there'd been some kind of hearing here in Cold Springs, and then the judge or psychologist or some damn body wanted Virgil's competency evaluation to be here as well. The problem was, Virgil didn't. The man refused to speak to anyone.

That was fine by Luther. He'd looked in on Adam's father from time to time, when he was dozing, or pretending to. No wonder Virgil was crazy, sleeping at odd times and never more than an hour or two at a stretch. And he *was* crazy—Luther had no doubt of that, evaluation or not. Once when Virgil was lying on a bunk, face to the wall, he'd turned to look at Luther over his shoulder, as if he'd felt the deputy's eyes on him. Little hairs had prickled on the back of Luther's neck, like they had on the mountain in the dark, not so long ago.

Multiple agencies were still processing the crime scenes at the rock pinnacle. Days after Luther froze his ass off while hoping he wasn't watching Adam Rutledge die, they'd found the first set of human remains. These had been preliminarily identified as young Sarah Edmunds, a girl who'd disappeared from Beecham County twenty years ago, within months of Danny Carpenter's kidnapping. They were still waiting for additional forensic analysis, but so far, there was no physical evidence linking Virgil Rutledge to the girl's abduction or death.

A few days ago, they'd uncovered a second set of remains: a young male, probably a teenager and probably of more recent vintage than Sarah Edmunds. Tracking down Danny Carpenter's archived records had proved challenging, and the experts hadn't examined the remains yet, so law enforcement refused to speculate on identity. And there wasn't as much of that—speculation—as you might expect, even among the community at large. It's as if people were too superstitious to speak of it.

In the meantime, Luther was stuck babysitting one of the local prosecutors and Virgil's assigned public defender. Grant had called to say he was on his way but running late. The Sheriff had sounded flustered and hadn't given an explanation, both of which were so uncharacteristic of him that Luther had spent the past ten minutes wondering what was going on with his boss. It beat listening to the lawyers (he couldn't remember either of their damn names) yammer at each other about timelines and motions and whatnot.

Luther shouldered his way to the counter, muttering a pardon when he inadvertently bumped Virgil's lawyer. (Defense attorney or not, she was a woman, and not bad looking at all if she'd stop scowling.) Pouring fresh water from a gallon jug, he flipped the switch, listened to the coffee maker pop with promise, and tried to think of a justification for leaving the room. Let the two suits (both navy blue) cross-examine the refrigerator for a while.

"Luther!" Deputy Beth Marshall called out from the front desk, and he latched onto her voice like a lifeline.

Although certain neither attorney would notice his absence, he excused himself and went to thank Beth on two counts.

"Good idea on the bottled water," he said, leaning against her desk. Minus the tap water's heavy sulfur and iron content, the coffee he made now was almost palatable. "And thanks for—"

Getting me out of there, he nearly said, but the deputy interrupted him with a pointing finger.

"Hello, Luther," said Iris Rutledge, the object of the pointing finger.

Luther had the feeling Iris Rutledge didn't much care for him. He wasn't sure why she wouldn't, other than general antipathy toward the Beck family. He couldn't hold that against her—hell, he didn't like his relatives, either. Still, dealing with her invariably made him uncomfortable.

"Ms. Rutledge, what brings you in?" he asked. She simply stared, and he felt a fool when his brain caught up to his mouth, as she'd likely intended. "Ah, so you're here to see your son?"

Virgil's attorney must have heard them from the other room, and she nudged Luther aside. Light brown hair in a simple bob with bangs, she didn't wear much makeup, and she'd entirely missed the mascara on her left eye this morning. It made Luther smile.

"Mrs. Rutledge," the woman said.

Iris flinched slightly as the lawyer took her by the arm toward a set of chairs pushed against the white walls. Luther always addressed Iris as *Ms.*, and the woman did not abide being coddled.

"Should we be talking in front of him?" Iris asked, ignoring Luther but indicating the assistant district attorney. The prosecutor smiled back at her, as much as the man was capable of smiling.

"It's okay for this," the public defender said, hunched over Iris, neither sitting nor standing. "But later, when we talk about your son's mental state in more detail, we'll do it confidentially."

"Sit down. You make my neck hurt," Iris told her, and the woman complied. "I haven't seen my son in at least twenty years, so at this point I'd say you know more about his mental state than I do. I take it from the way you lawyers are mincing around, it's not good."

"Miss Rutledge," the prosecutor said. Luther almost snorted when Iris glared at the man's intrusive knee as he sat on the arm of the chair next to her. "It's not often my colleague and I agree."

"How trying for you," Iris observed.

The man's lip twisted, as if he couldn't decide on the appropriate expression. "Yes, well, the fact is—"

"The fact is the judge has ordered a competency evaluation to decide if your son can understand the charges against him and assist me with his defense," the public defender cut in. "Unfortunately, he's been unwilling to cooperate."

"Unwilling or unable?" Iris asked.

Virgil's attorney raised her brows and shrugged lightly padded shoulders. "Either way, if the psychologist can't do the evaluation, the court can have your son committed."

Iris's eyes closed briefly, before she asked, "For how long?"

"According to statute, initially fifteen days. But he'd still need to be evaluated—and the judge would still have to decide if he's competent—before his case can move forward. With transport back and forth, and scheduling hearings... the timeline starts getting complicated."

Things were about to get complicated where Virgil Rutledge was concerned all right, but Luther wasn't sure the man's attorney grasped the magnitude about to rain down on her. No doubt the woman had spent a lot of hours over the past week with her nose in heavy law books and endlessly scrolling computer screens, trying to get a handle on the procedures involved with Virgil's kind of crazy. She'd probably even made a flow chart on a big sheet of paper and taped it up in her office. The problem was, Virgil's kind of crazy didn't much abide by flow charts.

Iris stared at the public defender, Luther suspected mirroring his own train of thought. Iris at least had an inkling of which way the tracks were running. "Is he on medication?" she asked.

Virgil's attorney pressed her lips together, then asked in a flat tone, "To treat a mental health condition?"

Iris almost laughed. "I guess he wouldn't be able to tell you about his history, would he? If he's not cooperating."

And crazy as a fucking loon, Luther thought.

The defense attorney frowned at the prosecutor, still leaning against Iris's chair. He raised his hands and retreated behind the reception desk while the woman escorted Iris to the far corner of the room, saying, "Let's discuss this in private."

LUTHER NEARLY JUMPED over the reception desk with enthusiasm when the Sheriff stumbled through the front door. If he'd had to hear that damned bore of a prosecutor talk about trout fishing much longer, Luther might have strung himself from the overhead pipe in the bathroom with his own belt.

Grant's pale cheeks were flushed and his auburn hair unruly, his broad-brimmed hat nowhere to be seen. The man's eyes skated around the room, as if he'd forgotten why he was there as soon as he'd crossed the threshold. Luther moved quickly to intercept him.

"The attorneys—and Iris—are here about Virgil Rutledge," Luther said, voice low. "You okay?"

Grant nodded, but still didn't seem entirely present, not acknowledging anyone as he approached the reception desk. Beth glanced at Luther uncertainly.

Luther said, "Sheriff, Mr. Rutledge has been secured in Interview Room One. I believe Ms., uh..." He stared at the public defender, waiting for her name to drop from the sky. "Virgil's attorney would like Iris to go in with her."

"Actually, Deputy Breck, I've changed my mind," the lawyer said. "I'd like to meet with Mr. Rutledge alone first."

She smiled at Luther as she spoke, and seemed surprised when he couldn't help but smile back. He was certain she knew *his* proper name (*nicely played*), and now he was determined to find out hers. In fact, he was so determined, it took him a moment to realize that Grant still hadn't spoken.

"Shall I lead the way, *sir?*" Luther asked, hoping the rarely used formal address would snap Grant out of his fugue.

Grant's eyes finally focused on Luther as he said, "Thank you, Deputy."

The prosecutor stepped outside to make a phone call, but everyone else followed Luther. The Beecham County Sheriff's Department was small. They only had one true interview room, halfway down the short, broad hallway, but sometimes used a file room or conference room in a pinch. A simple bench stood against the wall opposite the interview room, bolted to the floor.

Luther motioned Iris to sit, but she shook her head. The one-way mirror, a staple of cop shows, was nowhere to be seen. Instead, the interview room had a small, high window in the wall with recording equipment installed inside, tucked away from angry, grabby hands. The window had an adjustable Venetian blind on the outside and was broad enough to accommodate a couple of people standing side-by-side. The officers used it for security purposes when the cameras weren't on.

Standing by the door, waiting to enter, the defense lawyer asked, "You've turned off the monitoring equipment?"

Luther found himself smiling again. "Of course," he said.

The Sheriff nodded his approval, and Luther stepped in front of the lawyer to open the door. Virgil sat with his back to the wall, wearing a blue jumpsuit and restraints, in a chair behind a bolted table. Deputy Gerald Hayes, a big sonuvagun with a neck nearly as thick as his bearded, blonde head, stood next to him. The room was so small, Luther stepped back outside once the lawyer cleared the entry. Deputy Hayes left her alone in the room with her client once he was satisfied everyone was settled and secure. Luther twisted the blinds slightly, just enough to see inside.

"Are you supposed to be doing that?" Iris asked.

"I don't know how you feel about his lawyer, but would you want to be left alone with your son in his current mental state, with nobody watching?" Luther asked. He motioned for Iris to take a place at the window, and she reluctantly joined him.

Physically, Virgil looked healthy, more healthy than he would've expected. It struck Luther that, while Virgil was older than him, he and Virgil were probably closer in age than he and Adam. Deep lines in Virgil's face contradicted an overall sense of raw vitality about the man. His hair hadn't been cut yet, so it hung to his shoulders, but it had been washed, with shades of gray and brown and blonde fighting for dominance. Luther watched Iris as Iris watched her son intently. Her demeanor gave away nothing, but within moments she turned from the window.

"She's wasting her time," Iris said.

Grant stepped to the window, taking the spot she'd vacated. "Why? What do you see?"

"I can just tell," Iris said.

Luther and the Sheriff observed as Virgil interacted with his attorney, or rather, failed to interact with her. The public defender's back was to them as she spoke to Virgil, shoulders and upper body shifting slightly, occasionally using her hands. He sat immobile and never responded, just stared at the window, as if he could feel the officers watching. No doubt he could—anyone could—with their silhouettes visible through the narrowed blinds. *But those eyes... Those damned, uncanny eyes of his belong in another world.*

Soon the Sheriff shuffled over and sat next to Iris, and Gerald took his boss's place at the window. Grant rested his head in his hands, as if massaging the back of his skull. It did nothing to improve the tidiness of his hair.

"What's wrong, Grant?" Iris asked.

"I just left the hospital," he admitted. "Dad had a bad fall this morning."

"Is he all right?" Iris asked, before Luther had a chance.

Grant simply shrugged.

"Bonnie should have called me," Iris said.

"I doubt she's had a chance," Grant said.

The old Sheriff Mason had been good to Luther, both when he'd hired him and in their years working together. Better than Luther had any right to expect. Luther said, "You know, I can handle this. You don't have to be here."

The ghost of a smile lit Grant's face. "Thank you, Luther. But my mother is with him now, and he's pretty out of it. They'll be doing hip surgery tomorrow. His prognosis is good."

"I'll drop by the hospital later," Iris said. "See if she needs some relief."

Movement in the interview room caught Luther's eye—Virgil was leaning across the table—and Gerald yelled, "Sheriff!"

Rather than wait for the man's response, Gerald strode to the door of the interview room and charged inside, allowing Virgil's yells to carry into the hallway. Luther followed quickly to the open door, but waited for a request for assistance to enter. With an inmate restrained in such a small room, Luther could easily do more harm than good by adding his bulk to the space.

"He'll do it again!" Virgil's voice was pleading.

"Sir, you need to settle down," Deputy Hayes said, and motioned Virgil's attorney to move slowly toward the exit.

Luther helped her through the doorway then stood, watching and waiting. The soundproofed walls seem to absorb the sliding, clattering of the metal chain as Virgil's hands came together. He started to rise, but Gerald put his hands on Virgil's shoulders and firmly pushed him back into his chair.

"You need to stay seated, sir," the deputy said.

"But he's not finished! You have to stop him, because he'll never stop on his own."

"Hey! I don't want to hear it." Gerald was an easygoing guy, but an edge had crept into his voice.

Luther was reminded of the moment when Virgil tried to reason with him in the cave on the mountain. But the man didn't seem to have any more common sense than he'd had a week and a half ago. Luther braced himself, ready to move, until Virgil reached across the table and pressed his forehead flat against its surface between his outstretched arms. Luther let out his breath and looked to the other deputy. "You got this?"

Gerald nodded, and Luther went back out into the hallway, closing the door behind him.

"I don't understand," Iris was saying. She and Grant were the only people in the hallway.

"Where's the girl? I mean, the woman," Luther stuttered. "His lawyer. Where is she?"

Grant inclined his head, indicating she'd gone in the opposite direction. Luther headed that way, knowing he didn't have much building to search. He found her in the reception area, sitting in Beth's chair.

"Ma'am, is Beth—"

"Deputy Marshall went to get me a glass of water," the lawyer said. Her face was pale, except for two red spots on her cheeks.

Luther kneeled next to her chair. "Are you okay, Ms....? I don't recall that we were ever properly introduced."

"I'm Faith Callaway. And you're —"

"Not named after a haircare product," Luther said, earning a smile. "I'm Deputy Luther Beck."

"I know," she said. "But you're not quite what I expected."

Luther, unsure what to make of that, felt a flush of his own and tried not to be distracted by it. "Did he hurt you?"

"No! Not at all. He just wasn't..."

"He wasn't what you expected either?" Luther grinned. He might not have Adam Rutledge's dimple, but he could be charming when the occasion called for it. "If you're going to stay in this business, you might need to work on managing your expectations. So what was all that about back there?"

She looked down at her lap and shook her head, hair swirling around her chin. "You know I can't tell you."

Before Luther could follow up, he felt someone behind him... Iris, flanked by the Sheriff. Luther stood slowly, ignoring the angry pop of his knee.

"What was he saying?" Iris asked. She was nearly as pale as her son's attorney. "Who was he talking about?"

"I'm sorry—as I told the deputy, I can't share privileged communications," Ms. Callaway said. Then she softened and added, "Besides, trust me, Mrs. Rutledge, you don't want to know."

4

———

"**M**an, you best get where you're going, because that battery is shot."

Adam barely heard the driver's parting words over the sound of the tow truck's diesel engine. The truck rumbled up the hill until it reached the first driveway on the left, then carefully turned around and came back down. The driver raised a finger from the wheel toward Adam as he passed.

It had taken longer to jump Adam's little hatchback than to haul it back onto the road. The tow truck driver had only charged fifty bucks (he called it the "JJ Special"), but it'd probably cost Adam another hundred and fifty to replace the battery. He still had a little money tucked away—he always kept a "blow town" kitty— but with no money coming in and no idea what was on the horizon... maybe he could squeak a couple more weeks out of this battery. He needed an oil change, too, and probably new spark plugs. The car's engine miss was showing its ugly head too often for comfort when the prospect of restarting a stall was so uncertain.

The rearview mirror seemed off kilter. Adam adjusted it before encouraging the whining car up the mountain toward JJ's, inadvertently catching sight of the darkness ringing his sunken, blue eyes. The mirror probably got moved during the tow, or—*scary thought*—maybe Adam didn't sit as straight as he used to a whopping two weeks ago. He turned at the second driveway, taking it faster than he should have to keep the RPMs steady. He was nearly alongside JJ's vehicle when he noticed Evie's bicycle on the ground, and braked hard to avoid crushing it. The car stalled at the sudden stop. Adam heaved a relieved sigh as he switched off the ignition. The way things were going lately, he'd have done more damage to his car than to Evie's bike.

JJ, standing on the front step, had seen the near miss. "Evie!" she yelled into the house. "What did I tell you about your bike? You're lucky Adam didn't run over the god—"

He grinned as JJ caught herself and rolled her eyes.

"—The god blessed thing. And hurry up if you don't want Rachel to start without you. They already left and we need to get gas on the way."

"I could drive," Adam said.

"No thanks," JJ snorted. "I'd rather not have to push start your car in the middle of town." She put a hand on his shoulder, part affectionate and part directional, as they meandered away from the house. "You look like shit."

"Thanks," he said. He was getting a little tired of hearing that but tried to let it go, studying JJ in the dusky light instead. Her voice had a grating quality, and she looked as though sleep hadn't been her number one priority lately, either. "You're not exactly projecting rainbows and buttercups yourself."

They walked over to a thick poplar tree, the one that had borne their initials since childhood. "One of the nurses at the hospital quit, so I'm stuck working crazy shifts for a while."

"And?" he asked, knowing there was more. The two of them slid down, backs against the tree, until they both sat on the ground, shoulders touching. It had warmed up considerably since the recent early cold snap (the one that gave Adam hypothermia), but he wouldn't want to sit on the cool earth for very long.

JJ sighed. "And Marcus has been hassling me. Calling at weird hours, showing up outside Evie's school—"

"Has he showed up here?" Adam asked.

"No."

She'd said it too fast, and he didn't believe her. "JJ..."

"He hasn't!" she protested, but quickly softened to, "Not exactly. Not to the house. But Otto said there was somebody he didn't recognize parked on our road."

"And you think it was him?"

She didn't answer aloud, but he felt the motion of her nod. "Have you told Grant?" he asked.

"No! He's the Sheriff, and I don't want things to be weird between us."

"You mean you think it would be awkward if the boy you *like* had to arrest the boy you *used to like*?" Adam asked, letting his voice slide into a higher register.

JJ smacked him, just as Evie burst through the front door. "Did you feed Trooper?" JJ asked.

Now it was Evie's turn to roll her eyes, before banging back inside the house. JJ groaned theatrically as she stood, offering Adam a hand. He took it, rising more slowly than she had, trying to hide it when his head swam.

"You sure you're okay?" JJ asked.

"Yeah. Listen, don't you think it'll get weirder between you and Grant if he hears about this from someone else first?" Adam asked. Still lightheaded, he clamped his mouth against the urge to pant for oxygen.

JJ's eyes turned hard. "Who's he going to hear it from? You?"

"Don't be stupid!" Adam said, wrapping his arm around the tree to prop himself upright. "If you don't want me to tell him, I won't. But this is Cold Springs, not..."

His brain ground to a halt as he tried to maintain all necessary bodily functions and come up with the name of anyplace bigger than their town. Which would be pretty much anyplace in the country.

"Plattsville?" JJ joked. The next town over, it wasn't exactly a booming metropolis. It was bigger than Cold Springs, and they'd invoked it ironically like New York City when they were kids.

Evie emerged from the house carrying a plastic novelty cup as if it were filled with liquid gold rather than dog food. The clatter of kibble into Trooper's bowl (a former saucepan, now missing its handle) was somehow reassuring. Adam watched as the dog waited patiently for the eleven-year-old to step back, still clutching the cup the way a much younger child would. She looked up at Adam.

"Where's your costume?" she asked.

They were going to the Volunteer Fire Department's Trunk-or-Treat Halloween celebration. Halloween wasn't until Monday, but the adults running things decided they'd much rather have the weekend to recover from the festivities.

"Was I supposed to wear a costume?" Adam asked, walking with Evie to JJ's Bronco while she locked up the house.

"I am!" Evie said, unnecessarily. She wore jeans tucked into cowboy boots, a matching cowboy hat, a brown vest and red bandanna over a white button-down shirt, all topped off by a low-hanging, double holster and a shiny sheriff's badge.

"Your mom didn't dress up," Adam pointed out. Both he and JJ were wearing jeans and flannel shirts over T-shirts, as did most people in Cold Springs this time of year.

Evie's snort eerily echoed her mother's. "She never does. But I thought at least you would."

"It seems I'm forever disappointing the Tulley women," Adam muttered.

JJ didn't comment.

~

Twenty minutes later, they were on Main Street looking for parking, along with everyone else in Cold Springs. Vehicles crept by the school grounds, eyes peeled for parking spots and unruly children. Parents had angled cars in alongside the edge of the road on the school side. The opposite side had no shoulder, just a guardrail against the steep bank that fell to the river below, thus no parking. The school parking lots were full, as was the playground's basketball court. Even the paved loop that bisected the small campus (the main school building lay on one side, with the cafeteria and machine shop on the other) was choked with cars and people. Adam was half surprised they hadn't filled the baseball field, too.

"Mom! Mom, there's Rachel's car!" Evie said.

Adam felt a rumble in his stomach as he recognized her father Otto's pickup in the growing darkness, but there was no one in it.

"I know, sweetie, but I have to find a place for my car."

"Mom!" Evie whined.

Adam was surprised when JJ caved, asking him in a soft voice, "Would you mind taking her to find the Nicholsons, and I'll catch up?"

Adam could feel Evie's wiggling excitement in the seat behind him. "Of course not," he said, then whispered, "You owe me."

"No kidding. Evie, wait for Adam to get out first, and hold his hand while you cross the street. Do not run off—stay right next to Adam at all times. Got it?"

"Got it, Mom. I'll be good."

"You'd better be."

A shiver ran through Adam when he got out of the SUV and the cool night air hit a sheen of sweat he hadn't noticed before. *Suck it up, Rutledge.* He opened Evie's door and quickly wiped his clammy hand on his pants.

"I'm afraid your steed is bedding down for the night, Sheriff Tulley, so we'll have to go on foot. Shall we mosey?"

Expressions warred on the girl's face. She tried to look older and cynical and above it all (*like JJ*), but excitement won out. She jumped down onto the asphalt, catching Adam's hand on the way. Adam had a flash of Rachel, of her tiny, cold hand in his, and steadied himself against the vehicle until the sensation passed.

Evie held Adam's hand as they threaded through the traffic

and the parked cars cozied along the road. She let go once they reached a gap in the chain-link fence and stepped onto the grassy play yard. He allowed it, but kept his hand on her shoulder, trying not to grip it too tightly. *Beware JJ's wrath if I let her child out of my sight, even for a moment.* The crowd was thick, though you could still squeak through, and pretty well mixed age-wise. Costumeless teenagers traveled in packs and had mastered the cynical look Evie tried earlier. Younger kids moved in slightly smaller groups that orbited around central cores of taller adults.

"There's Jacob!" She pointed toward one of the costumeless, teenaged packs, but didn't wave. Adam barely recognized Rachel's older brother, having only seen a photograph of the boy taken before his most recent growth spurt. Evie pulled Adam by the arm and said, "I know where to meet Rachel."

It was easy to see her best friend when they got close—or it would have been if the light were better. Few people stood beneath a familiar old oak tree where she and her parents waited. The delicate child wore a vivid red cloak, hooded over her long, dark hair. He wasn't sure why, but it turned Adam's stomach a bit to see her in it. Perhaps because she looked so pale and vulnerable, and even a little frightened.

The girls clasped hands, leaving the adults to stare at Adam. Otto had foregone the opportunity to dress as a Viking (Adam couldn't help but see the large, bearded man that way) and was dressed much as Adam was. "Adam," he said, nodding.

"Where's JJ?" Dorothy snapped.

Apparently Rachel's mother's opinion of Adam had not improved with her daughter's recovery. Wearing a black gown with ragged edges, Dorothy crossed her arms over her chest, squishing an amount of décolletage that verged on the unseemly for a family gathering. Adam quickly looked away.

"She's looking for parking," he said. "Rachel, you should have told us to bring Trooper. He could have been your wolf."

Rachel didn't seem thrilled by the idea, but Evie gave him a look that said, *Oh, sure, you wait 'til now to share the scheme that lets me bring my dog.*

"Mom made my costume," Rachel said, holding the cloak out to show a white, puffy-sleeved shirt tucked into a red skirt beneath it.

"She did an excellent job," Adam said. "I've never seen a finer Red Riding Hood."

"She made her costume, too," Rachel added. "My mom's a witch."

Adam avoided looking at Dorothy, but glimpsed Otto's smile in his peripheral vision and struggled not to answer it. "You know, Evie's mom and I used to sit under this tree when we were your age."

"I didn't know the tree was *that* old!" Evie exclaimed, although she obviously did. Still, it gave the adults an excuse to laugh away some of the tension.

They decided to start their rounds and let JJ catch up. Adam was surprised when the girls flanked him, neither quite taking his hand but both staying close. He glanced over his shoulder and saw that the Nicholsons had fallen a few steps behind, snuggling and giving the girls some privacy.

"Where to first?" Adam asked. "The Bouncy House?"

The big inflatable looked less like a house than an oversized life jacket. It made a good landmark, though, standing brightly in the upper field.

"I don't feel much like bouncing right now," Rachel said, then veered abruptly to, "Why doesn't my mom like you?" She stared at the ground ahead of them, as if the answer weren't important to her.

Adam blew out his breath. Feeling queasy (*yes, Iris, I know you told me the sandwich was bad*), he concentrated on choosing his words carefully, knowing there was a good chance Rachel would repeat some version of them to one or both parents. He seized on his rolling stomach.

"You ever get really seasick?" he asked.

"I've never been on a real boat," Rachel said. "Just a canoe."

"I have, but I was too little to remember it," Evie chimed in. "Mom said I was fine, but my dad got seasick."

And probably complained about it the whole time, Adam thought, then regrouped. "What about carsick?"

"Yeah, I've been carsick bad before," Rachel said. "I puked all over my backpack and Mom got mad at Dad because he was driving and she said she told him not to let me eat that many pancakes at grandma's."

"I'll bet you didn't want to eat pancakes again for a while."

"I was okay with pancakes, but I couldn't do sausage," Rachel admitted, mouth wrinkled in distaste as she looked at him.

"Well, it's like that," Adam said, hoping he wasn't reaching too far with the metaphor. "When your mom sees me, she thinks of what happened to you, and how she was so scared it made her sick."

"But it wasn't your fault!" Evie protested.

"No, but it wasn't the sausage's fault that Rachel got sick, either. We can't always help the way we think about things. Sometimes we just have to wait for it to pass."

Maybe he shouldn't have chosen a food analogy. Adam's stomach cramped and rumbled, and he suddenly realized that some things refused to wait.

"Excuse me, girls," he said, and jogged desperately for the nearest portable toilet.

5

"Not bad for a bunch of rednecks," Luther said, scanning the transformed school grounds. Squealing children in cheap, plastic costumes were lined up to get their faces painted at a booth to the right. The ring toss across the way drew a decidedly older audience, with more excited fathers than daughters and sons tossing plastic circles at Coke bottles.

"I think hillbilly is the preferred term," Grant said.

Luther smiled. "Are you sure you want to be here? You know it's not a big deal for me —"

"Thanks, Luther, but it'll do me good to get my mind off things." Grant arced sideways to avoid a waist-high kid racing by, slopping a bright red beverage like a contrail. "For a little while, anyway."

Both men wore their khaki uniforms. They wandered through the crowd, tipping their hats, nodding and smiling and making small talk. It was the kind of gig Luther looked forward to once in a while, so long as you didn't have to bring down the law on a bunch of rowdy teenagers. Eventually they made their way to the Strongman High Striker, manned by none other than Luther's brother, Leslie.

"It looks like Les is having way too much fun," Grant observed.

The man had certainly gotten into character, wearing hiking boots and jeans with his flannel shirt sleeves rolled up to his elbows and some kind of crazy hat that Luther thought was supposed to suggest a lumberjack. Les's voice was loud and boisterous, and his grin was wide. It was good to see his brother having fun, but he *was* still his brother.

"You know he just volunteered to do that because he thinks it'll improve his chances of getting laid," Luther said, then looked around to see if anyone overheard them. "Sorry, Sheriff."

Grant laughed. "I don't suppose there's any shame in that, Luther."

The deputy turned in a slow circle, taking in the crowd around them. "Come to think of it, I haven't seen JJ yet..."

Grant gave him stink eye, but it was hard to take a blushing man's anger seriously.

Les waved as Luther and Grant approached. "Can I interest either of you gentlemen in a contest of manly strength?"

Grant held up his hands. "Not me, thanks. I can barely lift my head tonight, much less that big hammer."

Luther said, "Well, I guess somebody has to uphold the Department's good reputation. All right, I'll take some of that."

Les handed Luther the heavy hammer with a smirk. "Let's see what you got, old man."

Luther strode forward and extended the hammer toward the bell, like a baseball player calling his shot. Then he squatted a bit, shimmying his hips back and forth. When he turned toward Grant, he recognized a few other faces gathered around, including Virgil's public defender, Faith Callaway. He gave her his biggest, best grin and said, "You know, it's all in the hips."

"Are you going to hit that thing, or are you trying out for one of those dance shows?" she asked.

Les cackled, and Luther grinned even wider. He felt almost giddy with anticipation as he bent his knees and swung the hammer forward and down with both arms. A resounding clang cut through the air, and Luther raised his hands over his head in triumph. Ms. Callaway clapped her hands slowly, as if she'd either seen better, or she hadn't but didn't want to admit it.

"Who's next?" Luther asked, and held the hammer toward Grant with raised eyebrows. Grant shook his head, but Luther noticed Adam approaching. "You want to take a turn?"

Adam demurred, holding up a hand much as Grant had, except Adam appeared to be in pain. In fact, Adam looked like shit, pale and sweaty and slightly hunched. Luther handed the hammer back to his brother and took a bow before joining Grant and Adam. "You okay?"

"Yeah," Adam said, unconvincingly. Then he clutched his midsection. "Actually, no. I think I got a touch of food poisoning."

Luther took a step back involuntarily, thankful he hadn't shaken the man's hand. "There's real bathrooms open over there in the schoolhouse."

"Thanks," Adam said. "I think I really just need to go home. Have either of you seen JJ? I came here with her and Evie."

"We haven't, but I'd be happy to give you a ride to Iris's," Grant offered.

Adam swallowed hard and turned an interesting shade that seemed more leprechaun than human in the mix of carnival and street lights. "Thanks, I might just take you up on that if I can't find her," he said, leaving the men behind with a little wave.

In the past few minutes, the sky had slipped from dusk to full dark. Luther watched the plaid of Adam's shirt as he set off through the throng, traversing the long field toward the beckoning lights of the schoolhouse restrooms. He shook his head. "That guy couldn't catch a break unless it was a compound fracture."

"It does sometimes seem that way," Grant agreed.

Luther's thoughts returned to Virgil, to the crazy things the man had said on the mountain about the first son being resurrected, and then the crazy things he'd been saying today. "Do you think there's any way to ever make Virgil right?"

He expected the Sheriff to be philosophical, say something

like, how do we even know what right is? Or what right is for him? Instead his boss simply responded, "I don't know."

Luther looked around, wary of eavesdroppers. He leaned in until he and the Sheriff were shoulder to shoulder and pretended to watch kids race across the way. "Did you hear all that crazy shit Virgil said today?"

Grant lowered his voice. "I heard enough."

Luther glanced over at Faith Callaway, in a crowd of people, head tilted to laugh with another woman about her age. "I tried to get her to tell me what it was about."

Grant shook his head. "Luther..."

Luther ignored the man's disapproval. "She wouldn't tell me. 'Course, I didn't try that hard. The thing is, all that stuff he was saying, about somebody who couldn't be stopped —" He hesitated and almost didn't finish, but over the last month he'd felt as if he and Grant had developed a better relationship. At least, he hoped so. Still, his voice dropped almost to a whisper. "So I asked Gerald what he said. He was talking about Adam."

Grant pushed his hat back and rubbed his forehead. "Yeah, I was afraid of that."

A frustrated energy rose in Luther, and he worked to keep it under control. That's something else he'd been cultivating over the past month. "You know it's bullshit."

"Of course I know it's bullshit," Grant said, pulling his hat back down firmly and showing a little energy himself. "But Adam's position in this town, however long he chooses to stay, is tenuous enough as it is. That's why I didn't say anything, and why we need to keep it between ourselves."

One of the volunteer firemen caught Grant's eye and waved the two men toward his booth. He probably wanted to point out some underage drinkers. Luther had seen a couple of flasks himself, but tended to let that kind of thing go so long as the kids didn't get obnoxious or behind the wheel. Together, he and Grant made their way toward the Pin the Tail on the Goblin, smiling and genial with everyone they passed. How many could have guessed their thoughts?

Grant leaned into Luther and said, "God forbid we have another kid go missing. If these people heard what Virgil said about his son, he'd be lucky if they didn't string him up."

6

It was disorienting, approaching the entrance of a place Adam had spent so much of the first twelve years of his life but hadn't set foot inside since. The school in Cold Springs served kindergarten through junior high. Local students attended a consolidated county high school when they reached ninth grade. The structure had been built around the same time as the War Memorial Building down the street, and it showed. Pale, concrete steps practically glowed against the brick backdrop, red in daylight but dark at night. The steps led directly onto an asphalt basketball court, crowded with cars Adam had circled around, not trusting himself to negotiate such close quarters. *Just a little farther.*

A man bumped Adam's shoulder hard as he passed, and Adam stumbled, dropping to his knees on the asphalt under a wave of intense nausea. The bright steps left an afterimage on his retina, fuzzy white lines superimposed over everything that passed in front of his eyes. When he stood and turned to get a better look at the man, he'd vanished. Which, in Adam's current state, merely meant the man was more than six feet away.

Wide, concrete-topped, brick sections bookended the steps. A few young couples sat there, nuzzled close enough to provoke parents, while far enough apart in the bits that mattered to suggest intervention was unreasonable. Adam nearly tripped over one young man's lazy leg as he walked past; only his crawling pace saved him.

Once inside, the hall lights that had seemed so promising from afar made Adam squint. His legs responded on a peculiar delay, but he kept walking, past classrooms with closed doors on both sides, past an emergency exit on the left, past—wait, *water fountain*. Its shiny reflection was a sliver of glass in his brain, and the button was worn to a tarnished roughness. The icy water felt so good sluicing down his throat, Adam could have cried. If only he could fill his belly with gallons and gallons...

A sudden pressure reminded him why he'd come in the building in the first place. There—up ahead. *Please, God, don't let there be a line.*

The door swung inward so easily, Adam nearly fell into the bathroom. Of its four painted plywood stalls, the nearest was the only one occupied. Adam headed for the last one, snugged against the wall and across from the urinals. He made it inside, slid the bolt home with shaking hands, and got his pants down just in time.

It was not pretty, but at least there was plenty of toilet paper.

The person on the far end had departed, and a few more had come and gone by the time Adam began considering whether it was safe for him to leave. There was something comforting about being there, something beyond the reassurance that he wouldn't have an accident in public.

And then he remembered. He'd spent a lot of time in these bathroom stalls after Danny was kidnapped. When it got to be too much—that sense of his classmates' eyes upon him—he'd ask for a bathroom pass and just sit in a stall, until someone came to get him or he heard the sounds of the bell to change classes. He wasn't sure how he'd passed the time. Maybe sleeping, since he hadn't done a lot of that then. An involuntary smile snuck onto his exhausted face. *Some things never change.*

He pulled his pants up and made his way to the sink, fingers shaking almost as badly as when he'd entered. After washing his hands, he splashed water on his face and held it against his forehead in cupped hands. He wiped the drops from his eyes with the heels of his hands and felt heat radiating from his forehead. Even through blurry eyes, the sight of his face in the mirror—white, chapped lips and sallow skin drawn tightly across his skull—was shocking. It was time to go home.

Adam extended a hand in the hallway, tracing the wall with two fingers to keep oriented while his vision fuzzed out. He felt the surfaces change beneath his fingertips: painted wall, doorframe and door, painted wall, poster paper, painted wall... *water fountain!*

Even walking slowly, the impact bent him double over the low-hung fixture and his left, tracing arm flung forward, settling in the wet, metal catchment. Adam stared at the floor, concentrating on a small puddle until its edges became clear. Maybe he should just stop here, sit *right here* and wait to see if JJ found him. She'd yell at him, call him a doofus, or something worse if Evie wasn't with her.

Adam stood as straight as his aching guts would allow. She'd do that anyway, wherever they found each other. He followed the lights to the exit.

Pushing the door open and stepping carefully down the stairs, Adam found himself on an empty sidewalk. Facing a flagpole. *What the hell?* He must have gone out the side exit. At least he hadn't set off an alarm. He looked around. The traffic on Main Street had cleared, and although there were a few scattered figures elsewhere, the crowds had gathered in the fields far off to his left where the games were set up. He could not face the press of people again. Physically, he couldn't handle it, and mentally... it was undoubtedly a side effect of his sickness, but he had a strange feeling, just short of paranoia, that someone was watching him. It'd be better to wait for JJ at her car. Too bad he didn't know where she'd parked it.

Adam sighed and put his hand to an ache in his head. *I can do this.* JJ was the type of person to park far away and be done with it rather than circling. She'd been heading toward the center of town when she'd dropped off him and Evie, so Adam would walk in that direction until he found her Bronco. He felt cool metal beneath his hands as he picked his way through parked cars and crossed the street to the empty side.

Trees clung to the steep embankment, creating a narrow, now leafless fringe at the edge of the road. Adam knew a river ran far below him, but he couldn't see it in the dark. He couldn't hear it, either—no matter how much he strained—over a white noise that filled his head. The low metal guardrail was at trip-the-human-and-toss-him-to-his-death height. Adam stepped onto the edge of the road when his calf bumped the guardrail, preferring to take his chances with slow-moving cars. A dirt lane lay ahead on the right, across from the school property boundary, and cut back and forth to reach the floodplain below. Beyond that, the earth filled in again, hosting a small cemetery. It was buffered from the road by an old, iron fence and a stretch of trees, with a shoulder once again wide enough to allow cars to park alongside the road.

Adam made it as far as the cemetery property when he began to feel truly awful. This time, he needed to vomit. Trailing a hand on the cars as he had the wall of the hallway, he told himself that was something to be grateful for, not having to drop his trousers next to someone's plastic carnations. This close to Halloween, people would get upset and think it was a prank, never knowing—

He shuffled quickly into the trees, falling to his knees as he began to heave. Tears filled his eyes as he went past the point of having anything to purge. He fell onto his side and curled his knees to his chest, trying to soothe aching, cramping muscles. It was dark here, but a streetlight glowed in the distance. Darkness began to swallow that glow, starting at his peripheral vision and working its way toward the center.

Just before he lost consciousness, he thought someone stood over him, that a figure said his name in a vaguely familiar but oddly singsong voice. *Adam... Oh, Adam...*

7

He could do it right now. Step on Adam's throat, and be done with it. If he wanted to be less obvious, he could cover his mouth and nose with his hand, although it probably wouldn't fool law enforcement. Hell, he could probably just roll Adam on his back and wait for him to drown in his own vomit. Pathetic. He didn't understand the man's fascination with Adam... Except it was also his.

He reached down and grabbed the front of Adam's shirt, close enough to smell the odor of sickness. What had the idiot done this time? He pulled, until Adam's body shifted and his head lolled to the side, then risked a little bit of illumination from the mini-flashlight on his keychain.

Wow. The hollow-cheeked face was almost unrecognizable from the man who'd so recently arrived in Cold Springs, and yet... yet there was a hint of the boy who'd occupied this body. He ran a thumb across a scruffy indentation that always dimpled when Adam smiled, but there was no reaction. He'd hoped he would smile, even involuntarily. If he had, maybe, just maybe he would have softened. Maybe he wouldn't have gone through with it.

But this was a golden opportunity, if he hurried. He switched off his light and gave Adam a last pat on the chest.

"Don't worry. I'll be seeing you again."

8

———

The child's voice was so soft, JJ had to squat to hear her.

"I don't feel very good," Rachel confided.

"Do you need to go to the bathroom?" JJ asked.

"I just want to go home," she whispered. "Will you tell my mom?"

"Of course." JJ smoothed the girl's hair away from her forehead; she didn't have a fever. She'd seemed anxious all evening, and she could simply be overwhelmed by the crowds. Rachel was a sensitive child, and JJ thought she'd been doing remarkably well since her ordeal.

Evie gave her mother a dirty look when JJ reached toward her next, as if JJ might remove her precious cowboy hat. She touched her daughter's shoulder instead. "How about you, kid? Have you had enough excitement for one night?"

Evie nodded. She looked tired, doubtless because she'd been up late the night before, wandering from room to room in her costume. JJ had been afraid she'd find her wearing it in bed this morning.

Dorothy stood a few feet away, laughing and ogling her

husband Otto's ring-tossing prowess. She'd probably had more fun than the kids, but JJ didn't begrudge her. The kidnapping had put Dorothy and Otto's marriage through the wringer, and JJ was glad to see them relaxed and having a good time, even if it was just for an hour or two. Although she did wish Dorothy would stop shoving her damn boobs in everyone's face.

Rachel was disappointed that JJ and Evie couldn't leave with the Nicholsons, but they still had to find Adam. JJ found it strange she hadn't seen him all night and might have gone looking earlier, except she'd had all eyes on Rachel and Evie. Despite Evie's early excitement, both girls had been subdued, and JJ had worked harder than usual to get them engaged with the festivities. And, okay, maybe she'd held back looking for Adam because she was annoyed that he'd left Evie with Dorothy and Otto with no explanation. She kept thinking he'd show up and apologize, but he never did.

JJ and Evie approached the High Striker, where Les was passing the hammer to the next shift. He ducked beneath the rope they'd strung around it to keep anyone from being clobbered.

"Les!" JJ yelled.

Country music played loudly from a pickup parked behind the High Striker, so she had to grab his arm to get his attention.

"Hey, JJ! You having a good time?" he yelled.

She motioned him away from the music blast zone. "I'm looking for Adam. Have you seen him?"

Les smiled. "Yeah, I saw him a good while back. He looked sick as a damn dog, so you might want to check the bathrooms. I'd make him walk if I were you. But I value my car upholstery."

"Gee, thanks, Les," she said, shaking her head. *Asshole.*

She and Evie checked the portable toilets with no success. Then they checked each of the major attractions—still no luck. By the time they reached the schoolhouse, Evie was dragging.

"I don't want to have to go in there again before Monday morning," Evie said.

But JJ gave her daughter a stern look, and she followed without further complaint. They checked the ladies room—just because—and asked a man escorting his young son to check the men's room. The two emerged a few minutes later and said it was empty. JJ watched them exit the building, then took Evie by the hand. "Come on."

"Are you serious?" Evie asked, horrified.

The man had been right; it was empty inside. JJ pushed the doors open and checked the stalls to be sure. "Dammit!"

JJ looked to Evie. She tried not to curse in front of her daughter, but the girl hadn't noticed. Evie was transfixed by the two yellow-splattered urinals on the far end of the room. "That is so gross!" she said.

"Yeah, boys can be pretty gross," JJ said, leading her out of the bathroom. She stalled out in the hallway, unsure where else to go. Evie took the opportunity to drink from the water fountain like a dying dog in a desert.

"Save some for the rest of the town," JJ said.

Evie stifled a burp and wiped a hand across her face. "If he didn't feel good, maybe he went to the car."

Yes, that makes sense. "Kid," JJ said, "sometimes I forget you're not just a pretty face."

"I've got a mean free throw, too."

JJ smiled and gave her daughter's cowboy hat a gentle push. Damn, Evie was smart. Always precocious. She hated to think what she'd be like in a few years. Her puberty might kill JJ.

They left the noise of the gathering behind and walked up the street. She'd parked a little ways past the cemetery, but Adam had no way of knowing that, so JJ kept her eyes open. She saw only a couple of teens sitting on the ground next to a vehicle, backs against its door. JJ stopped when they reached the entrance to the cemetery. Could Adam have gone in there? It was possible, but why? She sighed. If she didn't check, she'd never sleep, wondering all night if the dumbass was curled next to a tombstone.

"You think Adam is in there?" Evie asked.

"I don't know," JJ admitted. "What do you think?"

JJ held in a laugh as Evie's theatrical sigh mirrored the one she'd released just moments earlier.

"Well, let's go," Evie said, taking her mother's hand.

JJ determined they'd stay on the paved circuit. A single light held sentinel next to a flagpole at the center of the graveyard, and the area near the entrance received some illumination from the streetlights. However, once they reached the first row of graves, they were on their own.

"Did you ever go in the cemetery on Halloween when you were a kid?" Evie asked.

"No," JJ said automatically, then smiled as she reconsidered. "Well, there was one time, but it was the day after Halloween. Me and Adam and Danny—"

His name was out before she could stop it.

Evie said, "That's the boy that was kidnapped like Rachel."

Nice job; no getting around it now. It was probably best to be open anyway. JJ worried about Rachel dealing with her kidnapping experience, but—knowing how Danny's disappearance had shaped her and Adam—she also worried about her daughter, about the lifelong imprint a friend's absence could leave.

JJ stalled, dropping her daughter's hand to pull out her cell phone and trigger the app that made it an anemic flashlight. Finally, she answered, "Yes, sweetie, he was kidnapped like Rachel. Danny read something somewhere that made him think the really scary ghosts waited until the night of November first to show themselves instead of Halloween. So Adam and I told your Grandpa and Iris that we were going to Danny's house, but we really stayed around school."

"What did Danny tell his parents?"

"I don't know. They didn't really keep tabs on him the way our families did," JJ admitted. "Danny brought his dad's camera so he could take pictures of the ghosts. We goofed around until close to dark, then walked over to the cemetery and hid behind a big tombstone."

JJ pointed toward the back, beyond the reach of her light. It had seemed ginormous when they were children, but looking at the nearby gravestones decades later, it was impossible that even the largest could have shielded the three of them from view.

"What did you see?" Evie asked. Her hand had slipped into JJ's again, and JJ smiled in the dark.

"Well—"

"Stop right there!" a voice boomed from the shadows.

JJ dropped her cell phone and—suddenly blinded by blazing white light—shoved her daughter behind her. "Who's there?"

The beam of light lowered to her waist but, eyes still dazzled, she couldn't distinguish more than a shape in the dark.

"Sorry, ma'am. It's Beecham County Sheriff's Deputy Hayes. I was doing a quick pass by the cemetery when I saw a light and wanted to make sure there weren't kids up to no good."

"My mom's not a kid," Evie protested.

"Gee, thanks for that," JJ said, knocking Evie's hat askew as she reached back for her daughter. "Deputy, we were looking for a friend who isn't feeling well, and we thought maybe he'd come in here to, you know..."

"Throw up," Evie clarified.

"I haven't seen anyone," the man shape said, coming closer. "And I've been dropping by every half hour or so. Let me walk you back out to the street."

~

JJ WAS DISAPPOINTED but not surprised that Adam wasn't waiting by the car. "Evie, I need you to help me out," she said, once they were in and buckled up. "Keep your eyes open and yell if you see Adam."

"Okay," she said. "Mom, would that guy have arrested you if I wasn't there?"

"Not this time, babe." JJ drove slowly down Main Street. All of the businesses were closed except the gas station and its convenience store, the VFW post, and probably the bar on the far side of town. She'd see in about a minute.

"So what happened?" Evie asked. "When you were in the cemetery with Adam and Danny."

JJ tried to switch gears in her mind, but it was hard to push her anxiety for Adam away. It was also hard to remember what was funny about the story, what punchline she'd intended to share with her daughter. "Well, we didn't see any ghosts."

"Duh!" from the passenger seat.

"We did see some bigger kids. Older kids who must've had the same idea as Danny. They jumped out and chased us through the cemetery." She couldn't remember who the older kids were now, except the punk who'd kicked Adam when he fell. JJ'd thrown a rock at his head, distracting him long enough for them to escape. Always a bully, the guy had died in a car accident not long after Adam moved away. She'd wanted to tell Adam the asshole had gotten what was coming to him, but she never got the chance.

"Were you scared?" Evie asked.

JJ made a U-turn in the bar's parking lot, the edge of Cold Springs proper. She hadn't been scared—angry, but not scared. There hadn't been time. But she lied and said, "I'm sure I must have been."

"Did you get in trouble?"

"No, I didn't." Her dad had been suspicious, and Iris had wanted to know where Adam got the nasty bruise on his leg, but the two of them had managed to skate by. Danny, on the other hand... The guy who'd kicked Adam had also broken the camera Danny was carrying. Danny never said, but JJ was pretty sure his father had beaten the crap out of him.

JJ slowed to a crawl when they reached the school grounds again. She made a complete circle, driving the loop through the school and passing the property from the road one last time, but Adam was nowhere to be seen. There was nothing else to do but head home. Maybe he'd gotten a ride with someone back to her house and his car.

As they left the town's last streetlight behind, Evie asked, "Mom, do you think Adam's okay?"

"I'm sure he's fine."

Except, of course, she was lying.

9

A vehicle had parked on the road between JJ's neighbor's driveway and her own. Its headlights lit up her rearview mirror as she passed, and when she turned into her driveway, they followed.

Shit.

"Pumpkin—"

"I'm not a pumpkin. Pumpkins are round," Evie said.

"Whatever," JJ replied. Her child's incipient body issues were the least of her worries at the moment. "I want you to go straight to the front door and inside the house as soon as I stop the car. Okay?"

"Why? Is there—"

"Evie, okay?"

"Okay," she said grudgingly. "But if the door's locked, I'll need a key."

JJ parked the car, pulled her keys from the ignition and passed them to her daughter. Evie headed for the front door, but more slowly than her mother would have liked. JJ walked around the back of her Bronco, intending to release Trooper (his barking suggested he'd like nothing better), but headlights moved up the driveway so quickly she was afraid to cross in front of them. The vehicle almost seemed aimed at her.

JJ stepped back, alongside the solid Bronco, ready to run. Blinded by headlights, she heard more than saw the machine grind to a sudden halt, throwing gravel and sending her heart thumping against the walls of her chest. It was a pickup, probably red as Otto had described, though it was hard to tell in the dark, and it was so close she could've touched it with an outstretched leg. Or it could have touched her. She held her breath as the driver's door opened.

"JJ, aren't you looking lovely this fine evening?" The voice was smooth and sweet and made her want to vomit. She should have known...

"Marcus, were you trying to fucking run me over, or are you still just the shittiest driver I've ever met?" It didn't pay to let the man know he'd spooked her.

"Jesus, JJ, watch your mouth," he said, but JJ barely heard her ex-husband over Trooper's barking. Marcus glanced toward the tie-out. "That damn dog never did like me."

"Trooper, enough," JJ said. He stopped immediately, but his silhouette showed rigid posture and ears standing at attention.

"Nice trick," Marcus said, then raised his eyes toward the front porch, calling out, "Hey there, pumpkin!"

"I'm not a pumpkin," Evie said.

JJ almost laughed, even though her daughter had ignored her instructions to go inside. *At least there's one Tulley woman who can resist the man's charms.* But then Evie descended the steps anyway, coming to join them in the headlights of Marcus's truck.

"I can see you're not a pumpkin," Marcus said. "Obviously, you're a cowboy."

Evie let out a long-suffering sigh. "I'm not a cowboy. I'm an Old West Sheriff. Didn't you see my badge?" She pointed to the shiny plastic gold star pinned to her vest.

Marcus stepped closer and squatted down for a better look. "I do now. But why would you want to be a sheriff instead of an outlaw?"

JJ had a strong inclination to smack the man. "Marcus, just because you don't have a moral compass doesn't mean your daughter was born without one."

Marcus pretended to ignore her, but JJ knew she'd gotten to him. He pointed toward their daughter's holsters. "Do you know any gun tricks?"

"No, I don't care much about guns." Evie reached around her back to retrieve her lasso. "But the Sheriff said he'll teach me some rope tricks."

JJ felt a cold stab of apprehension when Marcus spoke. "He did, did he? Well, not with that fake piece of crap."

The lasso *was* a fake, some kind of synthetic material stitched together to look as if it were coiled when you couldn't much more than choke a cat with it. And Evie knew it was fake. But her father had still offended her. JJ imagined she could hear her daughter's molars grinding when she spoke.

"No, not with the toy. He'll teach me with a *real rope*. And he said he'd show me how to tie up bank robbers, too."

"Well, darling," Marcus said, touching his daughter's cheek. "I could teach you to do tricks with a *real gun*."

"Evie, it's time to go in and get ready for bed," JJ said.

"Mom—"

I cannot strike my daughter's father in front of her. Of course, that wasn't the only possibility. *Nor can I let him strike me.* "Now, Evie. Straight in. Bath, and then PJs."

Marcus watched their daughter cross the yard to the house. His face was shadowed, but JJ didn't need her eyes to see it; he was etched in her mind. He had the most amazing hazel eyes, with full lashes—but not too full—perfectly proportioned to convince a woman (or at least her ovaries) that he was a sensitive man. Then the lines alongside his mouth... *that's a man with a sense of humor*, you'd think. Top it all off with thick hair that ranged from dirty blonde to light brown depending on the season, and killer abs. The man had kept barbells in their garage and actually used them.

It was only after Evie's booted feet clomped on the front steps and she banged the front door behind her that Marcus's gaze swung to JJ. "Sheriff, huh? Would that be *Grant?*"

And there it was. It was a mystery to JJ how perhaps the most attractive man she'd ever met could be so goddamned ugly. "Marcus, we've talked about this. If you want to see Evie, you need to call first. And I'd really prefer to deal with your parents about visitation. You need to leave now."

"Why, is Grant coming over? Is he going to give Evie some of those lessons tonight?"

Marcus stepped closer, so close JJ could smell the end of a long day on him (*God help me, he still smells good*), but JJ held her ground. He shifted his feet a little, and JJ ran through options in her head —how far it was to Trooper (*far enough*), how far it was to the shotgun in the house (*too far*), how far it was to the gun locked in the Bronco's glovebox (*impossibly far*).

"Or maybe the lessons are for you," he said, reaching toward her. "You know I love your hair, your beautiful, long—"

JJ caught his hand, but gently, not wanting to provoke him if she could help it. "Then you shouldn't have used it to drag me across the living room. Do you have any idea how much of my beautiful, long hair fell out after that?"

"Ha!" he laughed. He lowered his hand when she let go, but somehow his face seemed closer. "You're right; I shouldn't have done that. But then, you shouldn't have called your daddy, either."

JJ smiled and prayed he could see it, prayed he could see her contempt. "Actually, I didn't. And before you say, *he's not here to protect me anymore*, let me tell you that Evie is the only reason I haven't had you arrested—or better yet, blown your goddamned brains out. But I've been working a lot of hours lately, and I'm not in the best mood, so you best be getting your ass to whoever'll take it."

She turned on her heel and strode toward the front steps.

"JJ!" he said, not quite angry and not quite yelling. But that's when he was most dangerous. "JJ!" A little louder.

Just a little farther... The motion-sensing porch light that had timed out flashed on again. She heard his feet on the gravel behind her, but didn't dare run.

"JJ!" he said, touching her arm as her foot landed on the bottom step.

She swung around.

"You left these," he said, jingling a set of keys.

Her hand began drifting like a magnet before her brain could protest, *but you gave your keys to Evie.*

Focused on the keys flashing in his hand, JJ didn't see Marcus's other hand whip out to the back of her head. His fingers dug into her hair and he jerked her head back until she stared at the dark sky. Her spine cracked, and tears sprang to her eyes as delicate hairs ripped from the back of her neck. Her left arm was trapped between them, so she torqued her hips around to maintain her balance on the step, bringing her almost to his eye level. Marcus leaned close, so she could hear him over Trooper's lunging barks.

"See, this is the reason we couldn't stay together. You've never shown me the proper respect. You never even *took my name*," he said, in the same pleading, sultry tone he'd use to charm a woman in a bar.

JJ struggled to swallow, to speak, her throat bent back at an extreme angle. "Marcus, don't do this where Evie can see us. You don't want her to hate you."

"Like you care," he said.

"I do care," she whispered. "I still remember what it was like... in the beginning. When it was just the two of us. And then when Evie was little." JJ sucked air in a strangled sob. "I just wish..."

"You just wish what, baby?"

"I just wish—"

You'd stay the fuck out of my life. JJ's right hand shot up like a rocket, the heel of her palm striking Marcus's nose. He released her, grabbing at his face and dropping to his knees, and JJ kicked him in the chest to finish his fall. Her follow-through carried her off the step and she landed awkwardly, but she was halfway to Trooper before her ex's body hit the ground. Her shaking fingers and aching hand fumbled with the dog's tie-out.

I should have checked him for a gun.

Except, for all of his badass talk with Evie, she'd never known Marcus to carry concealed. She just needed to get in the house with her dog and her shotgun and everything would be okay. He was a coward at heart, so she had no doubt he'd leave.

Make that *little* doubt.

"Heel," she said to Trooper, voice still a little raspy.

Marcus had made it as far as his knees by the time she returned to the front steps. His lips curled back, and his teeth shone white in the porch light, except where blood covered them. She hoped he'd bitten his damn tongue off. There was blood below his nose, too, but it was hard to say whether she'd broken it. *Right on the schnoz, Dad. Just like you taught me.*

Trooper growled beside her, and JJ put a calming hand on the ruff of his neck. Then she pulled her cell phone from her pocket to take a picture. The damned thing was dead—must have been from using it as a flashlight—but she went through the motions. Hopefully he'd think she'd taken a photo of him anyway.

"I'm going inside now. If you want to see Evie again, I better get a call from your parents or your lawyer. I don't want to hear your disgusting voice again."

He raised one knee and braced himself against it. "You think it's going to be that simple? Bitch?" he asked. His words had a hollow, echoing quality, and "think" sounded like "fink."

JJ leaned in, close enough to make him think she wasn't afraid of him but not close enough to be stupid. "Yeah, I do. Because if I ever see you on my property again, I'll feed your dick to my dog."

She strode up the steps with Trooper without a second look, slamming the front door behind her.

10

He'd scouted out the carnival this afternoon while the men were setting up—long before the unexpected pleasure of seeing Adam—and knew the Bouncy House was his best bet. A false sense of security came with those plastic, inflatable walls, or maybe just a diffusion of responsibility with such a density of children. Either way, the Bouncy House was one of those places where parents relaxed their guard, milling around outside with the other adults, enjoying a moment's respite while their kids worked out the pounds of sugar they'd ingested. It was also located at the periphery of the grounds next to a small neighborhood with a dozen or so houses. He'd parked his van there earlier (*can't have a party without balloons*), so if he moved quickly, he'd have an easy getaway.

So long as the kid didn't scream.

He'd come prepared for that as well.

He circled the Bouncy House, taking the crowd temperature one last time. On the back side, away from the lights, he slipped the brown robe from his trick-or-treat bag and pulled it over his clothes. He adjusted the hot, rubber mask on his head—the friendliest-looking bear he'd ever seen. Then he stepped over to the Bouncy House "window," too high and narrow for a child to easily bounce through, but low enough for him to see inside.

Children ricocheted off the walls and floor at crazy angles that made his stomach hurt, but there weren't as many as there had been earlier—maybe a dozen. He stuck his head in further and ran his eyes along the edge. *There...*

A few feet to the left, a costumed boy sat against the wall, legs crossed. Occasionally a particularly boisterous (or fat) kid produced waves that rocked the boy against the wall, and he'd tumble on his side. It was sad to watch. And it was perfect.

"Hey!" he called out to the boy, pitching his voice carefully to sound cartoonish but low enough to avoid attracting the attention of the squealers in the center. The boy looked at him. "Have you seen a pot of honey anywhere?"

It was impossible to gauge the boy's reaction through his plastic mask (Batman, no less), but he was certain he sensed confusion.

"How about Goldilocks? Brat blonde girl, about yay high," he said, reaching in to demonstrate. "You seen her?"

The boy shook his head, but didn't move any closer. The kid wasn't going to make it easy on him. "Let me ask you something," he said, gesturing for the boy to approach him.

The boy looked around, pale blonde hair flashing when he turned his head. Towhead, he'd always heard that color called. The boy could have been Goldilocks's brother. Whatever the boy saw —or didn't see, like anyone who cared what he did—he finally approached the man on hands and knees, rising and falling as the floor bounced. The man imagined he could hear the *flap-shushing* of the black plastic pants covering the boy's legs.

"Anybody ever call you Towhead?" he asked.

The boy shook his head.

"Well, you've led a deprived life. Towhead, I need your opinion on something. I have to go to a costume party tomorrow night, and I can't decide which one of these to wear." He bent down and pulled two rubber masks from his bag.

"What do you think?" he asked, holding them up for the child to see.

They were both science fiction, but while one looked vaguely Star Wars-related, he had no idea of the other one's derivation. He did know he'd nearly had to punch a guy with whining kids to get the last one in the store, and that seemed a good indicator of popularity. Red and white and roughly shaped like a full-head helmet (some kind of sci-fi soldier?), the boy reached for it immediately.

"This one, huh?"

The boy nodded. He held it out, and the boy took it reverently in his hands. "You want to try it on?"

The boy nodded even harder and nearly snapped the elastic band on his thin, molded Batman mask in his eagerness to remove it from his head. He was young—maybe eight or nine—and had a smattering of freckles across a cherubic face that belonged on the cover of a Christian pamphlet about heaven. The only mark on its stereotypical perfection was a scar on his upper lip. Related speech impediment? That might explain his reluctance to speak, and his isolation from his peers.

The boy manipulated the rubber mask in his hands, trying to make sure the head hole was open. "Wait," the man said. "There's a tag inside. Let me get it so you don't poke your eye out."

He squatted out of view, and instead of removing something from the mask, he added something. Something he'd practiced securing to the mouth and nose area, something that had done its job before. He looked around, but the children were oblivious, or at least not alarmed by him, and that's all that mattered.

"Here you go," he said, pinching the front of the mask as he helped the boy slide it over his head.

He heard a little noise—a grunt of protest—and pushed the mask against the boy's face while pretending to tug the back portion into place over his neck. After several seconds of maneuvering, the boy went limp, and the man struggled to hold the child upright without looking like that was what he was doing. Now for the tricky part. He pulled the boy toward him and lifted him up and over the window. He wasn't that heavy, but the angle was awkward, and he nearly dropped the child in the transition. He settled the boy against his chest, and that's when he noticed that he was being watched. *Dammit.*

He lowered the boy. He had to get the cotton pad out of the mask. It wouldn't do much good to grab the kid and accidentally kill him at the scene. But it was hard to get his hand in the mask while the kid was wearing it, and even harder to grasp the pad with his fingers and pull it out. This was something he should have trained for. Sweat ran from his temple in the hot bear mask.

Got it. He sighed with relief.

The kid across the way—an even younger boy in a Ninja Turtle costume—was still watching. He smiled, then remembered the kid couldn't see him through his damn hot mask. Instead he made a cartoonish dance with his shoulders, and the Ninja Turtle smiled. Then he slowly sank below the window, out of the Ninja Turtle's view, and popped up again. That won him a grin. He waved, and raised the towheaded boy's hand to wave goodbye as well. It was limp and wobbly on the end of his manipulated arm, but the Ninja Turtle didn't seem to notice. He stepped to the side, out of view, and carried the boy away in both arms.

He'd almost made it to the van when he met an elderly woman, probably one of the neighborhood residents, heading toward the carnival.

"Aren't you hot in that mask?" she asked.

He laughed and hoped the sound carried. "Yes, ma'am, I am, and you can bet I won't be a bear again next year. The darn mask is so big I can't carry it and my boy at the same time. A' course, I guess *he'll* be too big for carrying next year."

"Aww," she said. "It looks like he's done for the night."

He smiled beneath his mask. "Yes, ma'am. He surely is. If I didn't know better, I'd think he was never waking up."

11

———

I got lucky.

JJ knew that if she'd used a little less force, or been half an inch to either side, all she'd have done was piss Marcus off. She also knew she couldn't count on being lucky the next time. She'd never thought her husband would actually kill her, but now she wasn't so sure.

Trooper raised his head from the couch at the sound of her shifting the ice pack on her wrist. She should have iced it a couple of hours ago, but she hadn't wanted to in front of Evie. She didn't want her daughter to know what had happened, and—so far—it seemed she didn't. Thank God for small miracles. She told herself that's also why she hadn't called it in, but that wasn't entirely true.

JJ had known Grant since they were kids, but he was a couple of years older, so she hadn't known him well. Then he'd gone away to college and into law enforcement somewhere else. But even when he'd returned a few years ago, they'd never gotten reacquainted. Not until the incident with Marcus, the one where JJ's father—already sick with cancer—nearly beat the father of her child to death. Max Tulley might have finished the job, had Grant not arrived to stop him, but she thought he probably wouldn't have. Grant hadn't done much in the way of intervening, just been a calm, watchful presence. And then he'd driven Marcus to a hospital in the next county. *That's the way his daddy would have handled it*, Max had said. *Actually, no. Ulysses probably would have gotten in a few licks of his own.*

Grant dropped by a few times after that, just checking in, but stopped visiting when Max got really bad. Near the end, her father had asked people—the ones that knew—not to come by anymore; he didn't want to see them. Of course, everyone in Cold Springs, and people from places she'd never heard of, showed up for her dad's funeral, but she'd felt such relief when she saw Grant. He made her feel safe—not physically, but emotionally—in a way that no one else had since Adam left when they were kids.

A few months ago, she'd called the Sheriff's Department because of a break-in, something her gut wanted to lay at Marcus's door. She wouldn't have bothered, but a window had been broken and she'd (wrongly) thought her insurance would cover it. Grant began dropping by again regularly after that, and although they'd never been on a date, they'd gotten into a kind of routine. She didn't want to jeopardize that, whatever it was. But this had to stop.

She picked up her phone (the landline; the damn cell was still charging). Instead of calling the station, she called Iris's house. She'd already tried Adam several times, and reassured herself he was even more lax about charging his phone than she was about hers. She let Iris's phone ring and ring, and eventually the machine picked up, but she didn't bother leaving a message. Yet.

She wished she'd gone over there before putting Evie down for the night. She was worried about Adam. Instead of getting better, he seemed to have gotten worse—physically and mentally—since being released from the hospital, and he was reluctant to talk about it, or about what had happened on the mountain to land him in intensive care.

She could also use a little support herself right now. Not that she had any doubt about what his advice would be. He'd pushed her to go to Grant from the beginning, as soon as he learned what was happening. He was probably right. In fact, she knew he was right.

Trooper lifted his head again, ears alert. A moment later, JJ heard a vehicle approaching. By the time she'd untangled her legs and jumped down from the couch, she could see flashes of headlights through the trees. She turned off the lamp next to her so the living room was nearly dark.

Shotgun... She'd locked it up again, as she always did when it wasn't in hand. She scrambled toward the closet, then hesitated. Trooper was alert, but not barking, so she headed toward the locked front door instead. She recognized the headlights now, just as Trooper had recognized the engine sound. It was Grant in one of the Department vehicles. Her heart lifted, then seized nearly as quickly. Decision time.

She turned on her porch light and watched, Trooper standing next to her, as Grant parked the cruiser. *Deep breath.* He cut the headlights and the engine. Opened his door. *It's time to tell him,* she thought, and with that certainty felt a burden lift from her chest.

She smiled at the thought of seeing Grant—she should've put hot water or coffee on—but her smile faltered when he didn't come inside. Instead, Grant walked over to Adam's car, still parked and waiting for his return (and probably a jump-start). The Sheriff pulled out a flashlight and circled Adam's hatchback slowly, shining it through the side windows and the back glass to illuminate the interior. Then he examined the ground around the car and felt its hood before finally extinguishing the flashlight and advancing on the front door. JJ turned the doorknob to meet him, but she'd forgotten the door was still locked. She disengaged it as he was lifting one hand to knock, his hat held in the other.

"What's wrong, Grant?" she asked, because something obviously was. His body was rigid, his lips pressed tightly together.

"Where's Adam?"

"I don't know."

"What do you mean, you don't know? Isn't that his car in your driveway?" he asked, voice challenging.

JJ's temper flared in response. "You know damn well it's his car. Just like you know damn well I gave him a ride to the trunk-or-treat tonight. But I lost track of him and I haven't seen him since. Now, what the hell is going on?"

"There's been another kidnapping," he said. "An eight-year-old boy from the trunk-or-treat."

JJ gasped. "Dear God, not again."

Grant continued, "We got an anonymous tip that Adam's the one who took him."

12

Luther wasn't sure of his chances of finding his brother at home. It wasn't yet midnight, possibly still early by Les's Friday night standards, and Les wasn't answering his cell phone.

Early. Early days... *that's the bullshit law enforcement aphorism when you know you're already fucked.*

He drove too fast. It had been three hours since the boy went missing, since he and Grant and a couple of volunteer firefighters had set up a checkpoint and searched every vehicle leaving the vicinity of the school. Then he'd coordinated follow-up searches of the grounds while Grant took the boy's parents home. They weren't completely flipping out yet, which to Luther's mind meant they got a gold star. Beth had offered to stay with them, but the DA's office was sending someone, freeing Beth up for her now familiar job of setting up a Command Center. Grant was heading to the Nicholsons now, to prevent Dorothy from freaking when she heard the news and to confirm Rachel hadn't seen something unusual tonight, whatever that meant. He'd also muttered something about checking out a tip from the lunatic fringe.

How was this happening again? Virgil Rutledge kidnapped

Rachel, and he was in custody. Luther kept praying someone would come on the radio and say it was a mistake, that the boy (*Aaron Schofield; give him his name*) had been hiding under a tarp, that he went home with an uncle—anything other than all the coordinating chatter he heard now. Of course, he'd thought the same thing last month—hell, it wasn't even last month, just a few weeks ago—with Rachel. And it wasn't a mistake. But they did find her, in one piece. It could happen again.

It was surreal having another kidnapping so soon, but it did mean that they were still at the tops of people's minds resourcewise. Everyone with the Beecham County Sheriff's Department had been called in tonight, and Grant had even wrangled a few extra law enforcement bodies from neighboring counties that would arrive tomorrow. The State Troopers should be at the Command Center with Beth any time now, and the FBI had been notified. Some of the field agents were no doubt cursing the winding West Virginia roads already. At least they weren't icy this time.

Luther was surprised to find an extra vehicle parked outside his brother's trailer, one he didn't recognize. A small, older model sedan, he was careful not to block it in or park too close. Drunk people were hard on county vehicles, and any friends at his brother's house on a Friday night were likely either drunk or well on their way.

Les still had a stack of wobbly cinder blocks for a front step, so Luther stood on the ground next to the door and beat on it. No response, so he banged a few more times. "Les, come on, goddammit! Open up, now. It's important."

The door swung open and he found himself facing a set of knees that were far too attractive to belong to his brother. His gaze followed the bare legs up until they met a T-shirt... and little else. Luther quickly looked away, then stepped up on the blocks to get closer to eye level and avoid learning anything else he didn't need to know about this mystery woman. Except she wasn't a mystery woman. What was her name?

"Esther? Esther LaRue?" Luther asked.

"Long time, Luther. Come on in. Les is in the shower, but he should be out in a minute," she said, before backing away from the door and disappearing inside.

Luther climbed up and kept his eyes averted until they were both on level floor. Her dark, curly hair was decidedly mussed, hanging down over a navy West Virginia University T-shirt. "Esther, you mind putting on some pants?" he asked, as she stretched across the counter for a pack of cigarettes, revealing one fluorescent white cheek and a bit of lace.

She smiled. Her teeth weren't great, but her smile was so genuine you tended to forget. "Luther, I do believe you're a prude," she said, and picked up a pair of boxers from the couch.

Luther turned his head while she slipped them on. "Esther, did you take your kids to the trunk-or-treat tonight?"

He heard her patting the cigarette pack against her palm and figured it was safe to look again. She was technically clothed now, and Luther tried not to think "her" undershorts had been on his brother not so long ago.

"Yeah, I took them in and hung out for a while. Then Les and I left, and the kids stayed with my parents. Why?" she asked.

"Did you see a man in a big brown robe and a goofy bear mask?"

She laughed. "Why, did he steal all the pic-a-nic baskets?" When Luther didn't answer, her face grew serious. "No, I didn't. And I feel like that's something I would have noticed. Most grown-ups weren't wearing costumes."

"What about a little blonde boy in a Batman costume?" Luther asked.

She lit her cigarette and watched the first puff of smoke rise. "Was that Aaron Schofield? He's in my daughter's class."

"What can you tell me about him?"

She grabbed a jar lid and set it on the coffee table for an ashtray before sitting on Les's couch, legs crossed. "Cute kid, but not very social. I don't know who his friends would be. Is something wrong?"

Luther heard his brother's heavy footsteps in the hallway before he saw him. Thank God he was wearing pants, or at least gym shorts. "Luther, what's up?" he asked.

"I need the volunteer sheet from tonight. Wes said you have it."

Les smacked Esther's leg to make her scoot over. "Yeah, but I don't know what I did with it."

Of course he doesn't know what he did with it... deep breath. "Les, I need you to find it. Now."

Les must have recognized that tone of voice. He stood immediately and began looking around the living room, which was relatively clean by Les's standards. "Where'd I put my pants?" he muttered.

"They might be in the kitchen," Esther suggested. "Ask him about the bear."

By the time Luther realized she was talking to him, she'd continued without him. "Luther wants to know, did you see a man tonight in a robe dressed like a goofy bear?"

Les looked up from his search behind the recliner. "Is that a joke?"

Luther clenched his jaw, then reminded himself to release it. "No, Les it's not a fucking joke. Aaron Schofield was kidnapped tonight."

Les's mouth dropped open, and Luther heard Esther murmur, "Sweet Jesus."

"Okay. Now that we've established I'm not here for shits and giggles, did you see him, and did you see a man dressed like a bear?" Luther asked. *I'm so goddamned exhausted already. And this is only the beginning.* He sat on one of Les's chairs, just for a minute. He'd removed his hat and was massaging the back of his neck when Les answered.

"Found them," he said, lifting his pants and pulling his jean pockets inside out. One had a mashed, folded sheet of paper, and he handed it to Luther. "Here you go. I didn't see the kid, and I sure didn't see a bear. I helped set up early, then went down the street and grabbed a burger. I ran the high striker from opening until Esther came and got me. Must have been sometime around seven, seven-thirty. Came straight here and... well, you know."

Luther was shocked when the man actually blushed. He didn't know there was a Beck over the age of twelve that was constitutionally capable of blushing. He pulled a pair of glasses from his pocket and scanned the names. He recognized everyone on the list, and they'd already spoken with most of them. Luther stared at the sweat stain inside the brim of his hat, then slowly rose. It was going to be a long night. "Okay, then. I guess that's all. I better get this list back to headquarters. You want to walk me out?"

Luther gave Esther a nod and tried not to break his neck stepping off the cinder blocks outside. Les followed, tiptoeing barefoot across the gravel. He'd be lucky if he didn't get tetanus.

"You see anybody unusual while you were setting up? Anybody you didn't know, or anybody that didn't belong?" Luther asked.

Les leaned against Luther's vehicle. "I'm sorry, Luther. I can't think of anybody, then or later."

Luther held up the list. "How about somebody that didn't show up to help out that was supposed to?"

Les shook his head. "Nope. Nothing."

Luther nudged his brother out of the way and opened the door. "Okay. Thanks. And Les, don't tell anybody I'm coming. They'll probably hear anyway, but you never know."

"No problem, Luther."

Luther closed the door and buckled up. He knew he'd just wasted his breath. His little brother gossiped worse than a bored grandma in a brothel. Thinking of wasting his breath, Luther rolled down his window to get a last word in. "Listen, I know it's none of my business, but you and Esther..." Luther trailed off, unsure how to finish without pissing off his brother. "Is she on the up and up?"

If Les had been wearing his boots, he would have dug his toes in the ground. As it was, he avoided Luther's eye. "I might help her out from time to time, but that's all. There's nothing wrong with that."

"No," Luther agreed. "Nothing at all. You gotta work this weekend?"

Les shook his head. "No, I wish. And I'm gonna be short this week, too. Let me know if y'all need any help with searches or anything."

Luther nodded. "Sure thing."

He resisted the urge to ask his brother if he could be the rapist father of *this* kidnapped child.

13

—————

"You're not Batman," the kidnapped boy said. The fumbling grogginess of his voice made him sound even younger than he appeared.

"I'm wearing the mask, so I'm as much Batman as you were," he responded. The child's mask had seemed a good compromise, a way to hide his face when the boy was conscious without scaring him and making him scream. "Besides, you're too young to be Batman. Tell you what. I'll call you Batman, and you can call me Bruce Wayne. But I get to keep wearing the mask."

The boy's coordination was off, too, and he nearly stuck the straw up his nose trying to finish his milkshake. "Bruce" smiled behind his mask. "Make sure you drink it all. Chocolate milkshakes give you superpowers."

Eyes bleary, the boy still said, "I don't think so."

"Sure they do. Why do you think grown-ups don't want you to drink them?" When he heard the slurping sound of the last melty bits, he continued, "Now go pee one last time before bed."

"It's nighttime already?" The shadows beneath the boy's eyes were dark, a sharp contrast with his pale blonde hair.

"It's nighttime when I say it's nighttime." It was still nighttime

—around four a.m., in fact—and it had been a long night. His patience was wearing thin. "Now go pee."

The boy stumbled getting down from the chair, but Bruce didn't move to help. The boy knew where the bathroom was. He'd changed out of his plastic costume there earlier. The boy's current shirt was pink, but it fit. Bruce had stolen it from an unattended laundromat dryer last week, along with some other clothes (luckily for the kid, including the right gender of underwear). Find a laundromat next to a bar and have decent timing, and pretty much anything in the dryers is yours for the taking. If—as had happened on this occasion—someone wandered back from next door to make sure their britches hadn't gone up in flames, having an innocent face helped, too.

Bruce waited another minute or two and was about to check if the kid had passed out when the bathroom door flew open, as if he'd fallen against it. The boy walked to the bed and tried to climb on, but like many motel beds, it was higher than it needed to be. Bruce finished his French fries and gave the boy a boost. He'd be down for the count in a few minutes. The room was plenty warm—stuffy, in fact—and he left the boy on top of the blankets. The kid rolled over onto his back and that's when he saw it—the dreaded crumpling face that precedes a bout of wailing.

"Hey!" he said sharply, and the boy looked at him. "Who'd I tell you doesn't get to go to Disney World?"

The boy's lip trembled like a Hallmark movie, but he managed to say, "Crybabies."

"That's right. Mickey does not let crybabies in the castle." Bruce thought there was a castle, but he wasn't sure; he'd never been there himself.

"But when do mommy and daddy get here?" the boy asked.

"I told you, they're meeting us at the park. But they have to get away from work first. I'm just keeping you until then." He wondered if the kid would believe his story if he didn't have him doped to the gills. It was possible. He seemed pretty gullible, even for a kid. Still, best to keep him quiet. "How about a bedtime story?"

The kid rubbed his eyes, settling deeper into the pillow. "I'm too old for a bedtime story."

Bruce gritted his teeth. "Then I'll tell you a big kid bedtime story."

He picked up an old National Geographic magazine that had been in the room before him and flipped to a spread from the Serengeti. He sat next to the kid on the bed, cringing a little as his back touched the wall, a wall that probably hadn't been cleaned since the place was built. "You like lions?" he asked.

The kid nodded with closed eyes. It wouldn't be long now. Bruce spun a yarn as he turned the pages, one that involved a giraffe going to a buffalo dentist with an antelope hygienist. He'd had a bone stuck between his teeth, which no one could figure out because he was supposed to be an herbivore. Finally, the giraffe jumped up from the chair, flung off his costume and revealed himself to be a lion. He ate everyone in the office.

Bruce let the magazine fall shut and scooted to the edge of the bed.

"The end," the boy murmured.

"No!" Bruce rolled back toward the boy and slapped his hand over his mouth.

The boy's eyes opened partway, but—unlike Bruce—he was too far gone to be alarmed. That is, until the hand inadvertently covered his nose as well.

"You never *ever* say that. It's bad luck." Bruce's gaze jerked around the room, like a tweaker on a three-day high. The boy tried to sit up, to move away, but Bruce pushed him down with his other hand. This place was cheap, but the opaque, brown curtains did a good job of keeping out prying eyes. Still...

He felt a buzzing against his hand, and looked down to see the boy's face turning pink. "Sorry," Bruce said, sliding his fingers away from the boy's nose and feeling a burst of snot as the child sucked air in and out. "But you have to promise me you'll be quiet. And that you'll never say those words again. Okay?"

The boy nodded, and Bruce slowly released his hand from the boy's face. Then he tucked his own knees up and pulled the boy against his side. He listened to the boy's snuffles while he tried to calm his own racing heart, tried to tell himself it was just a stupid superstition.

"Shh," he said, "you'll be okay."

Probably. Although he had given the boy enough drugs to drop a horse. The boy's head relaxed against the pillows, and his breath evened out. Bruce would stick around long enough to make sure it stayed that way. He'd hate to have to take another kid so soon.

14

———

Thunk. Thunk. *The old man kept an axe on a stump near the pump house and then complained when it got rusty. That's what it sounded like—the axe striking the stump. Except a little bit different. He'd just finished weeding the beans and brushed his hands on his pants before circling the house.*

The stump was empty, no axe in sight.

The thick door of the pump house stuck at the base and groaned in protest. It finally came free, and he stepped inside, tugging the string for the overhead light. It felt cool inside. There was nothing out of place, except a few small chunks of insulation near the water tank. Maybe he'd bring the dog in later, see what a canine nose made of it. Dang rodents.

Thunk. Thunk.

He used his full weight to push the door shut before twisting the simple wooden latch to secure it. Then he followed the sound. Down the slope, through dense woods that sheltered the dark, even on a summer's day. He smelled something, something musky, organic.

Thunk.

Not musky. Bloody. The old man had been complaining about too many roosters; he must be getting rid of some of them.

Except he hasn't heard any chicken protests, and chickens do not do anything quietly. Plus it's an awful long way to go to kill anything you want to eat, anything you'd want to take back to the kitchen.

Suddenly he knew where he was going. There was a little area ahead, shielded from view, where a rocky chunk rose out of the leaf-strewn earth and the trail swung around it. That's where he'd find the old man. If he wanted to. And he wasn't sure he wanted to anymore. Maybe he should just turn around. See if his little brother had made it home yet and get him started on the rest of his chores (the ones he hasn't done for him already) so the old man didn't tan his ass.

Thunk.

But he had to know. So he kept walking, not bothering to move quietly, hoping that somehow his presence would be noted and whatever he heard would stop before he got there. And disappear, as if it had never been.

He reached the rocky chunk and hesitated. The smell was stronger now. Not quite as bad as when the men butchered in the fall, but bad enough to make his stomach churn. He rounded the lumpy bit of land, and there was the back of the old man in his work overalls. The bloody axe rested on one shoulder. A sugar maple clung to the bank next to the old man, spindly limbs outstretched, and he could swear the leaves were speckled with red.

But it was too late to turn back. He couldn't move, his feet rooted to the ground. His father turned, and the boy felt his pants go warm and wet with urine. His throat seized up, but he managed to choke out a single word.

"Please—"

~

THUNK—

Adam bolted upright in bed, sweating, too scared to scream. Too scared to breathe, he realized with a sudden gasp, lungs thirsty, ribs aching.

Bang, bang, bang, bang!

"Jesus!" Adam's heart thumped so hard, his entire body thudded with his pulse. He could see his fingers jump with it as he untangled them from a thin blanket in a dimly lit world. His blanket. In his bed at Iris's. And there was someone knocking at the door. He untangled the rest of his body and found he was still wearing the clothes he wore—yesterday? The room was dark except for a nightlight. No light shone through the curtain, but the sun came up late now. He glanced at the clock on the nightstand— 6:23 a.m. Okay, so it was Saturday, and he was wearing his T-shirt and pants from yesterday.

Bang, bang, bang!

Who knocks on the door at six a.m.? And where was Iris? *Iris...*

Adam jumped out of bed, kicking a trashcan oddly situated next to the bed. There was a nightlight in the hallway as well, and one on the stairs. He gripped the wooden rail and forced himself to descend more slowly than his frantic brain wanted. His knees were so weak, he nearly fell at the bottom when he let go of the railing. The porch light was already on—he could see it through the small window in the door—and he flipped the light on in the entryway before unlocking the door and throwing it wide.

An unfamiliar man in a green uniform (*state police?*) stood on the porch. *Is this what it was like for Iris?* The man removed his hat as Adam almost tore the screen door from its hinges.

"Is Iris okay?" Adam demanded. "What happened?"

"Adam Rutledge?" the man asked. He was about Adam's age— early thirties, with close-cropped dark hair—but his calm, deep voice seemed older.

Adam gripped the doorframe. "Yes, I'm Adam Rutledge. Please tell me what's happened to my grandmother."

"Nothing, sir. I'm sorry if I alarmed you. Your grandmother is fine. I'm here for another reason entirely. I'm Trooper—"

Adam didn't hear the rest. He sank down and found himself sitting on the floor, leaning against the door. He nearly fell on his back when the door drifted open further.

"Sir, are you all right?" the officer asked.

Adam flinched when he felt a hand on his shoulder. "Yes, I'm fine. I just, I was—" *Having a hellacious nightmare and thought I'd woken to an even worse one.* Adam wiped his eyes with the heels of his hands. "Sorry. Just give me a minute."

Adam got to his feet slowly. The officer stood on the threshold, neither in nor out, and the chilly air from outside helped clear Adam's head. "So why are you here?"

"Sir, there was a crime committed at the town festival last night, and we need to get statements from everyone who was there."

"Now?" Adam asked.

"Time is crucial, or I wouldn't be here. I can give you a ride to the Sheriff's Department right now," the man said.

"Uh, okay," Adam said, his head apparently not so clear after all. He was having trouble making the pieces of the picture fit together. The whole experience was surreal. Where was Iris? And how had he gotten to her house? The flannel shirt he'd worn the day before was draped across a dining chair, folded in half. His keys were on the table, and he found his wallet in one of the heavy shirt's pockets.

It wasn't until he'd locked the front door that the obvious question occurred to Adam. "Wait—what kind of crime?"

The state trooper didn't respond, except to tell Adam to get in the backseat (departmental policy). Adam climbed into the Impala, his torso muscles protesting as he crunched down to sit. "What crime?" he repeated.

"Kidnapping," the trooper said from the front as he started the vehicle. "A young boy was taken last night."

That's when Adam knew he was in trouble.

15

Bruce sat outside the Sheriff's Department, sipping a lukewarm, bitter cup of coffee. It was midmorning—after ten a.m., he saw by his watch—and Adam had been in there for a long time. Adam wasn't alone—there'd been vehicles from multiple law enforcement agencies coming and going with witnesses all morning—but he did seem to be special in the amount of time they were taking with them. The poor guy must be a real sight by now, considering how bad he'd looked the night before.

Bruce almost felt guilty for calling in the tip. But not quite.

An older model sedan pulled into the parking lot. *Well, well, well. If it isn't Iris Rutledge.* Someone—or more likely, multiple some-ones—would be getting an earful in the next few minutes. At this point, they'd have nothing to hold Adam with, so presumably they'd let him leave with Iris shortly.

Bruce started his vehicle. He should be going anyway. The drugs would be wearing thin on his little Batman by now. He'd been conservative because he wasn't sure how the child would metabolize the cocktail. This was, after all, a learning experience.

He'd always believed in lifelong learning, which was why he had one more errand to run before checking on the kid. And this was one he rather thought he'd enjoy.

16

─────────

There's nothing like wearing vomit to give you confidence while being questioned by the police. Adam had realized that a few hours ago, first left alone in a room. There was no clock, but he'd remained alone long enough to notice an odor and sincerely wish he'd changed T-shirts before coming in. The fluorescent lights made him feel hungover.

The state trooper who'd picked Adam up had returned to question him. Adam explained that he'd been sick (he could've sworn he saw the trooper look at his shirt then) and that he wasn't entirely clear on all of the events of the evening. He had no recollection of seeing the child, or of seeing a man dressed like a bear. He described his movements, as best he could remember them, and was left fumbling to explain how he'd made his way home with his vehicle still parked at JJ's.

The state trooper had been cordial enough—not rude, but not friendly either—and had brought Adam a cup of water before leaving him alone again. Adam was too dehydrated to have to go to the bathroom, and thankfully his stomach and bowels seemed to have settled down. Still, he would've killed for a toothbrush and an opportunity to get cleaned up.

He'd put his head down on the laminate table and dozed off when the door opened again, and he finally saw a friendly face. Or at least a haggard, familiar face. "Grant!" he said with relief.

But Grant wasn't smiling, and another familiar face followed on his heels. A decidedly unfriendly one. "Thanks for coming in," Grant said. "I assume you remember Special Agent D'Antonio."

Adam didn't acknowledge the FBI agent as he sat next to the Sheriff. "Grant, I'm happy to do anything I can to help you find the boy, but I told the other officer everything I know. I was sick last night—I still feel pretty awful—so I didn't stick around and I didn't even see the boy."

D'Antonio leaned across the table. "There's someone else who says you did."

Adam was terrified and angry, both reflex reactions. "Then someone is mistaken. Look, the condition I was in, I wouldn't have seen *the president* unless he was standing between me and a bathroom stall."

"The last time I saw you," Grant said, "that's the direction you were headed, toward the schoolhouse bathrooms. Where'd you go after that?"

"I don't know exactly." Adam put his elbows on the table and rested his face in his hands. He wrinkled his nose; he smelled his own body odor in addition to the vomit. "It's like I told the state trooper, I decided to go wait at JJ's car, but I didn't know where she was parked. I walked toward town..."

He lifted his face. "I got as far as the cemetery, and then I got sick again. And that's all I remember."

"So you shit on somebody's grave?" D'Antonio asked.

"No! I wouldn't do that. I just—I had to vomit, okay? I tried to do it in the trees, but I'm not sure how far I got."

D'Antonio sat back in his chair and rested his clasped hands on his belly. "So somehow you got home to your grandma's without a car. Convenient. You know what that reminds me of? Your daddy, Virgil Rutledge. He kidnapped a child and somehow took her— what, maybe twenty miles?—off into the woods without a car. We never found a vehicle anywhere on the access roads around there. You know anything about that?"

Adam's stomach cramped and he felt a rush of heat in his head. He took a deep breath before answering. "No sir, I don't."

"Can you tell me again how you managed to find Rachel Nicholson? That was some damned good luck," D'Antonio noted with a touch of sarcasm.

"Yes, sir, it was," Adam agreed, voice calm. "Except for the part where I almost died."

"Do you know where Iris was last night?" Grant asked.

"I can guess, but I have no way of knowing. I haven't seen her since she dropped me off by JJ's to get my car towed out of the ditch."

There was a knock, and the door opened just far enough for someone to motion Grant to the door. "Excuse me," he said.

Adam was left staring at D'Antonio. The man smiled. "You really expect me to believe you don't know where you were last night or how you got home?"

"No," Adam said, and the man blinked, betraying a hint of surprise. "I don't expect you to believe it, but it's true. Look, I know you don't trust me—"

"I suspect the feeling is mutual," he said.

The corner of Adam's mouth curled in the smallest smile he could manage. "You're right, it is. But if I had something to do with this, wouldn't I have had a better story ready? Some explanation of where I was last night beyond 'I don't know'?"

D'Antonio nodded. "Yes, you would. Unless you didn't plan to do it." Eyes intense, he leaned forward so quickly his chair nearly went out from under him. "Come on, Rutledge—where's the boy?"

Adam could imagine D'Antonio beating him—torturing him even—to save the child. And he couldn't blame him. But he wasn't frightened of the man, either. Of course, Adam's instinct for self-preservation hadn't exactly been fully functional lately. He leaned in as well, close enough for the agent to smell the vomit on his shirt, and said, "I swear to God, if I knew I'd tell you."

The door swung open again to admit Grant. He looked at D'Antonio, something passed between them, and D'Antonio shook his head in frustration. Then Grant told Adam, "Iris is here if you're ready to leave."

IRIS SAT in the reception area, face flushed. On his way out, Adam had gotten pointed looks from a bunch of men he didn't recognize, but they were nothing compared to the scowl Iris directed at Adam's escort. She stood and walked outside to her car, not waiting to see if Adam followed.

Achy and lightheaded, Adam fell behind his grandmother crossing the parking lot. He tried to shade his eyes from the sunny sky, but that only made him realize how sore his abdominal muscles were from repeated vomiting, on top of all the previous abuse. Iris had already started the engine by the time he reached her car. She wrinkled her nose when he got in, then stared at the front of his shirt.

"The sandwich?" she asked.

"I guess so."

"I'm sorry, kiddo," she said, and pulled out of the lot and onto the road toward home. "Those are the kinds of things you hate to be right about."

Adam pulled the sun visor down, leaned back in his seat and shut his eyes. "I might need a lawyer."

"Let's not talk about that right now."

He reluctantly opened his eyes and looked over to see her gripping the steering wheel tightly, at exactly ten and two. "Iris, we can't pretend that, just because I didn't do anything wrong, everything will be alright."

She huffed. "I know that. I just don't want to talk about it while you still look—and smell—like death warmed over."

Adam smiled. "Fair enough. How'd you know to come get me?"

Iris spoke carefully, as if she were trying very hard not to be self-conscious. "I just got home about an hour ago. JJ had left a couple of messages, looking for you. But before I could track her down, Luther called."

"Really?" Adam was surprised. He hadn't seen Luther at the Sheriff's Department. In fact, he hadn't seen him since last night. "Why?"

"He didn't say in so many words, but I got the impression he thought they ought to be spending their precious time—that child's precious time—elsewhere."

Adam sighed and closed his eyes again. "I'm glad somebody did."

He dozed off and didn't wake when Iris pulled up in front of the house, not until she patted his leg. "Come on," she said. "Let's see if we can get you to something approximating human."

Iris vetoed his desire for a bath ("waste of hot water, not to mention in your current state you'd probably drown"), and Adam took a long, blissful hot shower instead. He shaved, put on a clean shirt and jeans and followed the scent of homemade chicken soup down the stairs. He was of two minds, or rather, two stomachs— one ravenous and drooling and one still looking for an excuse to purge. Iris must have seen the war on his face when he entered the kitchen. He took his usual seat at the table, and she set a half-full bowl of soup and a plate of saltines in front of him.

"Let's see how you do with that first," she said.

"Thank you, Iris."

She touched his face with her hand, teasing the spot that dimpled when he smiled. "Almost."

"Almost human or almost shaved?" he asked.

"Both," she replied. She served herself from a big pot on the stove before sitting next to him.

The first three slurping spoonfuls were manna from heaven. In the fourth, the texture of one of the noodles struck his contrary stomach as wrong, and the smell just seemed a little bit off. He set his spoon on the plate and decided to stick with saltines for a while, nibbling from the corners to the center.

"How's Harlan?" he asked, trying to distract his stomach by being mischievous.

"Quite well," Iris said, straight-faced, though he thought it took some effort. "He sends his regards, and wants to know when you're coming to see him."

Adam brushed some cracker crumbs from his face with a napkin. "Why doesn't he ever come here?"

"He doesn't like this house," Iris said, taking her bowl to the sink. "It's a hard place for him to be."

"What's that mean?" Adam asked, coughing cracker crumbs onto his shirt front.

"He won't say, specifically. But there are things that linger here, ugly things. Some of them I experienced myself—which is probably why he doesn't want to bring them up—but this has been my home for most of my life, and I've had more good days than bad," she said, rinsing the bowl and setting it in the dish drainer. "I suppose he can only see the bad."

Adam gave up on the rest of his soup, putting his own bowl in the sink. He brushed his shirt off over the trashcan while he was up.

"What were you really dreaming about yesterday, when you were screaming?" Iris asked.

Surprised, Adam turned too quickly, and leaned against the counter to cover a moment of dizziness. "Just what you said. I was dreaming about the accident that killed mom, like I always do."

Except this time I saw myself. He didn't dare share that revelation with his grandmother.

"So you haven't *seen*—" She hesitated. "You don't *know* anything about the boy."

"No," he said, truthfully. *I wish I did.* Another thought he didn't share, instead confirming, "It's not like with Rachel. I can't help them find him."

"Good."

He kept his face impassive, but Iris still became defensive. "I will not lose you, too."

"You won't lose me. Look, I told you I can't help them."

"I won't lose you to the law, either."

"They were only questioning me because I was there last night," he said.

"That's not the only reason," she countered, drying the bowls she'd already washed.

"It doesn't help that I didn't have an alibi," he admitted. "But that's why I said I might need a lawyer. Not that I think they consider me a serious suspect, but just to play it safe."

She crossed her arms firmly and stared at him. "A lawyer won't be enough."

His mind was still sluggish, but something in her eyes—a kind of fierce determination—finally clicked for him. "You think I should run?" he asked, incredulous. "Why in God's name would I want to do that?"

"Because they're going to come for you. And once that happens, no one will be able to keep you safe." She was so calm and certain, almost fatalistic.

"Iris, that's crazy. Grant knows—"

"No, *your father* is crazy. This is just plain common sense. And Grant Mason isn't the only one you have to worry about," she said, walking toward the stairs.

"What's my father have to do with it?" Adam asked.

"I'm not sure," she admitted, pausing on the stairs. "But with him already in jail and another child missing, who do you think they'll look to next? Unless they find something to point them somewhere else, who do you think their prime suspect will be?"

Adam fidgeted with the rounded edges of one of the staircase balusters. Iris was overreacting—he knew that—but he couldn't help but recall the way D'Antonio had looked at him, how convinced the FBI agent appeared to be that Adam was involved. That had been true this morning, and when he'd previously questioned Adam in the hospital about Rachel's disappearance. Iris was right about that part; if the boy wasn't found, D'Antonio was not going away.

His grandmother had gone ahead, and he mounted the stairs to find her waiting in his bedroom, sitting on the wooden chair next to the bed, the spot where she'd spent so many nights in his childhood. "What are you doing?" he asked.

"Watching while you pack a bag."

17

"Mom, you're making a mess."

Evie's voice pulled JJ back to the present, back to the little table outside the mall where she sat with her daughter and Rachel, holding an ice cream cone that dribbled onto her sore wrist and the cuff of her long-sleeved shirt.

"Damn!" JJ said, then looked at the girls apologetically.

"Don't worry, Miss Tulley," Rachel said, licking her cone carefully. "If I get secret ice cream, you can have a secret swear word."

JJ smiled and dabbed at her sleeve with a pile of napkins. She'd actually gotten a special ice cream dispensation from Dorothy when she'd offered to take the girls to the Plattsville mall to distract them—especially Rachel—from the missing boy. But Rachel didn't need to know that. "Thank you, sweetie. Sorry, my mind drifted off somewhere. Did I miss the identity of the latest, cutest boy in class?"

The girls were right on the cusp, at that age where they were starting to like boys but weren't always ready to admit to it. Today, Evie was leaning toward the latter.

"No, Mom!" She spoke in an indignant, how-did-you-function-before-I-came-along tone. "I was saying how stupid Trevor got us all in trouble in English and that's why the whole class has to write an essay this weekend."

"Well, then, I guess we'd better be finishing our ice cream so you can go home and get to work."

Evie rolled her eyes. JJ stuck her tongue out at her daughter, and Evie replied in kind. Thank God she wasn't a teenager yet.

"I'll bet she didn't hear me because she was thinking about the Sheriff," Evie stage-whispered. Rachel looked uneasy for a moment until Evie added, "She thinks he's cute."

Rachel relaxed and the girls giggled conspiratorially. JJ almost blushed as she attacked her ice cream, eating the chunk-filled, vanilla mess down to the pointed sugar cone. She had been thinking about Grant, but not the way the girls meant. She'd been thinking about him showing up on her doorstep last night, and what it meant for Adam. Iris had called earlier to let her know she'd picked him up from the station, and that he was sleeping. JJ needed to speak with Adam, but she was almost afraid to. Something wasn't right with him. After twenty years apart, she felt like she was losing him again. But this time, she wasn't sure he'd ever make it back.

She needed to speak with Grant, too. She'd never quite gotten around to telling him about the latest Marcus drama. She'd almost told Otto this morning when she picked up Rachel. Perhaps Marcus would take the wrong driveway the next time and find himself staring down the barrel of one of Otto's rifles. Or into his fists.

"Is he your boyfriend?" Evie asked.

There I go, drifting off again. She focused on her daughter and said, "I don't know what he is. What do you think? Would that be a bad thing if he was?"

Now it was Evie's turn to be uncomfortable. She shrugged. "He's okay."

"I think he's nice," Rachel volunteered.

JJ crunched the last bit of her cone and wiped her hands as best she could. Rachel looked at her expectantly. She knew

Dorothy was one of those people who smeared antibacterial gel compulsively, but it drove JJ nuts. It was bad enough having to use the stuff at work, when it actually made sense to do so. "Shall we go, ladies?"

The girls were subdued in the back seat on the way home. They'd passed through Cold Springs and reached the familiar straight stretch at the Howard farm, with its brown fields and small herd of cattle, when Evie spoke.

"Do you think they'll find Aaron?" she asked.

The boy was a year behind the girls in school, so of course he was on their minds. JJ, only half lying, said, "Yes, I do, sweetie."

"Why aren't you looking for him?" Evie asked.

JJ met her daughter's demanding, brown eyes in the rearview mirror before heading into a sequence of sharp turns. "That's what the Sheriff's Department is trained to do, and they've got all kinds of other people in law enforcement to help them."

"You found Rachel."

JJ tapped her brakes and steered around a rock in the road, tumbled from a nearby steep bank. "That was different."

"Your mom didn't find me," Rachel said, voice soft. "She carried me off the mountain, but Adam found me."

JJ tilted her head enough to risk a glance at the girl. She was staring out the window, as if at something far away.

"Except sometimes," Rachel admitted, "I think maybe I found him."

SOMETHING'S NOT RIGHT. Trooper wasn't standing at the edge of his tie-out, wagging his tail in greeting. JJ raised in her seat and finally saw him, lying next to his doghouse in a depression that hadn't been there—or at least hadn't been as deep—before.

"Girls," she said, parking her Bronco and tucking her cell phone into her pocket, "stay in the car until I tell you to get out."

The dog's water bowl was empty, with a pile of vomit nearby.

She approached the shepherd mix cautiously, but he didn't move until she knelt next to him and called his name. "Trooper?"

He thumped his tail once, and lifted his muzzle far enough for JJ to see the foamy strand of saliva that connected to the ground. *Shit.* His chest heaved a strenuous inhale, and she counted off the seconds (*six*) before the next one. She placed one hand gently atop his long skull and used the other to peel back his lips, revealing gums that were nearly white. A wave of grief swept through JJ, making her lips and eyes tingle.

"Mom?" Evie called behind her, and JJ started. "Is Trooper going to die?"

JJ squeezed her eyes shut and let anger rush through her, pushing the grief away, before turning to her daughter. Rachel stood behind Evie, face pink and on the verge of tears.

"I hope not, sweetie, but he's very sick," JJ said. "I need the two of you to run next door and get Otto. Hurry."

JJ watched the girls sprint through the woods that separated the Tulley and Nicholson properties while she pulled out her cell phone. Their vet was programmed in her contacts, but the woman's office wasn't open on Saturday afternoon. JJ stroked Trooper's flank as the phone rang (*so goddamn slowly*) on the other end. Finally, a recording greeted her with the number for the local vet currently on call. JJ wrote the number in the dirt with her finger, then punched it in. The tech who answered transferred her directly to the vet. She told him what they'd found. His office was half an hour away and she'd never been there before, so she tried to stay calm as he gave her directions.

"I'd advise you not to bring your daughter, and make sure she says her goodbyes," he said.

JJ hung up and pressed her forearm against her face to hold back the tears. Evie did not need this so soon after losing her grandfather. Deep breath. *Mother fucking sonuva fucking bitch.* She lifted her head and saw Otto emerging from the woods with Evie. At least they'd left Rachel behind.

"Good girl, Evie!" she called out before her daughter could ask about her dog. "Now I need you to go get the tarp for the back, and a dog towel."

JJ watched as her child grabbed the keys from the Bronco and sprinted toward the house, a girl on a mission.

Otto rubbed a knuckle on Trooper's head, in the ridge that rode up from between his eyes, his threat to kill the dog a few weeks ago apparently forgotten. "I'm sorry, JJ. He looks bad. He get into some poison?"

She shrugged, though that was her best guess, and the vet's as well.

"What do you want me to do?" he asked.

"I'll need your help getting him in the truck in a minute. I figured we'd fold the tarp in half and lay him on top to carry him." She paused to get her shaking voice under control. "The vet thinks there's a good chance he won't make it. Can I leave Evie with you and Dorothy?"

"Of course," he said.

"There's something else." She told him about the incident with Marcus the night before. He shook his head, muttering something under his breath that she couldn't hear, but suspected did not bode well for Marcus's health.

"Don't worry, JJ. Evie's safe with us. She always will be. But do you think he'll really come back?"

She sometimes forgot that Otto had maybe met Marcus once or twice, and certainly didn't know the man. Her hand met Otto's at the top of the panting dog's head, and she looked at him.

"I think the bastard already did."

18

———

"This is such bullshit," Luther said, for about the millionth time. "You know that, right?"

"I'm sorry, Luther." Gerald had said that multiple times, too.

"It's not your fault," Luther reassured him. "You didn't know the man had such a hard-on for Rutledge."

Special Agent D'Antonio had heard about the incident with Virgil Rutledge and his attorney and asked Gerald for his version of the events. Luther wasn't even sure if the disclosure was legal, but the deputy had told him what he'd heard. And of course, what he'd heard was a crazy man implicating his son.

"You're sure Adam Rutledge doesn't have anything to do with this?"

"Pretty damn sure," Luther replied.

D'Antonio tore into Grant after learning what Gerald had witnessed, spouting off about being blind and letting kidnappers go free. They went into Grant's office and shut the door so they could yell at each other in private. If D'Antonio knew Luther was the one who'd called Iris about Adam, Luther had no doubt he'd have been on the receiving end, too. After a few minutes, Grant and D'Antonio came back out and sent Luther to JJ's house. They'd gotten authorization for a search warrant for Adam's car, but the judge wasn't willing to go further than that over the phone and without more evidence. Grant and D'Antonio were waiting with the judge at his home now for the results of the search of Adam's car. Depending on what was found, the judge could authorize a search of Iris's home as well. Officer Kiss-Ass Kilbourne (so Luther called him, Kissy for short) had arrived a few minutes ago with the signed car search warrant. Luther had convinced him to wait until JJ returned home before executing it. Or at least, he thought he had.

Luther strode toward Adam's car, where Kissy was peering in the windows. He was a young guy—a punk with a badge, really. Not that Luther hadn't crossed some lines in his time, but he felt as though that's the only reason Kissy had joined the neighboring county's Sheriff's Department. Kissy had been on loan for the previous kidnapping as well, but even on brief acquaintance the man rubbed Luther the wrong way, so he'd managed to avoid him. Over the past twelve hours, Luther had decided the man was also jockeying for position, hoping to impress the FBI folks he interacted with so rarely. Not that Kissy would ever make it at the Academy, although Luther would surely like to see him try.

"What the hell do you think you're doing?" Luther asked.

Kissy grinned as he opened the passenger door of Adam's car. "Well, lookee here. He didn't even lock it."

Luther was carrying a few extra pounds, and he used every one of them to slam the door shut with his hip. Kissy stepped up to Luther, removing his campaign hat so they stood toe to toe. Gerald intervened, almost as quickly as he had in the interrogation room, looking uncomfortable. "Come on now, guys. We're all on the same side here, aren't we?"

Luther thought that remained to be seen, but he took a moment to remember why he was there. As much as it pushed his buttons that an asshole outsider wrongly and blindly suspected Adam of involvement, Adam wasn't in any danger. The boy was. And the sooner they eliminated Adam from their inquiries, the sooner they could find the real culprit, and hopefully the child.

"Fine," Luther said. "Let's just get this done."

The words were no sooner out of his mouth than JJ's Bronco came flying up the driveway. She was alone, and she already appeared frazzled, nearly falling out of her vehicle before a word was spoken. She looked around, taking in the two law enforcement vehicles from two different counties, and headed straight for Luther.

"Are you here about my dog?" JJ asked.

"I—uh, no. What about your dog?" Luther looked around and realized the dog was nowhere to be seen. Normally it would have been barking its fool brains out.

"Never mind," JJ said. "If it's not for that, why are you here? Is it about the boy?"

Luther took a deep breath and held up a couple of sheets of paper. "JJ, don't freak out. We're here to execute a search warrant on Adam's car." He nodded to Kiss-Ass, and took a few steps away from the car while the man got down to business. "We have no right to search anywhere else on your property, and we have no intention of doing so."

JJ's mouth dropped open. She closed it with her hand, then shook her head. "I don't have time for this shit. I have to be at work in a couple of hours. I'd like to shower the dog vomit off first, and oh yeah—head next door and tell my daughter that her dog isn't dead yet."

She was on the verge of angry tears, and her clothes were a little worse for wear, with unidentifiable stains on her T-shirt.

"JJ, is there something going on? Something you want to tell me about?"

She waved her hand through the air as if swatting a noisome fly. "You know this is a complete crock of shit."

Luther risked putting a reassuring hand on JJ's arm. She looked like she could use it. "Yes, I do know that. But some of the higher-ups don't, and the sooner we do this, the sooner they'll stop wasting time looking at Adam."

Kissy let out a whoop behind them that would've been appropriate at a monster truck rally. Luther turned to see him triumphantly holding an item about the size of a fat book in the air. "Waste of time, huh? Well, look what I found in the little peckerwood's hatchback."

Luther stepped forward for a better look, and his stomach roiled. It was a costume, a brown hooded robe still in its plastic package. Luther donned latex gloves, and Kissy handed the item to him. "Looks like a match to me."

"No!" JJ said. "You know Adam never locks his car. This doesn't mean anything." She turned away with her cell phone in hand.

"Hey!" Kissy yelled. "You can't do that."

The deputy grabbed for her phone, but JJ sidestepped him easily, making him look a cloddish fool. She put the phone to her ear and dodged him a second time, and Luther watched the deputy flush with angry embarrassment. The man's hand drifted to his waist...

"Kiss-A—uh, Kilbourne, I'll get it," Luther said, and passed the costume back to him. "Bag the evidence."

Luther held out his hand. "Don't worry, JJ. I'll give it back before I leave."

JJ made a face like she was ready to spit in his hand, but set her phone in it instead. He was sure she only gave it up because there was no answer on Adam's end.

While Luther was doing this, Kilbourne pulled out his smart phone and took a picture, then placed a call of his own. "Sir, this is Officer Kilbourne. Did you get the photo?" He tilted the phone away from his face and told Luther, "They're showing it to the judge."

"Luther, you know anyone could've put that there," JJ pleaded. He didn't respond, and everyone fell silent, staring at Kilbourne's phone. Waiting. It didn't take long.

"Yes sir, I'm still here." He paused, nodding as if the man on the other end of the phone could see him. "Yes sir, I'll head on over. As soon as I wrap up at the Tulley place."

The man hung up and tucked his phone into his pocket, then handed the package to Gerald and said, "You want to bag this? Make it quick if you want to go with me. Daylight's wasting. I'm heading to Iris Rutledge's house. We got the search warrant."

19

____

Adam sat on a stone in the middle of a clearing, soaking up the last rays of the sun. He'd warmed enough to roll up his sleeves a couple of hours ago, and his undershirt was sticky—though not drenched—with sweat. The surrounding woods were dim and cool as dusk approached, and soon the chill would reach him as well. But the moment of comfortable repose felt so good, he didn't want it to end.

He'd spent much of the afternoon in a surprisingly restful nap, then managed another half bowl of soup and crackers and ventured outside to work on Iris's garden. When his uncle was still alive, Adam's grandparents had cultivated row upon row of corn, potatoes, tomatoes, multiple varieties of beans, turnips, beets, a cabbage patch, and on and on. They'd also kept livestock—hogs and chickens, a few head of cattle for meat and milking, and the occasional sheep. Come fall, the kitchen was alive—and blisteringly hot—with the sounds and smells of canning. The men butchered then as well, and an assembly line of women packed the meat to be frozen.

Adam knew this from the stories Iris told, years later when it was just the two of them on the property. Even then, they'd kept a small kitchen garden with a few favorites, including Adam's crook-neck squash. In recent years, however, the garden fence had fallen into disrepair and Iris hadn't bothered putting anything out (without a barrier, the deer made short work of anything but tomatoes). Fixing the fence became Adam's project after he got out of the hospital, something tangible he could focus on when it wasn't freezing outside. He'd overdone it today, digging out rotten fence posts and dragging them into a pile, but it felt good to get something done, to have aches and pains of exertion rather than inexplicable injuries. He watched a pair of cardinals, perched on a remaining fence post, as they watched him in turn. He wondered if Iris fed the birds in winter, if perhaps they had some sort of race memory and were waiting for that day to come.

Most of Adam's thoughts that afternoon hadn't been devoted to nostalgia or philosophy. He'd woken from his nap, feeling almost refreshed, except for the picture in his mind of a little boy in a Batman costume. The picture hadn't *arisen* in his mind; it was planted there during his interrogation this morning by people who knew what he did not. Adam couldn't actually see the boy, only what had been described to him. And that wasn't enough. He needed to speak with Harlan.

Adam had kept these thoughts to himself. He felt certain Harlan could help him help the boy, but he was just as certain this would drive another wedge between Harlan and Iris. Rather than daydreaming of batter-dipped, fried squash and sweet iced tea, Adam had pondered how to ensure that whatever happened was all on him. None of the blame could fall to Harlan. He and Iris had a chance to be happy together for whatever remained of their lives, and Adam didn't want to jeopardize that. But he couldn't ignore the child.

Adam sighed and rose, stretching his hands over his head with a satisfied moan. He was brushing the dirt from the seat of his pants when he heard two things at once: a vehicle's tires—as if it had missed its turn and slammed its brakes to go back—and Iris screaming his name.

He jumped a fallen bit of fencing and ran toward the house, ignoring the familiar tug in his side.

"Adam!" Iris screamed again.

"I'm coming!" He met her just below the front porch. "Are you—"

"Inside!" Iris demanded, and turned on her heel back into the house.

By the time he made it through the front door, Iris was halfway up the stairs. He ran after her, and she met him at the top with the duffel bag they'd packed together a few hours ago. "You have to go," Iris said. "Now!"

Passing him the bag, she raced to the kitchen and grabbed a paper sack from the counter. The heavy duffel tugged at Adam's ribs, and he shifted the strap to the other shoulder. Iris unbalanced him yanking the bag toward her, unzipping it, and shoving the paper sack inside.

"Iris, what's going on?"

"JJ just called," she said. "They're coming to arrest you."

"Arrest me?" Adam heard a vehicle heading up the driveway, presumably the same one he'd heard turning around earlier. "This is crazy, Iris. I can't run. Maybe they'll take me in and question me again, but eventually they'll have to admit I didn't have anything to do with this."

Iris shook her head and forced him toward the hallway, as the vehicle's engine cut off. "By then it might be too late."

"Iris, you're overreacting—"

"No, I'm not," she insisted, still shoving him away from the front door. "I should've told you about Virgil, but I wanted you to rest, and I never had a chance. You'll have to take the bolthole."

She placed her hand against a section of wainscoting beneath the stairs, and somehow suddenly there was an opening in the wall.

Adam was so shocked, he didn't protest as she pushed him inside. Finally, her words caught up with him. "What about Virgil? What happened when you saw him?"

Iris held her breath, clearly not wanting to answer, but knowing

Adam wouldn't leave if she didn't. "He said you were behind kidnapping Rachel, and that you'd do it again. And now another child is missing."

There was a pounding at the front door, and Adam's legs turned to water. He tried to brace himself against the wall inside the bolthole and knocked a glass jar from a shelf. It hit the floor, shattering, and the air filled with the eye-watering odor of old canned tomatoes. Iris grabbed Adam's shoulders to steady him.

"I'm so sorry," she said. "Now go. Harlan will pick you up at the spot where you kids used to cross the road. It might be a while, so keep your head down."

"Coming!" she yelled. She grabbed his face and pulled it down so she could kiss him on the forehead. "I love you, kid. Be safe."

"I love you, Gram," Adam said, and watched her trembling hand cover her mouth before she pushed the door closed, plunging him into darkness.

Moments later, he heard the front door open over the sounds of Iris's protests. Standing in the dark, her voice in the distance, Adam experienced a moment of déjà vu. He'd been in the hidden space once as a child, escorted by Iris. A bare bulb hung from the ceiling in the space carved out under the stairs, but he didn't dare try it now. Iris had packed a flashlight in the zippered end of his duffel, and he rummaged in the dark until he pulled it free. He still didn't turn it on, stretching out his hands, turning and slowly shuffling forward. The flashlight he carried bumped a jar in the dark, causing a resounding *ting* and setting the jar wobbling noisily against its neighbors. Adam held his breath.

Two sets of footsteps approached from the entryway. He heard Iris's voice, but couldn't make out the words. Adam jumped as something thumped next to him on the other side of the wall. Was it the cop banging, trying to get in?

"I said, I need my medicine!" The wall thumped again, and this time when Iris spoke, her voice was closer to the ground, as if she were kneeling or sitting on the floor. "It's in the kitchen, on the counter next to the stove."

Had she fallen? What medicine did Iris take? Had he given his grandmother a heart attack on top of everything else? Adam ran his fingers across the wall, past the shelves, searching for the edges of the door so he could get to her. He opened his mouth to call out, when Iris's voice came through the wall clearly, almost next to his head, "Go—now!"

Thank God. Adam savored the sense of relief for a moment, touching the wall where he'd heard her voice, before switching on his flashlight and fleeing.

The old Rutledge house had served multiple generations, including some who'd made their meager fortunes distilling moonshine. Adam didn't know if the passage had been built for that purpose, or if it predated the Rutledge booze runners and they'd simply taken advantage of what was already there. The first portion, wood-framed with a level dirt floor, stretched for about twenty feet before hitting a right angle turn, presumably at the back end of the house.

Adam pointed his flashlight directly in front of his feet, stepping carefully, hesitant to touch "walls" recognizable as nothing more than thicker darkness in his peripheral vision. The floor here was made of rough, gray concrete with a sharp, downward slope. The air was cool and damp with an odor that reminded him of sawdust. Like many houses in the area, this one was tucked into the side of the mountain, using the earth to help regulate temperature. Adam believed he was passing from beneath the house itself to the neighboring dairy, also built into the side of the hill.

Adam arrived at one last turn, this time a hard left. The passage broadened a bit, and off to one side, the tarnished coils of the old Rutledge still reflected his flashlight's beam faintly alongside its big pot. Ahead of him was a plank wall with a wood scrap latch. He spun the simple catch and gave the wall a mighty shove —a bit too mighty. Adam flinched at—once again—the sound of breaking glass. The wall swung wide enough for him to step clear of it, pushing bits of broken glass and vegetable mush in its path.

As he'd suspected, Adam emerged into the dairy. From the

dairy side, the swinging wall was disguised by shelves full of canned vegetables with rusting lids that had likely gone toxic before Adam was born. He was careful not to knock any more to the ground with his bag as he pushed the wall shut behind him, but couldn't find a way to secure it. Perhaps the weight of the shelves kept it in place.

The dairy was a small space smelling strongly of lime, about ten feet wide by fifteen feet long, but shelves and empty, nested buckets along the walls made it feel more narrow. Dust motes swam in Adam's flashlight beam. He grabbed the handle on the thick, exterior door and pushed it hard, but it wouldn't budge. Throwing his full weight against it, he let out a loud, pained grunt as he struck the solid construction and his heavy duffel bag struck him. The door screamed as it came free of its thick, swollen frame.

Adam blinked against the meager sunlight still streaming through the trees. His eyes were drawn to the nearby freestanding pump house, containing the water pump and tanks for the well, but apparently no cops. Everything else was forest. Opening the door wide as he could, he shone his flashlight back into the dairy. The shelving looked like a wall rather than a door, but his boot prints were visible in the mixed vegetables on the floor.

A single siren whoop pierced the air, followed by the sound of another vehicle approaching the house. *Backup, or did Iris frighten the cop into calling for an ambulance?* Either way, he literally did not have time to cover his tracks. Shoving the door closed, Adam hurtled down the wooded ridge, duffel bag slamming against his hip.

20

─────

He races down the hill, as if the devil is at his heels. And maybe he is.

"Boy!" the old man bellows. "Don't you dare run from me!"

He doesn't slow down, but can't help glancing over his shoulder. The old man isn't as fast as he is, not running through the woods. But he'll never give up. That's the one thing he's always taught them—unlike the Pharaoh, you never give up on something you're chasing. But what if you're the one being chased?

There's a steeper section ahead, and he slows down, knowing how the wet leaves and the very earth beneath him can act as Judas. He glances over his shoulder again, and sees the old man making up distance. He cuts across the slope at a diagonal, aiming for a patch of woods where lightning took out some old trees and the little guys moved in with a frenzy of competition. The old man's too big to get in and out of that undergrowth as easily as he can.

Soon he's flying downhill through whip-thin branches. Green leaves slap at his skin and stick for an instant before letting go. He can't turn to look, can't see where the old man is, but surely he's fallen farther behind.

He crosses his arms in front of his face at the end, bursting through a last thick bit of vegetation. That's why he doesn't see the old man waiting for him. He doesn't see his big hickory stick either, until it's swinging through the air ("Spying bastard!" the old man yells) and cracks against his arm. He screams in shocked pain, and now he's tumbling, end over end down the mountain...

~

ADAM JERKED awake with the sound of a truck's horn—one quick toot. He blinked and looked around, struggling to find his place. *That wasn't me running.* Not anymore. He'd been dozing, slumped over his duffel bag, a tree trunk at his back.

It was nearly dark, and the pickup waiting on the road a dozen yards away was using its headlights, which made it even harder to distinguish its color. Adam threw his bag over his shoulder and crept closer, until only an old farm fence and some brush separated them, but he still didn't recognize the truck. Finally, the driver's door opened and a head popped up, pale in the dark.

"Adam—you out there?" Harlan Miller's voice was the kind of loud whisper you reserve for when you don't want to be heard, but you need to be. "Goddamn, son! Are you waiting for an engraved invitation?"

Branches and brambles clung to Adam's jeans as he scrambled to the waist-high fence and dropped his bag on the other side. A square section of the rusted wire bent but held while he stepped on it and swung his leg over. He tossed his bag in the extended cab space behind his seat before climbing in.

Harlan grinned. "I hear you're a wanted man."

Adam stared back at him; he didn't know what there was to be grinning about. Suddenly, Harlan didn't either.

"Shit. That was meant to be a joke, but the look on your face suggests I was a little too close to the mark. Helluva way to find out," he said, wasting no time putting the truck in gear and heading toward the highway. "You okay?"

Adam's stomach was cramping again, his body ached with the knowledge that he'd pushed himself too far in the garden this afternoon, and he was having trouble shaking the feeling of pursuit from his most-recent nightmare. Probably because he actually was being pursued by the authorities. But he said, "I'm fine."

"Like hell," Harlan said, veering around a pothole on the old asphalt road. "Sorry it took me so long to get here. Jim's out of town, but he called in and heard Iris's message on his machine, sent one of his kids over to let me know. I still haven't had a chance to speak with Iris, but I think she'll be at the hospital visiting with Mrs. Mason after her husband's surgery."

"So we're going to the hospital?" Adam asked. "Are you sure that's a good idea?"

"Probably not," Harlan admitted. "But at this point, I don't know what's a good idea and what isn't, because I don't really know what the hell is going on."

Adam told him what little he knew—that Iris had sent him away because someone came to arrest him.

Harlan blew out his breath. "You don't think that was maybe a little bit premature?"

"Probably," Adam admitted, and grinned when he realized how closely his tone of voice had echoed Harlan's from a moment ago. He looked over and caught Harlan's answering flash of teeth. The man struggled a bit when he reached the stop sign at the highway, trying to hold the big pickup in place on the incline.

"Whose truck is this?" Adam asked.

"Jim's," Harlan said, lurching forward. "Farm truck. His son brought it over and said Jim wanted me to use it. That should have been my first tip-off that things were serious. I think something got lost in translation, from Iris to Jim's machine to Jim to his son to me."

"Imagine that," Adam said, distracted by— "What in God's name is that smell?"

"Oh, good, you smell it, too," Harlan said. "I haven't had time to check the truck and I was afraid it was just me, kind of an olfactory hallucination."

"You get those often?" Adam asked. He couldn't place the odor, but it was potent and unpleasant.

"No."

Harlan's response was so brief, Adam knew he was holding something back. "Did you think it might have been related to the boy?" he asked.

"No," Harlan said, then softened to, "Not really. You know anything about the kid?"

"No, but I wanted to talk to you about it."

"So you finally want to talk to me, huh? I was starting to feel like a debt collector," Harlan snarked, glancing in Adam's direction. "Sorry. I'm afraid there's some crazy shit on the horizon, and I should have been getting ready for it. Let's just hold this conversation until I get the lay of the land from Iris."

Adam watched the road's texture (long, cracking tendrils here, a buckle there) and color (here nearly black, there bleached by salt) change as it passed through the truck's headlights, beneath and behind them. Trees thinned as they reached the outskirts of Plattsville, replaced by the occasional streetlight, and Adam slumped automatically in his seat. Where were they going, after the hospital? Where—and how—could this possibly end?

"Hey," Harlan said, drawing his attention. "Easy over there. We'll figure it out."

Adam smiled and shook his head, remembering an early conversation with the older man just a couple of weeks ago. *Not psychic, my ass*, he thought, wondering if Iris considered it potty mouthed if he didn't say it out loud.

Harlan laughed next to him. "I'll have to ask her," he said, as if Adam had spoken aloud.

The parking lot seemed surprisingly empty for a Saturday night, unless one knew Beecham County residents were the kind of folks who didn't go to the emergency room until they were bleeding out their ears. Saturday night tomfoolery usually didn't rise to that level, so long as the drunks stayed off the roads. Harlan parked in a handicapped spot in the front row. He reached past

Adam, pulled a handicapped card from the glovebox, and hung it from the rearview mirror.

Harlan grinned. "I don't know where the hell Jim got this—wily bastard—but I found it when I was checking the glovebox for the registration. There's even a cane in the back. Sit tight. I'll just be a minute, and we'll get back on the road."

Adam rolled his window down partway to let the stink out. He removed his seat belt and wriggled around, trying to get comfortable, while he watched Harlan enter the hospital. It was a nice enough building, with simple, contemporary lines gleaming white behind tastefully lit landscaping on this dark evening. In addition to its aesthetic appeal, the glass front had the advantage of showcasing Harlan's advance on the receptionist (no doubt charming her within an inch of her bed), before heading to the elevators.

Aesthetically appealing or not, Adam couldn't say he was glad to sit in front of the hospital again, having been so recently released. He felt antsy, agitated, as if something grave was right around the corner. He wanted to believe Harlan had planted that seed, the unjustified paranoia about craziness on the horizon. And yet, a moment later, it was upon them.

Adam watched in the side view mirror as headlights swung into the parking lot. He slouched, then slid off the seat entirely as the headlights drew near, ducking his head below the door. It was a squeeze, tucked in the footwell with the gearshift at his back, and Adam nearly lost an eye to the window crank, but he was soon glad of his caution. The headlights lit up the car interior above him, and he held his breath as the vehicle parked in the adjacent space.

No reason to be alarmed about a little old lady coming to check on her husband, he thought.

Except, it wasn't a little old lady.

He listened as the driver's door of the vehicle next to him opened, and slammed shut again. Then the passenger door opened as well. "I told you, I won't be long," said a voice a couple of feet away. "I just want to check on my dad real quick. You can wait in the car."

It wasn't an old lady come to check on her husband; it was Sheriff Grant Mason come to check on his father.

"That's okay," came Agent D'Antonio's reply. "I just finished up the media appeal. And there might be one or two people in there worth me talking to."

The agent's door slammed shut, too.

"I still don't like the language," Grant said, the tone of his voice suggesting 'don't like' was an understatement. "Adam Rutledge is a person of interest who may have information, not a suspect."

D'Antonio responded, "With all respect to your position in this community, a child's life is at stake. And that makes Rutledge a suspect."

There was a faint hollow, metallic sound Adam couldn't identify. Maybe Grant leaning against the car? "Well, with everyone moving on the roadblocks, hopefully we'll have Adam in hand soon and get all this straightened out."

"And find the boy," D'Antonio said pointedly.

"Look," Grant said, just as forcefully. "You don't have to remind me what my job is. I live here. I know that child; I know his family. And safely recovering him is my first priority."

The words were barely out of Grant's mouth when a cell phone rang. He said, "I'm sorry. Give me a minute." His voice trailed off as he stepped away from the vehicle.

Finding Iris and Harlan in the same room, it wouldn't take long for the Sheriff to put two and two together, and for Adam to end up in jail. He had to warn Harlan that the man was on the way.

Adam struggled to pull his cell phone from his pocket in the cramped space while keeping his head out of sight. If Jim hadn't gotten such a lumbering beast, perched high on its axles, he'd have been arrested by now. He couldn't risk his voice being heard and doubted his grandmother knew how to read a text. Harlan didn't have a phone. *JJ!* JJ worked tonight, and she kept her cell phone near because of Evie. He only hoped she could reach Harlan in time.

21

"What the hell were you thinking?" JJ demanded as she stepped into the room.

Iris rose from her chair alongside Ulysses Mason's bed and walked slowly, carefully to meet her. The woman looked old and worn out. "Perhaps we should take this somewhere else," she said.

JJ glanced at the sleeping patient before checking the hallway. It was empty, as it usually was in this part of the hospital, this time of night. There were few staff on duty, and even fewer visitors. She stepped back in and shut the door behind her.

"I think we'll be fine here," JJ said, but kept her voice low. "Why did you send Adam away? And don't try to tell me you didn't, because he wouldn't have come up with such a damn fool idea on his own."

Iris leaned in. "You said they were coming to arrest him—"

"I never said any such thing," JJ protested, voice rising. "I said they were coming to search your house, and that's all I said."

"Well, it was just a matter of time," Iris said with conviction.

JJ wanted to smack the woman for her damn arrogant certainty and all the trouble it had caused. "You know Grant won't let them railroad Adam. He's a good man."

Iris shook her head. "You sweet, naïve girl. Grant's got bigger things on his mind than Adam." She nodded toward the man in the bed. "Like his father, and the little Schofield boy. And Grant doesn't speak for everyone."

JJ still wanted to smack Iris, but there was some truth in what she was saying. The attitude toward Adam, especially among the non-local officers, was not good. They weren't crazy about JJ either, not after the earful they'd received at her home. She was lucky to have gotten a message to Iris via her landline.

"So where's he going to go?" JJ asked. "What's he going to do? Come on, Iris, what's your master plan?"

Iris was saved from a reply when the door behind them swung open as quickly as the safety mechanism would allow, nearly catching JJ in the rear end. Iris's mouth dropped open.

"Hey, darling," Harlan said with a grin. "Did you miss me?"

Iris threw her hands over her head, grabbing the roots of her long hair in frustration. "Harlan, you were supposed to be gone by now. You were supposed to be far away. *With him.*"

Harlan pulled off his cap and rubbed his own flattened, silver hair. "Well, Iris, excuse me for not reading your mind."

JJ could hear layers of subtext in his statement, but they were lost on her. And Iris and Harlan's relationship wasn't her primary concern right now. "I still think Adam needs to turn himself in," she said. "To Grant."

Harlan seemed to notice the man in the bed for the first time. He walked over to the former Sheriff, bent close, and nodded to himself. Then he began pacing. "No," he said. "I think Iris is right, as much as I hate to say it. There's something else going on here, and if Adam and I don't get to the bottom of it, I'm not sure anyone will."

"Harlan," Iris snapped, "that's not what I intended, and you know it."

JJ felt a buzzing in her scrub pants and looked at her cell

phone, reading the screen. "Shit," she said. "Adam just texted. Grant and some FBI guy are here. They're on their way up now."

Iris's face grew pale, and her hand strayed to her forehead. "No," she muttered. "Not Adam, too."

"Hey," Harlan said, grabbing her firmly by the shoulders. "We're not done yet. Whatever's going on, this is about Virgil, isn't it?"

Iris gazed up at him, his face a good head above hers. "Yes, I think it is. I don't understand how, with him sitting in jail, but it has to all be connected."

"Okay, then," Harlan said, pacing again between the door and the bed. "If Virgil is the key, we need to figure out what the hell he's been up to for the past thirty years. Who did he have a connection with?"

JJ went to the door and looked up and down the hallway. No one yet, but the man was on borrowed time.

"I don't know," Iris stammered. "No one. He disappeared and—wait, maybe Lawrence's brother."

"Virgil's uncle Teddy?" Harlan asked. "Where the hell would I find him?"

Iris's hands were shaking, and she'd started to pace, too. "I don't know. The last time I heard, he was in Virginia. Doreen might know where to find him."

"Well, shit," Harlan said.

Iris stopped where their pacing intersected, and managed a wan smile. "You know you were always *her* favorite, too."

Harlan barked a short laugh before embracing Iris. JJ checked the hall yet again, to give them privacy, and was about to warn the man to hurry it up when she heard his voice next to her ear.

"It's okay. We've still got all our clothes on." He turned back and locked eyes with Iris. His twinkled, but hers brimmed with tears. "Don't worry. I'll take care of him."

Iris's voice was unsteady as she said, "Don't forget to take care of yourself."

22

———

Adam rose slowly, contorting around the seat and console to peek over the dashboard. He doubted Grant and D'Antonio could see him as they neared the entrance. He hadn't gotten a response text from JJ. Harlan still hadn't emerged, and there was now no way for him to exit the hospital without bumping into Grant, unless maybe he took the stairs.

Harlan did not take the stairs.

Adam watched in horror as Harlan stepped off the elevator mere seconds after the two law enforcement officers entered the hospital. He held his breath while Grant wheeled toward the reception desk. D'Antonio continued straight to the elevators, and Harlan passed so near the FBI agent that their shoulders may have touched. *That's okay*, he reminded himself, *D'Antonio hasn't met Harlan*. But Grant... Harlan would still have to pass Grant on his way to the front door.

Harlan reached up with one arm, shielding his face while pulling his cap down lower. Instead of walking toward Grant, he veered in the opposite direction, where an ATM stood in the lobby. A moment later, Grant joined D'Antonio by the elevator, without a second glance at the ATM. Harlan didn't wait for the men to leave the first floor, just tucked his wallet into his pocket and left. The receptionist must have called out to him—Harlan raised a hand in acknowledgment, but he didn't stop or look back.

Adam let out his pent-up breath, but was still crouched on the floor of the truck when Harlan returned. "What the hell are you doing down there?" Harlan asked.

"I found the bad smell," Adam said. "I think there's something dead under the seat. Is it safe to get up?"

"Yeah, they're gone."

"Well, we better be, too," Adam said, stretching his legs gratefully as he told Harlan about the roadblocks.

"Roadblocks, huh? What the hell do they think they have on you?" he asked, pulling out of the parking lot in a more restrained manner than Adam could have managed.

"I wish I knew."

Back on the main road, they met a couple of cruisers heading in the opposite direction, lights flashing but no sirens.

"You'd think they had somewhere to be," Adam observed, dryly.

"They're blocking off the nearest interstate access. That's okay," Harlan said. "I've got a few tricks up my sleeve."

Instead of getting on the highway, about half a mile from the hospital Harlan turned on the first in a series of alternate routes. Leafless trees crowded the pavement—it all looked the same to Adam at night, and he was lost in no time. "Where are we headed?" he asked.

"That depends on what we run into," Harlan said, watching the road carefully. "We'll probably be okay, as bad as the coverage is around here, but if you've got some way to disable that cell phone, you might want to do it."

Adam looked at him in surprise.

"What?" Harlan said. "I'm not a total Luddite."

Adam struggled to get the SIM card out of his phone in the dark, without dropping it on the floor. The phone's back case fell on his lap. His hands weren't exactly shaking, but a vibrating hum ran all through his body, and he nearly dropped the battery as well. Finally, he pulled the small card free and tucked it carefully in the watch pocket of his jeans. He did it just in time, too. The truck lurched as Harlan crossed the road and pulled off on a primitive national forest access road.

"This'll bring us out past the Beecham County line," Harlan said. "Hopefully ahead of the next set of roadblocks, since I figure they don't have enough manpower on hand to get them all in place simultaneously."

Adam's teeth snapped together painfully as he bounced in his seat. "You sure this is still passable?"

"'Course it is. We'll be back on the highway in ten, fifteen minutes tops." Harlan grunted when the truck bottomed out on a particularly jarring rut. "Assuming we don't tear up Jim Henderson's truck in the process."

Even on high beam, the headlights were incapable of penetrating the darkness enough to reveal the road's hazards. Harlan slowed even more and revised his estimate. "Maybe twenty minutes."

The last twenty-four hours was catching up with Adam. He rested his elbow on the truck door and let his hand fall lightly across his eyes. So long as he kept his arm relaxed, absorbing the shocks of the road, his hand stayed put, blocking the glare from the headlights. He shut his eyes and tried not to be too attached to his physical discomfort, or his anxiety. To just be where he was, like some sort of Hindu or Buddhist or somebody else from a far-away land.

Harlan slammed on the brakes and Adam's relaxed arm flew from the door, smacking across the dashboard and catching his knuckles funny. "Ow!"

The truck skidded to a stop on the leaf-strewn, gravel track. About eighteen inches from striking the tree that lay across the road.

Harlan sighed. "Well, shit."

~

ADAM JOINED Harlan as he opened the half door to rummage in the back of the cab. "What are you looking for?"

Harlan shifted a big paper bag by its bottom (Adam heard the sounds of the truck's heavy snow chains inside) and dragged a toolbox out of the way before finding his prize. He grinned at Adam in the anemic light of the truck interior. "You can't have a farm truck without a chainsaw. Or at least, old Scout leader Jim can't. Only one set of earmuffs, though, so stand clear. I don't want Iris blaming me the next time you don't listen."

Soon the sound of the saw's engine ripped through the air like the toothy chain ripped through the downed pine tree. It made Adam paranoid—*who uses a chainsaw at night?* But the better question was, who cares enough about that answer to investigate? No one. He hoped.

It seemed wrong to simply stand around while a man several decades his senior dismantled a tree by a truck's headlights. Adam had offered to help, but Harlan knew his way around a chainsaw, and Adam definitely did not. Instead, Adam cleared the bigger limbs from the road as Harlan removed them, throwing the wood in the bed of the truck according to Harlan's instruction. Although tall (when standing), the tree wasn't particularly girthy. In less than ten minutes, Adam's strong, younger back was helping Harlan lift and swing the trunk away from the road, just far enough for the pickup to pass.

The rest of the trip to the highway was bone jarring, but uneventful. Harlan was quiet, but Adam wasn't sure he could've heard anything the man said anyway. The chainsaw still buzzed in his ears. More than half an hour had passed since they'd left the hospital parking lot. That was more than half an hour for road-blocks to be put in place. More than half an hour for officers to become acquainted with Adam's name and his face. When he finally saw the highway ahead, it was with a mix of relief and trep-idation.

The line between Beecham and Kirby County fell roughly at the crest of a mountain. The access road met the highway in sight of the crest on the Kirby County side. Also on the Kirby County side of the crest tonight: two Kirby County cruisers, one above the access road and one below, lights flashing. They couldn't have been there long. An officer near the lower car was still setting out flares. Presumably Beecham County had set up a checkpoint in the uphill lane on their side of the mountain as well.

"What do we do?" Adam asked, mouth suddenly dry.

"We keep going," Harlan said, turning left into the downhill lane. "Nice and slow, thinking happy thoughts."

The nearest officer placed his flare on the center double yellow line, then held up a bright red LED traffic wand and a reflective gloved hand as they approached.

"Crap!" Adam said.

Harlan glanced at him before slowing the truck to a stop. "I wish I'd gotten to you before your grandmother ruined your ability to swear. Listen, it'll be okay. Just look sleepy and keep your mouth shut."

The officer wore a reflective vest, but wisely remained in the other lane rather than stepping in front of the truck. He yelled something over his shoulder to a woman in uniform, standing behind the cruiser. Harlan rolled his window down, and the cool night air rushed in and chilled the sweat Adam had worked up moving the tree.

"Evening, officer. I hope this isn't about the illegal kindling," Harlan said, grinning and gesturing over his shoulder at the bed of the pickup. "My nephew and I ran into a little roadblock back there. Probably fell after that last bad storm. We had to cut our way through, and I didn't figure the park service would mind if we kept a few souvenirs."

The deputy took a step toward the bed and whistled. "No kidding? You're lucky you didn't cut your ever-loving arm off in the dark."

"I made my nephew do all the heavy lifting," Harlan said.

"He always does," Adam agreed, sinking into his seat and pulling down his cap.

Harlan laughed. "Plum wore the little pussy out. So what's going on back there—car wreck?"

The deputy looked toward his cruiser, where his partner looked to be getting on the radio. "No. We're looking for somebody that took a little boy in Beecham County. Adam Rutledge. You know him?"

Harlan stroked his chin. "Can't say as I do. Though the little bit I've heard about the Rutledges in general, I wouldn't trust any of them as far as I could throw them."

"Well, keep your eyes out. He's got a little blonde boy, eight years old."

"We certainly will," Harlan said, shifting his truck into gear.

The deputy tipped his hat and turned to leave. Adam's heart tap-tap-tapped in double-time. *Almost...*

Harlan started to roll forward, but the deputy raised a hand and swung his flashlight over the bed of the truck. Harlan waited, and pretended not to be bothered as the deputy glanced in the back of the cab.

"What were the two of you doing on national forest land this time of night?" the deputy asked.

"Well now, officer, that seems like the kind of question I might want to take the Fifth on, don't you think?" Harlan grinned. "It being a good few weeks before buck season. 'Course, I guess there's nothing wrong with scouting out your locations ahead of time."

The man patted his uniformed chest. "Do I look like the game warden? Y'all have a good night."

Adam gave a nod before resting his head against the truck window, facing away from the female officer as they passed. He kept his eyes locked on the cruiser lights and the stationary flares in the side mirror, until the first serious curve in the road hid them from sight. The sound of the tires on the road was almost indistinguishable from the roaring in his ears. Harlan cracked his window, adding the whistling of the passing air to the ambient noise.

"The first time we stop," he said, "I have got to find that damn smell. But I don't plan on pulling over until we're near out of gas—get some miles between us and all the crazy—so you might want to crack your window, too."

Adam cranked the window down an inch or two and felt the influx of cold air circle around to the exposed back of his neck. The stereo effect of the window noise made his head hurt.

"And don't be telling your grandmother I used that word back there."

"What word?" Adam asked.

"You know what word," Harlan said sharply. "The 'little kitty' word. She'd have my ass."

Little kitty? Ahh... Adam almost smiled at the thought of Iris tearing into Harlan. But before he had a chance, he found his head resting against the cold window again as he drifted off to sleep.

23

———

"Do you think they made it?" JJ asked, checking her watch for no good reason. Nearly ten p.m.

Iris sat back down alongside the old Sheriff. "I imagine if they didn't make it, we would've heard the commotion by now."

Leave it to Iris to be pragmatic. Except, there was nothing pragmatic about sending her grandson and whatever the hell Harlan was to her on the lam. "Iris, this is crazy. Nothing good can come of Adam running. What happens when he and Harlan get to another county, somewhere else where they know Adam is wanted, but don't know *him*? They're both liable to end up killed."

"Don't be ridiculous," Iris said.

She knew the woman was trying as much to convince herself as to convince JJ, but her temper rose with the flush that crept up her cheeks. Before it had a chance to boil over, a soft voice called out from the hospital bed.

"Iris?"

JJ started, wondering how much the recovering man had heard, and how much he had understood.

"Still right here, Ulysses," Iris said, running her hand over his head, where the gray buzzcut hair still showed an occasional hint of color. "Do you need anything?"

"What was all the noise about?" he asked, eyes not quite open.

"Nothing," Iris said. "I hope we didn't disturb you."

"Lawrence isn't bothering you again, is he?" the former Sheriff asked.

Iris's hand stilled in midair, as though she'd forgotten how to move it.

Lawrence... it took JJ a moment to remember that was Iris's dead husband, Adam's grandfather. She hated to see Grant's father slipping in time, but at least it meant he probably hadn't followed their discussion.

"No," Iris said, "he isn't."

"I must've heard something..." the man trailed off. He closed his eyes, but his voice seemed stronger when he continued. "Good. I thought we took care of that, but sometimes it's hard to remember."

The door to Mr. Mason's room opened before JJ could ponder the cryptic remark. The Sheriff (the current one) was still in uniform and held his hat in his hands. He stepped forward uncertainly, like a child who's come upon something he's not sure he's ready to see. "Where's mom?" Grant asked, looking to Iris instead of JJ.

Iris took Grant's hand and led him to her spot by the bed. "I'm watching him while she has a little break, but she'll be back soon."

"How's he doing?" Grant asked, reaching for his father's hand, but changed his mind when his fingers brushed the IV. Instead, he settled his hand on his father's forearm, thick with freckles and the same auburn hair Grant had inherited. The elderly man sighed, but didn't open his eyes.

"He's doing really well," JJ said. She wanted to put her arms around Grant, to give him some physical reassurance, but she had no more than spoken the words when a familiar-looking man in a suit entered the room. His smile glanced off JJ before settling on Iris. The expression felt more predatory than friendly.

"Ms. Rutledge," he said. "What a fortunate coincidence. I was hoping to get another opportunity to speak with you. I noticed the patient's room next door is empty. Perhaps you'd be so good as to join me there."

It was not a request, although JJ was certain that Iris would have been within her rights to refuse the man. However, Iris surprised her.

"I'm happy to do anything I can to help you find that boy," Iris said. "Grant, this shouldn't take but a minute. You stay with your dad and I'll be right back."

The woman occasionally drove her insane, but JJ found herself feeling suddenly protective of Iris. She gave Grant's shoulder a quick squeeze before following Iris and the suited man into the hallway. "Hey!"

Iris had already slipped into the unoccupied room, but the suit paused and smiled at her. "Yes?"

Now that she had his attention, JJ wasn't sure what to say. She settled for, "I didn't catch your name."

"Special Agent Rafael D'Antonio with the FBI. Don't worry, Ms. Tulley. You're on my list as well," he said, and leaned casually against the wall, arms crossed. An attractive man—early forties and literally tall, dark, and handsome, with the imperfection of a minor scar on his upper lip that added interest—he almost appeared to be posing. Presumably he hoped to disarm her with charm.

"What list is that?" she asked.

"The list of people I'd like to speak with. I'd particularly like to know why you phoned Ms. Rutledge while her grandson's car was being searched, considering you were specifically instructed not to do so."

Did he really know she'd called Iris? JJ wasn't certain and wasn't in the mood to call his bluff. But outright lying, that she could do.

"I was *instructed* not to tell Adam that his car was being searched, and I didn't do that. I called to let Iris know I'd be working tonight. She'd wondered if there'd be another friendly face around when she relieved Mrs. Mason."

"Really?" D'Antonio said, standing upright and stepping toward her. "I can't imagine why I don't believe you, unless it's something to do with your relationship with Adam Rutledge. Is that why you were so hostile to the officers at your home?"

"Hostile?" JJ matched his step forward with one of her own and felt her control slip. "Considering I found half a goddamned army in my yard—"

"Sheriff Mason tried to notify you."

JJ paused long enough to make a mental note to check her missed calls. "—Several of whom I'd never met before and aren't even from this jurisdiction, I think my reaction was justified, and a whole world away from hostile. Plus, I happen to have been dealing with some crazy shit in my own life—"

"Ms. Tulley, I'm sorry if I've inconvenienced you," he interrupted, voice dripping sarcasm, "but I'm trying to find a missing child. Just because this time it's a child you don't know personally, doesn't mean his life is any less worthy of protection. I don't know what Adam Rutledge is to you, but he's not worth that child's life."

D'Antonio stopped and stared at her, gnawing at his lip, doubtless trying as hard to get his temper under control as JJ was her own. Except JJ suspected it was easier for her, because she knew he was right. This was why she'd argued with Iris. Law enforcement should be focused on finding the boy, not on finding Adam.

Grant emerged from his father's room, glared at them both and said, "Try to keep it down. This *is* a hospital."

The chastened federal agent turned toward the room where Iris waited. JJ touched Grant's arm when he would have followed. He met her eyes, but only briefly. "Not now, JJ."

She couldn't meet his eyes, either, and stared at the shiny floor. "I'm sorry," she said. "I am so, so sorry. For all of it."

"Just tell him to come in," he said.

She nodded, but didn't otherwise move until Grant joined Iris and D'Antonio and closed the door behind him. Then she went to find some privacy of her own. The nurse behind the desk motioned for her as she passed, but JJ pointed at her phone. Things were more relaxed here at night, but she'd been neglecting her duties and needed to get back to work. Soon.

The break room was empty. She had a sudden magical thought—*maybe Adam's still in the parking lot*—and went straight to the window. She scanned the scattered beater cars and pickups, trying to distinguish signs of life or, failing that, see if she recognized any of the vehicles. No luck, and she had no more luck reaching him on his phone; it rang through to voicemail twice. He might not be avoiding her. After all, there were more holes in coverage than there was actual coverage in the mountains. And sometimes, a text could get through when a voice call couldn't.

Call me. You need to turn yourself in NOW, she typed.

Marcus, Trooper, Adam's flight and the boy's kidnapping—it was just too much, too fast. And too soon after she'd held poor Rachel in her arms, wondering if the girl would make it back alive or become the hurt her own daughter carried into adulthood. And yet, the thing JJ's selfish mind dwelled upon most was the distance in Grant's voice, and his profile as he refused to look at her. Did Grant think she'd somehow chosen Adam over him? JJ's eyes filled with tears. She held her breath to keep them inside, but one snuck out the corner anyway, followed by another, and another.

"Shit," she muttered, wiping at her eyes angrily before staring at her blank phone screen.

Then she put her phone back in her pocket, where it remained silent for the rest of her shift, like an unexploded bomb.

24

———

"Do you know someone named Adam?" Bruce asked.

The blonde boy sat cross-legged on the motel bed and stared. Bruce wasn't entirely sure whether the boy understood him. His pupils were about the size of the little dots scattered across the bedspread. (Bruce told himself the dots were part of the design.)

"Do you mean like the son of God?" the boy asked, pale brow wrinkled.

Good to know they still get to them early here. "No, not a Bible person. I mean a real person."

The child tilted his head, a parody of a confused child. "Is he a boy in my class?"

"No, I mean someone like—" he caught himself. He'd almost said *someone like me.* "I mean, someone like your dad. An adult."

"What's he look like?" the boy asked.

Once again, he'd almost slipped and said *a little bit like me.* Except with darker hair and that damn dimple. Of course, Bruce was still wearing the Batman mask so the kid couldn't see him. He grinned behind it. "Never mind."

There was no reason to think the boy would know Adam, since he'd been away for his entire life. But he wondered if not knowing Adam would make a difference. Perhaps he should have tried for the girl again—JJ Tulley's daughter—as had been his original intention. But now that he'd gone and taken the neighbor kid, it seemed unlikely JJ would lower her guard enough for her own child to be vulnerable. Still, it would've been nice.

But again, did it really matter if Adam knew the kid? After all, there was no reason to think Adam had known the neighbor girl, and Adam had found her just fine. Or so he'd heard. It was time for another experiment.

"We're going to play a little game," Bruce said. "Close your eyes." The boy did. "Now I want you to pretend like you have a friend named Adam, an imaginary friend. And you want him to come see you, so you say his name."

"Okay," the boy said, and called out, "Aaa...dam!"

Bruce almost laughed behind his mask. The boy sounded like he was yelling for his pet, and he liked the idea of Adam as a pet. Preferably his. "No, just say his name in your head."

The boy opened his eyes. "But then how's he supposed to hear me?"

He'd wanted the child coherent, but there was such a thing as too coherent. "Just do it."

"But why—"

He was on his knees and in the boy's face in one motion. "Because I fucking said so," he growled.

The boy's lower lip began to tremble. Bruce didn't want him to be scared, because that would make him harder to handle. But did the boy need to be scared for this to work? If you didn't have something to be scared about, you could just pick up the telephone; you wouldn't need some kind of mind-bending trick. Bruce didn't know the answer. "Don't forget to close your eyes," he said.

He watched the boy until the child began drowsily tipping over. "It's okay," Bruce said. "You can lay down now."

He waited even longer, until he was sure the child was asleep. Then he leaned over and whispered in the boy's ear, "Adam? Can you hear me? Adam, I'm right here waiting for you. If you want to save this child, too, you have to come find me."

25

─────────

The abrupt cessation of motion yanked Adam from a doze and his head from its resting position. He'd pulled his shirt collar up to shield his face, but his upper cheek was cold and damp from the window.

"Sorry about that," Harlan said. "The clutch on Jim's truck could use a little work. Or I could use a little sleep, one or the other."

Adam could hear traffic in the distance, but it was irregular, waves rather than a constant roar. "Where are we?"

"Far enough away to feel safe to stop. I'll get us a room."

The pickup sat in the poorly lit parking lot of a crappy, one-story motel, its details thankfully lost in the dark. Harlan hadn't parked by the office, but rather in front of a section of rooms that appeared unoccupied. There were no cars parked nearby, and no lights shone through the curtained windows.

Adam wiped his cold cheek and massaged the numb right arm he'd been leaning against back to life. His arm was just beginning to tingle when Harlan returned. The man opened the driver's door and locked it, then said, "Come on."

They'd been driving long enough for Adam's legs to turn to clay and for his arms and chest to tighten up from the afternoon's exertions and the previous night's vomiting. He groaned as he awkwardly pulled his duffel bag from the back. "Do we have a plan?"

"Son, I don't even have a spare pair of underwear," Harlan said. Adam's face fell, and Harlan said, "Don't worry—I won't try to borrow yours. I'll just go commando."

Adam shook his head, grinning, and followed Harlan to a door almost directly in front of the truck. Harlan fumbled with an old-fashioned key on a plastic ring. Finally pushing open the door, he said, "We do have a plan of sorts. There's enough distance between us and them to crash for a few hours."

A single large bed took up most of the room, and a single chair faced an empty space that should have held a television. Adam threw his bag on the chair, reluctant to set it down on carpet the color of dirt. "And what then?"

"We'll talk about it in the morning," Harlan said. "Get some sleep. I saw one of those twenty-four-hour drugstores just down the road, and I want to see if I can pick up a couple of things." He jiggled the key on its ring. "I'll be back in a bit, but like I said, don't wait up."

So Adam didn't.

～

He reached for the screaming child.

"Shush," he said. "It'll be okay." Except it wouldn't, and the child knew it. Had he heard the whispering voices, too? Or was it just that he, like his father, knew his mother was dying in the front seat?

The man fought with the child seat's straps and buckles at the best of times, and these were not those. He worked by feel, his back brushing against the roof of the car in the dark. His upper body twisted and hung too far forward for his own upright seat to support him. The boy wriggled, then wailed when his father fell forward, elbow mashing his little leg.

"Just settle down," he growled, blood running into his eye. He brushed it away, wiping his hand on the boy's overalls. They already felt sticky.

No, Virgil.

His wife's voice was faint. He was afraid to look at her, afraid of what he'd see, and afraid of what she'd see in him.

"I have to do this," he said. "I have to."

No, you don't!

This time, the voice boomed in his skull. He jerked his head toward her, certain he could feel her eyes boring through him, but her head still faced straight ahead. So he went back to work. The swinging arm of the child seat finally came free, and he lifted it over his screaming boy's head.

"He won't be harmed," Virgil said.

But he knew it was a lie, even as he spoke the words. Of course, his wife knew as well. She didn't respond—not directly—but he began to hear a different whispering, to feel a tingling across his skin.

He grabbed the boy awkwardly beneath the armpits and lifted, but the child's arms were still tangled somehow. He tilted him, this way and that, trying to pull him free. One hand remained caught in the strap that had secured his legs.

It has to happen now, his father's voice whispered.

"I know—I'm trying!" he screamed in desperation. Finally, he yanked the child toward him and heard a sickening pop, followed by the boy shrieking a shrill octave higher.

And then another hand appeared...

～

THE HAND TUGGED ON ADAM, and a strong, reassuring voice broke through the pained shrieking.

"Adam, come back to me. You're safe if you come back to me," the voice said. But another hand was clamped over his mouth, and Adam struggled against it. "Adam, don't panic. Just relax. I'm letting you go now."

Adam opened his eyes and sucked air like a landed fish. He was lying on a bed in a cheap motel room. A small lamp on the nightstand next to him had been knocked over. Its lampshade was askew, and it still gave off light at odd angles. Harlan stood by the bed, face shadowed, but silver-white hair shining. Adam surveyed the rest of the area, noting his duffel and a plastic shopping bag in the chair, but no other belongings. The door to the bathroom was ajar, and the light was switched on, illuminating a dingy white space. An empty white space.

There's no one else in here, no one but Harlan and me.

Adam gazed at his hand, at the wonky thumb that perpetually stuck out at odd angles. It rarely ached, but it did now, throbbing with the beat of his heart. He rubbed it with the other hand (*there's no one else here*) and slowly sat up. Then he set the lamp upright and got his first good look at Harlan. The man was pale, lips barely visible beneath his mustache.

"When did you start having visions again?" Harlan asked.

Adam's voice was grit in his throat. "What do you mean?"

"It's a pretty simple goddamn question," Harlan said. When Adam didn't answer, he continued. "You told me you were burned out, that you weren't seeing anything."

"No!" Adam countered. "That's what you said, back in the hospital."

"Well obviously I was fucking wrong." Harlan took a deep breath and sat next to him, placing his hands palm down on the bed. They were shaking, though not quite as much as Adam's own. "What you saw tonight, is that something you've seen before?"

Adam nodded and felt a chill on the back of his neck. He rubbed his hand against it, and his fingers came away slick with cold sweat. "I've had that nightmare off and on for as long as I can remember. But it seems different now, like I'm seeing it from a different place. It's the night my mom died."

"Well, I know that, son. I was there. But that wasn't any kind of dream or nightmare; that was a vision." He ran his hands over his face and let out a roaring groan. "How long have you been having this 'different' nightmare?"

Adam's wonky thumb had stopped throbbing, but it still

seemed especially cold. He fidgeted with it rather than looking at Harlan. "Since I was released from the hospital."

"Shit."

Adam noticed that, although they sat close to each other, Harlan had avoided touching him. Seconds ticked by as he waited for Harlan to say something else. Anything else. Finally, "But you haven't seen anything about the boy?"

"No, sir," Adam said. "I didn't know a thing about it until they started knocking on my door."

Harlan ran his hands over his head and dug his fingers into his scalp so enthusiastically Adam could hear his nails scratch the skin. Then he stood and said abruptly, "We're leaving."

"Now?"

"Go take a quick, cold shower—I don't want you falling asleep on me again—and we'll hit the road."

"Where are we headed?" Adam asked.

"The only person who can help us find Aaron Schofield also happens to be the only person who can help us figure out what the hell is going on in there," Harlan said, pointing at Adam's skull. "And how to stop it. But first we've got to find him. And fast."

26

———

To say Luther was uncomfortable with the direction things had taken in this case would be a gross understatement.

What a clusterfuck.

"Are you sure about this, Iris?" Luther asked. "What did his lawyer say?"

He knew Ms. Callaway was on her way, but he felt like this was something that was bound to come back and bite him in the ass.

"Luther, dear," Iris said, "you shouldn't wear your hat in the building."

He removed his hat automatically, and his head felt naked.

"I find it hard to believe that's what his lawyer said," Luther countered. He didn't stand a chance against Iris—especially after an exhausting night of knocking on doors—but he had to try. Besides, Grant and Special Agent Man had left him to deal with her.

Iris sighed. "She said it's not confidential, so it's up to me whether you sit in. For all I know, you'll be listening anyway. I might as well be able to see your face while you do."

Virgil Rutledge's transport had been delayed when the meeting with his attorney triggered a scene. Then once Aaron Schofield disappeared, they couldn't spare the officers for transport, and Special Agent Man wanted to keep Virgil close. Last night, D'Antonio had made a deal with Virgil's attorney, and she'd signed some sort of immunity agreement on his behalf. (Of course, with Virgil being nuttier than a fruitcake, Luther wasn't sure anything the man said or signed would mean a thing if he ever made it to trial.)

What amazed Luther was that somehow D'Antonio had gotten Iris to go along, too, presumably by playing on her fears for Adam. Her job this morning was to convince Virgil to resume antipsychotic medication, in the hopes of getting something more coherent and reliable out of him to help find the boy, and to see if he could tell them anything else helpful in the interim. That was assuming someone had a Crazy-to-English dictionary handy, because from what Luther had seen so far, they'd need it.

Iris watched the parking lot through the glass front doors. "His lawyer just pulled in. Are we supposed to wait for Grant and the FBI man?"

Luther would bet she remembered the man's name, but refused to use it out of stubbornness. "No. They'll be here if they can. We can't afford to wait, and we'll be recording it. Are you ready?"

Iris was dressed nicely in slacks and a cardigan—more appropriate to a Sunday service than a Sunday at the Sheriff's Department—and wore her long, white hair back in a bun, probably secured with something that violated the visitation rules. She fidgeted with her sleeve, tugging it further down her wrist. And that's when it hit Luther: Iris was nervous. Of course she was nervous! She was about to speak with the crazy son she hadn't seen in years—in jail, while her grandson was on the run under suspicion of kidnapping. No wonder she'd given Luther shit about his hat. How could he have been so blind? He supposed Iris was just one of those people that it was hard for him to think of as being human like everyone else. He touched her hand impulsively.

"I'll be right next to you," Luther said.

Her eyes crinkled as she smiled, and he noticed she'd worn a little makeup. She squeezed his hand briefly and said, "Just try not to knock me over on your rush to get out the door when things get crazy."

Virgil's attorney Faith Callaway hadn't worn a suit, but instead dressed similarly to Iris. Her soft brown leather briefcase smacked against her hip as she hurried up the sidewalk and in the door. She opened her mouth—probably to apologize—and stopped herself.

Luther took advantage of her hesitation. "Good morning, Ms. Callaway. If you're going to meet with Mr. Rutledge, you can either leave your briefcase with one of the other deputies, or you can submit to a search. Up to you," he said, smiling.

"Oh, I—" She patted the bag at her side protectively, face slightly flushed, and tucked her hair behind one ear. "Actually, I'll be watching from outside. Your interview room is crowded with three people, much less four. And I don't want to complicate Mr. Rutledge's interactions with his mother."

"Okay, then. Ladies, follow me." Luther led them down the hallway to the interview room.

Ms. Callaway set her briefcase on the wooden bench and asked Iris if she had any questions.

"No," Iris said, and reached for the door.

"Ms. Rutledge, ma'am," Luther said, stretching an arm out in front of her, "I need to go first."

She stepped aside and Luther entered the room. Once again, Deputy Gerald Hayes was standing, back against the wall, alongside an already seated Virgil. That left two chairs across from him, but Luther wasn't sure about the psychology of sitting next to Iris. Would it cause the man to distrust his mother, trust Luther, or something else entirely? Luther didn't want to stand at the wall as Gerald did, either. He wanted Virgil to relax, so much as was possible while wearing arm and leg restraints.

Iris entered on Luther's heels. He pulled one of the chairs out for her and, as a compromise, dragged the other chair to the end of the table. It was far enough from Virgil that if the inmate successfully made a move on him, Luther had no business wearing his uniform. (He also, in accordance with department policy, hadn't worn his sidearm into the room.) He nodded at Gerald to leave the room but said nothing, beginning his task of becoming invisible to the other two people. Instead of sitting at attention, Luther scooted his chair back and appeared to relax, almost slumping.

Iris sat straight enough for both of them, her usual adherence to near perfect posture. The tentativeness he'd seen in the hallway was gone; she had her game face on. Her voice was calm and even as she spoke. "Do you know who I am?"

Her son looked coherent, for whatever that was worth. He was wearing the same style of blue jumpsuit he'd previously worn. He hadn't shaved recently and his hair still hadn't been cut, but—again—it was relatively clean. If he concentrated, Luther could smell the slightest hint of body odor, but nothing unusual. As opposed to his almost colorless, spooky eyes... a man could live a long life without ever seeing their like.

Virgil inclined his head and replied, voice raspy and with a slight drawl, "Of course, I know who you are, Mom. I'm not crazy."

Then he grinned, the same grin Adam had inherited, with even a hint of the same dimple, but on the older man it seemed wrong, asynchronous. It reminded Luther of those little girls dressed up with high heels and makeup for beauty pageants. *If they'd handled snakes for the talent portion of the competition.* A chill ran up Luther's spine.

"Yes," she said, "yes, you are."

Virgil shrugged his shoulders. The metallic chatter of restraints at his wrists drew Luther's eyes to the muscles playing in his ropy forearms, and a rough white scar crossing one palm. Virgil turned to Luther. "I know who you are, too."

Luther held his breath, focusing on the creases in the man's forehead, the pale eyebrows that seemed too thin, to avoid falling into his eyes.

"Virgil," Iris asked, drawing her son's attention, "do you know why I'm here?"

"Not precisely," he said. His eyes flicked up and to the left, as if he were watching someone at the door. Luther fought the urge to turn his own head to see what was there.

"It's about the boy," she said.

Virgil's gaze returned to his mother long enough to say, "The boy is long gone," before looking again at the door.

Iris flinched slightly at his words. "Not that boy," she said. Luther assumed referring to Danny.

Virgil didn't seem to hear her, just kept staring over her shoulder, and added, "So is the girl."

Iris leaned forward. "Rachel Nicholson is fine."

"*Not that girl*," Virgil said, slowly and deliberately, meeting Iris's eyes until she sat back in her chair, a pallor washing over her face.

Sarah Edmunds, Luther thought. *He means Sarah Edmunds. The girl who disappeared a few months after Danny*.

Iris set her hands on her lap below the table, Luther suspected to hide their shaking. "Virgil, someone took a little boy a couple of days ago."

Virgil's eyes drifted away again, toward the door. Luther found himself succumbing to curiosity, to the horror movie inevitability of looking over his shoulder. And that's why he missed Iris launching from her seat. *Launching*... she was an elderly woman, for God's sake, so the word was a bit hyperbolic. But suddenly her ass was off her chair and her hands gripped Virgil's on the table.

Luther stood. "Ms. Rutledge, you need to sit, and you need to stop touching the prisoner."

Iris ignored him entirely, bearing down on Virgil with the considerable force of her personality and her thin, bony hands. "They think Adam took the boy. They're chasing after your son—my grandson—and he's going to end up dead."

"No." Virgil jerked his hands from Iris and twisted away in his chair.

"Iris, you need to sit," Luther reiterated, but she remained standing.

Virgil drew his arms to his sides and began curling in on

himself. "I killed the first son—twice. I damned myself to hell so she could live. So she could be resurrected."

"Charlotte is dead," Iris said. "Nothing will change that. But you can still save your son. You need to take your medication so you can help us—"

"For Christ's sake, Iris, stop," Luther said, but it was too late.

Virgil bolted from his seat, screaming, "The first son was not resurrected! He cannot be the doer of evil in this world—it's his doppelgänger!"

Luther heard the door to the interview room open as he shoved Virgil's chair out of the way. "On your knees!"

Instead, Virgil faced Luther and said, glacial blue eyes wide enough to expose the whites, "*You* have to stop him! *You* will be there at the end."

"Get down!" Luther said, grabbing Virgil's shoulders and pushing him toward the ground. Virgil didn't resist, but he nearly head-butted Luther inadvertently as he first fell to his knees and then toppled forward. Luther tried to keep the man from cracking his head open on the floor.

Gerald (*when did he come in?*) edged between Luther and the downed man. "I've got it, sir," he said.

That's when Luther noticed that Iris was gone; the other deputy had taken her place in the small room.

"Sir, I'll take it from here," Gerald said.

Luther saw determination and a hint of uncertainty in the deputy's face, perhaps because he was familiar with the legendary Beck temper. He didn't want to go against Luther, but he would if necessary, to protect the department.

Luther nodded and got to his feet slowly, one knee protesting. "Thanks, Deputy Hayes," he said, and headed for the door.

He understood Gerald's reaction, his interpretation of the situation, but the man was all wrong. Virgil Rutledge hadn't pissed Luther off. The man had frightened him.

27

Adam was no stranger to long miles and longer hours on the road. Still, sitting in Jim Henderson's truck was getting old.

They'd crossed into Virginia before stopping at the motel, but that didn't give Adam a sense of where they were now, much less where they were going. They'd eaten breakfast about half an hour ago, after exiting the interstate. The landscape was a little flatter than Adam was used to, with fewer trees and more empty pastures browned in anticipation of winter. The gray sky didn't help his persistent headache, but did seem in keeping with the depressing miasma that had settled over the area. His eyelids fluttered.

"No sleeping," Harlan said, as he'd done half a dozen times in the past few hours.

Adam stretched his eyes wide. "Are we almost there?"

"Yes," Harlan replied.

"You said that fifteen minutes ago," Adam pointed out.

"This time I mean it."

Adam believed him. Harlan wasn't exactly fidgeting, but he lacked his usual air of self-containment. Even when they'd been searching for a still-missing Rachel, there'd been a kind of certainty about Harlan, a sense that the answer lay outside him. That, although it may mean tragedy, a failure would do nothing to change Harlan's core. Now, there was a subtle but undeniable air of brittleness to the man. His eyes flicked to the passing fields on their left more often than seemed necessary. His dark brows had crept closer to each other than was usual, and his mouth pursed.

"And where are we going again?" Adam asked.

"To see a woman who hates my guts."

"How much does that narrow the field?" Adam sniped.

Harlan winced, then said, "She's the ex-wife of the guy we need to find. Do you trust me?"

Adam's laugh was bitter, and he hated himself for it. "It's a little bit late for that question, isn't it?" When Harlan didn't respond, Adam said, "Yes, I trust you."

Harlan signaled and turned left onto a paved road that led them through a collection of a dozen or so dingy-looking houses that could loosely be called a neighborhood. All were single-story with some kind of siding, most had dogs on tie-outs, and a few had cars "parked" in the front yards that looked as if they weren't going anywhere anytime soon. Harlan shook his head and muttered something under his breath. Then he said, "I'd rather not tell you any more about either person right now. I have my reasons, and I promise I'll explain afterwards."

Adam took a moment to consider while Harlan slowed the pickup, looking for a particular house. "Okay," Adam said. "I don't much like it, but I can wait. This time."

Harlan glanced at him. "Good," he said, trying unsuccessfully for a smile. He pulled into a driveway that looked no worse than the rest, and yet had a feeling of darkness about it, a sense that it was much more unclean than it appeared. Harlan parked alongside the single beater car. A fat Rottweiler lay on top of his doghouse. Adam wondered how he'd hefted his bulk up there, and how the structure managed to hold. The dog barked a few times, but didn't seem motivated to get down.

After a minute or two that seemed much longer, an elderly woman emerged from the front door and crossed her arms, waiting at the rotten balustrade that enclosed her porch. She was almost gaunt beneath a flannel shirt and overlarge jeans, and her long, straight gray hair was gathered in a ponytail at the base of her neck. Her nose—and the rest of her relatively unlined face—was narrow, patrician even. She could have been beautiful, but everything seemed to turn down—the corners of her eyes, her mouth, even a slight sag in her jaw emphasized the creases of her cheeks—as if she were displeased with the world and had been for a very long time.

Harlan gripped the steering wheel and expelled a deep exhale. "This woman cannot be trusted to reliably do anything except cause other people pain. If she figures out who you are, and she thinks turning you in will do that, she won't hesitate to put the law on our asses. So stay in the car."

He got out of the pickup and said, "Hello, Doreen."

She didn't respond. Harlan walked to the top of the porch steps and leaned against the newel post. It was nearly as rotten as the railing; Adam hoped the man didn't bust through. The woman he'd called Doreen was speaking now, but Adam couldn't hear their conversation. He watched; it didn't seem to be going well. Harlan shook his head in disgust, and the woman's lips curled back in a sneer. Not going well at all.

And Aaron was waiting.

Unless the child was beyond waiting for anything anymore.

The urge to act wrenched Adam, but to do what? And he was so exhausted. Stretching his legs until his feet hit the rise of the wheel well, his eyes drifted shut.

An image immediately popped into his mind, *a blonde woman with a narrow face and a waist nearly as tiny.*

Adam gasped, jerked upright, and stared at the woman Harlan had called Doreen. Her facial features, especially the narrow slice of her nose, were unmistakable. Adam closed his eyes and saw Doreen again, but forty years younger. The likeness, lacking depth and detail, reminded him of a ghost image left behind after staring at something bright.

Was this what Harlan had been trying to prevent, keeping him awake? Perhaps, but Adam knew there was something useful there, at the edge of the other side, something that would help them find Aaron. And Harlan wasn't there to stop him.

Adam breathed deeply, relaxed his shoulders and shook out his hands. Doreen faded, and instead he found himself *in the woods again, woods he now recognized as being behind Iris's house. The boy's feet led him inexorably forward, toward the spot where he'd previously heard the axe chopping... But he couldn't remember what happened then. This time, it wasn't the sound of an axe drawing him forward, but the sound of voices. It was the sound of Doreen and the old man.*

There was less visual clarity than in Adam's previous visions, and he couldn't distinguish their words. The emotions also weren't as visceral, or smothering. He felt anticipation and anxiety, but neither was overwhelming.

The boy rounded the rocky outcrop to soft sounds of both protest and agreement. Doreen was draped over the old man (Lawrence; that's what he calls Lawrence), *arms over his shoulders, her meager chest pressed against his. Lawrence pushed her away, even before he saw the boy* (his words were still lost to Adam). *Doreen stumbled, but was undeterred. She reached for the waistband of his pants and dropped to her knees in front of him as she unbuckled his belt and slid it from his pants. Lawrence grabbed her shoulders and gave her a shake. The face that looked up at him was wide-eyed with adoration. Lawrence's expression softened, his hands went to his zipper... And then he saw the boy.*

At first, the old man laughed. But Doreen was angry. She grabbed the stunned boy by the arm and yanked him forward, until he was standing in front of Lawrence. Then she picked up the old man's belt from the ground and handed it to him. The boy put his hands on the rough rock wall and braced himself; to do otherwise would only make it worse. The old man began by using the looped belt, and as much as it ached and burned, it was familiar. But then something happened—did Doreen say something?—and his swings became wild and flailing. The boy crumpled to his knees, but Lawrence only struck him harder. The boy shrieked when the metal buckle hit his ear—

Adam opened his eyes, sucking air, and planted his hands on the truck's dashboard to steady himself. His fingers sought out his ear, half expecting it to be bloody, but a ghostly stinging was all that remained.

What the hell just happened?

But Aaron couldn't wait for him to figure it out. Adam got out of the truck, legs buckling beneath him as he stood (*not as solid as I thought*). He carefully placed one foot in front of the other, advancing step by step to the front of the pickup. He leaned against the bumper and hoped he looked more casual than semiconscious. Doreen stared as if he were an actor she was trying to place.

"Do I know you?" she asked.

"No, ma'am. We've never met." He let his tone say more than the words when he added, "But I know you."

Harlan scrutinized him. Adam wasn't sure what the man saw, but it was something he didn't like. "Get back in the truck, son."

Adam ignored him, and Doreen turned to Harlan. "Who is he?"

"I'm telling you, it's not worth it," Harlan said significantly, glowering from beneath his brows at Adam. "We'll find him, one way or another."

"Uncle Teddy, or the little boy?" Adam leaned on one hip and crossed his arms, bracing a foot against a dead potted plant. "You mean to tell me you really don't care if an innocent child lives or dies?"

Doreen smiled, but it was an ugly thing. "I should've known you were a Rutledge. The math doesn't work for poor Bo, so you must be Virgil's bastard."

"Did you forget? Virgil and my mother *Charlotte*—" Adam emphasized his mother's name, "were married. Is there anything you'd like to say about her?"

Doreen paled, her lips blanching to the color of her hair, and Adam continued, "I didn't think so."

Harlan tramped down the steps, now looking almost alarmed. "It's time to go," he said, taking Adam gently by the elbow.

Adam stayed rooted, and Harlan didn't force it. Adam paused, gathering himself, then said, "You never had children, did you? They can be very inconvenient. Especially when they see things they aren't supposed to."

Doreen drifted toward the top step and wrapped her hands around the rotten post. Adam grinned, and felt Harlan stiffen next to him. "Come on, Doreen. You know where I'm going with this. Why don't you just tell us where Teddy is?"

Doreen shook her head. "You've got that same crazy smile your daddy had. Do you talk to trees and rocks too?"

An even bigger smile spread across Adam's face. "I talk to whomever and whatever will listen. Who do you think I should tell the real reason Lawrence beat Virgil within an inch of his life?"

Doreen gripped the post more tightly, and a little piece chunked off and fell to the steps beneath her.

"I'm sorry, Doreen. I'm not being very specific, am I? I'm sure my grandfather beating my father wasn't anything unusual. Virgil must've been around ten years old that time Lawrence used his belt. Down over the hill. By the..." Adam closed his eyes, and a word came to him. "By the *altar*. The *sacrificial altar*. Do you think everyone knows what kind of offerings you wanted to make there?"

Doreen's face flushed and she began muttering under her breath—curses or Bible verses, Adam wasn't sure there was a difference for her. Then she said, "You'll go the same way he did."

Adam stood and boomed, in a voice not quite his own, "Where is Theodore?"

The woman flinched. Her eyes flashed to Harlan as she answered, "The place where Lawrence took us, that first time. He left it to Teddy when he died."

Harlan nodded his understanding. Then she spat at Adam— actually *spat* at him—but the saliva fell far short of his feet. He leaned against the pickup hood and tried to keep the swaying inside. Doreen paused in the doorway for a parting shot. "You know you'll burn in hell. Standing right next to your daddy."

She slammed the door shut after her.

Hell, maybe. But *standing*, Adam wasn't so sure.

28

———

"What the hell was that all about?" Harlan asked.

Adam waited until they got out of sight of Doreen's house, but he couldn't wait any longer. "Pull over," he said.

Harlan edged the pickup onto the narrow shoulder with a jerky stop. Adam stumbled out of the truck and made it a few feet from the front tires before falling to his knees and vomiting his crappy diner breakfast. *Even worse the second time.* When the heaving stopped, he noticed he had one hand and knee on gravel and one on asphalt. He wondered which would feel more restful against his cheek. A couple of paper towels and a bottle of water swam into his peripheral vision.

"Thanks," Adam said. He sat on his heels and poured a little water on the towels before wiping his face, then took a few swigs to swish and spit. He felt better, but not by much. He rocked back onto his butt and hung onto his raised knees like the gunwale of a heaving ship.

"Did I tell you I got rid of that smell last night, while you were sleeping?" Harlan asked. Adam grunted. "You were right; it was a dead squirrel under the passenger's seat. It would've been mummified by spring."

"Nice," Adam said, holding the plastic bottle of cool water against his forehead.

"Yeah," Harlan agreed. "I figure so long as we don't end up in a shootout with the poh-leece, and fill the gas tank when we bring it back, Jim's coming out on top."

Harlan hopped up on the hood of the pickup like a man half his age and made himself comfortable. *Suck it up*, Adam thought, and joined him, with a little help from the front bumper. "So who is Doreen?" Adam asked.

Harlan raised his eyebrows, as if surprised by the question, then nodded to himself. "You know who Teddy is?"

Adam rubbed the bridge of his nose and tried to ignore the smell of vomit. "If I could just put together the pieces of what you said and what she said. And what I said..."

How can I not know? How can I not remember what I said? Harlan gripped his arm through his jacket, and Adam felt the panic recede far enough to breathe.

"Theodore is your grandfather Lawrence's brother," Harlan said. "I guess that makes him your great uncle. Doreen is Teddy's ex-wife."

"Why does she hate you so much?"

"Nope. Your turn. What happened back there?"

Adam lay back against the windshield, belatedly thinking of all the dead bugs and bird poop that resided there. "I saw something while I was waiting in the truck. Something about Doreen and Lawrence a long time ago."

"*You* saw something?"

Adam lifted his head. "You know what I mean."

"I think I do," Harlan said, almost apologetic, "but I'm afraid I need to hear you say it out loud."

"Virgil saw it," Adam said, and let his head rest against the windshield again, hands covering his eyes to protect them against the midmorning glare.

"You've been seeing your mother's accident from Virgil's point of view, haven't you?"

"Yeah, I guess so," Adam admitted.

"But what you saw at Doreen's was different, wasn't it?" Harlan asked. "I mean, different from your previous visions."

Adam took his hands from his eyes and sat up, ignoring the aching muscles in his chest and abdomen. "Yes. Do you know why?"

"I have an idea," Harlan said, "but you're not going to like it."

"Well, gee, there's a shocker," Adam said.

Harlan laughed and Adam grinned, a little of the tension dissipated. But not for long.

"Okay. You know how with Rachel, at first you didn't understand the significance of your dreams—your visions—until you realized you were seeing through her, watching what happened with her?"

Adam nodded. "I realized it with your help."

"And eventually she came to know you were there as well."

Adam motioned impatiently and Harlan continued. "The vision you just had of Doreen—and all of your other recent ones—have come from Virgil's past experiences. Agreed?"

Adam nodded and brought his feet up to sit cross-legged. "So?"

Harlan sighed. "I was hoping you'd get there on your own."

"Dangit, Harlan, do I look like a man capable of great intellectual or intuitive leaps at the moment? I am hanging on by the barest thread to—" He didn't know how else to say it. "To everything."

Harlan put a hand on Adam's bony, jean-clad knee and said, "Well, hang on tight then, because I think this thing is two-way now. I think *Virgil* is seeing through *you*."

Adam's mouth dropped open, but he closed it quickly as his stomach clenched and threatened to heave. "No," he whispered, when his esophagus stopped spasming.

"It's more than that. When you confronted Doreen, I saw him

in you," Harlan said, pointing two fingers at his own eyes to demonstrate.

"You mean, like I was *possessed?*"

"Not exactly. Or rather, not entirely," Harlan said. "I don't know how to explain it. There were things you said, things you knew that *just Adam* wouldn't know. Like who Uncle Teddy is. And there was a sense of dissonance about you, of watching two overlapping personalities at once. I believe even Doreen saw him in you—especially when you talked about Charlotte—and it spooked her."

"Did you know about this, what Virgil was doing?"

"I suspected he could see through you—that's why I didn't tell you more about our plans ahead of time. I didn't want to risk drawing Virgil out by talking about Doreen. She wasn't exactly his favorite person, either."

"Why not?" Adam asked.

"Well, it sounds like you saw part of the reason, although I never knew it. Presumably she was afraid he'd tell what he'd seen about her and Lawrence, and she punished him for it. And chances are, that wasn't the only thing Virgil had on her."

"Why didn't he say anything?"

"I imagine he figured Lawrence would kill him," Harlan said matter-of-factly. "Your grandfather was a hard man."

Adam's mind kept skittering around the edges of the deepest pit, afraid to fall in, but he had to know. "Do you think Virgil can see through me anytime? Like now?"

"When you saw through Rachel's eyes, could you do it all the time? Whenever you wanted?"

"No, but I didn't know what I was doing."

Harlan gave a wry smile. "That's true, but your father's raw gifts never equaled yours. I don't think you're an open book for Virgil yet, but I don't think he's going to stop, either. It's only going to get worse. That's why I didn't want you to sleep—you're more vulnerable when you're sleeping. To be honest, I never imagined he could do what he did back there *while you were awake.*"

Adam put his face in his hands and squeezed his throbbing head. "Great."

"On the bright side, in addition to helping us find the boy, there's nobody I'd trust more than Teddy to help us figure out how to stop Virgil from turning your brains to mush. And now we know where to find him. Roughly."

"Is he in the 'love Harlan' or 'hate Harlan' camp?"

This time Harlan's smile reached his eyes. "Iris is a lonely singularity on the one end, but I would say Teddy is in the healthy middle ground."

"So why does his ex-wife hate you?"

"She blames me for a lot of things that went wrong with Lawrence," Harlan admitted.

"And she loved Lawrence," Adam said with certainty. When Harlan raised a single brow, Adam added, "It's a sense I got from Virgil."

Harlan said, "He ought to know."

Adam thought back to the short interaction on her property. "She also hates you because she's afraid of you, afraid you'll see things about her she doesn't want anyone else to see."

"Is that coming from Virgil, too?"

"Maybe a little," Adam said. A cool breeze had picked up, and the heat of the truck's hood felt good against his back. "But I think it's mostly from me. It makes sense, especially when you think about her rocky relationship with Virgil, and what you can do."

Harlan snorted. "You don't know the half of it."

"Which is why you're going to tell me," Adam said.

"Indeed, I am," Harlan said. "But not half a mile from the woman's house."

The truck shifted as Harlan moved, and his fingers brushed the skin of Adam's bare wrist...

Doreen stood in front of the kitchen sink, hands wet to her elbows.

"Everyone knows," she told Iris.

The boy watched Doreen's hand stray to the counter where the knife sat, still bloody from quartering the meat she'd put in the oven. She stepped forward, blocking the view of her hands, but he knew what she was doing. He just couldn't speak; terror had taken his voice. He knew when her fingers closed on the handle—

Adam jerked upright, shaking himself away from Harlan and free of the images. "Jesus!" he hissed, sliding off the truck and landing on the opposite side.

"Easy, Adam. You know Iris doesn't approve of blasphemy," Harlan said, face serious.

"Did she try to kill Iris?" Adam asked.

"What?" Harlan asked, confused, but his face quickly cleared. "Doreen, you mean. Come to think of it, I guess she did. Though she didn't put much effort into it."

Adam caught a flash of blood, but it wasn't Iris's. "Harlan, show me your arm," he said.

Harlan balked, and for a moment Adam thought they were at a standstill. Then Harlan shook his head and muttered, "God-dammit." He slid his right sleeve up to show a pale line of scar on his forearm, almost as pale as the hair that surrounded it. "It wasn't as bad as it probably looked to a ten-year-old Virgil."

"If you still have the scar after forty years, I think it probably was," Adam said.

Harlan gave a sad smile. "Touché. You okay?"

And he realized, he wasn't. Adam covered his mouth with his hand, trying to hold the panic in. He babbled through his fingers, "I don't want this-I don't want this-I don't want this."

Harlan stretched his arms across the hood of the pickup, palms down, as if the truck were a metal horse to be calmed. "Adam, let's bring the crazy down a notch, buddy."

Adam let his hand fall away and said, "I don't want this. I don't want to see these things. And I can't make it stop."

"You know," Harlan said, "some people say everything happens for a reason. Maybe you're meant to see these things so you can..."

Harlan trailed off, surrendering to dead air. But his attempt at an inane platitude was both so heartfelt and incongruous, it did more to pacify Adam than any reasoned argument could have.

"Yeah," Harlan acknowledged, "I think those greeting card people are full of shit, too. But like I said, if anyone can help us get a handle on this, it's your Great Uncle Teddy. Now get in the truck and let's find the crazy sonuvabitch."

29

Luther banged on the door until his knuckles hurt. *Goddammit, Les, answer.*

It was almost exactly the middle of the day. His brother ought to damn well be up by now, even on a Sunday. Luther hunched his shoulders against a sudden brisk wind. He hoped the weather wasn't about to take a turn, too. That was the last thing they needed.

He'd snuck in a couple of hours of sleep the night before, but Luther was getting pretty close to running on empty. And empty was a common theme in the investigation right now. They'd found nothing to point them toward anyone besides Adam. Two officers from a neighboring county had let an elderly man and someone matching Adam's description past their roadblock last night, but his colleagues thought it was a coincidence, someone who happened to look like Adam. Luther didn't believe Adam had anything to do with the boy's kidnapping, but at least if they picked him up, everyone—especially D'Antonio—could look elsewhere.

The door to Les's trailer opened, and for the second time in a weekend Luther found himself seeing much more of Esther LaRue than he should.

"Luther," she said, and stepped out onto the cinder block steps, closing the door behind her. She wore another ratty WVU T-shirt, and it made Luther cold just standing next to her. He looked away, afraid he'd see goosebumps on her long legs, or worse, something even more intimate.

"Goddamn, Esther, put some clothes on."

"This isn't a great time to see Les," she said, gripping her elbows in the cold.

Luther was exhausted, and his temper was short. "Well, why the hell not? I'm sorry I didn't clear His Highness's schedule ahead of time—"

The door suddenly opened behind Esther, and Luther caught a flash of her underwear (*cotton this time*) when she lost her balance. Esther wobbled, throwing the cinder blocks beneath her off true as well, and fell against Luther. He grunted as he caught her awkwardly, trying to avoid clutching any sensitive bits.

"Luther," Les said, squinting against the overcast sky that filtered through the leafless trees as though it were a beach in August. "Come on in."

Inside, the curtains were drawn and the lights were off. The smell of burnt toast was thick in the air. There were other scents, too—a hint of sex, and the body odor of at least one person who was not entirely well. Luther wanted to open a window. "You doing okay, Les?" he asked.

"Yeah," his brother said, retreating to the darkest corner in the room and scrubbing his face with his hands as he sat down. "But I might be coming down with something. That time of year. So what's up?"

Luther crossed the room, pulling a couple of sheets of folded paper from his pocket. "I brought your volunteer list—I was hoping you could take another look at it. Can you think of anyone else not on here who might have been at the trunk-or-treat Friday night?"

Les took the list and leaned toward the nearest window without opening the curtain. "I don't know, Luther. I can't think too straight right now, but... Hey, wait a minute. I think Jim was there, and he's not on the list."

"Jim Henderson?" Luther asked. One of Jim's sons had been in the same class with Les and Adam. Come to think of it, he'd also supplied JJ with the little ATV that had brought her and Rachel Nicholson partway down the mountain.

"Yeah, Jim was there for a little while. I remember he stopped by—must've been before seven o'clock—to see if we needed help. Things were running pretty smooth, and he'd said something about leaving early the next morning to visit his daughter, so we sent him on home."

"She still live over by Wheeling?"

Les shrugged. "I don't know."

"I think she's in Ohio somewheres now," Esther said, appearing with a cup of coffee for Les. He took it without a word of acknowledgment. "So y'all still haven't found little Aaron?" she asked.

Luther shook his head. "I gotta be going. Jim Henderson lives near here, right? Toward Pine Gap?"

Les took a big slug of coffee before replying. "Okay, so when we took Pop's fancy toy to find the Nicholson girl, remember the first road we passed before Old Man Hodgkin's place? Where Wes almost hit a poultry truck that time?"

If he didn't actually hit it, how the hell am I supposed to know where it didn't happen? But Les was trying to help, so Luther moderated his response. "No, Les, I don't have a clue."

Esther sat on the edge of Les's chair and put a hand on his shoulder. "Why don't you ride over with him? It won't take long, and it'd be good for you to get out of the house." She leaned against him and sweetened the pot. "If you're nice, I'll even do the dishes while you're gone."

"If I drove slow enough, you think you could do my dishes, too?" Luther joked. He should be so lucky as to have dirty dishes; he hadn't been home enough to dirty any. Esther grinned, but his brother looked reluctant. "It would save me some time and curs-ing, Les, if you feel up to it."

Les said, "A'right. Just let me change my pants and get a jacket." He chugged the rest of his coffee before patting Esther's bare knee. "Thanks, babe."

～

LUTHER RAISED his collar against the wind. "Damn, it is getting chilly," he said, climbing in the car.

Les, sweaty from being inside, grunted in agreement and adjusted his sunglasses.

"How long you been dating Esther?" Luther asked.

"Off and on a few months."

"You never mentioned anything before."

Les shrugged. His reticence reminded Luther of the single occasion he'd fetched his much younger adolescent brother from school. "You remember that time mom sent me to pick you up? I think you were in junior high."

Les grunted. "Hell, yes. You drove up in your cruiser. Half the kids thought I was being arrested."

"Must've done wonders for your street cred," Luther said.

Les laughed. "Yeah, until they realized I *hadn't* been arrested and you were my cop brother. I had to punch somebody about it a couple of days later; I can't remember who."

Luther had been long gone from the Beck household by then, and although he checked on his mom regularly, he hadn't exactly been engaged in his brother's life. It'd been struggle enough to keep his own nose clean. "Why'd she send me to get you anyway?"

"Turn right up there," Les said, pointing. "I got kicked off the bus for a couple weeks for fighting. She figured dad would whoop my ass something fierce if he found out, so she signed all the papers and picked me up from school. I guess something came up that day."

Luther pulled onto a gravel road that looked vaguely familiar.

He drove slowly, afraid of bottoming out the county car. The heavily forested ground sloped alternately on either side, like a bed sheet snapped to attention but taking its time getting there.

"That's where I park to go mushroom hunting," Les said, gesturing as they passed a small turnout about a mile down the road. "There's a good spot the next hollow over."

Of course, he pronounced the word *holler*, like most people did. Except for Dead Hollow. Luther wondered why that was, then reined his mind in from its wandering as Les continued.

"You still want to go with me in the spring?" Les asked.

"Hell, yeah. I love morels—as long as you're cooking them, I'm in," Luther said.

"A'right." Les smiled. "You can bring the beer."

The forest dissipated until the road passed between two pastures. Luther hadn't remembered the old metal gate that lay ahead. Fortunately it wasn't locked, just loosely secured with a loop of heavy chain. He opened it and drove through. He caught his toe on the cattle guard when he secured the gate behind them and felt a twinge in his back.

"Sucks getting old," he said, groaning as he got in the car.

"They say it beats the alternative."

"True enough," Luther said. "Doesn't Harlan Miller live out this way?"

"Yep," Les confirmed. "His property's right after Jim Henderson's."

Trees quickly returned to swallow the road, creating a heavy canopy overhead. Luther wondered if anyone had bothered to check with Harlan Miller about Adam. If not, it was a major oversight, but an understandable one. Did anyone in law enforcement outside of Luther and Grant even know about Adam's recent connection to the older man?

"That's the Henderson place coming up on the left," Les said.

Most of the property was visible from the road, and there didn't seem to be any activity outdoors on this clear, Sunday afternoon. He suspected no one was at home. "Let's check Harlan Miller's place first."

"You're driving," Les said.

Luther wasn't sure he'd ever been to Harlan's cabin. It wasn't far past the Henderson place and wasn't hard to find, so long as you didn't miss the turn for the winding, wooded driveway.

"Nice place," he said. The bright white chinking between the logs fairly gleamed in the sunlight.

Les grunted in agreement. "I'd hate to think about hauling all those logs in here. Supposed to be nice inside, too, but I've heard he's a bit of a neat freak."

Harlan's pickup was parked next to a substantial, tarp-covered woodpile, with additional wood stacked alongside the house under the roof overhang. No smoke rose from the stone chimney, but the weather had been decent for a few days. Luther parked his vehicle and cut the engine.

"Stay in the car," he told his brother. "This shouldn't take long."

Luther knocked on the heavy front door, but there was no response. He hadn't expected one. The place had the air of being empty, though not of having been so for long. Luther made a quick circuit around the cabin, but didn't see anything unusual. Harlan's heavy-duty trashcan, lid weighed down by a brick, held a bulging garbage bag.

"Critters'll be in there in no time," Les said, startling Luther. "Should've dropped his trash at the dump. I guess he didn't mean to stay away long."

"Or he was in a hurry," Luther said, glowering. "I thought I told you to stay in the car."

"I got antsy."

"Well, let's antsy your ass back to the car." Luther examined the parking area more closely on the way back. "You know of Harlan having any other vehicles?"

"No." Les patted the pickup as they passed. "Takes pretty good care of his truck. This sure as hell ain't the one that played cozy with all those tore-up trees in the driveway."

If Harlan hadn't gotten a ride with Iris (and Luther had seen Iris this morning, so she wasn't his full-time chauffeur), then how did the man get wherever he was going?

It was about a half mile back to Jim Henderson's place. Harlan's had felt like a hermitage, but at first glance, Jim's property was almost inviting. Luther reconsidered his assessment as the driveway took them between rolling fields to the homestead. He'd been here once before and recalled that, although it backed up to forest, it still felt too exposed to be inviting. A mid-sized collie mix barked a few times from the front porch as they arrived, but he was a halfhearted alarm system at best.

"This time, stay in the goddamned car," Luther said, then added, "Please. Me wondering where you are is not helpful."

"And if you're not being helpful..." Les muttered.

Luther cracked a smile. "... Then you better be getting beer."

It was something Pop used to say, when he'd send the boys to the ice chest or the refrigerator, usually while he stared at a non-functioning vehicle in their driveway. Because of the age differ-ence, by the time Rudy Beck was sending little Les for beer, the man was usually watching Luther's feet sticking out from under the car.

The collie strolled down to meet Luther, then followed the deputy back up to the porch and lay down on a dog hair-covered welcome mat. Despite the mat's promise, there was no one to welcome Luther at the Hendersons, either. The dog's water bowl was full, and somebody was obviously coming by to feed him, but Luther didn't fancy waiting around for that to happen. He returned to the car.

"You want to come with me for a minute?" he asked Les.

The dog loped over when Les got out, allowing a quick scratch behind his ears. He fell in behind the two men as they approached a pickup parked in front.

"This is Jim's truck?" Luther asked.

"Yep," Les answered, rocking on his heels as though stillness was death.

There were additional wear patterns on the ground next to it. "His wife have her own car?"

"Yeah," Les said, scuffing at the ground with his foot. "I don't remember what. Some kind of blue Toyota, I think."

It made sense that Jim and his wife would take the more comfortable car for a long road trip to see their daughter. Luther and his entourage followed a path that swung around the house to the barn, worn by human feet as well as various farm equipment and recreational vehicles. Next to the barn, there was a patch of brown dirt with plenty of tire tracks.

"Jim have a farm truck, too?" Luther asked.

Les tilted his head back to gaze at the overcast sky through his sunglasses. "Yeah, I believe he does. One of them big, heavy duty ones."

Back at the car, Luther checked in with Beth while his brother got settled. "Hey, I'm at the Henderson place. How's it going there with our favorite crazy prisoner?"

She sighed. "He finally stopped screaming, but only because they gave him enough sedatives to take down an elephant."

"They who?"

"Who can keep it straight anymore? Ultimately, I think the Feds got authorization, but it's above my pay grade. Didn't make his lawyer happy, I can tell you that. Can't say as I blame her."

Luther thought of the petite public defender, probably in over her head but no doubt spitting fire. "Why's that?"

"Well, I didn't want to listen to him scream, but that was just noise. Now—I don't know. Something's upset him that makes him try to stay awake, but he can't explain it. It's sad, really. And a little creepy."

Luther couldn't say he was surprised—there was a lot of creepy going on around Virgil Rutledge—but it made him uneasy as well. "I gotta run my brother home real quick. Can you help me out with something?"

"Go ahead."

"I need contact numbers for Jim Henderson and his wife, and I need you to run them both through the DMV and see what vehicles they've got registered in their names..."

"Okay."

"I also need the name of the Kirby County officer that thought he saw Adam with an old guy last night. Thanks, Beth."

Luther glanced over to make sure his brother was belted in. Sweaty and feverish, he looked like shit. "How you doing over there?"

Les sniffed. "I'll live."

Luther turned the car around easily in the broad driveway. "You work tomorrow?"

"No, I'm off."

"That's probably a good thing. I'd hate to think about you driving a truck tomorrow."

"Yeah, but it's hard as hell to get a solid forty hours in anymore. I could use the money," Les admitted.

Luther gripped the steering wheel and braced himself to say something that went against his nature and could open him up to a whole bunch of pain in the ass. "You know, Les, if you need a little to tide you over, I can help."

Les sniffed again and wiped his nose on his sleeve. "I appreciate that, Luther, but it doesn't seem right."

"Why not?" Luther asked, warming to the idea. "Who the hell else should be loaning you money besides your brother? Besides, what am I gonna spend it on? I got no real hobbies, no wife and kids. I don't even have a girlfriend to take to the movies."

"That's okay—who wants to drive fifty miles to a theatre for some weepy horseshit anyway," Les said, but Luther caught him smiling.

"I'm guessing you do," Luther teased.

"Yeah, maybe I do," Les admitted as Luther turned onto his road. "I'll think about it."

A few minutes later, Les climbed out of Luther's car like an arthritic old man. Cold air pushed the hard-won heat from the interior as he stood with the door open.

"Feel better, man," Luther said. "I'll try to drop by and check on you sometime tomorrow."

Les waved a hand. "Don't worry about it. I'll be fine. Listen, you want to go over to the cemetery with me next week?"

It took Luther a moment—their mother's birthday. He couldn't remember the last time he'd been out to visit her grave. "Yeah, that'd be good."

Les nodded and a sudden gust of wind caught the door as he closed it, nearly taking Les over, too. He leaned toward the window and shouted, "Good luck finding the kid!"

Luther waved an acknowledgment and backed out onto the road. They needed a lot more than luck, but he couldn't help feeling something was about to break. He just wished he knew which way—for the angels or the other bastards.

30

"Y ou sure we didn't miss a turn?" Adam asked.

"I'm sure," Harlan said. "I've only been here once, but it was pretty unforgettable."

He stopped the truck when they reached a stone cairn. The stack of gray, lichen-covered rocks stood the height of a man, with a two-foot-high weathered, wooden cross protruding from the top. The cross was made of raw poles rather than flat, milled lumber, and Adam couldn't tell how the crossbar had been secured. There was a matching cairn on the other side, as if they marked an entrance. Beyond the cairns, the road was bound by rows of evergreen trees on each side and disappeared from sight as it curved ahead. Additional stacks of stones appeared periodically between the trees, but none of those incorporated crosses.

Adam shivered involuntarily. He'd thought he was over the food poisoning, but his nausea and feverishness had grown worse throughout the day. Harlan asked if he was okay, and Adam nodded. "What is this place?"

Harlan muttered at the clutch under his breath before he got the truck moving again. "Well, I don't know what it is now, and I can't rightly say I know the word for what it used to be."

"I find that hard to believe," Adam said. "You're not a man who suffers from a shortage of words."

Harlan laughed. "Smartass. I really don't know what to call it, though. Not a mission exactly... What do you call a cult's summer home?"

"A cult? Seriously?"

"I probably won't use that word in front of Teddy, although I doubt he'd really mind, and it's as good a word as any. See, back in the day, your grandfather Lawrence had a little religious group," Harlan said, raising the truck's sun visor to accommodate the day's fading light.

"Iris said—"

"Whatever Iris said, I can guarantee it wasn't much, and it was selective," Harlan said, with energy.

Piney branches had grown together, like threaded green fingers, shielding the property from view on either side. It was disconcerting, and Adam kept expecting someone or something to slide the limbs away and peek through. "Was Iris in his group?"

"Oh yeah," Harlan said. "She was part of it by virtue of being Lawrence's wife, but I wouldn't call her a true believer."

"What about you?" Adam asked.

Harlan grinned. "I wasn't exactly what you'd call a true believer, either. But I was part of it for a while, until I either came to my senses or your grandfather kicked me out. It depends on which story you hear."

"And which story do you tell?"

"I try not to tell any of them." Harlan glanced over at Adam. "I'm sorry, I'm not being cagey. I don't talk about this, and Iris doesn't talk about this, and no one else knows. Well, no one we ever see, anyway."

Harlan slowed the truck as they approached a fork in the road. On the right side, a faded sign mounted on a tree depicted a small ball of flame, much like the symbol you'd see on a fire extinguisher. On the left side, a slightly less faded sign showed a pyramid. Harlan took the path to the left.

"Are you sure this is the right way?" Adam asked.

"Quite sure. I don't know what's down the right path now, but if it's anything like it used to be, I'd just as soon never travel that road again."

"What happened to not being cryptic?" Adam asked, just before a stomach-churning sense of disorientation struck. He shuddered as an image flashed in his mind, of *white robes and blood and flames and the bleating scream of a literal sacrificial lamb*.

Adam flung open his door, and only his still-fastened seat belt prevented him from falling from the moving pickup.

Harlan slammed on the brakes, stalling the truck. He stomped the emergency brake, slid over and reached across Adam to close the swinging door. "Adam! Look at me."

The world streaked by Adam's eyes as if he were spinning in a centrifuge. He could hear Harlan's voice, but wasn't sure where it was coming from.

"Adam!" Harlan grabbed Adam's face with his bare hands, and an electric jolt knocked Adam's head back and turned the world red. Harlan jerked his hands away.

"Shit!" he said, grabbing a dark-stained hand towel from the edge of the seat. He used the dirty towel to cover his hands before placing his palms flat against Adam's cheeks. "Adam, come back to me. Focus on me."

And Adam did, corralling the images that flew by until he fastened onto Harlan's dark brows and his deep-set brown eyes. Harlan's silver hair blurred like a halo around his head, but the eyes —the eyes stayed solid. And then the pressure around Adam's skull fell away, so suddenly his chin hit his chest. The smell of dirty, old oil overwhelmed him, and he started to heave. He threw his arm across his face—striking Harlan's jaw—and held his breath, trying to keep everything inside. It worked, until his next inhale, when he began shivering uncontrollably.

"Can you hold it together for a few more minutes?" Harlan asked.

Adam nodded, unsure if the gesture was distinguishable from

the rest of his shaking. Harlan started the truck and roared through the gears, flinging Adam's head against the seat. Adam thought of the scarred trees in Harlan's driveway and wanted to say something funny about them, but he couldn't. He couldn't make the words come.

He had a sense of trees transitioning from rows to natural forest, conifer to deciduous, but somehow couldn't capture individual trunks with his eyes. There was a bit of fence, a tumbled gray structure, then another structure that was mostly standing, before the house came into sight ahead of them.

"Almost there, buddy," Harlan said, short of breath.

The house didn't look in much better shape than the structures they'd passed earlier, and Adam was surprised when a figure came running out the front door and down the porch steps.

"How did he know?" Adam said. Or at least, he thought he said. He wasn't certain he'd spoken the words out loud, because that's when his eyes rolled back in his head. Adam fell forward, felt a band of pressure across his chest from the seat belt, and then nothing.

31

"Adam?" It was Harlan's voice.

Adam was lying on a bed. He felt the mattress shift and tried to open his eyes, but there was something heavy on top of them.

"Okay," Harlan said. "I'm going to remove this from your eyes. Don't try to take in too much too fast. We think the stimulation helps set you off."

The pressure on Adam's face eased, and light bombarded his eyes. His vision was blurry, with loops and dark circles, the way it would get when he and JJ and Danny pressed against their eyeballs as kids. Eventually, he became aware of a ceiling above him, sheets of thin plywood secured with screws. He tilted his head and saw the tops of tongue and groove walls, and then an indistinct version of Harlan's face entered into his field of vision.

"You scared the shit out of me, son," Harlan said. "And I have to say, you do that entirely too much."

"Where are we?" Adam asked.

"Your uncle Teddy's house. He's in the other room. I need you to drink this," Harlan said. Adam felt hands on his shoulders, lifting them up, and a pillow sliding beneath. Then steam blanketed his face and warm ceramic pressed against his bottom lip. "I know, it smells like ass. I'm afraid it always smells like ass."

Adam tasted the hot liquid. It wasn't the same tea that Harlan had given Adam in his home, but Harlan was right—it did smell and taste equally vile. After a few sips, Adam lifted his own hands to hold the small cup. He flinched and nearly dropped it on his chest when his fingers brushed Harlan's.

"Don't worry," Harlan said, "I'm wearing gloves. You think you're up for a little socializing now?"

"Sure," Adam said. His tongue felt odd when it hissed, then curled to make the R. He braced himself with his elbows and sat up.

"Easy there—we don't want you cracking your head open on the floor. And there's no rush," he said.

Adam couldn't distinguish subtleties of facial expressions yet, but he knew that was wishful thinking on Harlan's part. "Yes, there is a rush," he said. "We have to find Aaron. How long have we been here?"

"About an hour. Maybe more."

Adam stood shakily, and Harlan steadied him by the elbow. "Your eyes are still getting their proper shape back, so just think of this as the elderly leading the blind," Harlan said.

There was a short hallway, barely lengthy enough to earn the name, before Adam found himself in an open living area not that different from Harlan's cabin. If, that is, Harlan left his cabin unoccupied for twenty years. The layout was similar, but this house felt like a photograph with a fancy, vintage filter applied. It wasn't particularly dirty, but everything appeared as though it had been left in the sun too long—the walls, the floor, even the furniture had faded fabrics. The light coming in the windows diffused through the surrounding trees and didn't seem strong enough to account for the effect. Finally, Adam realized that the house was just old. After all, his grandfather had been bringing people here decades ago.

Harlan led Adam toward a sofa upholstered in an unrecognizable plant pattern. A voice—not as deep as Harlan's, more midrange, sounding as if it traveled through the man's sinuses and exited his nose—called out from the kitchen. "It's probably best we meet before your vision returns entirely. It can be a little disconcerting."

The man stepped forward, wiping his hands on a green apron. He held out his hand, and then pulled it back. "Sorry, that was stupid. I'm your great uncle Theodore, Teddy for short."

Even slightly blurred, the resemblance to Adam's father Virgil was unmistakable: the same bump on the narrow nose, the same deep lines bracketing his mouth, the same shape of the eyes and slightly protruding chin. Teddy's hair was short, gray-blonde with a pronounced widow's peak. Adam wondered if he'd see that shape on Virgil's head, were the man to get a haircut. Or maybe he'd have to wait a dozen years.

"How did you know we were coming?" Adam asked.

"Doreen called and let me know you were on the way," Teddy said. "The woman's ways are mysterious. Fortunately, she didn't know about Virgil being arrested, and I didn't tell her. She thinks Virgil is dead."

"A lot of people thought Virgil was dead," Harlan said. His tone seemed to convey a certainty that Teddy had never been one of those people, maybe even that Teddy had been in touch with Virgil.

Teddy pressed on. "Harlan tried to catch me up while you were... indisposed. I'd heard about Virgil's arrest, but I didn't know about this new kidnapping."

Harlan sat on the arm of a chair so he could face both Adam and Teddy. "Adam and I have been trying to figure out where Virgil's been the past few years—hell, the past twenty years—to see if we could find some clue there that'll lead us to an accomplice."

"We don't mean you," Adam said, afraid of offending his relative in their first few minutes of acquaintance.

"Speak for yourself," Harlan said.

Adam waited for a laugh, but there wasn't one.

"Come to the table and we'll put our heads together, see what we can figure out," Teddy said.

Adam reached the head of the dining table under his own power, but just barely. The spots had cleared from his eyes, but his peripheral vision was still iffy. It was disconcerting when a flannel-sleeved arm appeared and set a steaming bowl in front of him. Teddy and Harlan sat across from each other and bowed their heads. Adam didn't recall ever hearing Harlan say a prayer, or anything that could remotely be mistaken for one, but it seemed that's what they were doing. After a moment, they nodded to each other and picked up their utensils.

"Why do you get plates of food and I get a bowl of broth?" Adam asked.

Harlan shook his head and gestured at Adam with a slice of bread. "It's a lot easier to clean up broth than it is to clean up chewed food." He slathered more butter on his bread, and added, "Keep that down and we'll revisit the situation."

Adam stared at the blue enamelware bowl, and at the neglected, wooden table it rested upon, its finish worn in uneven streaks. The bowl began to shimmer in front of him. It gave off the same scent of chicken and herbs, but he saw it resting on a different table (white laminate with multicolored flecks) in a different time.

"Adam, you still with us?" Harlan asked, voice gruff.

"Yes, sir," Adam said.

"What did you see?" Teddy asked.

"Just this... this broth in this bowl—"

"Describe the table you saw," Teddy said.

Adam looked at him in surprise, but did as he asked. Teddy nodded, and rose from his seat. "Y'all go ahead and eat. I need to get this started," he said, walking behind Adam into the kitchen.

Harlan stared at Adam while speaking to Teddy. "What do you think? Six hours? Eight?"

"For what?" Adam asked. "What's going on?"

"We need to loosen the hold he has on you," Teddy said. "One way to do that is to make you unavailable—basically knock you out."

"Loosen whose hold?" Adam asked.

"Your father," Harlan said.

Adam closed his eyes. The broth was shimmering again, and it wasn't helping him deal with his frustration. "I can't sleep indefinitely. Not if we're going to figure out who has Aaron."

"Adam—"

Adam slammed his hand on the table and the bowl of broth bounced. "There's a kid out there in trouble!"

"I'm sorry, son," Harlan said, voice firm, "but the sad fact is there's always a kid in trouble somewhere, and you dying isn't going to change that."

Adam shook his head. "This isn't going to kill me."

"Actually, it damn well could," Harlan said, pointing a spoon at him for emphasis. "But let's say it doesn't. How about going through the rest of your life being as crazy as your father? How does that sound?"

"I am *not* crazy like Virgil," Adam said, because that's what he had to say, what he had to tell himself. No matter what doubts he might have.

"Just because you're not crazy *now*, doesn't mean it won't *make you crazy*," Harlan said. "And you wouldn't be the first one to go down that road. Believe me."

"Harlan," Teddy cut in, "I'm not sure you're helping. Adam, what we're talking about, it isn't just sleep. It's beyond sleep, because you're vulnerable when you're sleeping. This is beyond his reach."

Teddy brought a tea tray to the table. Instead of a teapot with delicate cups, it held a saucepan on a knitted potholder, accompanied by metal cups. The elderly man poured from the saucepan with more dexterity than Adam could have managed and set the half-full cup in front of him.

"Drink up."

Adam leaned over and looked at the liquid inside. It was translucent enough that he could see a dent in the bottom of the cup. "Okay," he said, and drained it in one hearty chug.

The liquid tasted strange, like mushrooms and pine and sulfur, and a funny tingling spread through his body almost instantly. He saw an image in his mind of a dark curtain being drawn, but it couldn't hold back the flood of nausea and pain that rolled over him. One eye winked shut momentarily, and Adam's head jerked.

This is bad.

He pushed his chair back from the table, but it was too late. Adam fell to the floor, all loose joints and funky angles, head slamming against the hard wood.

And then he began convulsing.

32

Bruce sat outside a crappy apartment building, a hundred and fifty miles from Cold Springs and about twenty from the boy. It was good to have some distance from the kid. He'd tried using him to contact Adam again, with no better success. Either he was missing something, or Virgil was wrong about Adam. Bruce knew he just needed to be patient, but patience didn't come easily to him. It was also getting harder to get the dosage right, to keep the boy both compliant and breathing. Ultimately though, he might have to kill the boy, and he wasn't looking forward to it. He didn't like killing kids.

But the world doesn't stop spinning when things aren't going your way. A man's still gotta make a living.

He got out of his vehicle and knocked lightly on the cheap door of the ground floor unit, afraid his knuckles would punch right through. The man (*Chip, like the brown paint peeling off the exterior*) who quickly motioned him inside was in his mid-twenties, but there was no innocence left in him. He reeked of pot, and his potent body odor suggested he'd been metabolizing harder drugs and alcohol and not much else. Chip seemed only half present, and what awareness remained in his eyes sought out the package. It was always about *the package*.

Cash in hand, Bruce held up the baggie and watched Chip's face turn feral. Chip had dirty blonde hair (really dirty, not like a fancy model trying to slum it) and was skinny to the point of emaciation. *Not my type,* he thought. And he did have a type, for what he was contemplating. However, it'd been a rough few days, and this was a good opportunity to test something. So he was willing to make an exception.

"Chip, buddy, I've got your regular, but I'm rolling out something new I thought you might be interested in..."

BRUCE LOOKED at the body on the filthy floor, filthier now that Chip had vomited. Really, he should've left long ago, but the first use of a new cocktail required careful observation. It had taken the tweaker longer to stop convulsing than he'd thought it would. Still, enough was enough. Chip was hanging on, but he wouldn't be for much longer. Bruce stood in the center of the room, unwilling to sit on the folding chair furniture, or any other surface in the hovel. He turned in a circle, reviewing the scene. That's when the picture on the screen caught his attention.

The television was on, but the sound was off, as it had been when he arrived. Bruce looked around for the remote, but didn't see it. He moved closer to the TV anyway, as if to hear its muted soundtrack. A banner headline, **Possible Child Kidnapping Suspect**, ran under a photograph of Adam Rutledge. It wasn't a posed photo, more like a surveillance one, and he wondered where they'd gotten it. *Shit.*

His body shook with frustration. He wanted to kick the dying man on the floor, but it wouldn't do to have signs of anything other than an overdose. Instead, he pulled out his cell phone and made a call.

"Hey man, it's me, Mitch," he said, in a voice Chip wouldn't have recognized as he paced around his body. "I just saw some crazy shit on the news. Should I be worried about getting in and out of Cold Springs with product?"

The man on the other end sounded grim. "Hell yeah, you should be worried. They've been doing checkpoints and shit. All because that dumb fucker ran when they went to pick him up. Hopefully, the cops'll shoot him."

Bruce blew out a frustrated sigh. "Well, shit. This puts me in a bad position. But you can hold off for another day or two, can't you?"

Bruce stepped on Chip's limp hand and nearly dropped his phone, waving his arms to regain his balance. He gave Chip a dirty look, as if it were the dying (*dead?*) man's fault. *One good kick to the face. Just one...*

The man on the other end of the line didn't seem to notice. "Sure, I guess I can wait. Or I could meet you somewhere else."

I'll bet you could, you worthless fucking addict. "Yeah, that's a bad idea. Don't worry, I'll be in touch when things cool down."

Bruce hung up. He knew better than to scream, even in this shitty apartment building, so he dug his fingers into his skull and screamed on the inside. *What kind of stupid sonuvabitch runs when the cops have no real evidence against him?* The foundation of his strategy had just gone out the window: Adam wasn't about to come looking for him—even with him holding the kid—while he was on the run from the cops. And what if the cops killed Adam? This necessitated a change in plans. *Dammit.* He'd have to get rid of the kid tomorrow.

There was no reaction from Chip when he kicked him in the kidney on the way out the door.

33

Adam became aware of lying on the floor, of aching pains in his limbs where they'd struck his chair and the table. He couldn't see—at least, nothing he could make sense of—but his mind was filled with waves of light of different colors, dominated by a washed-out red background with punctuating lines and shapes of fierce indigo.

"Sweet Jesus." That was Uncle Teddy.

Then Adam was being lifted, hands at his shoulders and calves. The motion was awkward and swaying. His boots and then a shin banged against something before the blood rushed to his lowered head. *Going down porch steps.* The quality of the light in his mind changed once he was outside. He tried to say something, but he had no words, no way to speak them. He just wanted to tell them, *It's okay. You can leave me here. I'm done.*

Air brushed his areas of exposed skin—face, neck, hands and ankles, one side of his stomach. *It's cold*, he thought, but still could not say. His body could, though, and although the racking convulsions had stopped, he began to shake.

"Shit!" That was Harlan. "Put him by that tree."

Adam felt the ground beneath him, cool and slightly damp, and he could smell the mulchy odor of rich soil and rotting leaves. *Yes. Here. Just leave me here.*

But there were hands under his shoulders again, tugging him until he could feel the incipient swell of a neighboring tree trunk through the ground.

"Adam," Harlan said, and Adam felt his gloved hand against his cheek. "This isn't going to be pleasant, but just remember. You can trust me."

Then Harlan was next to him, on the ground. He knew that—he didn't know how he knew—until somehow Adam could see them all from above: Adam's body, shielded by Harlan (thank God —the sight of his jean-clad, shivering legs was disturbing enough), and Teddy standing on Adam's other side, with a wispy, endearing bald spot at the crown of his head. Harlan removed his gloves and grasped Adam's bare hand with his own, volatile one.

The old man lay on the ground, dead. He had to be dead—there was so much blood and his mouth hung open. A rifle lay on the ground and Harlan kneeled next to Lawrence, face angry.

Adam jerked away. He dug his heels into the earth and kicked, but Harlan grabbed his wrist and pushed his chest back down to the ground. "Shh, relax."

An incredible pain shattered Adam's skull, and he had no choice but to relax, to lie still and hope he died. Harlan kept one hand on his wrist and placed the other palm on the ground. And then, something happened. The pain eased, and Adam watched it and the flashing lights—the ones he'd seen in his mind—travel through Harlan's hands and through Harlan himself, finally draining into the earth. Harlan's words in the hospital about Adam healing Rachel came back to him: *Like using your blood to put out a fire when there's a bucket of water handy.*

"Exactly," Harlan said, as if he had spoken out loud. "Now let somebody else do the bleeding for once."

Teddy appeared—Adam hadn't realized he'd left—with a navy wool blanket and a piece of cardboard. He tossed the cardboard on the ground next to Adam and spread the blanket over him. Adam smelled a slight odor of mustiness and cedar even though the blanket only reached his chest. Teddy made his way awkwardly to the ground, tugging the cardboard beneath his rear end. Then he leaned against the tree, grunting as he settled into place. He said, "It's going to be a long night."

Night? He was right; it was dark already. When had it gotten dark? The blanket began to feel less like a blanket and more like a restraint. Adam squirmed beneath it, but he lacked the strength to get as far as his elbows. He couldn't even lift his head. His eyes fell shut.

Adam felt the back of a weathered hand brush his forehead and sighed.

"He's okay," Teddy said. "Considering. How'd he get to be grown without knowing about all this?"

"Huh," Harlan grunted. "You really have to ask?"

Adam was warm—warmer on one side than the other—and content to just be and breathe. And listen.

"Iris," Teddy said, answering his own question. "She never wanted to believe, and honestly, only someone who *disbelieved* as much as she did could have lived with Lawrence as long as she did."

"Yeah," Harlan said.

There was a whumping sound (*new log on the fire*), followed by renewed popping and crackling. Without the men's voices as a tether, Adam began to drift away. Until, "Teddy, what do you think his chances are?"

"Good," Teddy said, a little too quickly. "I think they're good. I'll regret how Virgil turned out until the day I die, but the fact is, he never had a chance. His boy does."

And Adam was gone.

～

"*Charlotte?*"

The boy wailed and wriggled in his arms, stretching out a chubby hand with its now misshapen thumb, desperate to reach his mother. Virgil touched the flesh of her bloody arm with a firm finger, and it was like poking a particularly bony cut of meat—yielding, but not responsive. "I know you're still in there. I love you, and I'll make this right."

He slammed his head into the car frame as he backed out of the car with the boy in his arms, but it was just one more sensation in a hurricane of sensations. The boy screamed and tried to climb over his shoulder, to his mother. That's when Virgil began to cry. No matter what happened, whether he was successful or not, nothing would ever be the same. They could never be the family he'd imagined. He felt a piece of himself dying with every step he took away from his wife. But this was the only way. And it had to work. Why else would the wreck have happened here, so close to a place that was so special to his father, and to his father before him?

It was dark, he didn't have a flashlight, and he hadn't been here since he'd married Charlotte, but his feet still knew the way. The ground was mostly level and perpetually blanketed in leaves, but they were the softer, quieter leaves of summer, the ones from previous seasons well on their way to returning to the earth. In the fall, there was a crisp edge to the top layer of leaves underfoot that had only just released their hold on life. Sounds traveled differently then, too, and even more so in the winter. The summer canopy absorbed sounds that traveled unimpeded past the leafless trees and snow-covered ground of winter. He told himself that's why he couldn't hear anything from the wreck, from Charlotte or from anyone come to rescue her from outside.

The boy's cries had also diminished to a vague mewling. As they neared their destination, he looked less for his mother and clung instead to his father, burying his face against Virgil's bloody neck. Finally, there was a soft glow ahead, as the barest hint of light reached them from above. Death brings clarity, *his own father had said. Which was why Lawrence Rutledge came to this place of death, of barren trees and hostile soil, to pray. And to offer sacrifices...*

～

ADAM GASPED. The organic strobe of the campfire and the evergreen boughs overhead helped push the panic away. The other world had lost its hold. Adam didn't know whether it was because he'd pulled himself free, if that world had lost interest in him, or if someone else had pushed it away. But right now, it didn't matter. He shivered, and the motion drained his remaining strength. His eyes drifted shut again as Harlan draped another blanket over him.

"It's okay, son," Harlan whispered in his ear, placing his hand on Adam's forehead as he had in the hospital. "Don't worry. We're right here."

34

The hospital was quiet, late on a Sunday night. Luther found Grant and Agent D'Antonio in the hallway outside the old Sheriff's room. "How's he doing?"

"Good, I think," Grant said. "Yesterday's surgery went well. I didn't get a chance to speak with him today, but I just peeked in and Iris said he's recovering."

"Do you need a minute?" Luther asked, glaring at D'Antonio. He dared the man to say they didn't have time, even though he knew they really didn't. Dislike wasn't rational.

Grant shook his head and motioned in the other direction. "Let's meet down there."

Luther felt entirely too much like a spy, or more accurately a member of a doomed conspiracy, as Grant led them to an empty patient room. But it had to be done. Recently someone—perhaps multiple someones—had been a little too free with what was said in confidence at the Command Center. Luther had his own suspicions, namely Kiss-Ass Kilbourne, who seemed to be doing everything he could to make his mark. Tonight's debriefing had included a clarification of the proper modes of communication with the public and the press. Luther had added, "In other words, keep your goddamn mouths shut." It may have been the first thing he'd ever said that won D'Antonio's approval. Still, in an abundance of caution, the three men had agreed to meet privately at the conveniently located hospital.

The empty room, semi-private, held two hospital beds with a couple of awkward chairs for each. Luther grabbed a chair from the far side of the room while D'Antonio shut the door behind them.

"Who wants to go first?" Grant asked.

"I will, if you don't mind," Luther said. "I still don't think Adam is behind this, but I have made some progress on tracking him down." Luther explained how he'd come to suspect that Adam was traveling with Harlan Miller. "I've been trying to reach Jim Henderson, but a truck registered in his name is unaccounted for, and I think that's Rutledge and Miller's mode of transport."

D'Antonio nodded. "We'll put out an APB. Any idea where they're headed?"

"Not a one," Luther admitted. "Which, I'm sorry to say, just leaves Iris and JJ."

Grant nodded. "JJ said she'll stop by when she has a chance, and Iris is still here waiting for my mom, so I'll take care of them shortly. In the meantime, we finally got something solid on the tip line. A woman who lives behind the school saw a man in a bear suit carrying a child to a van."

Luther's eyes widened. "She have her finger up her ass all weekend?" he asked. Grant winced, and Luther said, "Sorry, boss."

"It's the best lead we've got," Grant said. "She's working with someone right now on the van's logo. It looks like a party supply place."

There was a knock at the door, and a moment later JJ entered, dressed for work in two-tone scrubs.

"Thanks for dropping in, JJ," Grant said. He stood and offered her his chair. "I'll get right to the point. We know Adam is with

Harlan, and we need to know where they're going. Before someone gets hurt."

Instead of looking angry, as Luther had expected, JJ looked embarrassed. "I'm sorry. I don't know."

"JJ—"

"No, I really don't. I swear," she said, focused on Grant as though no one else was in the room. "I haven't seen or spoken to Adam since I dropped him off at the school Friday night. Now, Harlan and Iris were talking fast in here—"

"Last night?" D'Antonio barked.

"Right before you came in," JJ confirmed, "and I couldn't follow what they were saying. I didn't know the people they were talking about and it was all in shorthand, you know?"

"What do you know about Iris and Harlan's history?" Grant asked.

"Until a few weeks ago, I didn't even know they knew each other, much less had a history," JJ admitted.

"Ulysses would know," Luther said.

Grant shook his head. "Maybe. But most days, even Dad doesn't know what Dad knows."

"I could ask him," Luther said. "Maybe it'd be less confusing for him then, since he only knows me through the department."

Grant shrugged. "I don't mind if you want to try."

"Ms. Tulley," D'Antonio cut in, "if you don't remember names, what can you tell us about the context? Anything you remember."

JJ shot a quick look of distaste at the federal agent before answering. "Harlan said something about Virgil being at the heart of this, about trying to figure out who'd know what he'd been up to for the past twenty years."

"Mr. Rutledge did agree to resume antipsychotic medication—"

"When?" Luther asked.

"I just got the call in the lobby," D'Antonio said, nodding toward the front of the hospital. "But he still won't be capable of helping us out—should he choose to—for some time."

So who might Virgil have stayed in touch with over the years? *His family.* Luther didn't say it out loud. He didn't have to; he saw it in Grant's eyes, too. "I'm on it," Luther said. "Right after I speak with your dad."

~

"SO HOW ARE the nurses treating you?" Luther asked, shifting in his seat. Hospital chairs never felt big enough to accommodate a man of his size.

The man in the bed smiled. He looked better than Luther would have thought. "Don't you be harassing any of those fine young ladies, Deputy. They don't need the distraction."

"Yes sir, Sheriff. I imagine you're distraction enough."

Ulysses Mason nodded, and his smile slowly faded. Luther watched a kaleidoscope of expressions cross the elderly man's face as he drifted inexorably away, while clinging tooth and nail to the solidity of the known. "I haven't seen you in a while, have I?"

"No sir," Luther said, and brushed at the lint on his hat to avoid seeing the confusion in his eyes. "I wanted to drop by, but I've been busy."

The old Sheriff lifted a hand toward the neighboring night-stand. Luther handed him his water, and Ulysses maneuvered the cup and straw mostly successfully, getting just a few dribbles on his sheet before handing the cup back to Luther. "My son has been busy, too. I hear you found the girl. Sarah's parents will be glad to put her to rest," the old man said.

Sarah Edmunds. Somehow the man had heard about her remains being identified and, in a moment of lucidity, connected that to one of the cases he'd never solved.

"Yes sir," Luther agreed. "They surely will."

He didn't mention Danny, so perhaps he hadn't heard about the second body. Luther didn't visit the old man regularly—he found their time together an unholy mixture of depressing and disconcerting—but he'd done it often enough to know that time was very fluid for Mr. Mason. His mind traveled back and forth among the decades as if that dimension no longer had meaning for him. So when he spoke again, it wasn't the temporal shift that Luther found jarring, but rather the almost superstitious sense he'd had before that the old man still made important connections, that he saw things that others could not.

"Have you been keeping an eye on the Rutledge boy like I asked?"

Like you asked damn near fifteen years ago.

"Yes sir," Luther said. He told himself he wasn't lying, except in his experience any time such a reassurance was needed, the truth was already lying in a puddle on the floor with skid marks down the middle. "Speaking of the Rutledges—"

"Iris sits with me when Bonnie isn't here," Ulysses said. His brow wrinkled with concern. "I'm glad we got past all that, that she and Bonnie can be friends again."

"All what?"

"After Lawrence..." Ulysses trailed off, and suddenly his eyes grew hard, almost shifty. It was a transition Luther had witnessed before in people battling dementia. "It doesn't matter. He's gone."

"Yes, sir, he is," Luther agreed. "Is he the one that introduced Iris and Harlan Miller?"

Ulysses pursed his lips and shook his head slightly, like a disappointed father. "Don't you believe what people say about them, Luther. Some people just like to cause trouble, that's all."

"What kind of people?" Luther asked.

Ulysses waved a dismissive hand. "The talk started with Lawrence's *congregation*."

"That's right," Luther said. "I remember Pop saying something once about Lawrence's loonies."

Luther cracked a smile as he spoke, but Ulysses didn't. "Remember what I told you, Luther. Father or not, you need to stay away from Rudy Beck."

"Yes, sir," Luther replied automatically.

He'd told Luther the same thing years ago, when he'd first

applied to the Sheriff's Department. Straight up—*stay away from your dad. That man's not worth your time.* No wiffle-waffling around about family, like everyone else did. It was one of the reasons Luther had trusted Ulysses Mason from the start, one of the reasons he'd shared his deepest secrets with the man.

"So Harlan Miller was part of Lawrence's religious group?" Luther guessed.

Ulysses nodded, fighting lazy eyelids.

"Anyone else come to mind?" Luther asked.

Ulysses closed his eyes, and Luther waited for the sound of a snore. Instead, the old Sheriff said, "His brother."

"Harlan's brother?"

Ulysses opened his eyes. "Not Harlan. I don't know that he ever had one. Lawrence's brother, Theodore, was part of it. And his wife, too. Never turn your back on that woman if you know what's good for you. Are you married?"

"No, sir. I haven't been lucky that way. I should be going now," Luther said, rising and placing his hat back on his head.

"Thanks for stopping by," Ulysses said. "You been running like you're supposed to?"

Luther patted his belly, where he kept a few extra pounds, and grinned. "Does it look like it?"

This was a bit of a running gag with them. On good days, Ulysses would say, *Not unless it's to the fridge.* Today, although he'd done well during their conversation, he simply smiled uncertainly. Luther let it go, not wanting to cause the man stress.

Luther was nearly to the door when something occurred to him. He turned and said, "Funny, Harlan Miller doesn't strike me as the religious type."

Ulysses nodded. "Not unless it was some serious, old-time religion. The kind that doesn't talk about God."

Luther stroked his chin and felt a little scruff there. "What do you mean?"

"Harlan's got a reputation with some of the old-timers for

having The Sight. I saw a bit myself, from time to time, and it's kinda spooky."

"Huh," Luther said, noncommittally, before giving a final wave and closing the door to the room behind him.

Great—that's all I need. Another crazy-ass crackpot to deal with.

35

Adam smelled the fire first. Then he heard its crackling, popping hunger for fuel, and then he saw its glow flickering through his eyelids.

He opened his eyes and saw the familiar evergreen boughs above his head. His feet were warm from the campfire, but his face had the flushed feeling that comes from being simultaneously hot and cold.

"Hey there, Rip Van Winkle," came Teddy's voice, a moment before his face passed into Adam's field of vision. "Welcome back to the land of the... well, not quite dead, anyway. You think you're ready to sit up for a minute?"

Adam's throat had glommed shut, and he gave a small cough to clear it. "Sure," he croaked.

A noise from the dark woods nearby startled Adam, and he lifted his head. Harlan appeared, adjusting his upper layers (corduroy jacket, flannel shirt, and presumably undershirt) where they hung over his pants. He blinked as he approached, eyes adjusting to the light. "Goddamn, Teddy. You need to explore the waste technology of the twentieth century, much less the twenty-first. It's been a number of years since I've shit in an outhouse at night, and I have to say I did not miss the experience."

"I could use a hand here," Teddy said.

Together, the two elderly men lifted Adam so his back was against the tree. Adam expended no effort whatsoever, and yet he felt short of breath. Harlan held him steady, while Teddy tucked a blanket behind Adam and wrapped it around his shoulders. Now Adam could see the fire, and the licking red and white and orange of its flames were mesmerizing...

"Hey," Harlan said, giving Adam's shoulder a gentle shake. "Let's not sail away quite yet."

Harlan slid one of a pair of folding, canvas camping chairs in front of Adam to block his view of the fire. Freed from that enticement, Adam turned his head to take in the rest of his surroundings. They sat in the forest, maybe twenty yards away from Teddy's front door. The sky was dark, so overcast he couldn't even distinguish clouds. He thought they were closer to dawn than dusk, but for now the only light came from the campfire and what was probably the kitchen window. As Adam stared at the house, trying to fix its layout in his mind, Teddy emerged carrying a tray. He set it within reach on one of the chairs and approached Adam with a steaming ceramic cup.

Adam's chest squeezed with fear. His hands twitched at his sides, resisting the impulse to knock the cup from Teddy's hand as his great uncle squatted next to him.

"No," Adam said. "No way. I'm not drinking that again."

Teddy extended the cup carefully with both hands and said, "It's sweet tea."

Adam reluctantly accepted the offering and held it to his nose. It did not smell like ass. He took a sip... sugary sweet black tea with a generous dollop of milk. The hot liquid felt soothing against his gunky throat, and the sugar and caffeine tingled through his system.

"Besides," Harlan said, "it wasn't the tea that almost did you in."

Adam was afraid to ask what nearly had.

"Don't worry—we'll get to that later. Can I get you anything?" Harlan asked.

Adam shook his head deliberately, afraid his entire body would topple over.

"Can you speak now?" Harlan asked, sitting next to Adam on the ground. The tree's trunk was wide enough to provide postural support for both men.

Adam swallowed hard to clear his throat. "If I have anything worth saying."

Harlan grinned and squeezed his shoulder. "All right, just drink your tea. I'll do the talking for a while. Teddy, feel free to jump in when I start making shit up."

Teddy dragged the other chair to join them, passing a cup to Harlan and choosing one for himself before getting comfortable. Raising his own beverage, he said, "I always do."

Adam suspected the two men were drinking "corrected tea," unless they hadn't bothered with the tea part at all.

"It's time for a bedtime story. Way past time," Harlan said. "Tonight, our subject will be why Doreen hates me."

Teddy snorted in the dark. Harlan flipped him the bird, and Teddy flipped him right back. *A hundred and fifty years of maturity*, Adam thought, groggily unsure of the math.

"It all goes back to Lawrence. I told you your grandfather had a religious group, just as his father did before him. When I met Lawrence, he had a small group of crazies—no offense, Teddy— and he wanted to bring me into the fold."

"You need to tell the boy why he wanted you," Teddy said.

"The *boy* is as old as we were then," Harlan remarked.

"Like I said, *the boy*." Teddy smiled.

Harlan curled a lip in response. "Fine. Lawrence was interested in me because of my—what was it you called it, son? *Woo woo?* Because I am who I am. Apparently, your *great* grandfather had some similar gifts of sight, and that helped him build his little flock. But your grandfather Lawrence didn't have it—"

"Harlan, that's not true."

"Fine, he had a little here and there, but nothing like Teddy. Lawrence had just enough to give him a taste, to help him understand what else was possible. And that chafed his ass to no end. Still, Lawrence was also a pragmatist, so he was always looking for people who could do what he could not, people he could use to build his following."

Harlan paused for a sip, and Adam commented, "I wouldn't think you and he would've had... compatible dispositions."

"No doubt," Harlan admitted, "but it took us a lot longer to admit it than you'd think. Lawrence could be a very charismatic man, when he chose to be, and he did *know things*—or at least, he was good at making you think he did. He strung me along for a couple of years, saying he'd help me gain insight, control over my abilities."

Teddy burped from his chair. "You know that's not the only reason you stuck around. You were in love with Iris."

Harlan glared at Teddy. "It's true I didn't want to leave her. And, husband or not, I was afraid to leave her with Lawrence. But that's neither here nor there. As Adam said, the man and I weren't compatible. I've never had a very high opinion of religion, and I have an even worse one of the men like Lawrence who use it. The power dynamic in his group was unhealthy and unsustainable."

The indictment rolled off Harlan's tongue easily, and Adam suspected this was a discussion the two men had had before. In fact, they seemed barely aware Adam was there, an addition to their usual shared audience.

"Don't forget the snake handling," Teddy added.

Harlan ran his hands over his forearms, as if chasing away the crawling sensations. "That was downright stupid. I couldn't believe it when Lawrence brought Virgil—*not even a teenager*—into the snake handling bit."

"He thought Virgil was special. *Chosen*," Teddy said. "That he wouldn't be harmed."

Harlan shook his head and looked ready to argue the dead man's motivation.

"They actually used poisonous snakes?" Adam cut in, both fascinated and appalled.

"Rattlesnakes, copperheads, maybe a cottonmouth once in a while," Teddy said. "Now don't get me wrong, they didn't do it all the time. Just every once in a while, when Lawrence said the spirit moved him."

Harlan countered, "Lawrence did it when he needed to, when he thought people were losing their faith *in him*. It had nothing to do with God and everything to do with keeping the congregation in line."

Teddy's mouth set in a hard line.

"You know it's true. It came back to bite him in the ass, though, didn't it?" Harlan took a sip and smiled. "Well, the hand, anyway."

Teddy knocked his canvas chair over as he stood. "The man almost died!"

Adam watched, too weak to intervene if he'd wanted, as Harlan pushed up off the tree and got in Teddy's face. "He lost a goddamned finger is all. And whose fault was that?" Harlan demanded.

"Doreen thought it was yours, that you pushed him because you knew he'd go to the snakes. She said you meant for him to die."

Harlan's voice dropped, in volume and in register, and Adam could barely make out his words. "And what do you think, Teddy?"

The men stared at each other, the night silent save for the popping of the flames. Finally, Teddy replied, "I think I'm too old to have the same goddamned argument every time I see you. Even as rarely as that is."

Harlan turned toward the fire, while Teddy righted his chair and spun it to face Adam. He sank back down with a sigh. "I mostly agreed with Harlan back then, and I wouldn't have stuck around as long as I did except I was trying to keep an eye on your dad. The way my brother—your grandpappy—treated him..."

Adam's head seethed with emotions—anger and frustration that no one had protected Virgil, sorrow that the child he'd seen beaten was beyond his reach and beyond his protection, and fear that another one was as well. The swirling was so powerful, his forehead dipped toward his chest before he could stop it.

"Sorry. He's the last thing I should be talking about now," Teddy said. "After the incident where Lawrence lost his finger, I drifted away from my brother and the rest of the congregation. My wife Doreen was angry—Lordy, she was pissed—at me and at Harlan. She stuck close to the core group for a while, as I pulled farther away. Eventually, I decided to move from Cold Springs, and she went with me. She didn't want to, but I think Lawrence convinced her it was her duty." Teddy laughed, a hollow sound. "Probably tired of her hanging on him all the time. In any case, we were miserable together, and when Lawrence died, she finally left me."

A recurring vision of his bloody grandfather lying on the ground, Harlan crouched over him, made Adam flinch.

"You okay?" Teddy asked.

Adam nodded, but pressed an elbow against the tree to maintain his balance. Harlan sat next to him on the ground again, and their shoulders bumped briefly.

Teddy held up his ceramic cup. "Harlan, you need a top-up?"

Harlan said no, and Adam intuited the man had his mind set on doing something that required a clear head. He wasn't sure he'd ever seen Harlan, hollow-eyed and haggard, look more like he needed a drink. "Don't abstain on my account," Adam said. It came out more sharply than he'd meant it to.

"Don't stay awake on mine," Harlan said.

Adam realized then that he *was* bone tired. It was hard to keep his head upright. In fact, it was easier to lean against Harlan, who was closer than he'd been just a moment ago.

"Grab my cup!" Teddy said, and Harlan did, catching both it

and Adam. He gently lowered Adam the rest of the way to the ground.

Adam stared at the dirt, watched tiny, dark organic bits form airborne clouds when his breath exhaled. Harlan set Adam's empty cup next to him. The cup... the tea...

"Suffin a mitch!" Adam said. *Wait, that's not right.*

"Language, son." Shadows gathered in the hollow between Harlan's nose and cheek, and between his nose and mustache, as he smiled. "Just rest."

36

––––––

JJ should have gone off shift twenty minutes ago, but she'd already missed having breakfast with Evie (*what would I do without Otto and Dorothy?*). There was nothing waiting for her at home except sleep and the lazy, recovering dog who'd want to join her in it. And she wouldn't be able to sleep, not the way her mind was spinning. She hadn't left the house at all yesterday except to get Trooper from the vet, and things had been quiet—too quiet. It was only a matter of time before the situation escalated with Marcus.

Escalated... *where the hell do you escalate to after poisoning a dog?* JJ didn't know, but she was certain her ex-husband had set himself on a path of no return. She was less certain what she should do about it.

When she wasn't obsessing over Marcus, JJ was checking her cell phone compulsively. She'd been entirely truthful—for once—when she'd told Grant and the FBI jerk that she hadn't heard from Adam, but she kept hoping for a voicemail or a reply text, anything to let her know he was okay. To make matters worse, she feared— because she was such a latecomer to truth-telling where Adam was concerned—Grant had lost faith in her. She'd missed seeing him before he left the hospital last night, so she hoped Grant would visit his father first thing this morning. Instead of heading home, she busied herself with a clipboard that didn't need her attention, wondering how much longer she could stall. Her heart leapt when she finally heard the elevator doors open and saw him doff his hat.

"Do you mind?" her co-worker asked, smiling disingenuously as she watched Grant approach. "I need to hit the little nurses' room."

JJ rolled her eyes, but was grateful. She felt awkward enough without an audience, and doubtless Grant did, too. He rocked slightly on his heels, standing over her, trying to find words.

"Your dad's still sleeping," she said, having checked on him herself a few minutes earlier.

"Good," he said. "Listen, I just wanted to say I'm sorry."

"Why?" JJ asked, surprised. "What do you have to be sorry about?"

He traced his hand along the counter, knocking a stray pen on the floor. He picked it up and set it back carefully, then stuck his hands in his pockets. "I'm sorry I had to put you in that position, with Adam. I know he means a lot to you."

"I feel like I betrayed him," JJ admitted, the words out before she could stop them.

Grant nodded, in that way he had of expressing understanding rather than necessarily agreement. JJ felt his solid presence next to her, tugging at her like gravity. Why wouldn't the damn man just move closer, so she didn't have to?

"I'm sorry," he repeated, and started to make tracks.

JJ grabbed his arm to stop him. "I'm sorry, too. I should've told you sooner. But, it's hard not to feel like I have to protect him."

Grant turned and faced her, folding his hands loosely around her upper arms. They seemed to be supporting each other, rather than him holding her up. "You are protecting him," he said. "Finding Adam is the best way to protect him."

"Yes, but it's also the best way to place him in danger," she pointed out.

He didn't disagree, but he leaned forward and kissed her forehead. "I'll try to keep him safe," he said, and squeezed her hand. His long, smooth stride quickly ate up the distance to his father's room, almost before she could tell he'd moved.

She appreciated the thought, keeping Adam safe, but she wasn't sure it was a promise Grant had the power to keep.

~

JJ WAS CROSSING the parking lot, still riding a Grant-doesn't-hate-me buzz, when Otto called.

"What's up, Rachel Papa?" she asked, tucking her cell phone in her shoulder crook as she unlocked her Bronco.

"Don't freak out," he said.

Nothing good follows those words, she thought, recalling Luther's preamble to searching Adam's car. "Then don't freak me out. What's going on?"

"Marcus is at the school."

JJ couldn't breathe. Her throat seized up, and it was like trying to suck air through a coffee stirrer.

"JJ? Are you still there?" Otto asked.

She climbed into her vehicle and sat, not breathing, but not getting drawn into panic, either. Waiting for the stirrer to become a straw. Finally, she sipped enough air to ask, "What do you mean, *at the school?*"

"I was stuck in the line-up after I dropped the girls off, and I noticed his truck parked behind me almost down by the cemetery. I'm sure it's fine—Evie is safe inside—but I couldn't get turned around and I'm running late for work already. But I thought you should know. You're not freaking out, are you? Do you want me to go back?"

JJ swallowed the bile that had risen in her throat. "No. You're right—Evie will be fine, but thanks for letting me know."

She hung up, calmly set her phone on the passenger seat, and started the SUV. *I should call the Sheriff's Department.* She backed out of her spot and signaled as she turned out of the parking lot. *I should tell Grant.* She made a complete stop at the four-way inter-section before joining the highway that connected Plattsville and Cold Springs. It was the same route she took every morning and evening, between her house and work, so she could have been heading home on autopilot. Except she wasn't. She fumbled with the mass of keys hanging from the ignition, detaching the one for the glovebox and setting it on the seat next to her phone.

I should kill the sonuvabitch.

Marcus wasn't at the cemetery when she got there, or anywhere else in the vicinity of the school. She stopped anyway (tucking the glovebox key in her pocket) and spoke with the Vice Principal of the school for a few minutes. He didn't know the gory details of JJ's divorce, but he did know she had sole custody, and Otto and Dorothy were the only other people authorized to pick up Evie. He was very accommodating, and she should've felt better when she left, but she didn't.

She'd been in such a hurry, JJ had left her jacket in the car. Her scrub pants were like paper, and she rubbed her forearms where they peeked from beneath a long-sleeved T-shirt. But when goose-bumps prickled on her biceps, it wasn't because of the cold. She was being watched.

JJ stood on the sidewalk and listened to the wind whip the flags on the pole above her, the fasteners jangling discordantly like her nerves. Shielding her eyes against the morning's white glare, she surveyed the grounds and parking areas, much as she had looking for Adam Friday night.

And there was Marcus's red truck, parked on the side of the road partway between the school and the River Lounge, the restaurant where Dorothy worked. It was the same direction as her own vehicle, so JJ told herself she was just going to her car. Until she realized she was running.

Marcus tipped his baseball cap at her, started his truck, and made a U-turn on Main Street. JJ cursed her awkward purse banging against her side and her chunky-soled shoes that threw off her running stride. At least she was parked pointing in the right direction. She followed and saw a flash of red vehicle ahead as he turned off the highway onto a two-lane road that was technically still within the town limits. The speed limit was twenty-five miles per hour, but when she made the turn herself she could tell he must be doing nearly twice that. It was a residential area and she hated to be an idiot, but the kids were in school and she didn't recall any roaming animals in the neighborhood.

I will not spend my life looking over my shoulder.

She closed the distance between them to a few car lengths before the street dead-ended and he made another in a series of turns that led them toward the park where she'd spent so much time with Adam and Danny as kids. *Where the hell is Marcus going?* Multiple roads split off from that area, some simple park access cul-de-sacs, but most were private lanes that meandered off into the boonies. Just before the park, a section of road wound endlessly around a slab of mountain and she lost sight of his truck. *If he dodges me now, he's gone.*

JJ took the curve too fast, tires skidding and squealing in protest as she drifted across the center line into the path of a cement truck. It blasted its deep, angry horn, and JJ fought the urge to jerk the wheel. Her heart was racing when she came out of the turn, and she pulled over in the parking area across from the empty basketball court. She removed her shaking hands from the steering wheel. Marcus was nowhere to be seen.

And what would you really have done if you'd caught him?

She stared at her locked glovebox. JJ had a feeling that soon, she'd find out.

37

———————

Adam woke to an overcast sky with a dry mouth, too-tight boots, and a cold ache in his bones. But he was alive, and that was something.

The woods were quiet. The occasional bird plucked at dried seed stalks or rustled in the leaf litter. A slight breeze passed through the trees like the mountain's breath. And nearby, the loudest sounds were generated by an old man in the kitchen—the bang of a skillet on a burner, the protesting whine of a water pump, and the occasional creative expletive.

With so many blankets piled atop him, Adam felt like a hungover mummy. It was almost more than he could manage to pull himself free. Then there was the matter of standing, but the tree behind his head helped with that. He trudged slowly past the canvas chairs from the previous evening, a forgotten rake long since rusted, a small plastic tub of patching putty, and other random yard detritus that Teddy probably didn't see anymore except to step around. Adam was thankful of the rail at the front porch steps, the same rail his feet had struck when Harlan and Teddy had carried him the night before.

Harlan met him in front of the door with a small glass of

orange juice. Adam looked at the beverage uncertainly. "I know," Harlan said, "I prefer mine with vodka, too. But trust me, it'll help."

Adam shrugged and drank it in three gulps. The acid burned its way down his throat and threatened to come back up, but the sugar made his head a little less foggy.

Inside, Teddy stood next to the stove, dropping slivers of butter into a cast-iron skillet. There was a bowl of eggs next to him, and a plate of something blotting on paper towels. He pointed to a coffeemaker at the end of the counter. "Coffee's on. Fried okay for your eggs?"

Adam's stomach roiled at the thought of eggs, and he didn't trust himself to speak.

"Fried will be fine," Harlan said, fixing Adam with a stare. "Although I'd pass on the coffee if I were you. No offense, Teddy, but that'll peel the paint off the walls."

Teddy looked around the kitchen and living area, where walls alternated between bare, weathered wood and grimy sheetrock. "I wish I could say that's what happened here. This place hasn't seen a can of paint since Eisenhower."

The smell of ham—fried in the same skillet before the eggs— hit Adam's nostrils and brought a surge of nausea with it. "I need to sit down," he said, lips numb and an ocean rushing in his ears.

Harlan helped Adam to a dining chair, handed him a glass of water and sat next to him. "Teddy and I have been discussing the situation," Harlan said.

"You mean who could have taken the boy?"

"Not exactly," Teddy said. "Don't take this the wrong way, but if it's not you—or me, for that matter—then I don't have a clue who it could be. I can't think of anyone else with a connection to Virgil."

Adam put his head in his hands. "Okay, fine. Then what about locations, places whoever might have taken the boy?"

"We can try that," Teddy said, "and we probably should, but that assumes our mystery man took him to a place connected with

Virgil. Considering he took the child *without* Virgil, that might be a faulty assumption."

Teddy set plates of ham and eggs in front of Adam and Harlan before serving his own. "Almost forgot," he said, returning a moment later with a stack of toast, a jar of jelly, and a spoon. He unscrewed the jar lid. "Does grape jelly mold?" he asked.

"Everything molds eventually," Harlan said, grabbing a piece of toast to dip in his runny eggs. "Son, the first few bites are the hardest, but you'll feel better after. And don't start with dry bread."

Adam stared at his plate: white bread toast; three eggs, their yolks mounded and the whites bubbly crisp and browning at the edges; and a slab of country ham so red it was almost purple, with a small bone shaped like an eyeball. He started with a forkful of egg, figuring if he could keep that down, he could keep anything down. He added a chunk of bread to hide the revolting bright yellow, viscous yolk from his sight. Chewing was okay; it was swallowing that made him shudder. *One down.*

"Harlan tells me you haven't seen anything about this boy," Teddy said. He drank a glass of milk, and that turned Adam's stomach almost as much as his own food.

"No, sir, I haven't," Adam confirmed, choking down another bite.

"So what about with the girl that was kidnapped a couple of weeks ago? Tell me how that worked. Did you seek her out? Was she alone when you saw her?"

Adam set down his fork, grateful for an excuse to let his food settle. "I definitely didn't seek her out. The first time I was sleeping, and I saw her being kidnapped, but didn't know what to make of it. I didn't have any sense of who did it, except that it was an adult male."

Teddy sawed into his ham with his knife and motioned for Adam to continue. "What else?"

Adam closed his eyes, trying to recall. "The next time, I was also asleep. Rachel woke up and she was being held in a dark room somewhere. A blinding light came on—"

His eyes flew open, and he slapped his hand over his mouth and the nausea.

Harlan gripped Adam's bicep, squeezing hard. "It's bad manners to vomit at the breakfast table." He told Teddy, "That's when Adam spoke *through* the girl to Virgil, not that he knew it at the time."

Adam swallowed hard. It helped to remember there was no porcelain God to pray to, only an outhouse. He continued, "The next time, I was exhausted, dozing off in the shower, and she reached out. She was having a bad asthma attack and somehow transferred that to me."

"Max Tulley's girl probably saved them both when she found Adam and did CPR on him," Harlan added.

"You ever go the other way? Reach out to her?" Teddy asked, mopping his plate with his toast.

"Once all by his lonesome, when he managed to cut himself through her," Harlan said, raising his brows significantly, "and then once later with me—"

"You give him anything to help him get through?" Teddy cut in.

"Yeah, but nothing like what you've got here. The girl was scared to death trying to escape, had another asthma attack in the process, and almost killed both of us. I had to pull him out. Then Adam did it once more by himself up on the mountain—when I'd warned him not to—to figure out where she was."

"She was unconscious," Adam said.

Harlan pursed his lips and stared at the paint-thinning coffee in his mug. "After he found her, he healed her."

Teddy put his own coffee down with a thud. "Using what?"

"Himself. How long were you in the hospital?" Harlan asked.

Adam didn't answer.

Teddy shook his head. "And I thought Lawrence was reckless."

"The difference is, Lawrence made informed decisions, albeit ill-considered ones. Adam just makes it up as he goes along."

"Well, it's a good thing his elders are here to look out for him now." Teddy picked up a toothpick as if it were a digestive, shut his eyes and swiveled the stick around his mouth. "Just give me a minute."

Adam finished his breakfast while Harlan bused his portion of the table. The ham was a little tough and on the salty side, but intensely flavorful. Harlan was right, he did feel a little better now. He burped softly, finished his glass of water, and was considering whether he was desperate enough to brave the outhouse when Teddy spoke.

"Okay, here's the way I see it. In the first case, we've got a kidnapped girl with a strong latent gift reaching out to Adam in times of extreme stress. We've got Adam vulnerable to receiving these... transmissions when he's at the edges of consciousness. Of course, the more he opens his mind, the greedier the gift gets. And then we add Virgil. I'd say his presence around the girl acted as an amplifier. Good so far?" Teddy asked.

Adam and Harlan nodded.

"In the second case, we've got a few factors working *against* any kind of connection happening. The chances of the boy having the same gift that the girl did are pretty astronomical, unless they were both specifically targeted for their gifts, which is damned unlikely."

"Why?" Adam asked.

"How would *you* sniff out a latent gift?" Teddy asked.

Adam's mouth hung open.

"Yeah, me either," Teddy said. "So now we've got a boy with little or no latent abilities. We've got Adam, no better trained but probably pretty well burnt out after healing the girl. Before that, when you fought Virgil to keep her, did you get any kind of visions or anything from him?"

Adam's breakfast found its way back up to the base of his throat, and he swallowed it down carefully before replying, "Yes. Images, flooding over me. I don't know what."

"And what was Virgil's condition at the time?"

"I don't know what you mean," Adam said.

Teddy leaned toward him, voice intent. "Yes, you do. Don't try to be politic. Was your daddy crazy?"

Adam nodded reluctantly.

Teddy looked to Harlan. "Virgil forged a link with Adam on that mountain. Now, not only is he *not amplifying* for the kid, he's masking anyone else's transmissions by flooding Adam with all of his own crazy shit. Adam, that's what happened to you last night—hell, it's probably been happening for weeks. And that's what those vile concoctions you drank were supposed to mitigate."

As much as he didn't want to revisit the misery of the last twelve hours, Adam needed to, and to face his panic about the future. "Why am I okay now? Is this something I'll have to deal with the rest of my life? Do I have to move to Alaska?"

"That might help," Teddy said. Harlan glared at him. "What? It's true. Proximity is a factor."

"What we did last night was triage, just stopping the bleeding to save your life until we can figure out the rest," Harlan explained. "We don't know why you're okay now. It could be something on Virgil's end, something that made him incapable of control yesterday having resolved today. It could be he overwhelmed your connection last night—fried it—and it'll take time to regenerate. Or it could be you, that you're beginning to develop your own defenses, to shield against him. We just don't know."

Adam pushed his own anxiety away to concentrate on what mattered. "So where does that leave us with Aaron? Are you saying we came here for nothing, that we've got no way to find him?"

Teddy rose from the table and took his plate to the sink. "Lord, save us from your goddamn martyrs," he muttered. "In the first place, the trip wasn't wasted because we saved your life. I hear that doesn't mean much to you lately, but without me and Harlan you'd be dead or no better than a turnip right now. I don't know you very well, but you are reasonably presentable, and it would be nice to see the Rutledge line carry on."

He paused to run water noisily over his plate. "In the second place, I do have an idea about finding the boy. But it requires us to leave this humble abode and take our show on the road. What do you say?"

Adam looked at the old man, a self-described hermit, and suspected his great uncle's life was about to spin out of his control. At the very least, it was taking a direction the man couldn't have imagined twenty-four hours earlier. "I say, thank you. When can we leave?"

Teddy stared across the table at Harlan, and something passed between the men. "Yeah," Harlan said. "He's got more of his mother in him than he's got of Virgil. I'll help you pack stuff up."

Adam's duffel was still in Jim's truck, so he had nothing to do but watch Teddy and Harlan in the kitchen, pouring pots of liquid into Mason jars and stacking small wooden boxes of herbs.

"Goddamn, Teddy, you've got enough for an army here," Harlan said.

"You can't be too careful," Teddy replied.

Adam's stomach rumbled painfully, and he resigned himself to his first outhouse experience. As he headed for the door, Harlan called out, "Don't forget to check for snakes."

Teddy laughed, and Adam flipped them the bird. The old coots were a bad influence.

It was cool outside, chillier than Adam remembered, maybe because his blood had gone to his belly to digest half a pig. He crossed the yard and stood in front of the roughly four-by-six wooden structure, vaguely disappointed there wasn't a moon carved in the door.

It wasn't the most pleasant experience, but Adam emerged some time later untraumatized. He found a bar of soap at the outdoor tap next to the front steps and washed his hands. Wiping them dry on his pants, he stared at the spot, leaves and soil disturbed, where he had lain the night before. *Dead to the world.*

Adam heard the creak of feet on the warped steps behind him and felt Teddy's hand on his shoulder.

"You okay?" Teddy asked. He hadn't changed his dirty jeans,

but he'd added another long-sleeved shirt and was wearing a squared-off trucker cap on his head.

Adam nodded, speechless.

"You know, it's good to finally see you again, despite the circumstances. It's been a long time since your daddy brought you out here," Teddy said.

Adam heard the bang of the front screen door as Harlan joined them. "I don't actually remember meeting you," Adam said. "I guess I was too little."

Teddy laughed, and pointed around back of the house with his hat. "You weren't too little to shoot targets in the backyard. And you were a natural. You hit every damn—"

Teddy paused, as Adam and Harlan went rigid next to him. "What's wrong?"

Adam said, "Up until all this craziness, I hadn't seen my dad since my mother died."

Teddy rubbed his face in consternation and pulled his hat down tight. "Wait a minute—but you were just a wee thing then."

"Exactly," Harlan agreed.

Teddy asked, "Then who the hell was the kid Virgil brought with him?"

38

"Just wait a damn minute," Harlan said. "Let's not jump to conclusions. Teddy, when was this?"

The man's face went gray as his hair. Adam dragged a canvas chair over. Teddy sat down so heavily, the flimsy thing nearly toppled with him. "Hell, I don't know. One year's pretty much the same as another to me."

Harlan paced in front of the steps. "How old was the kid?"

Teddy leaned forward, elbows on his knees, and massaged his temples. "Twelve, maybe. I think one of them remarked about him not being thirteen yet."

Adam went to the truck and retrieved his wallet from his duffel bag. Inside was a photograph, edges jagged where a child had trimmed them with scissors, and colors faded, giving the image a yellowish hue. Adam handed the photo to Teddy. "Is the boy in this picture?"

Teddy squinted, then reached in his front pocket for his glasses. "It's been a long while, and the two boys look alike, but I'm pretty sure it was the one on the end."

Adam took the picture from Teddy's hand and sat on the ground before he fell down. He dropped his head between his knees and heard Harlan's voice far away. Holding the photo up, he waited for Harlan to pluck it from his numb fingers and said, lips equally numb, "It's Danny."

Harlan held the photograph close to his face, then moved it a few inches farther away, trying to get the best view. "Are you sure?"

"Of course I'm sure. That's me in the middle and JJ and Danny on the ends. It's at JJ's house, on her eleventh birthday. We'd just carved our initials on the poplar tree behind us," Adam said. Harlan and Teddy were staring at him; he realized Harlan's question had been directed at Teddy. "Sorry."

Teddy waved a hand dismissively. "Yes, I'm sure that was him, but Virgil didn't call him Danny. Although come to think of it, I don't recall him ever calling the boy Adam, either."

"So what the hell did he call him?" Harlan demanded. "Hey You?"

Teddy shrugged. "Probably, something like that. Or boy, or son, or kid. I don't know. They weren't here all that long."

Harlan sighed and dragged the other chair to sit next to Teddy. "Okay. Let's hear it."

But part of Adam didn't want to hear. He found himself digging the inside of his ankle with a fingernail, as he had when he was a child trying to stay rooted to this world. Now, he wanted nothing more than to escape it. It had become unfamiliar in the blink of an eye (*Danny alive, all this time?*), and his instinct—as always—was to run.

"I was as close to Virgil as anybody was when he was growing up. I guess that's why he showed up on my doorstep after Charlotte died and stayed with me for a while. I saw him maybe two or three times in the ten years after that, until he showed up with the boy."

"Why? The other times I mean," Harlan clarified. "What did Virgil want then?"

Teddy lowered his head at Harlan. "You know damn well what he wanted—he wanted help!" Teddy pointed at stacked boxes and jars on the porch, waiting to be loaded. "He *needed* help, trying to hold it together. He'd start to unravel, and that's when his daddy's voice would return, constantly whispering in his ear. I'm amazed Virgil didn't blow his own brains out long ago."

"So you'd doctor him," Harlan prompted, adding to Adam in an aside, "Lawrence called Teddy his apothecary."

Teddy nodded. "Virgil'd stay here a couple weeks—the only time he ever stayed as long as a month was when Charlotte died—and then he'd up and leave. Sometimes he didn't even say goodbye."

"Was that what he wanted when he came here with the boy? Help?" Harlan asked.

Teddy paused to consider, and in that still moment, he looked like a confused, old man. "He didn't say straight out, but he seemed different. Not quite as... *unhinged* as he usually was when he showed up, but not in his right mind either. Virgil was anxious, but he wouldn't say why, and that was unusual—let me tell you, he'd shared some elaborate theories with me over the years. He and the boy only stayed a couple of days. I woke up one morning and they were gone."

"What can you tell us about the boy?"

Teddy raised his eyebrows and grimaced. "Well, this might be one of those hindsight things, but their relationship seemed a little off."

Adam stopped digging at his ankle long enough to ask, "What do you mean, *off*?"

Teddy searched Adam's face, then said, alarmed, "Oh, I don't mean anything sexual! It was nothing like that. It was more like... I don't know, like sometimes it was hard to tell which one of them was really in control. Virgil even asked me if I could see something *about* the boy, or *on* the boy, like attached to him."

"What kind of thing would be attached to him?" Adam asked.

Teddy took his hat off and waved it around. "Damned if I know, but Lawrence had Virgil believing in some crazy stuff."

"Rather than *what* Virgil thought was there, the better question is *why* Virgil thought something evil might be attached to the boy," Harlan said.

"He wouldn't say. But he was upset when I took the boy out back with my twenty-two rifle. We did some target shooting, and like I said, he was a natural. But there was a few minutes when Virgil and I weren't right there on top of him supervising, and the boy kept shooting. I didn't notice at the time, but a couple days later I found a bunch of dead birds over where he'd been shooting."

Harlan's face twisted in distaste.

"Now before you start," Teddy said, "I know how you feel about guns. But it's natural for a boy to be curious about guns and mortality, and if he happens to hit a few targets that move, you don't necessarily need to be calling a psychiatrist. Of course, maybe that opinion's colored by the fact that, until five minutes ago, I thought the boy was Adam, and I got no worries about him."

"I'm glad *you* don't," Harlan said. "Okay, let's say for the sake of argument that Danny is our kidnapper, that he helped Virgil kidnap Rachel and then kidnapped this boy on his own."

Adam nearly fell rushing to his feet. "Now, wait a minute. Even if Danny is still alive—and that's a big if—that doesn't make him a kidnapper."

Harlan sat casually in his chair, ankle crossed over his knee and elbows resting on the frame, and looked up at Adam. "I agree. But at this point, he is the only person we can name as a possibility. Teddy, if Danny is the man we're looking for, how does that affect the plan you mentioned? And by the way, what *is* your master plan?"

Teddy pulled a flask from inside his jacket, took a swig, and handed it to Harlan.

"It's that good, huh?" Harlan asked.

"I'll let you be the judge," Teddy said. "I do think it has a little better chance of success if Danny's the man we're looking for. See, I figured if we can't get to the boy, maybe we can get to the man who took him."

Adam sat on the porch steps across from the men as Harlan took a big belt from the flask. Harlan didn't hand it back to Teddy but said, "Go on."

"The way I see it, Adam can get in the kidnapper's head with our help. And once he's in *his* head, we can figure out where the man has the boy."

Adam held out his hand for the flask. He tilted his head back, and pure lightning hit his throat. "Jesus," he wheezed, "did you drain this from a battery?"

"Consider that your introduction to the other mind-altering Rutledge legacy," Teddy said, with a brief smile. "Adam may not know what the hell he's doing, but he's got potential."

"If I'm so clueless, why don't you wise elders get into his head?" Adam asked, pointing with the flask, trying to pretend his question was born of logic rather than fear. Of course, he wasn't fooling Harlan.

"I wish we could," Harlan said gently, "but it doesn't work that way. These gifts—if you want to call them that, and I don't know that I would—come in all flavors and sizes. By the time you get to our age, what you can do is pretty much locked in. Teddy and I both get the occasional hit of prescience. We see lingering energies, and have some variations on connecting with people, but neither of us can tap in to someone we don't already have a direct connection with. I couldn't do it with Rachel, and I can't do it with this man."

"But we can piggyback on you," Teddy added, "so our job is to amplify what you already have as much as we can. I mentioned proximity before. It's true that we don't know where this man is, but proximity isn't just about the miles. It's also easier to reach someone if you work from a place that means something to them, that has resonance. This house doesn't mean anything to him, but plenty of stuff does in Beecham County."

Adam took another hit from the flask. It didn't burn as badly the second time. "Except they're looking for us in Beecham County, and probably anyplace within a hundred miles of there."

Teddy closed his eyes. "Why don't y'all load that stuff in the truck, give me a minute to think?"

Adam rose and would have given the flask back to Teddy, but Harlan took it and tucked it in his own pocket. "He doesn't need that to think, but moving's thirsty work."

They decided to pile everyone and everything into Jim's pickup. Teddy had insisted that the glass jars and herbs go inside the truck, so Harlan emptied most of the items from the extended cab into heavy duty garbage bags before moving them to the bed of the truck. He did, however, draw the line at putting Jim's chainsaw in the back. They also left Adam's duffel inside the cab, stacked on its end.

Teddy didn't so much as blink at all of their banging around. His eyes remained shut, but he swayed slightly, as if he sat in a rocking chair. They left him in the yard and went inside to forage food for the road.

"Do not touch that grape jelly," Harlan said. "The last thing we need is you getting food poisoning again."

Adam made peanut butter and honey sandwiches while Harlan closed up and shut off whatever he thought appropriate, considering they didn't know when Teddy would make it home.

"Come on," Harlan said, grabbing a bag of sandwiches and heading out the door. He stood in front of Teddy's chair and said loudly, "All you need to do is lock the front door, unless you want to grab a spare pair of underwear or some such foolishness. Where are we going?"

Teddy opened his eyes. "Virgil had the girl at that little cabin up near Pine Gap, right?" Harlan nodded and Teddy continued, "I've got a pretty good idea of somewhere else Virgil would have spent time with Danny, if it is Danny. Someplace we took Virgil when he was a kid, over in Watkins County."

"Watkins County? Damn, then we better hit the road. We got half a state to cross, and then some. I finally got the hang of that shitty clutch, so I'll drive," Harlan said.

Adam glared at him, but Harlan just grinned. "Fine," he said, handing Adam the flask from his pocket. "You're a loud thinker."

~

WITH HARLAN DRIVING, Adam was stuck in the middle of the two older men, his feet riding up on the drive train hump and knees in the air. If it'd been warmer, he would've climbed in the back. He was afraid Harlan would slam the gearshift into his thigh, or worse.

For the first twenty minutes, the truck was mostly free of conversation, as Teddy directed them step by step to another interstate. From there, the route was a straight shot for a couple of hours, so Teddy elaborated on his plan.

"Having a decent location will give us a boost," Teddy said.

"We hope," Harlan replied. The closer they got to Watkins County, the less sanguine he was about their prospects. "I gotta be stopping somewhere soon to get gas."

"We don't know that Danny has much, if anything, in the way of a gift—"

"We don't know it's Danny," Adam reminded them.

"Fine, whoever it is, there's no reason to believe he'll be particularly receptive. But if it is Danny, he had a relationship with you, and he still has a relationship with Virgil."

It had begun to rain, and Harlan fumbled around the steering column until Adam pointed out the windshield wipers. That in hand, Harlan turned briefly toward Teddy. "I don't like where you're going with this. We just got Adam free, and I don't know if any of us have the strength to go through that again."

Adam bowed his head, and couldn't help but think he'd never be free. "You think we can use my connection to Virgil to get to Danny."

He didn't argue about whether it was Danny, because Teddy was right. It would work better—they had a better chance of finding Aaron—if it was Danny. And deep down, he knew that alive or not, the Danny he'd grown up with was gone.

"It won't be easy," Teddy admitted. "We have to keep your connection with Virgil active enough for him to help link us to Danny, but tamped down enough that things don't get crazy again."

"You mean we have to keep him from killing Adam. For fuck's sake, Teddy, just come out and say it. I'm sorry, but I'm not crazy about throwing the kid under the bus."

"That's where our magic elixirs come in," Teddy said, gesturing over his shoulder.

Harlan shook his head and abused the gearshift—and Adam's knee—as he downshifted for an exit with a gas station. "Yeah, that and a handful of magic goddamn beans will get you a bed in Weston."

Weston was the home of an infamous state mental hospital, invoked regularly on the schoolyard when Adam was a child. He'd imagined it as something out of *The Shining*, all malevolence and shifting, twisted angles.

"They don't send people there anymore," Teddy said.

Harlan ignored him and whipped the truck into the gas station so fast Adam was afraid he'd hit a pump. Harlan rolled in next to one, cut the engine and slammed the driver's door after himself.

"You getting out?" Adam asked.

Teddy shook his head, staring out the window. The view wasn't much—stained pavement and a small convenience store, all cinder block and dirty glass. The weedy patch beyond wasn't exactly the epitome of natural beauty either, and even the rolling brown hills in the distance looked tired.

Adam carefully maneuvered his legs around the gearshift and slipped out the driver's side door. They'd left the rain behind, but must have gained some altitude. Although midday now, it was cooler than it had been this morning at Teddy's.

Harlan stood next to the pickup, pumping gas. "They made it

so you can't jam your cap in the nozzle anymore," he complained. "You gotta stand here like a dumbass and get a hand cramp."

"You need gas money?" Adam offered.

"No, thanks." Harlan squinted at the sky over the neighboring field where a few turkey buzzards circled on lazy wings. "You feeling anything today?"

"From Virgil, you mean?"

Harlan cocked his head. "Or anyone else."

"Not really." Adam closed his eyes and lifted his face to the sun. Except for some minor aches, not helped by being cramped in the truck, he probably felt the best he had since his release from the hospital. And there was nausea, a low-grade queasiness now so ever-present he almost had to think about it to notice it was still there. Plus something else...

"What is it?" Harlan asked.

"I don't know," Adam admitted. "Uneasiness, I guess, but not connected to anything I can put my finger on."

The pump stopped, and Harlan set it back in its cradle. "I gotta pay inside. You might want to hit the head while we're here."

Adam fell in beside Harlan. A dark-haired, young man leaned across the counter to stare at them, paranoid or bored.

"I've got that same feeling," Harlan confessed. "That something's rippling, something's in motion that we can't see yet. Hang on to that feeling. It might just save our lives."

39

The doors to the Sheriff's Department couldn't open fast enough to accommodate Luther pushing his way through. "Beth, where are the Big Cheeses?" he asked, pausing at the front desk to give his good sense a chance to catch up with the rest of him.

"Grant's in his den," she said, glancing up from a computer screen full of property records. "Agent D'Antonio was in the break room with Deputy Kilbourne a few minutes ago."

"You mean Kiss-Ass?" Luther asked.

Beth smiled before she could stop herself. "You noticed that, too, huh?"

"Martians could see that man's big, puckered lips from their home planet," Luther asserted on his way past her to Grant's office.

Luther knocked on the closed door. Grant called him in, but he was deep in conversation with D'Antonio. Luther didn't care, throwing himself in the chair next to the federal agent and his hat on Grant's vast desk. He turned to address the agent.

"Adam Rutledge has an alibi for the Aaron Schofield kidnapping—Jim Henderson."

"Who's Jim Henderson?" D'Antonio asked.

"Volunteer Fire Department, and Harlan Miller's nearest neighbor. He dropped by the trunk-or-treat Friday night to help out, but they didn't need him so he left. That's when Jim says he found Adam Rutledge passed out—sick as a dog—at the edge of the cemetery across the road. He took Adam home to Iris's, helped him inside and up the stairs when no one answered, and put a trashcan by his bed."

"Time?" Grant asked.

"He stumbled across Adam sometime around seven p.m. By the time he left him at Iris's, it was after eight."

Grant blinked slowly, perhaps consulting his internal timeline. "And Aaron Schofield had already been kidnapped."

"If that's true, why the hell didn't this Henderson guy come forward before?" D'Antonio demanded.

"He was visiting his daughter in Ohio and didn't find out about the kidnapping until he got home today," Luther said. "And before you ask, Harlan has a standing invitation to borrow his farm truck, so he didn't think anything of it not being there."

Luther chose not to mention that he hadn't believed Jim when he said he routinely loaned the truck to Harlan—no point in muddying already turbid waters.

The intercom on Grant's desk buzzed, and Beth's voice said, "Sheriff, you need to take this one."

Grant picked up the line, and spent a lot of time listening. Luther couldn't make sense of the Sheriff's brief responses, so he passed the time by watching D'Antonio. The agent leaned back in his chair, eyes closed. He hadn't taken the news about Adam well, but Luther had to admit—he didn't think it was about ego. Like the man or not (and he didn't), D'Antonio's mission—like his—was to find the Schofield boy. He'd just been convinced Adam had taken him.

When Grant hung up, his bloodshot eyes held more animation than they had before the call. "Remember we'd come up with three possibilities on the van from the scene? One of them, registered to Randall Vogler, just parked outside a motel in Loganville."

"Description?" D'Antonio asked.

"Driven by a lone man in his mid-thirties." Beth entered, handing Grant a printed photo. Grant glanced at it, then passed it around. "Meet Mr. Vogler."

Luther pulled up a map in his mind. "Loganville—shit, that's more than two hours away."

"Luther, you can drive." Grant nodded at D'Antonio. "They don't have SWAT, so your guys sent a team coming from the other direction on the interstate. They'll probably beat us there."

"Is that a challenge?" Luther asked, grinning.

40

A couple of hours and a bag of sandwiches after filling up, Jim's pickup was headed—southeast? Adam had lost track—on a state road, paralleling one of the many branches of the Potomac River. Adam found the sight of the water calming, stretching almost from the road's shoulder to a steep bank on the other side. Sometimes deciduous trees, pale and naked silhouettes against the reddish-brown leaf litter, crowded the shore. Other times, a sheer rock face drew Adam's attention, and once even a cave, low down near the water line.

As his mind calmed, questions floated to the surface. "Why would Danny take a child?" Adam asked. "It seems crazy that he'd grow up to take a child, after being kidnapped himself."

"You may have hit the nail right on the head—*crazy*," Teddy said. "Being raised by Virgil would certainly put him on the road to crazy."

"Crazy isn't contagious," Harlan countered. "What if he's not doing it because of some weird shit that people like to read about or watch in serial killer movies—what if it's strategic?"

"Why strategic?" Adam asked. "What does kidnapping a kid get him?"

"You," Harlan said, halfway between a question and statement. His voice grew more sure as he said, "Who found the girl last time? Not me. Not JJ. And not the authorities. You did."

Adam shivered in his seat. "So you think the boy is bait. To get me physically, or to get me—" he waved his hands in the air around his head. "Whatever you want to call this. Psychically, I guess."

"I'm guessing physically," Harlan said, "but we just don't know."

Adam jumped when Teddy's arm cut in front of him, switching on the heat in the truck. Trying to, at least.

"Damn thing doesn't work." Teddy held his other hand in front of a vent before twisting the knob back to Off. "Just because somebody's got a strategy, doesn't mean it's a good one."

The river receded from the road, then swung close again, alternating back and forth as the miles passed, but always staying in view. They passed an empty park with restroom facilities and a baseball field, the backstop threaded with autumn leaves. The occasional house or well-kept trailer flying an American flag sat near the road, but there were no towns in evidence, and no businesses.

Teddy nearly hit Adam in the nose, extending his arm across the cab, when the state road swung away from the river in a sudden curve.

"Go that way," he said, indicating a smaller paved road that continued to the left.

The pickup took the turn hard, and the stacked jars rattled against each other in the back of the cab. Adam hoped none of them broke and soaked his bag with ass tea. He tried to recall which end of his duffel was on the bottom, and what was packed where. His cell phone, for instance. "Maybe we should try to call Iris, or JJ, or Grant, or somebody, and check in."

Harlan geared down as the road ahead climbed abruptly. The truck whined, then lurched as he took an even lower gear. "Too risky," he said. "Law enforcement will be monitoring their calls, and even if we tried to contact Grant, I doubt he's really the chief in charge right now." He inclined his head toward the mountain, rising alongside and ahead of them. "Besides, good luck getting a signal."

"Believe it or not, you might be able to get one along the high ridges when we get closer," Teddy said. "Some damn fools tried to put in an off-the-grid retreat center or some such shit. Apparently, they didn't want to retreat from their phones. It was too expensive to lay down poles all the way in, but they did manage to get a cell tower put up over yonder."

Teddy pointed out the window at something no one could see. Then he laughed. "Funny thing is, it didn't do them a damn bit of good. They were too far down in the holler to get reception. Never even finished building their yurt."

The road kept gaining altitude, curving and switching back on itself so it wasn't straight up. It was still unnerving, always having a deadly steep drop on one side or the other. There was no shoulder, just a moment of false security before the tree canopy descended swiftly with the slope of the land that supported it. The paved area didn't stretch much wider than the pickup, and Adam shuddered to think what would happen if they met another vehicle.

The treetops wreaked havoc with the light, even midday. Sudden shafts of sunlight blinded Adam and—coupled with shielding mountains intermittently plunging them into darkness— gave him a pounding, dry headache. Being squashed between the two men as they swung from side to side up the winding road didn't help, either. If the heater had worked, Adam would be climbing over Teddy to be sick, and possibly falling off the moun- tain in the process.

"You think the authorities know about this place?" Harlan asked.

Teddy grunted and shifted in his seat, mashing Adam even more. "Watch out," he said, fumbling around Adam's hip to unbuckle his own seat belt. "Screw it—if we go over that edge, I'm dying anyway—might as well be comfortable. It's possible some- body knows, and they'll figure it out eventually. I believe it's in my name. Technically, we've already passed the property, but you're gonna see a road up ahead that cuts back and takes us to the house."

In a few minutes, they reached the turnoff and found themselves descending the mountain they'd just spent so much time and gasoline ascending.

"Shit," Harlan said. "A man can only gear down so far."

The access road was unpaved and steeper than the path that had brought them to it, clinging to the edge of the mountain with the wall of earth to their left and precipitous slope to the right. The truck's brakes protested even more loudly than the engine as Harlan tried to keep them from racing to the bottom.

"You're gonna burn those brakes up," Teddy said.

"You think?" Harlan asked sarcastically. "You volunteering your caveman feet?"

He pressed a little too firmly, and the truck fishtailed on the gravel, adding a desperate scraping sound to the occasional brake squeal. Harlan let off, got the pickup under control, and settled back into hold and release, hold and release, until he reached the trench.

Years of runoff from above had gouged a trench across the road, bisecting it at about the halfway point. From there, the water had stayed on the road instead of continuing down the side of the mountain to the floodplain below. This created a channel in the road, a few inches deep, all the way to the bottom where the road reached level ground. Harlan thunked across the initial trench, then hugged the embankment to the left as long as he could to avoid getting locked into the channel.

The end was tantalizingly in sight when Harlan had to abandon his strategy. The channel swelled abruptly to at least two feet wide before splitting in half. Harlan couldn't dodge both ruts. He drove the left tires into the shallower one and tried riding the track the rest of the way down, but its zigzagging path threatened to yank the steering wheel from his hands. He steered out of it and the truck jumped free, only to have the right side slide toward the other rut. The truck dropped into it with a teeth-slamming thud, giving the vehicle a precarious, off-kilter aspect.

"Sonuvabitch," Harlan said, while Adam and Teddy braced themselves against the dashboard.

The rut veered toward the steep side drop-off and pulled the truck with it. Harlan tried to steer out again, but this time it was too deep to climb out.

"Hang on!" Harlan said, as the trapped wheels followed the track off the road and over the edge of the mountain.

It wasn't like driving off a cliff—the drop to level ground was about a dozen feet and had some angle to it. But it wasn't like a gentle ramp, either. Adam's heart flew to his throat. The front bumper caught the ground first, and the truck slammed, bottoming out soon after. The seat belt cinched tightly across Adam's lap as he jerked forward. Teddy grunted and went airborne, striking his face against the windshield. Breaking glass tinkled in the back.

The truck came to a slow, rolling stop, and Harlan said, "Well, we're here. Everybody okay?"

Adam felt fine, but blood speckled his right hand. Teddy pushed against him as he settled his rear on the seat and tilted his head back, hand over his nose. "A little less than okay," Teddy said, "but don't stop now. I sure as hell don't want to have to walk the rest of the way and bleed all over my shoes."

They were only a few hundred yards from the structure, a simple, wood-siding house with an outhouse and the decayed remnants of a fence on one side. Single-story and no bigger than a room or two, it was raised a couple of feet off the ground, but Adam couldn't see any sign that the river had encroached in recent years. A forested corridor hid the river from view, thinning to scattered trees in front of the house. The house also backed up to thick forest, and a path led away from it into the trees.

Teddy got out of the truck as soon as Harlan cut the engine. Harlan followed and, after a little grouching from both men, began examining Teddy's nose.

"I don't remember seeing one, but could you double-check whether there's a first aid kit in the truck?" Harlan asked.

They'd done such a thorough job of moving things, it didn't take Adam long to confirm there wasn't. While he was digging, Adam retrieved his cell phone from the duffel and slipped it into his jacket pocket. He tried not to overthink it; he just wanted to make sure he had options. "Sorry," he called out, "no luck!"

"Then we'll wing it," Harlan said, cleaning Teddy's face with a bottle of water and an old handkerchief while the injured man leaned against the hood of the truck.

"Do I want to know where that came from?" Teddy asked.

"Where do you think? My back pocket," Harlan replied, but when Teddy pulled away, he relented. "Relax; it hasn't been used. Keep pressure on it 'cause it's still bleeding a little, but it doesn't look like you broke it."

"Not broken—damn," Teddy said, even more nasal than usual. "That was probably my last chance to have an outlaw nose to impress the women."

Adam stared at the smoke-colored, unpainted boards of the house. The angles of the structure were mostly true and the windows were intact, but it looked like it belonged in a coffee table book about haunted, rural America. "We actually going in there? I mean, to do the thing?"

"Yes," Harlan said, still wiping blood from Teddy's face, "and sooner rather than later. Start unloading the truck."

"Not everything," Teddy said. "One rack should be plenty. The rest is just in case."

Only one of the jars had broken, on the far side away from Adam's bag, sparing his belongings. He set his duffel and the top rack of Mason jars on the hood, gathered the broken glass in a spare garbage bag, and used paper towels to sluice the liquid out of the truck as best he could. At least it was one of Teddy's less aromatic concoctions. He put the garbage bag of glass and paper in front of the house by the steps.

The door was open.

Harlan and Teddy had waited for him to be otherwise occupied before going inside. What had they feared—or hoped—they'd find before him? He carried the rack of jars up the steps, a line of dampness from the breakage soaking through his shirt before he reached the open door.

"No dead bodies?" Adam asked, blinking in the dim space. "Where do you want these?"

After the ghost tour exterior, the interior was a letdown. It was essentially one large room, with a partial wall providing structural support and a sense of division. The section to the left was smaller and functioned as the kitchen, with empty, built-in shelves and counter space and a sink, although Adam wouldn't hold his breath on water coming out if he turned on the tap. A camping stove, without gas, sat on the far edge of the counter. He put the rack of jars next to the stove, leaving some working space between them and the sink.

The two older men still hadn't spoken. He found them in the larger section, almost as immobile as the two plastic-sheathed cots and chest of drawers that comprised the room's furniture. Teddy and Harlan sat on a cot already. The mattress crinkled as Adam sat on the other one. "So?" he asked.

"This was Virgil's place," Harlan said, nodding toward the chest of drawers.

The cane from Jim's truck leaned against the dresser—he wasn't sure which man had carried it in. The top surface held an old-fashioned oil lamp and a familiar photograph. Adam picked up the tarnished metal frame and wiped the dusty glass front with the bottom of his shirt. It held the same photograph that resided now in Adam's duffel but usually sat next to his bed, wherever that was. He ran his thumb across his mother's face, then reached for the key he always wore, pulling the chain from beneath his shirt.

"That was your mother's," Harlan said, not a question.

"Yes," Adam said, "but I don't know what, if anything, it opens."

"It doesn't matter," Harlan said. "It acts as a focus. Any time things go south and you're not sure what's going on, center on the key. Otherwise, it's too easy to get lost."

"What do you mean, lost?" Adam asked.

"We're going somewhere they don't exactly make roadmaps for, and I can't pretend to understand the route that gets us there. But I do know that not everybody comes back," Harlan said.

"Since we don't know for sure it's Danny, what you want to do is think about the boy first," Teddy said, and held out a piece of newsprint with a photograph of Aaron. "Harlan got this from one of the papers. He said you were just at the boy's school, so maybe think about him there. If that doesn't work, then think about Danny—hell, think about them both at the same time, if you can manage it. We'll be there with you, but we won't be as deep, so we can nudge you in the right direction."

Adam took the paper from Teddy, and his own photo with JJ and Danny from his wallet. "Okay. That's it? That's all the plan we've got?"

"That's all you need to do on your end," Harlan said. "Teddy will take care of bringing Virgil in, if he doesn't show up on his own, which he probably will, so try not to freak when he does."

Easy for you to say. Adam didn't say it out loud, but Harlan smiled.

"Yes, it is. What about you, Theodore—how's the nose?"

Teddy said, "I think it's done bleeding."

Harlan motioned him toward the window where he could see better, then tilted Teddy's chin back. "Yeah, it looks good. Just keep that handkerchief close. Okay, let's get this thing going," he said, tossing a folded blanket on the floor.

Adam stood, uncertain.

Harlan stared at him. "Are you ready, son?"

Adam tried to lay out the sequence of events in his mind—if we do this, then this... But he found it too abstract to hold it all in his head.

"So let's say I get through to Danny. I can't really do anything, but I see where the child is," Adam said, and swallowed hard, bracing himself to go on. "What if it's too late? What if it's taken us too long to get to this point, and now that he knows we're on to him, he decides to just kill Aaron?"

"That is a risk," Harlan admitted, sitting on the blanket on the floor, back to the cot. "But the alternative is doing nothing, and then he has no reason to keep the boy alive at all."

Adam was terrified that he would be the cause—not the cause exactly, but the trigger—for the child's death. He'd spent his life avoiding making decisions, running away lest the wrong choice make things worse. But Harlan was right. This time, he couldn't live with himself if he did nothing.

"Okay," he said, sitting cross-legged on the dusty floor next to Harlan. "Let's do it."

41

———

Even with Luther driving like a maniac, they'd reached the motel a full half hour after the FBI team. Upon their arrival, D'Antonio had joined his colleagues. A small team of agents surrounded the one-story building, and the only other two "residents" this time of day (an obvious prostitute and her terrified john) had been quietly escorted elsewhere.

Grant and Luther sat in an unmarked Sheriff's vehicle at a laundromat across the street from the motel. When Kiss-Ass, still in Beecham County, had heard about the arrangements, he'd complained that he'd want to be closer to the action. *Action, my ass.* Luther figured he didn't get paid enough to sweat his balls off in Kevlar for the privilege of busting people's doors down and getting shot at. And yet, his body vibrated with not knowing whether there was a child breathing on the other side of the Room o8 door. The curtains were shut, and no one had exited since the teams had mobilized.

"What a shithole," Luther said.

"Yes, it is," Grant agreed.

"You think that place was ever anything other than a shithole?"

Luther asked, drumming his fingers on the steering wheel incessantly. "I mean, they had to have clean sheets on opening day."

Grant leaned against the window, chin resting on his hand, his surface calm a stark contrast to Luther's undisguised agitation. "Who knows? Maybe they brought the sheets with them from another shitty motel."

"These people didn't even know what the owner looked like," Luther said, angling a thumb over his shoulder at the laundromat sign, "so they're sure as hell not washing their bedding here."

"Maybe they stole them," Grant said, watching the motel with eyes that were marginally less fatigued than Luther's. The Sheriff had quickly dozed off and slept for the entire drive, which D'Antonio complained was the best way to avoid getting carsick, considering the speed with which Luther had taken the mountain turns.

The background radio chatter changed abruptly, and Luther leaned in to turn it up a notch. Grant raised a pair of binoculars and said, "Sounds like they're getting ready to move in."

"Could he have snuck out between the sighting and getting the first team in place?" Luther asked.

"I don't know," Grant said. His voice was still relaxed, but Luther noticed the Sheriff's jaw clenching almost in time with his own finger tapping.

The radio went silent, and even across the street the tension of imminent action was palpable, tingling waves passing through Luther's body. He rolled his head on his shoulders, trying to get the kinks out. He stretched his neck, looking over his shoulder at the sidewalk behind them. And that's when he saw him—a man wearing a baseball cap over dark hair, average height, mid-thirties, his own head swiveling like a bored kid on a stool.

"I doubt he's worried somebody stole his Jockey shorts," Luther muttered, monitoring the man in the rearview mirror while he shifted his weight and prepared himself to move.

"What?" Grant asked, lowering his binoculars and turning to Luther in confusion.

Before he could explain, sound and motion broke out across the street. The man behind them stopped to watch as figures in protective gear quickly breached the flimsy motel door. Then he dropped his head, tugging his hat lower, and turned to walk in the opposite direction.

Luther yanked the keys from the ignition, tossed them at Grant, and said, "Cover me."

He stretched his legs into a long stride and closed most of the gap between them before the man glanced back. The man's eyes grew wide as he took in Luther's uniform.

"Mr. Vogler? Randall Vogler," Luther said, voice calm but unyielding. "Sir, you need to stop right there."

The suspect paused. "What's this about, officer?" he asked.

"We just have a few questions." Luther stepped closer. "I need you to turn around and lock your hands together. Don't even think about running; it'll only make things worse."

Luther reached for his cuffs as the man turned, brought his hands together... and ran.

"Dammit!" Luther ran after him.

A single derelict building, set far back on its lot, lay between them and the corner. They passed it, and the suspect wheeled right at the next block. Luther's ankles wobbled as he followed—he hadn't tied his boots tightly enough that morning—and he struggled to keep up. A convenience store lay ahead, with a vacant, overgrown lot beyond that. The back of the lot had a chain-link fence perimeter, giving way to an improvised dump on the other side that was swallowed within yards by forest. *No, no, no...*

"Stop!"

Vogler cut across the vacant lot.

Much of the space had been paved years before, but was now overgrown with weeds that hid the buckled and cracked concrete. Luther felt a twinge in his hamstring as his foot landed on a raised section at an awkward angle. The sound of brown stalks and blades whipping against his legs was soon lost among his rhythmic panting.

Vogler stumbled when he looked over his shoulder, but remained a couple of body lengths ahead and closing on the fence fast. Luther's chest ached with every wheezing breath, but he dug deep and gave it one last kick. His vision browned around the edges and he heard the jangling of chain link ricocheting against the metal fence posts as Vogler scrambled up. Luther leaped, slamming the man's lower body against the cross post before he could slip the rest of the way over. Vogler grunted, and they rebounded off the fence with the force of Luther's weight. Luther landed on his back, with the suspect on top of him. The deputy rolled them both over, so Vogler was belly down on the ground beneath him.

"Don't fucking move," he panted, twisting the suspect's arms into position and snapping the cuffs on him with shaking hands. He climbed off the man, but stalled out on all fours in the dirt.

"You okay?" Grant asked. The Sheriff stood over him, holstering his weapon.

"Yeah," Luther gasped. "Just got the wind knocked out when he fell on me."

"So that's when that happened," Grant said, eyes up and surveying the area. Agent D'Antonio's khaki pants and FBI jacket could be seen cutting through the weeds as he approached.

"You got the patdown or you want me to do it?" Grant asked.

"No," Luther said, trying to get his breathing under control. "I got it."

His hands were still shaking, but not so much that he didn't feel the bulge in Vogler's back pocket. He tugged a latex glove over his sweaty hand before pulling a packet free. "Well, well, well..."

Luther held it up for Grant to see—a couple of folded lottery tickets, commonly used to contain heroin. Then he tucked the evidence away and helped Vogler to his feet. "Apparently our friend here is a gambling man."

D'Antonio's face was grim. "Maybe he is, but he's not our kidnapper. We didn't find the boy."

42

———

"What's the big roller coaster called again?" the boy asked, yawning so widely his jaw popped.

"The Space Rocket," Bruce said, although that didn't sound right. Not that it mattered. The kid wasn't going to tell anyone.

"I'm tired," the boy said. "Why am I so tired? I sleep all the time when I'm with you."

"I guess it's still not enough," he said. "I guess you need more sleep."

And the boy would be getting it soon.

The boy sat next to him on the bed. He'd been good so far, aside from a few moments of sniveling, and he'd been pretty self-contained. But now, unexpectedly, the boy leaned against him. "Are you telling the truth? About mom and dad waiting for us at Disney World?"

Bruce bristled. "Are you calling me a liar?"

The boy, oblivious to nonverbal cues, placed both hands on the man's arm and stared up at him. He was the perfect child, the Gerber baby at nine years old, except his hair was getting lank from going without washing. "You're not lying because something happened to mom and dad, are you?"

Bruce was struck dumb, but his mouth remained set and his gaze firm as a tear bled from the corner of the boy's eye.

"Are you?" the boy repeated.

Before he could stop himself, Bruce rested his hand on the crown of the boy's head, and he pulled him securely against his side. "I wouldn't do that."

"Promise?" The boy's voice buzzed against his side, but he was fading. The boy's head grew heavy and his face slid down, leaving lip slobber on the man's shirt.

"Time to go to sleep, buddy," he said, placing the child's head to rest on the pillow. "You know, I'm going to go with you, because I want to ride the Space Rocket, too."

It was true, the part about wanting to ride the roller coaster. He'd never ridden one, and it wasn't exactly the kind of thing you did for the first time as an adult. Not unless you were with a child. The closest he'd ever come to a roller coaster was probably the rope swing over the river at the park when they were kids. He hadn't thought of that in years—what made him think of it now?— but he could still remember that exhilarating rush when you let go of the rope and gravity took you, the sound of laughing voices calling out from the bank. He could even smell the funky tang of the river, a little like rotten vegetables.

Bruce shook himself free of the vivid memory, almost surprised by the sight of the semiconscious boy next to him.

"We'll sit in the front car of the roller coaster," he continued, "because that's the scariest one. That's where grown men scream like little girls."

The boy mumbled, "—not gonna scream like a girl…"

"I know you wouldn't," he said. "You're just about the bravest kid I know."

The boy was lying on his belly, so Bruce rolled him over gently. The boy sighed, but his eyes stayed closed. The man found himself stroking the boy's greasy hair. *Goddammit.* But it had to be done.

His hand slid to the boy's forehead, and he stopped, short of breath. *It has to be done.*

The man gasped when the boy opened his eyes and asked, "Do you really look like Bruce Wayne?"

He'd gotten so used to the feel of a mask, he'd nearly forgotten it was there. And it didn't matter. In the end, none of it mattered. He slid the Batman face up over his own. The plastic chin caught on his lip, making a soft popping noise, before he set the mask aside. The boy reached up and touched the brown scruff on his face, smiling dazedly before closing his eyes again.

Bruce put his hand on the crown of the boy's head one last time, then slowly slid it down his forehead... the rest of his face... until it covered the boy's nose and mouth. And he pressed gently. So gently. Part of him hoped the boy would struggle, thinking that would make it easier to press harder, hold longer if he had something to fight against. But the boy didn't struggle, and his eyes didn't open. *Has it been long enough yet?* He didn't think so.

And then the boy spoke.

Danny, no...

And his words ripped through Bruce's mind.

43

A dam fell through the air, shrieking with pleasure, as he hit the river and plunged to its soft bottom. He gazed up through the tannic water, rippling with sunlight, and thought—as he did every time, lungs straining—*I'm not going to make it.* But he did, bursting into the air, flinging water from his hair and mouth as he heard Danny and JJ laughing... Except that wasn't Danny he heard laughing; Adam heard himself, and shuddered with the sense of divergence.

But then something shifted—he was shaken loose—and Adam was somewhere else, *someone* else. He was with the boy, Aaron. His eyes were shut in a stupor that felt both reassuring and wrong, like the moment you begin to realize you've eaten too much candy and are going to be sick. Because with the boy's eyes closed, Adam couldn't see anything, and some part of him remembered *that's why I'm here. To see.*

Adam felt a hand on his own—in his own physical body—and with it, a lifting of the fog. In order to see, Adam needed to go back where he'd been before. *Back to Danny.* Adam felt the key around his neck, and remembered the cool river water, the simultaneously hilarious and revolting sensation of a piece of slimy grass stuck to the side of his face. And he felt himself return, except this time his body was bigger, more sure. He *(Danny)* sat sideways on a cheap motel bed, leaning forward. One palm was damp. *Why is it damp?* Somehow Adam knew the why was important.

It was damp from pressing against a child's mouth. Damp from the child's breath, trapped beneath it. Danny's hands were suffocating Aaron.

Danny, no...

The hands hesitated and released their pressure, but remained pressed to Aaron's face. Fear and anger knit together into something stronger as Adam screamed, *No!*

Pain ripped through Adam's skull, as though his brain were covered by skin that was being peeled slowly away. The primal, deafening sound that accompanied the pain made him wonder if his ears were bleeding. Part of Adam knew that *he* was making that sound happen—*not alone; with some help*—but he didn't know how to stop.

Harlan's fingers squeezed Adam's so tightly the pain cut through everything else. That's when Adam realized—it wasn't that he didn't know how to stop, it's that he didn't *want to*. Harlan tried to push him out, to make him stop, but Adam was unwilling to let go of what he desperately wanted to destroy. Just a little longer...

Enough, Harlan's voice said, before giving Adam one last mighty shove and releasing his grip on his hand.

Adam's palms fell to the floor and his head dropped to his chest. He opened his eyes, frantically searching... *there*. His kneecap shifted sideways painfully when it struck the hard wooden floor. Adam scrambled forward and got his head over the trashcan just in time, vomiting until he thought he'd die—either choke to death or asphyxiate. Finally, ears ringing, he was left with the sour smell, his throat acid raw and his eyes tearing. Adam coughed, wiped his face with his hand and saw a light smear of blood. He blinked away the tears in time to see a red drop fall. His nose was bleeding. Not like Teddy's had been, pouring everywhere, but a small trickle.

He looked over his shoulder and saw Teddy and Harlan still sitting, eyes shut. Harlan roused first. Adam made his way to the man on still-shaky knees and sat on his heels, watching Harlan blink and waiting for him to speak. He was afraid to disturb him, unsure whether Harlan's eyes saw what was in the room in front of him or some other place entirely.

Harlan's entire body jerked, as though flinching from something Adam couldn't see, and he inhaled a big wheezing breath. He tried to speak, but it seemed his vocal cords wouldn't cooperate. Harlan cleared his throat, closing his eyes momentarily as if doing so pained him, and said, "Bring us three jars."

The kitchen of the tiny house seemed a world away now. "Which ones?"

Harlan licked his lips and swallowed noisily. Adam could hear the stickiness of his throat. "Should have an A on the lid."

Adam braced himself against the cot, standing on unsteady legs. He made it to the kitchen in a kind of fugue where each step was lost to him by the time he'd taken the next one. Adam stared at the rack of Mason jars. Carrying three at once was a challenge. He grabbed one firmly in his hand, hugged the others to his belly with the same arm, then used his free arm to support the jar bottoms.

By the time he reached Harlan, Teddy was coming around as well. Harlan took the jars and swirled one in his hand before passing it back to Adam. "Drink this."

There was a sensation of cool liquid in Adam's mouth, but nothing else. He watched as Harlan swirled the other two jars, removed their lids, and handed one to Teddy, who still hadn't spoken. Blood trickled from the man's nose, and Adam put his hand up to his own. It seemed to have stopped. He nodded at Teddy. "Your nose is bleeding again."

Teddy blotted his nose with a handkerchief before sipping at the jar with a shudder.

"I can't taste it," Adam said. He seemed to have lost his sense of taste.

"Lucky you," Teddy croaked.

Thirsty, Adam drank halfway through the quart jar before finally asking, "What just happened?"

Both men continued sipping at their own beverages.

"I know it was Danny," Adam said, "and I know he had the boy. Is Aaron okay? Where are they?"

Harlan stretched his legs out straight and slid down to his elbows. Any lower, and he'd be lying down. "I don't know. I don't know if the boy's okay, and I'm not sure where they are. A cheap motel, but one cheap motel looks pretty much like any other."

Adam set his jar on the floor next to him. *All for nothing.* He'd run away from Cold Springs—probably made things worse by doing so—and it was all for nothing. They'd learned *nothing*.

"Easy," Harlan said. "That's why we had Teddy on the team, too. While you and I anchored ourselves to Danny, your uncle was digging around, trying to find stray bits of impressions and information that no one thinks is important enough to protect."

He turned to Teddy, and for a moment Adam thought Harlan's uncertainty matched his own. Then Teddy said, "Loganville. He's in Loganville, across from a used car lot."

Harlan said, "That's not more than an hour or so from here."

"True, but I doubt he's going to stick around and wait for us. Best thing to do is call it in. What do you think the chances are that the path around back is a quicker road out?"

"You'd know better than we would," Harlan said. "There are a lot of things around here you'd know better than we would."

Adam watched the two men staring at each other, unable to figure out the source or the meaning of the uneasy undercurrent. It had been there before they'd embarked, but not nearly so strong.

"Drink your tea," Teddy said. "I need one of those sandwiches. Adam, you got the keys? Not sure we didn't lock up out of habit."

Adam found them on the nightstand and tossed them to Teddy, who caught them and asked, "You want one too?"

The thought of peanut butter turned Adam's stomach, but that same stomach felt as if it were eating itself. "Sure," he said.

The worn springs of the cot protested as Teddy pushed off, standing only on his second attempt. He had a bit of a limp on his way to the door that Adam hadn't noticed before, a slight drag of his left leg that reminded Adam of someone else. He waited until Teddy had passed through the door before asking, "What really happened? What's going on?"

Adam got the impression Harlan was only half listening to him, head cocked at an angle as if he were listening instead to a storm on the horizon, trying to calculate when it would arrive. "Harlan!" he said.

Harlan finally met his eyes, and once again, Adam saw the same uncertainty he felt.

"I'm not sure," Harlan admitted, and headed for the door. As he reached the threshold, the sound of the pickup's engine cut through the air. "Shit!" Harlan shouted, and broke into a lurching, old man jog, Adam close on his heels.

Teddy must have decided the unfamiliar path around back of the house wasn't worth the risk. He was turning the truck around, pointing it back the way they'd come. It took a moment for the implications to sink in: *Teddy is leaving the property, and leaving us behind.*

"Teddy!" Harlan bellowed, but stopped a few yards past the front steps. So did Adam. Either Teddy would stop, or he wouldn't. Chasing him wouldn't make a bit of difference, and Adam really didn't have it in him to keep running.

Teddy paused, truck idling. "I'm sorry," he said. "I'll call it in on the way. And I'll send someone for you."

"Eventually," Harlan said.

Teddy pursed his thin lips, at best slightly apologetic. "Eventually," he agreed.

"This about Virgil?" Harlan asked.

Teddy shook his head, but Adam thought it was less an answer than a refusal to answer.

"You don't want to be part of this," Teddy said. He nodded in Adam's direction. "And they're not done with him yet. Keep an eye on Adam."

The truck kicked up gravel as it sped toward the steep road and Teddy battled the temperamental clutch.

Harlan said, as a cloud of dust enveloped them, "I always do."

44

———————

"Harlan, what the hell is going on?" Adam asked, as soon as the dust cleared.

Harlan sighed. "You gotta be tired of hearing me say this by now, but I don't know." He walked back to the steps, where Teddy had left the remaining bag of sandwiches and two big bottles of water. "Come on, let's get in the house. Something about being in the open here makes my skin crawl."

Adam followed Harlan inside because he didn't know what else to do. His head ached, he felt shivery all over, and he suspected his nose had started bleeding again.

Harlan plopped down on a crackling cot and pulled a couple of peanut butter sandwiches from the bag. "And paper towels, too. Iris would be proud," he said, handing a sandwich to Adam as he sat on the opposite cot.

Adam was so thirsty, it was a physical pain, his gums and lips and fingers throbbing. Cracking the seal on one of the water bottles, he started to chug it, but stopped after a few swallows. Thirsty or not, it may have to last for a while. "So Teddy's not coming back?" Adam asked.

"I'm afraid not," Harlan said, between bites. "Or at least, not anytime soon. We're on our own, until someone comes to get us."

"Who's someone? Someone, the law? Someone, Iris? And when do they get here?"

Harlan shrugged, trying to swallow a mouthful of sticky peanut butter and white bread. Adam nodded. "I know, I know. You don't know. How about telling me what you do know—what exactly did we do here?"

Harlan wiped his mouth and leaned back against the wall, looking as if it would take much more than a peanut butter sandwich and a bottle of water to perk him up. "Well, we got through to Danny. No, *you* got through to Danny, and Teddy and I were just along for the ride. You spoke to him—*through* him—when he would've killed the boy, but I genuinely don't know what happened after that."

Adam put the water bottle between his knees and fidgeted with the cap. "I did more than speak to him, though, didn't I? I know that much, but I don't know what I did."

"That's because you weren't the only one doing it," Harlan said, kneading his hands against his eyes as though trying to push them through the back of his skull. "I'm sorry, but I have got to lie down," he said, and proceeded to do so.

Adam wouldn't be put off so easily. "It wasn't *you* helping me. You tried to stop me. Was it Teddy?"

"Not exactly," Harlan said, resting the heels of his hands over his eye sockets, "except insofar as he acted as a bridge."

Suddenly exhausted himself, Adam lay back on his own cot. A layer of dust on the plastic tickled his raw throat and made him want to cough again. "So it was Virgil. Was he—were we *together*—trying to kill Danny?"

Harlan lifted his hands and turned his head to look at Adam. "Yes, son, I believe you were."

Then he rolled over and closed his eyes. Despite everything, Adam found himself doing the same.

~

THE FIRST THING Adam noticed when he woke (*I'm in the old house near the river*) was the change in the light coming through the windows. He must've slept for hours.

The second thing he noticed was that Harlan was gone.

Adam jumped up from the cot, only to sit down just as quickly when a wave of dizziness swept over him. He put his head between his knees and waited impatiently for the sensation to pass. Then he stood—more slowly this time—and headed for the front door.

"I'm in here," Harlan said from behind him. Adam tried to hide his relief as he followed the voice to the narrow kitchen. He found Harlan squatting next to the empty pantry shelves which, it turned out, weren't quite empty after all. "Can of Vienna sausages if you're feeling brave," Harlan said. "What's the date say?"

Adam leaned over the sink to maximize the light from the window. The gray stamped numbers were barely distinguishable against the metal. "Next year," he said, giving it back to Harlan.

The sound of the peeling lid was loud in the small space. Harlan handed Adam a fork. Adam didn't bother to ask where he'd found it, just wiped the utensil on his pants leg and speared one of the cylindrical meats. He stared out the window and wondered how far it was to the river. "Is this something I need to worry about? I mean, for the rest of my life. Is my father gonna try to use me as a hitman?"

Harlan responded as if Adam's question hadn't been a non sequitur. "I hope not. This wasn't quite like what happened with Doreen. It wasn't so much that Virgil was in control of you, as that he was able to... give you a nudge."

"The desire to save that boy by killing Danny came from me— it was *in me*," Adam said, somewhere between a question and a statement.

"Maybe," Harlan admitted, then waved his laden fork philosophically. "The *thought* was there—the awareness of the *option*—

but I don't know how much of the *desire to execute it* was. Virgil's the one who knew *how* to do it, or at least had an idea."

"Do you know how to do it? Kill someone like that?"

"No. I suppose, given enough time and sufficient motivation, I might be able to figure it out," Harlan said. "It strikes me as something Lawrence would have tried to teach his son, albeit second-hand. Lawrence had a lot of arcane knowledge, but thankfully he didn't have that kind of power himself. Neither did Virgil. That's why he needed the rest of us. I'll be honest—I don't know what the hell went on between him and Teddy, but when Virgil tried to draw from me, I stopped him. I didn't care what it was for. But you —you have a well of untapped power; all he had to do was nudge and ask."

"I should have stopped him, too," Adam said, tossing his fork in the sink.

"You would've, if you'd known. You wouldn't have killed Danny on your own. I know that," Harlan said.

"My mom wouldn't even have thought of it."

Harlan raised a dark brow. "Your mother was an amazing human being—no question—but don't go canonizing her. She was a healer by nature, but she would have done anything to protect the people she loved, especially you."

Adam's hand strayed to his neck.

"That key of hers you wear," Harlan said, pointing with his fork. "I told you, I suspect it's symbolic and doesn't actually open anything, but it is a powerful symbol. It reminds me of something I came across years ago. I asked her once where it came from—"

"When?"

Harlan waved vaguely. "Doesn't matter. We only met a couple of times. It was before she married your dad. Anyway, she wouldn't tell me where she got it. All she'd say was that it would keep her safe."

Adam rubbed the key between his thumb and index finger, so slowly and delicately he could feel it catch on the lines and whorls imprinted on his skin. He said (without bitterness or self-pity—

he'd given up those years ago), "I guess she wasn't wearing it the night of the accident."

"Of course not. *You* were." Harlan tossed his fork in the sink next to Adam's and turned the tap. It was—as Adam had expected —dry. "Damn. Shall we hike down to the river to wash the only two fucking forks in the house?"

45

Danny held a hand up and watched it shake. *Stop*, he thought, squeezing his fist until it did. Then he swiped his fingers across his upper lip. Nothing, not for an hour or so. He'd just checked in the rearview mirror, but he didn't trust his nose not to start bleeding again. This wasn't the time to think about what happened in the motel room (*or my hands will start shaking again*). This was the time for business, and for tidying up loose ends. He squeezed his eyes shut, took a deep breath. When he exited his car, he'd become someone else.

Danny knocked on the trailer door and waited. And waited. Finally, he heard heavy footsteps on the other side.

"I hope I'm not interrupting anything," Danny said. The man who opened the door smelled of desperation and other unpleasant odors. But the smells of addiction were also the smells of job security. "Is this a bad time?"

"No, not at all, Mitch. I just—I thought I wouldn't see you for a while because, you know..."

"The checkpoints are gone, so I didn't see much of a risk." At the moment, he was much more worried about the body in his trunk than about drugs or other contraband. "Are you going to invite me in?"

The man seemed to realize for the first time that he wore nothing but boxers and an undershirt. He tugged at the shirt's hem self-consciously and bent forward to push the door open wider. Danny's hand strayed toward his belt. *If that fly comes open, I might just cut your stupid throat on the doorstep.*

Danny caught the flimsy screen door before it could fall shut again and stepped up on a wobbly cinder block. The man had already disappeared inside, but he heard him call out, "Sorry for the mess. I've been feeling kinda off this weekend."

Kinda off was a familiar euphemism for withdrawal in Danny's business. The general state of hygiene and housekeeping within the trailer confirmed his diagnosis, although the dishes had been washed recently. He was used to seeing sinks filled with crusty dishes from days long past; withdrawal made his customers forget about food and cleaning. But they never forgot about him. Again, that usually meant job security. Except when it meant trouble.

Squalor made Danny physically ill, no matter how many times he saw it. That's why he used to carry a roll of peppermints, but a supplier had turned him on to some cheap Chinese candies. The ginger did a better job than mint at keeping his stomach happy. He pulled one from his pocket and popped it in his mouth, tucking the wrapper in a pants pocket.

"Got an extra?" the man asked, now wearing sweats and a T-shirt.

Danny handed him one. The man fumbled (*sweaty hands, along with everything else*) to get the candy unwrapped and in his mouth, then tossed the wrapper on the cluttered coffee table.

"Thanks. My guts are killing me," the man said, sitting in a dingy armchair and rocking back and forth. He couldn't stay still, not to save his life. "It's funny."

"What's funny?" Danny asked, knowing withdrawal rendered a coherent train of thought improbable if not impossible.

"Your candy," the man said. "Small world—I had some of your

candy, and my brother asked me about it. I couldn't remember where I got it."

"Really?" Danny knew the man was stupid, but he didn't think he was *that* stupid.

The man gave a tentative grin. "Okay, I could remember, but I wasn't about to say I got it from my drug dealer."

Danny cringed when the man cracked the hard candy between his teeth. He wiggled his jaw around, then coughed as a chunk went down the wrong way.

"You okay?" Danny asked.

The man coughed once more before answering with an irritated throat, "Yeah. Listen, I'm not like a lot of these people you sell to... I never took no heroin."

"No," Danny agreed. "No, you didn't."

"I've been thinking maybe I want to quit."

Danny paused, face frozen. He could work with this. "Good for you," he said.

"Yeah?" the man asked, uncertain.

"Yeah." Danny-Mitch smiled and raised his hands. "Hey, I just give adult customers what they ask for. I don't push anything they don't want."

The man nodded. "I think maybe I don't want this anymore."

"Okay," Danny said. "But cold turkey isn't the way to do it. No offense, but you look like shit."

"Ha!" The man wiped sweat from his puffy face. "That's 'cause I feel like shit."

"I can help you out." Danny produced a tiny bag with a couple of capsules. "This is the same stuff they give you if you go to a fancy detox. I only have one dose on me, but it lasts for twenty-four hours. I can drop by with some more tomorrow."

The man took the pills from him. "Thanks, man. How much do I owe you?"

"That's on the house."

"Seriously?"

"Sure. You saved my ass, letting me know about the checkpoints." Danny smiled. "But I'm not a total philanthropist. You can pay me for the rest tomorrow, same as you've been paying."

"Sounds good." The man picked up an open can of soda from the coffee table and raised it high in a mock toast, before using it to wash down the pills.

Danny nodded. "Your life will never be the same."

46

———

So close, Luther thought. And yet they weren't, and that was the problem. They were back where they started. Nowhere.

Grant had sent Luther back to Beecham County while he coordinated something else that would come to nothing. Luther felt hollowed out inside. He just wished he knew if the boy were still alive. He couldn't remember the last time he'd been really drunk, but right now he wanted nothing more than to get totally shit-faced. Hammered. Smashed. It would be worth the killer hangover for a couple of hours of forgetfulness.

Obviously, that wasn't an option—he'd grab a couple hours of sleep and get back to it. One foot in front of the other.

He reached the lights at the outskirts of Plattsville and realized he couldn't remember the last time he'd eaten. There wasn't a damn thing to eat at his house, either, except maybe an expired box of something in the back of a cabinet. The little market in Cold Springs would be closed by now, so Luther turned in to the grocery store parking lot to get something to throw in the microwave and maybe a carton of milk. *If I have any sense, I won't be buying a case of beer.*

The parking lot was poorly lit, but he still recognized a familiar vehicle and a familiar driver. JJ Tulley stood next to her old Bronco, kicking the back tire. Luther pulled into a space near hers, wrong way around so his driver side was facing her.

"Goddamn motherfucking son of a fucking bitch!" she growled.

She must've seen him get out of his vehicle, but apparently her synapses weren't firing enough to recognize him. Luther stood next to her and said, "I don't think that's proper inflation technique."

JJ simultaneously gasped and threw an elbow in his direction, which Luther managed to sidestep. "Hey, easy!" he said.

"Goddammit, Luther, you scared the shit out of me." JJ's hand went to her mouth, and Luther thought she was dangerously close to tears. She must've had a shitty day, too.

"You have a spare?" he asked, squinting at her tire in the feeble light.

"Of course I have a goddamn spare," JJ said. "I'm not an idiot."

Luther pulled a small flashlight from his belt, squatted down and ran the light over the tire, then whistled. No wonder it was flat. She hadn't picked up a nail, as he'd assumed; someone had slashed the sidewall of her tire. "Who'd you piss off?" he asked, without thinking.

She didn't answer, and Luther glanced up quickly, feeling like a shitheel and afraid he'd triggered a bout of crying. Except, he should have known better; it was JJ, after all.

"Thanks, Luther," she said, shoving a crumpled piece of paper in her pocket, "but I can get the tire. You head on home."

Luther ignored her and went to the back of the Bronco. He tried the latch, but it was still locked. "You can open this, or we can stand here arguing until your milk spoils."

She stood, considering, and finally tossed him a fat mass of keys. By some miracle, he managed to catch them and went to work.

"So what's going on, JJ?" he asked, feeling a suspect-chasing twinge in his back as he lifted her heavy spare—an old, full-sized tire—in one hand and the jack in the other.

JJ followed, grabbing the wrench, and went to work loosening the lugs before Luther had a chance. He stood, feeling extraneous, admiring her determination as she gritted her teeth and strained to make headway.

"It's Marcus," she said, so close on the heels of a grunt that at first he didn't recognize the words.

JJ tossed him the crumpled paper she'd hidden away. Luther pulled out his glasses and flashlight and squinted at a sloppy scrawl: *Whose car was parked outside your house all weekend, SLUT? Maybe he'll let you borrow it.*

"How long?" Luther asked.

"Long enough," she said, panting with effort. "I think he poisoned my dog Saturday."

"The dog that wanted to eat me?"

She nodded.

Sonuvabitch. Getting her protectors out of the way showed a scary amount of premeditation, and dedication.

JJ paused to wipe the sweat from her upper lip with her forearm. Luther gently took the wrench from her hand and loosened the remaining two nuts. When he was done, she jacked the car up and he finished removing the tire. She rolled it away and lifted it into the back while he secured the spare.

"You want to come to the station with me when we're done here and file for a TRO?" he asked.

"No. I'm sorry, Luther," she said. "I didn't say anything before because I don't want to be a bother—a distraction—while you're looking for Aaron."

Luther stood, wiping his hands on his pants. "I thought you said you weren't an idiot." But he smiled, and he thought he felt her smile in return. "Besides, unfortunately there's not a whole lot for me to be doing right now that'll find that little boy."

Luther thought perhaps he'd spoken too soon when his cell phone rang. Anything important and case-related should come over the radio, but a man could hope.

"Just a minute," he said, holding up a finger. "Yeah."

"Luther, you gotta get over here now," a woman said, voice so warped with crying he could barely make out the words. "I don't know what to do."

"Who is this?" Luther asked, putting a hand over his free ear to hear better. "Esther?"

"I found him lying on the floor, and he's not moving!" Esther wailed.

Les—shit. Luther stubbed his toe when he kicked the jack over. What the hell was he supposed to do from the IGA parking lot? "Well, call the goddamn rescue squad."

Esther sniffled on the other end, but she sounded more coherent. "Les always said not to call the squad if something happened, because he could lose his job."

"What?" Luther yelled at the phone, certain he hadn't heard her correctly.

"Luther, I think he overdosed," she said, now clear as a bell.

Luther was aware of JJ standing near him, watching him, aware of the heat still radiating from his vehicle in the cool night air. But he felt as though his higher brain function had shut down; Esther's words just didn't make sense. "*Overdosed?*"

"Yes, overdosed! Are you listening to me, Luther?" He heard her take a deep breath on the other end, as if his confusion helped to fuel her calm. "Look, I'll stay with him as long as I can, but I can't be found here. If my ex finds out about this, I'll lose my kids." And she hung up.

Luther's lips felt numb, along with his cheeks and the rest of his face. Overdosed? His little brother? Maybe Esther was overreacting. But maybe she wasn't.

"Luther, are you okay?" JJ asked.

Esther was right about one thing. If word got out that he'd been using drugs, Les could kiss his State Road job goodbye. They had a zero tolerance policy for their drivers, and—for good or ill—he'd already helped his brother get around one DUI. *Shit.* Les lived about fifteen minutes away. Luther looked at the light bar across the top of his vehicle. He could make it in ten, and then he'd figure out what to do.

"Luther!" JJ shouted in his face. "Who overdosed?"

He stared down at JJ, still wearing her nurse's scrubs. "I need your help."

~

"Is it Les?" JJ asked, holding fast to the oh-shit bar as Luther took a curve twenty miles per hour faster than he should have.

"Yes," Luther said, concentrating on the road. But something in the tone of her voice... "Did you know he was using?"

JJ shifted her bottom more squarely onto the seat. "No, I didn't. But I'm not surprised. We've had double the number of overdoses come through the ER this year, and it's not even November."

That's right; it was Halloween tonight. Luther should have been rounding up hell-raising kids, not looking for a missing child and checking out his brother's overdose. *Doubled?* He knew there'd been an increase in drug trafficking in the area, but on his end he certainly hadn't seen it double. Perhaps the effects hadn't trickled down yet. Or perhaps he just hadn't been paying attention, as he apparently hadn't been paying attention to his brother.

"So you don't know how long he's been using?" JJ asked. "Or what he's into?"

"No. I had no idea," Luther said, face flushing with shame. When was the last time he and his brother ate a meal together? Or even had a decent conversation? The twelve-year difference in their ages meant they hadn't been close growing up, but he felt as though that had changed when their mother began to decline. So when had it changed back again? Les had nearly gotten into trouble over illegal ginseng harvesting a while back, but things had been strained before that. And then he remembered.

"He hurt his back," Luther said. "At work, about eighteen

months ago. They had him on some kind of pills. Goddammit, I should've seen it."

But in retrospect, he probably hadn't seen a lot in his life over the past few years. He'd been cruising since his mom died, going through the motions, not really engaging with anyone or anything.

"Do you know how bad he is?" JJ asked.

"I don't know," Luther said. His SUV kicked up clouds of dust, reflecting like fog in his headlights, as he turned onto Les's road. "I couldn't really get much out of the woman who called."

"Do you have any Naloxone?"

Luther glanced at JJ. "Nalox—" He swerved to avoid hitting a garbage can spilling from someone's driveway.

"Shit, Luther!" JJ gripped the dash.

The near miss had given his brain time to make the connection. Naloxone: administered in case of opioid overdose. "No, I don't have any. The Sheriff's Department's been on a list for a while, but I guess it's a damn long list because it hasn't shown up yet."

Les's pickup was the lone vehicle in front of his trailer. They'd made good time, and he'd thought Esther would still be there. What could have spooked her into leaving? His chest grew tight as he hit the brakes, slammed the SUV into park, and ran toward the door. He was moving too fast when he hit the cinder blocks, and one flipped beneath him as he yanked open the front door. His knee hit the threshold of the trailer hard, and he crawled the rest of the way inside. His vision went dark with the sudden pain, and he blinked, standing awkwardly while his eyes cleared.

The room was dim, the only illumination coming from the bulb over the kitchen stove and a small lamp in the living room. Les lay face down on the floor, with a stinking pile of vomit next to him. Luther rushed to his brother and knelt on aching knees. "He's got a pulse," he called over his shoulder. At least, he thought Les did. Luther's own heart pounded so hard, it seemed the entire world shook with it.

A light came on overhead—barely strong enough to reach the

floor—then JJ appeared next to Luther and nudged him out of the way. "Les... Leslie, can you hear me?" Time paused while she held her fingers to Les's neck, silent. "Help me get him over."

On JJ's count, she and Luther rolled the bulky man onto his back. Les remained still as JJ rubbed his sternum with her knuckles, and when she checked his eyes, the pupils were too tiny for Luther to see. He deluded himself (*that's because I'm not wearing my glasses*) until JJ turned to him and said, "Call it in."

Luther paused, unsure. "He'll lose his job," he said, but it sounded stupid even to his own ears.

"Luther, your brother is dying," JJ said firmly. "Call it in."

So Luther did, while JJ checked Les's airway and timed his breathing. And, as usually happened, the protocol helped calm him. "On their way," he said. "What do you need?"

"Go through the house and find all the drugs you can—pill bottles, baggies, whatever. They'll want it at the hospital."

"Got it," he said.

Rummaging in the kitchen for a grocery bag without gaping holes, Luther heard plastic crackling as JJ unrolled the Ambu mask from her keychain and secured it to Les's face. She'd already begun rescue breathing when Luther passed on his way to the hallway. (*He'll be okay; my little brother will be okay.*)

The bathroom was disgusting, with toothpaste and dirt and varieties of grunge he didn't want to think about on every flat surface. The medicine cabinet contained several prescription bottles—most empty, some with a few pills, but all expired. He also found a joint in a baggie and nearly left it, thinking somehow to protect his brother, but ultimately deferred to JJ's medical judgment and threw it in the bag. There was nothing of interest in the toilet tank or under the sink.

Next he went to the spare bedroom directly across the hall, flipped on the light and surveyed the room. It was full of dust-covered boxes and not worth the effort with the clock running. The master bedroom—that's where he would find the things his brother didn't want anyone else to see.

And he did.

Lying on Les's bed, arms crossed on his chest, was the body of a small, blonde boy.

"JJ!" Luther screamed. "Get in here!"

He felt like he was moving in slow motion as he rushed to the bed, but his brain still screamed, *where's JJ? What's taking her so long?* "JJ!"

She appeared in the doorway as Luther bent to pick up the boy, oh so gently, one hand supporting Aaron Schofield's dirty blonde head.

"Oh, Luther," she said, shaking her head, tears in her eyes.

They were too late.

"No," Luther whispered. "No, no, no..." He slid his other arm beneath Aaron's knees and the boy's head lolled awkwardly to the side... and righted itself.

JJ's hand flew to her mouth, and her eyes locked on Luther's. His brother approached death a room away, but they both smiled. Because the boy was alive. Aaron Schofield was alive.

47

———

"Am I on? Is it time?" JJ asked automatically, pulling a borrowed blanket from her face. Her feet hit the floor before her eyes were even open.

"Time for what?" asked a voice that wasn't one of the nurses. "To solve another one of my cases?"

JJ blinked, rubbed her eyes with the heels of her hands, and swallowed hard. Her mouth was sticky, and she wondered when she'd last brushed her teeth. She was still in uniform, she was on the couch in the break room... her eyes finally came unglued. Grant was sitting next to her.

"Hey, sleepyhead," he said, smiling and brushing her hair back from her face.

JJ smiled back at him, but it was short-lived. "Has there been a change?"

Grant shook his head, but continued to stroke her hair. "Aaron is still groggy, but fine—his parents are with him—and Les hasn't regained consciousness."

JJ turned toward him, indulging in the feeling of his hand against her face, before asking, "How's Luther?"

"I don't know," Grant admitted. "I haven't seen him yet. He was gone when I got here."

"I assume his father hasn't shown up."

Grant dropped his hand and made a noise that might've been disgust if there'd been more energy behind it. "I wouldn't hold my breath waiting for Rudy Beck."

JJ leaned, elbows on her knees and forehead on her hands. There was something she'd wanted to tell Grant, something that had bugged her. She rubbed small circles above her aching brows, and it came back to her. "So, if Les hasn't regained consciousness, we still have no idea how Aaron got to his trailer."

Grant raised his hands. "JJ—"

She sat up quickly. "You don't really think Les had anything to do with it, do you?"

"JJ, I can't talk about an ongoing investigation."

"I know, I know. But there's something weird about his overdose."

Grant raised an eyebrow. "Weirder than finding a kidnapped child in his bed?"

She shook her head impatiently. "No, you don't understand. Have you spoken to Les's doctors? Or the first responders?"

"No, not yet."

"Les presented symptoms of a depressant-type, rather than a stimulant-type overdose."

Grant sighed. "Which would include the opioids he's apparently addicted to."

"But it wasn't an opioid overdose," JJ said. "I rode to the hospital with Luther. When we got here, I heard one of the EMTs say that administering Naloxone didn't do anything."

Grant spoke slowly, his exhausted mind finishing his train of thought as he finished the sentence. "Because Naloxone only works with opioid overdoses."

"Exactly," JJ said.

"Could the EMTs have administered it incorrectly, or used the wrong dosage?" he asked.

She frowned. "It seems unlikely, with the amount of practice they've had lately."

Grant pinched the bridge of his nose. He looked exhausted, as though someone had sucker-punched both eyes. "Did you tell Luther?" he asked.

"No," she said. She'd never had a chance.

Luther had carried the boy to the living room and watched over him while JJ resumed rescue breathing on Les. The emergency response time was decent, and Aaron's condition was good enough for her and Luther to follow the ambulance, transporting the boy in Luther's vehicle. They hadn't spoken, but she'd thought the deputy had done a remarkable job of holding it together. The typical controlled chaos had enveloped her when they reached the emergency room—with the addition of law enforcement from several agencies clamoring to interview her—and by the time she'd thought to look for Luther, he was gone.

"Good," Grant said.

It took JJ a moment to recover the conversational thread. "You mean you don't want me to tell him about the Naloxone?"

"I'd prefer you didn't, if you can help it," he requested. "As I said, I haven't seen him yet. But Luther was pretty strung out even before Les landed in here, and I shudder to think what'll happen the first time someone's stupid enough to talk about his kidnapper—"

"Pedophile," JJ cut in.

Grant nodded, and continued, "His *pedophile* brother within Luther's earshot. I'd rather he didn't hear about the medical anomalies until I've had a chance to see if there's anything to them."

JJ considered. "I won't lie to him if he asks, but I won't volunteer anything, either."

"Okay," he said, with a hint of a smile, before putting a reassuring hand on her knee. "How are you doing?"

JJ slid her hand over the top of his, linked their fingers, and twisted her hand so she could stare at his palm. A freckle at the flex in his wrist drew attention to the blue artery there, but she could trace patterns of circulation throughout his pale skin. Someday, she hoped she'd have the opportunity to memorize every vein, every line.

"I'm fine," she said. *For now.*

Grant lifted her hand to his lips and kissed it gently, at the split between her fingers. JJ shivered and tried to focus on his words instead of her libido as he asked, "If you're fine, then why are you still here?"

Why *was* she still here? For a while, she'd been answering questions, and waiting to answer questions, and waiting to answer someone else's questions... but why had she finally lain down on the couch in the end?

"Shit," she said, throwing her hands in the air before digging them into her long hair. She felt a dull ache at the back of her head she couldn't immediately identify. "My Bronco's still parked at the grocery store. With a flat tire, and a spoiled carton of milk. No, wait—Luther and I changed the tire before he got the call."

"The call?"

"The call from the woman who found Les."

48

"The boy's alive, in case you're wondering," Luther said when the woman answered the door. "Les is still touch and go, but the boy will be fine."

"Praise Jesus," Esther muttered.

Luther rolled his eyes. He didn't know if she could see it, beneath his hat in the glare of her porch light, but he didn't care. "You gonna let me in?"

"Luther, this isn't a good time—"

She didn't protest when he pushed past her into her living room. He was finding it difficult to breathe. He removed his hat, and used that familiar motion to try to get his temper under control.

"What the fuck were you thinking?" he asked, and felt he'd been mostly successful. "How the hell could you leave them there?"

Esther looked like a different woman fully dressed, even in jeans and a long-sleeved T-shirt. Like someone who could be in the PTA.

"I don't know, I just panicked. I told you, I can't be a part of this. I am not losing my kids," she said.

Luther pressed the heel of his hand against his forehead hard, rotating it as if it could somehow pierce his skull and make it to the center of his brain. "Not being part of this is not an option, Esther. I'll have somebody come around to take an official statement from you, but in the meantime, there are some questions you need to answer, and you need to answer them now."

"No," she said, crossing her arms, "and you can't make me."

Luther took a deep breath. Between the exhaustion and the endless stress and the sudden shock, he really wasn't feeling well. It didn't help that he'd never eaten. He turned slowly in place, eyes and ears open. The television was off, and he didn't hear anything except a cycling refrigerator. Esther stood near the door, rather than between him and the hallway that led to the kids' bedrooms. He concluded her children weren't at home, and he spoke freely.

"Esther," he said through gritted teeth, "don't dick me around. We just found a kidnapped child in my brother's bed, and he's not in any condition to explain how the boy got there. If you're so goddamned worried about being involved in this, what do you think's going to happen when everybody finds out you're Les's fuck buddy?"

Her lip began to tremble.

"Sit down," Luther said, motioning her to an armchair and taking a seat across from her. "Did you see anyone else at Les's place tonight?"

Esther started to cry in earnest, face pinkening as tears made tracks in her makeup. "No, no one."

"How about on the road?" he asked, calmly, as if he were interviewing a witness about any other case. "Did you pass any cars on your way there?"

"Maybe, I don't know. I don't remember."

"Was he expecting anyone?"

"Not that I know of."

Les pulled out his phone and looked at the call log on the screen. He hadn't bothered to check in the dark grocery store parking lot, but now he could see that she'd used her own cell phone. "How long were you at Les's before you called me?"

"Not long," she said, reaching to the coffee table for a tissue. "Just a minute or two. I called you, and then I went to the bathroom..." She trailed off.

"You wanted to make sure you hadn't left anything in his house, so no one would know you'd been there," Luther suggested. "And that's how you found the boy."

"Yes," she whispered. "That's why I was over there in the first place—I'd left my wallet, and mom still has the kids, so I thought I'd drop by and surprise him."

"And that's when you left," Luther said. "When you found the boy in his bedroom, you left."

She made a sound of assent and hid her eyes in her tissue. "I can't believe I did that. I have children. How could I leave that boy? But I thought he was..."

She'd thought he was dead. It was understandable. Luther had thought so as well. And JJ's face when she'd seen the child... But he was okay. Aaron was going to be okay. *Thank God.* But what the hell was going on? And if his brother survived, how the hell would he keep him out of prison?

Luther's mind was so detached from his body, he didn't hear his cell phone ring. Ultimately, the feeling of Esther's expectant stare upon him made him notice the insistent sound. He glanced at the screen. *Grant.* He'd known the man would catch up to him eventually.

"What is it?" Luther asked. "Is Les okay?"

"He's no worse," Grant said.

Which also means he's no better.

"I know you're upset, Luther, but there are people chomping at the bit to get on this. To get at you, for that matter. Who let you know Les overdosed?"

"A friend of his," Luther said, Esther's weepy eyes upon him.

"Did she know about the boy?"

Luther noticed Grant had already guessed it was a woman, and chose his words carefully. "Not when she called me."

"Is that where you are now?"

"Yes."

"You know you can't be there," Grant said, and the sound of his heavy exhale rattled over the connection. "Be careful, Luther. Assume anything you say or do will be broadcast in court someday."

Luther didn't respond.

"You get anything useful?" Grant asked.

"No," Luther admitted, "but I'm not done yet."

"Well," Grant said, "when you are, get over to the Command Center. We're calling a briefing."

"Okay," Luther said, fingers of dread tickling at his major organs. "I'll be there in twenty."

Grant hung up, and Luther rested his forehead against his phone and sighed. *Concentrate on the task at hand.*

Esther's perfect face had melted while he was distracted by Grant's call. A tissue lay on the coffee table, smeared with foundation and mascara, and she clutched a fresh one in her hand.

"So Friday night," Luther said, "you came home from the trunk-or-treat with Les?"

She nodded. "Around seven or seven-thirty. And we stayed in the whole night, until you showed up to get the list of volunteers."

Luther felt some of the pressure release in his chest. She may not be a defense attorney's first choice of witness, but Esther did give his brother an alibi for the time of the kidnapping. So if he hadn't kidnapped Aaron (and Luther never thought he had), what connection did Les share with the boy that he'd ended up in his trailer? He felt a little tickling at the edge of his brain, the seed of an idea, but was afraid to approach it head-on and scare it away.

"When I dropped by Les's yesterday, you told me it wasn't a good time, and he said he thought he'd picked up something. What was really going on?"

Luther waited impatiently while Esther stared down at the

tissue in her hand and squeezed it like a snotty stress ball. He leaned forward and placed two fingers on her knee, so she couldn't avoid seeing them.

Finally, her eyes were drawn inexorably up Luther's hand and arm to his face, and she admitted, "I knew Les was an addict. But he didn't do drugs."

Luther held his breath to keep from yelling, *Use the goddamned present tense.*

She continued, "What I mean is, he took what he needed to take—never in front of me—but he didn't take drugs just because."

"He wasn't a recreational user."

"Yes," Esther said, almost grateful. "That's exactly what I mean. So mostly you couldn't tell, unless you were paying attention and knew what to look for."

"And you do?"

"I had an ex... Look, you probably think I'm a lousy mom, but there are things I'm not going to expose my kids to again."

"Is that why you and Les never did anything together with your kids?" It was a shot in the dark, but Luther hit the mark.

She nodded. "We've been together off and on for a while, and we've had a lot of fun, but I guess you could say he was on probation. We never talked about it, but I was hoping he'd get it together."

"So what happened this weekend?"

"Les didn't say, but he was acting off on Saturday. He even smoked a skunky joint he'd gotten off some kid at the trunk-or-treat, which did not make me happy. So I checked his medicine cabinet. I'm not saying he didn't have pills stashed somewhere else, but all the bottles in the bathroom were empty."

So his brother had been in withdrawal on Sunday. And yet somewhere he'd picked up enough pills to overdose and have a few extra on hand by Monday evening. "Do you know who his dealer was?"

Esther shook her head. "Like I said, we never talked about it. We just pretended... But if I had to guess, I'd say he wasn't local.

Would you go to somebody local if your brother was a Sheriff's deputy?"

Luther dug his knuckles into his brows. He had to get to the Command Center. All eyes would be on him as it was; he didn't need to walk in late, too. He'd try to get a line on the dealer after the briefing. Luther couldn't stand around the hospital, waiting to see if his brother woke up or died, and he didn't think Les would expect him to. He'd much rather have his name cleared.

"I know you must think I'm an awful person, but I do hope Les is okay," Esther said. "He was good to me, and lately not many people have been."

Luther rose slowly from his chair, adrenaline spent. Yes, he did think Esther was an awful person. But so was Les. So was he. So was everyone, at one time or another. At the door, he said, "I'll keep this as quiet as I can. Try not to worry about your kids."

49

———

Despite his best intentions, Luther didn't make it to the Command Center briefing. There'd been rumblings there a few weeks ago, when Rachel was missing, and now at least half the assholes in the building would think his brother was a freaking pedophile. In the end, he found himself parking in front of the Sheriff's Department instead.

The few cars scattered around the parking lot likely belonged to officers picking up department vehicles or riding with someone else. The front door was locked, and most of the lights were off. Still, no doubt there was someone in uniform wandering around the halls or taking a dump, ostensibly ready to field any emergencies. Luther went to his desk and peeled off his coat. He settled to cogitating, as Rudy Beck would have said. A dangerous proposition.

Luther considered his first step. Photographs of Les's place (*the crime scene*) would have been downloaded at the Command Center, but if there was some way to access those remotely, Luther was damned if he knew it. He leaned back in his chair and put his feet on his desk. He didn't have what you'd call a photographic memory, but he was pretty good at remembering visual things and recognizing the unusual. Luther shut his eyes.

Mouth open and face slack, the flesh hung heavy and loose beneath Les's stubbly chin. Flecks of vomit had caught there, and on his blue lips. His lips were so blue, like a corpse on an examining table— Luther nearly fell from his chair rising to stand. *Jesus Christ.* A choked sob caught in his throat as he paced around the office. *Jesus, Les.* Luther pinched his nose between his fingers hard, willing the tears to not fall.

He took a wheezing, uneven breath and wiped his eyes. This was not going to work. Visualizing his brother dying next to a pool of vomit wouldn't do anything except make Luther useless, which was close to being the case already.

So if he didn't have easy access to the evidence gathered tonight, what did that leave? There was the trunk-or-treat scene of Aaron's abduction, but the bulk of that material was also at the Command Center. And there was Rachel Nicholson's abduction. If he went on the assumption that the two kidnappings were related, what unanswered questions remained about the Nicholson case?

One D'Antonio constantly revisited was how Virgil Rutledge got to and from the cabin out by Pine Gap, or anywhere else for that matter. They'd never found an abandoned vehicle near the cabin's access roads. He certainly hadn't hitched a ride with Rachel tucked under his arm. There were no witnesses to Rachel's abduction, and they hadn't gotten any usable tire tracks from there or the DNR cabin where they'd found some of Rachel's belongings. The anonymous tip that led them to the scene had pointed at a dark van. Granted, a van was the stereotypical pedophile's ride of choice, but that anonymous tip felt more suspect to Luther by the moment. He needed to track down the original tip sheet, and a recording if they had it.

That brought to mind the white van spotted at Aaron Schofield's abduction that led them to the raid in Loganville and the arrest of its owner, Randall Vogler. Despite the drugs he was carrying, the man had no prior arrests. After waiving his rights, he'd said his wife had kicked him out of the house a couple of weeks before (the Feds were tracking her down) and his business van was the only vehicle he'd had access to since then. Vogler claimed that Friday night, while the boy was being kidnapped, he'd gone to a Halloween party with some friends. If his alibi checked out, it seemed unlikely Vogler was directly involved with the boy's kidnapping, but D'Antonio felt—and Luther agreed—there was *something* there. For now, he was being held on the drug charges and they were working on getting the van impounded for forensic analysis.

Luther swallowed, and his tongue stuck to the roof of his mouth. The missed meals and crappy coffee had left him with a vile taste, and he wished he had a toothbrush. He stood and walked toward reception. He'd stopped keeping peppermints at his own desk, but maybe Beth had some in the candy dish out front...

The candy. What ever happened to the goddamned pinwheel candy he'd noticed at the DNR cabin, that Les had been chomping on at the Command Center? That candy had set Luther's search for his brother in motion. When he'd finally tracked Les down at home, they'd argued—Luther felt the thin red line on his hand from the freshly healed cut. Luther had bagged the candy he'd found in Les's house, intending to run it for prints. But they'd taken Virgil into custody soon after, and processing the candy slipped his mind. Had he left it in the vehicle?

Luther's hip bumped painfully against the front desk as he hurried outside without his coat. If the parking lot were better lit, Luther would've seen his exhalations. The cold jolted him a little closer to awake. He'd been driving the department's SUV that night. He dug everything out of the glovebox and piled it on the passenger's seat, even shone a flashlight around the area and beneath it, but the candy was nowhere to be found. Someone must have tossed it by now.

It was his own fault, but he couldn't get too upset. Learning anything from the candy had been a longshot. Maybe... He jammed everything back in the glovebox. Then Luther sat in the dark and called up the scene from Les's trailer again. This time, he tried to look past his brother's body, to the coffee table next to him. Had there been a pinwheel wrapper there, or was his wishful imagination creating it?

He knew one way to find out. Grant wouldn't have called everyone in for the middle-of-the-night briefing, but Luther was sure he would've wanted Beth. And, although they had gotten off to a rocky start, Luther thought Beth was starting to soften toward him. He hoped he was right on both counts, and pulled out his cell phone. It rang several times before she answered.

"Luther, where the hell are you?" she asked, voice a loud whisper. "You know you're supposed to be here."

Luther opted for honesty. "Would you have showed up, if you were me?"

"I don't know," she admitted.

"And what do you think the chances are I would've made it out of the building without laying somebody out?"

She made a sound that was close kin to a laugh. "Point taken. What do you want?"

"I need you to check something for me, if you can, without making a spectacle of yourself," Luther said. "Have the photos from Les's place been downloaded?"

"You don't ask much, do you? Tell me what you're looking for, and I'll give you a call back in a minute."

Luther did, and true to her intent if not exactly to her word, Beth called him back in four minutes. "You were right—there was an empty wrapper, and it was taken into evidence. I'll see if I can't encourage it toward the front of the line on fingerprints."

Luther smiled. "Thanks, Beth. I owe you a beer."

"You wish," she said. "You owe me at least two."

Luther shivered, the cold finally catching up with him. He locked up his vehicle and headed inside. Then he cleaned out the coffee pot and prepped the next batch. Back in his office, he set his head on his desk, just for a minute. Or maybe just a couple of hours...

50

————

Adam wasn't sure what had roused him. The only sounds were the shush of his found blanket against the crackling plastic beneath him, and the reassuring rhythm of Harlan's breathing across the room. Adam had nearly drifted off again when the thought arose, *But Harlan's not in his bed.*

It was dark in the old house, but not pitch black. Harlan sat in the sole chair next to the window, chin upon his hand. He'd pulled the curtain to one side, leaning to see outside without being seen. A patch of reflected moonlight found its way in through the gap, coming to rest on the bare floor.

"Did I wake you?" Harlan asked, without looking in Adam's direction.

"I don't think so. What woke you?"

"An old man's prostate," Harlan said.

He was lying. "What do you see?" Adam asked.

"Nothing," Harlan said. "Just trees. There's nothing out there to see."

"That's not what I meant. *What do you see?*"

Now Harlan turned to face him in the dark. "Nothing," he repeated.

He was still lying. Adam knew Harlan had seen something in his mind that, for some reason, he wasn't willing to voice. But he also knew no amount of pushing would convince Harlan to share before he was ready. "Do you think Teddy meant to leave us here, from the start?" Adam asked.

Adam couldn't see his face, but the silver of Harlan's hair showed faintly in the dark. "No. Teddy and I don't always agree on everything, but he wouldn't do something like that just to spite me. And he certainly wouldn't involve you."

"So you think something happened with Danny and Virgil to trigger him. Could he have been communicating directly with Virgil then? Like a conversation?"

"Maybe," Harlan said. "Hard to say. It's something Teddy and I don't talk about much, the details. After years of Lawrence and everyone else picking away at what we can and can't do, we tend to want to be private about it."

So Teddy could have left as a result of something Virgil "told" him. But Adam could conjure another possibility. "You also said Teddy can see the future, that you both can."

"I did not!" Harlan's raised voice went raspy. They'd found a couple of gallons of bottled water tucked beneath the sink, but they'd been rationing it, perhaps too cautiously.

"No one can 'see the future,'" Harlan said, rising and pulling the curtain shut. The room went even darker, and Harlan's footsteps advanced slowly toward his own cot. "At most, we get glimpses of things that might happen."

Adam heard springs creak and the mattress crackle as Harlan lay upon it. "Do you ever try to change what'll happen, because of that glimpse?" Adam asked.

Harlan sighed. "Three a.m. is too goddamned late to be having this kind of conversation."

"Why, do you have plans for tomorrow?"

"No, but you do," Harlan said.

"What do you mean?"

Harlan shifted and grunted on his thin mattress, then said, "You managed to hang onto your cell phone, didn't you?"

Adam had—it had been in his pocket rather than his duffel, which was who-knew-where by now—but how had Harlan known?

"You left it on the goddamned nightstand, Sherlock," Harlan said, answering the question Adam hadn't asked aloud. "I have a feeling Teddy's gonna be too busy to worry about getting us a ride out of here anytime soon. You need to hike up the mountain tomorrow and see if you can reach someone, before we start eating each other's toes."

"You're going to stay here?" The thought made Adam uneasy, but he couldn't say why.

"Son, do you know how old I am?"

"No, sir."

"Old enough to pull the age card while you go on walkabout. Shouldn't take more than a few hours, without me slowing you down. Now get some sleep."

But sleep was elusive. Adam felt split inside. He worried about Aaron Schofield—was the child still alive, and was he *whole*? Where was Danny now, and what was his endgame? What would happen when Adam returned to Cold Springs—would he be arrested? Would Iris and Harlan? When he thought of JJ, he felt a niggling, inexplicable anxiety, similar to the uneasiness he'd felt at the prospect of Harlan alone tomorrow. Finally, the specter of his father invading—or simply destroying—his mind hung over him.

At the same time, Adam was so exhausted he felt empty inside. And, stranded in this simple house, he was so physically isolated from the seething anxiety the rest of the world represented, it all seemed unreal.

"Harlan, you awake?" he asked.

"What?" As in, *what do you want now*. Not, *what did you say*.

"Did you kill Lawrence?"

"Does it matter?"

Adam's elbow banged against the wall as he put a hand under

his head. "I imagine it did to Lawrence. And he was my grandfather."

Harlan's sigh felt palpable in the dark, like a wave across Adam's skin. "No, I didn't kill him."

"Virgil thinks you did. He saw it."

"He doesn't know what he saw."

"I know what he saw," Adam said. "He showed me, multiple times, when he was in my head."

"And?"

"I can't decide if he was trying to warn me out of genuine concern, or just to confuse me," Adam admitted. "Either way, he didn't want me to trust you."

"Did it work?"

"Why do you think I can't sleep?" Adam had meant it as a joke, but neither man laughed.

"Good night," Harlan said.

Adam rolled over to face the wall, but instead of finding a better sleeping position, something poked him in the ribs. It was his cell phone jammed in his jacket pocket, the cell phone he now recalled tucking there, out of Teddy's and Harlan's sight, in a moment of judicious paranoia. And he hadn't consciously thought about it since. So how had Harlan known he'd kept the phone?

51

Danny tried to catch a few hours of sleep at an interstate rest stop with tractor-trailers stacked like cordwood at the far end. He leaned his seat back and thought he'd sleep like a baby. After all, no one knew this vehicle, and the boy had never been in it. He'd left the motel room clean, or at least clean enough not to cause suspicion. It was done. He was clear of it. Why wouldn't he sleep like a baby? Or rather, why didn't he?

Because Danny still wasn't done (*fucking Adam*) and he couldn't help but think he wasn't clear of it, either. His head had a dry ache, and the inside of his skull felt oddly tender and alternately hot and cold, like a bad sunburn. He was occasionally racked by shuddering chills, and he'd compulsively checked the rearview mirror while driving—not for pursuing law enforcement, but for blood. He'd even had to pull over once for a nosebleed.

It was hard to believe Virgil had been telling the truth after all. Adam had gotten to Danny—*in Danny*—somehow, and he wasn't sure the man was entirely gone. Adam had been easy to recognize—he'd spoken in Danny's head, for Christ's sake—but Adam hadn't been alone. Danny didn't have whatever weird powers Adam had, but he'd been poked and prodded by Virgil enough over the years for him to recognize that feeling, for him to smell the man that had been his father trying to penetrate his mind.

There'd been others there, too. One had stayed in the shadows, close to Virgil, while the second had attached himself to Adam. He didn't know who they were, but it didn't matter. The real danger had come from Adam and Virgil. The crazy old man and his favorite son, back together again. Virgil must be thrilled. *Sonuvabitch.* How could he turn against Danny like this? What had Adam ever done for him?

Maybe Virgil was back in one of his psychotic spirals, the ones that had terrified Danny when he couldn't bring himself to run away from their life together. Virgil would get lost in archetypes and symbols and epic struggles he saw manifested in bizarre ways in the world around them. He'd speak to voices Danny couldn't hear, on and on and on, and eventually Danny thought he heard them, too. That is, until Danny figured out on his own how to make them stop. But this... Danny couldn't figure out how to make Adam stop. And so he hadn't slept well, constantly vigilant not for a tap at his car window, but a tap at his mind.

He gave up before the first hint of light, turned on the radio to hear the news, and learned the boy had been found—alive. After a shocked moment of recrimination (*what the fuck was I thinking letting him see my face?*), Danny grew philosophical. It was unlikely the boy, having seen him briefly while drugged out of his mind, would be able to identify him. It was equally unlikely they'd find any physical evidence on the child that could connect him to Danny. Plus anything forensics found was useless without something from Danny (or his vehicle, clothing, etc.) for comparison. That meant, barring some new information from outside, it became an investigative loop where the authorities had to suspect him in order to know they should suspect him.

Honestly, the boy surviving was a bit of a relief. He'd believed the child was dead (Danny had been unable to find pulse or breath, but he wasn't at his best at the time), but Danny's heart had never been in killing him. The deputy's brother, on the other hand...

Danny had never cared for Leslie Beck, and probably daydreamed of killing the bully when they were children. Danny sat in the parking lot for twenty minutes, switching compulsively among the half-dozen staticky stations, and didn't hear a word about the man. The reports didn't even say where the boy had been recovered. So was the fat-ass dead or alive, or somewhere in between? And did they believe Les was involved?

Danny hadn't expected Les to be a serious suspect, but he'd figured it would muddy the water for a while, finding a dead child in the bed of a deputy's dead druggie brother. Maybe Les was dead, and the authorities were trying to make sense of the scenario before letting the press in. Or maybe Les was alive, talking to the authorities right now about his friendly neighborhood drug dealer.

No, Danny couldn't believe that. It was possible that the man had survived—Danny had wanted Les's death to look like an accidental overdose, and he could've miscalculated the dosage of the cocktail he'd given the overweight addict. But even if he had, he found it hard to believe that first, the man had recovered enough to speak with the authorities, and second, that he'd do so if he had. Les Beck had inherited his father's distrust of law enforcement, and, if conscious, he may initially have hopes of retaining his job. Once he'd realized that ship had sailed, Les still had no reason to talk because he had no reason to think Danny/Mitch had meant to kill him. So far as Les knew, he'd overdosed on his own, and his no-snitch code would kick in. (Again, he had all of his father's alternative ethics, but with none of his critical discernment.)

Except... Danny had left the kid in Les's bedroom. Thinking they were both dead. *Goddammit!* He'd been so absorbed by outsmarting everyone else that he'd outsmarted himself. Danny white-knuckled the steering wheel of the parked car, rolling his grip back and forth, teeth grinding. In his peripheral vision, he saw an SUV pull into the neighboring spot. He breathed deeply and stared at the little insignia on the driver's air bag, pretending it meant something. One thing he'd learned over the course of his convoluted life was that you had to rein it in while people could see you.

There was nothing to be done now except to not be so goddamned stupid the next time. *The next time.* What did that even mean? He couldn't think long-term right now; he had to concentrate on making it through the next few days. He still had options, but before he made a plan, he'd really like to know where he stood with Leslie Beck.

Danny started the car, drove up the long on-ramp and merged into the interstate traffic, getting heavier as the morning began in earnest. The next sign showed the exit nearest Cold Springs was just a few miles ahead. Virgil would declare that serendipity a sign, and maybe he'd be right. A few minutes in the town had low risk (Les Beck was the only person who'd seen him, and even he didn't know who Danny really was) for a potentially great peace of mind benefit. And who knew how inspiration would strike in his old hometown.

52

———

"**M**om! Did you hear me?" Evie demanded.

JJ lifted her chin from her hands. "Evie, I think everyone in the restaurant heard you."

Otto smiled at JJ sympathetically. He'd met her at the diner with the girls so she could have breakfast with them before school. Of course, they'd made those plans before JJ had spent the night being interrogated and napping on the break room couch. One of the deputies had given her a ride to the grocery store to get her car this morning, and she'd driven straight to the diner. Thank God for strong deodorant and the bottomless cup of coffee. Still, she supposed if Otto could sit in a booth designed for a man half his size and pretend to be interested listening to their girls prattle on about Phys Ed class, she could too.

"Sorry, sweetie. If it makes you feel any better, dodgeball scarred me too. I still have flashbacks." JJ reached across the booth and ostentatiously covered Otto's ears with her hands. "It's even worse when you get boobs."

Evie rolled her eyes, but Rachel laughed. Of course, JJ managed to knock over the bottle of syrup with said boobs while sitting down. She slammed her napkin onto the sticky mess. "See what I mean." She sighed when she saw that some of the syrup had dripped onto her scrub pants. She'd been working so many crazy shifts lately, she wasn't sure she had an extra pair in reserve. "I'd better go take care of this. I'll be back."

Evie sighed dramatically, as if her mother had asked her to hike Spruce Knob barefoot rather than simply slide out of a booth to let her pass. JJ tried to muss her daughter's hair in revenge, and Evie knocked the ketchup over dodging her.

"That one is all on you," JJ said, pointing for Evie to clean up the smear on the table.

On her way to the bathroom, JJ passed Luther sitting alone at the counter—also still in uniform—and sat on the stool next to him. "Any change?" she asked.

"No," Luther said, drinking his coffee as though it were a necessary chore. By the looks of the bags under his eyes, it was. He raised his mug for a refill and went back to his pancakes. "Still critical, but still alive. Thank you."

JJ shrugged. "I did what I could." She knew Les wasn't out of the woods yet, so she suppressed the urge to offer words of comfort.

"You said you guys have seen a lot of drug overdoses this year. Mostly opioids?" Luther asked.

"Yes," she said, then held her tongue. They were ranging into uncertain territory now, where she'd have to choose whether to tell Luther everything she knew, or everything she suspected.

"Any idea where all the drugs are coming from?" Luther asked.

It was not the question she'd expected, though it probably should have been. "I don't. And I don't know how much anyone else at the hospital will know either, but I'd be happy to ask around if you'd like."

"I appreciate it," Luther said.

JJ nodded and rose to leave, but Luther tapped her back down. "Not so fast," he said, then leaned closer and lowered his voice. "You need to come by today about the TRO."

JJ shook her head. "No, I don't. I was upset, and I overreacted."

Luther rested his silverware on his plate and swung on his round stool to face her. "You did not overreact. I told Beth what happened. She can't do anything until you come in, but she's expecting you."

JJ's face tingled, and her breath stuck in her throat. "Luther, you interfering, overbearing, nosy..." She was at a loss for more words.

Luther wiped the corners of his mustache with a napkin and fluttered his eyelashes. "You got any more of those fancy compliments for me?"

JJ breathed through her nose, and the air whistled inelegantly. "No," she said, "not right now. I don't want to use them all at once."

Luther fluttered his eyelashes again. *Stupid man.* She smiled and smacked him on the arm as she passed. He might be stupid, but against her better judgment she was starting to think he was okay. Or maybe it was just another side effect of the exhaustion.

JJ pulled ineffectually on the bathroom door. How many years had she been coming here, *pushing* on the damned bathroom door? She compensated for her initial failure by pushing too hard, bumping someone on the other side. *Dammit.* She released the door and waited for it to open from the inside.

"I'm sorry," JJ said, as a permed gray head appeared through the doorway. *It would be cranky, old Ms. Hildebrand.*

"JJ Tulley, I don't know what the hell kind of fire you think you're rushing off to!"

Watch your temper. She wasn't about to cause a scene by yelling at an old woman. And yet, when JJ opened her mouth to reply, a scream rang out.

JJ closed her mouth in surprise. A moment later another shrill scream *(that definitely wasn't me)* pierced the air behind her. *It was one of the girls.*

53

Luther spun toward the bloodcurdling sound, dropping his fork on the floor. A stunned man stood in the diner's entryway. In his early thirties, he was about six feet tall, medium build, with short, dark brown hair just beginning to curl. He looked almost as exhausted as Luther felt, and he was in need of a shave. The man's eyes locked on Rachel, who was screaming her ever-loving head off. Then his gaze swung to Luther as he rose from his stool. Luther was certain he'd never seen the man before, but he was equally certain the man recognized him, not just his uniform.

The man blinked, then turned and ran out the door.

Luther followed. He still felt the aches from the previous day's chase and knew he didn't have a chance in hell of catching the man, but by God he was going to try. The door shut just before Luther reached it, and he fumbled to open the damn thing. He finally slammed his weight against it, falling awkwardly through, and paused outside the diner. *Where the hell is he?* Small businesses stretched on either side of the restaurant, but there were plenty of buffering trees and parking lots between them.

Otto burst out the door behind Luther. "Where —"

"I don't know," Luther said, as a blur of movement down the street caught his eye. "There!"

The two men sprinted down the sidewalk. Short distances had always been Luther's strength, and he'd tied his boots more tightly today. It didn't matter—they reached the next corner in time to see a sedan peel out of a closed used car lot. "You get the license?" Luther panted.

"Just a partial," Otto said. "One C-K. I didn't catch the rest."

Luther couldn't get his breath to save his life. He might have to take the old Sheriff's advice and get back on the running regimen. "Yeah, that's all I got too."

There was no point in pursuit. By the time Luther made it back to his vehicle, the car would be long gone. It was already out of sight. "You have any idea who that was?"

"Never seen him before," Otto said.

There was a low hum of disturbed conversation when they entered the diner, louder than it had been five minutes ago, but not a mob scene. Nina had been working the tables there for forty years, and she had a gift for getting people to settle down and act their ages. Rachel sat between Evie and JJ, and JJ had her arms around the girl. Rachel's face was so pale, it reminded Luther of the last time he'd seen her in JJ's arms, when JJ carried her down off the mountain. The image was so sudden and tangible, he paused to steady himself against the counter.

As soon as she saw her father, Rachel tore herself from JJ and tackled Otto, disappearing in the huge man's embrace. "Shh, baby, you're okay. You're okay now."

Luther knelt next to the frightened girl. He didn't want to startle her by touching her, so he waited for her to look at him. "Rachel, sweetie, your daddy's right. You're safe now. But I need to know, can you tell me who that man was?"

Rachel looked at him, at Otto, at JJ, and at every other adult in the restaurant as if they were all the biggest idiots she'd ever seen. Finally she said, "That's the man who took me."

~

"RACHEL," Agent D'Antonio said, sitting next to the Sheriff behind his desk, "you never mentioned before that two men took you."

And you never mentioned before that you're a complete asshole, but somehow I figured it out, Luther thought. He straightened from his lean against the filing cabinets and began, "Sir —", but Grant raised his hand to give Rachel an opportunity to answer.

"I don't remember everything. And I didn't remember the younger man until I saw him this morning," Rachel said, squeezing Otto's hand tightly.

"Rachel," Grant said, "I have a couple of pictures I'd like you to look at and tell me if you recognize the people. Can you do that?"

She nodded, and Grant slid a photograph across his desk. Luther stiffened. The first picture was of his brother, Leslie.

"Of course I know him," she said simply. "He lives here."

Grant paused, and Luther could tell he was struggling to find the right words, ones that wouldn't suggest an answer to his question. Impatient, Luther blurted out, "Did he ever hurt you?"

Luther avoided Grant's gaze and found D'Antonio glaring at him instead. Rachel just looked confused. "No," she said. "He stinks sometimes, like at the trunk-or-treat, but I guess he's okay."

Grant flipped the photo over and slid another one across the desk, this time of Virgil. Instead of picking it up, Rachel stood from her chair and stared down at it. She said, in a small voice, "That's the man who chased me through the woods when I tried to get away."

"And what about the other man? The one you saw today?" Grant asked.

"The other man is the one who grabbed me on our road. Down from Evie's driveway."

Grant slid the photo away and tucked it in a folder, then set the folder out of sight. "The last time we talked, you couldn't remember anything about when he took you. How about now?"

Rachel sat back down and looked at her father. It seemed to Luther that she desperately wanted to crawl in Otto's lap and disappear. "Not exactly. A lot of the time I was sick and I couldn't breathe."

"Do you remember anything about the car you were in?" Grant continued.

She looked up toward the ceiling. "Not from the beginning. But later, I think there was a van. A white van."

"Rachel," D'Antonio said, "did you ever see the two men together at the same time? The man in the picture who chased you and the man from the diner this morning?"

"No." She glanced at Otto before continuing in a whisper. "But I think I heard them talking to each other. When I was dying."

Otto tensed, and Grant looked away. Only D'Antonio appeared unmoved. "Do you know what they were saying?" he asked.

She shook her head. "But Adam might know."

The agent's breath caught; if Luther hadn't been watching him, he'd have missed it. "What do you mean Adam might know? Adam Rutledge? Was he with them?"

Rachel looked to Otto. "I don't want to get him in trouble," she whispered.

"You're not going to get him in trouble," D'Antonio said, but Rachel wasn't stupid. And now the man was eager.

"Dad, I'm going to be late for school," Rachel said. Luther's heart went out to her. The poor child must be desperate if she was begging to go to school.

"Okay, sweetie," Otto said, before turning to D'Antonio. "We're done here."

"Rachel, why would Adam know? Was he with those men, too? Are they his friends?" D'Antonio asked.

"I said, we're done here." Otto placed his free hand—the one that wasn't occupied with his daughter—palm down on the desk. Luther bet Otto could flip the heavy piece of furniture with just one of those massive hands.

Rachel answered anyway. "No, they're not his friends. And he wasn't ever with them. He was with me. In my head, before he found me and Evie's mom took me down the mountain. That's how he heard them, too."

Grant said, "I'm sorry, Otto, but if I could just ask Rachel one more thing. Do you have any idea where the man who took you lives? Or where he's going?"

"He doesn't live here," she said. "But I think he came to the trunk-or-treat. That's why I felt sick."

"You can call us about speaking with her again later." Otto wrapped an arm around his daughter and led her toward the reception area where JJ and Evie were waiting for them.

Rachel hesitated at the door. "I think he's going home."

"You think who's going home?" Grant asked.

"The man who took me."

"Why is that?" Grant asked.

Rachel shrugged. "I don't know. I just do."

"What I meant was, why does he want to go home?" Grant clarified.

"Because it's the only place he feels safe."

54

Evie insisted that she and her mother wait at the Sheriff's Department while Rachel was being questioned. Beth, the deputy on the desk, was kind enough to tolerate Evie's persistent, hovering questions (*Have you ever used your handcuffs? Do you know how to pick a lock? How fast could one of the cruisers go if you floored it on the straight stretch out by the Howards' farm?*). That allowed JJ to sit on a plastic chair, purse on her lap, motionless except for her churning brain. What the hell was going on?

The man from the diner had been running by the time JJ turned, so she hadn't gotten a look at his face. There'd been no security footage from the diner or anywhere on the street where he would have passed. No doubt they'd generate sketches from the witnesses—including Rachel—but so far no one except Rachel admitted to having seen him before.

How could this stranger have kidnapped Rachel? Virgil Rutledge had taken Rachel—JJ and Adam had rescued her from him! Or had they? Virgil had certainly tried to kill Adam when he ran with Rachel. Virgil had said he thought she was dead, but what else had the man said? JJ went back to the cold mountain in her mind, back to the crazy man tied on the ground. *I was trying to protect her. From him... He's the one who did it. He's the one who always does it. And I can't stop him. You have to help me stop him...*

The best-case scenario appeared to be Virgil Rutledge wasn't working alone. The worst case didn't bear thinking about.

Motion caught JJ's attention as Otto emerged from the back, gently shepherding his daughter. A small girl—almost delicate— Rachel looked downright tiny in front of Otto. JJ rose, but Evie beat her to the pair and took Rachel's hand unselfconsciously.

"Did you know there are cops that work with dogs? That working with dogs is their actual, everyday job?" Evie took Rachel to Beth's desk to see something—JJ assumed photographic evidence of the best job in the world.

Otto's face was pinched, with fine lines around his mouth and forehead, and his bottom lip lifted in the center as if it were on a string.

"You okay?" JJ asked.

He jerked his head in something approximating a nod, and JJ watched his shoulders inch slowly away from his ears.

"You talk to Dorothy yet?" JJ asked. Otto looked heavenward in reply. "So she's freaking out?"

"Ha! Freaking out doesn't begin to cover it," Otto said.

"At least it happened at the diner and not at the River Lounge," JJ said, referring to the restaurant where Dorothy waitressed.

This time, Otto genuinely laughed. "Yes, I am thankful for that. Although Dorothy probably would have taken Luther's gun and shot the guy, which might not have been a bad thing."

Otto's voice trailed off and his jaw clenched beneath his sparse beard. Whoever the stranger was, he better hope Otto never got his hands on him.

"So what's your plan for Rachel today?" JJ asked.

"Dorothy wanted her to go home, but she's at work right now, and Rachel wants to go to class, so..."

"You want us to drive to school with you?"

The girls heard JJ's offer, and Rachel's face looked particularly hopeful.

Beth approached and cleared her throat. "Ms. Tulley, don't forget you have some paperwork to finish up for us."

Damn—the TRO. JJ was too flustered to come up with a convincing excuse. "But you don't need that right now, do you? Evie has to get to school."

"It is important for the, uh, *investigation* to make sure we've got our information straight." Beth stared at Otto significantly as she emphasized the word investigation. She continued, "And I'm sure Mr. Nicholson and Rachel wouldn't mind taking Evie to school with them."

Otto regarded both women, then said, "Of course. No problem at all. And either Dorothy or I will be picking up Rachel this afternoon—remember, it's a short day—if you'd like us to bring Evie home, too."

JJ glanced at the clock and did some quick calculations (*mechanic about picking up a couple of retread tires, grocery store to replace the spoiled milk and everything I forgot, nap, fix dinner, back for late shift*) before admitting, "That would be perfect, Otto. Thanks."

She was lucky to get a goodbye out of Evie, so focused was she on Rachel and her well-being. Evie was still holding Rachel's hand as they left the building. JJ hoped her daughter didn't become overbearing in her protectiveness.

"Your daughter is quite a girl," Beth said.

"Huh," JJ said, neither agreeing nor disagreeing. "You're quite a woman yourself, implying to Otto that you needed me to help find the man who kidnapped Aaron Schofield and possibly his own daughter. I could hardly say no, could I?"

"I was giving you an easy excuse to stick around," Beth said, retreating behind the main desk, which was almost as tall as she was.

JJ snorted, but followed her. "Really?"

"Fine." The deputy's broad face was unyielding as she countered, "I was trying to make sure your daughter doesn't come home from school one day to find her mother's bled out on the floor."

JJ opened her mouth, but Beth continued, "I know what you're going to say, and don't. I've been a cop for eight years, and I'm guessing you've worked in the ER at least that long. We both know it's not true. *He will.*"

"Don't tell me what my husband will and will not do," JJ shot back. "And don't think you know me."

She huffed out of the office, wishing the damned door would slam after her. Outside, the morning sun blinded her exhausted eyes, and she blinked to find her Bronco where she'd parked it beneath a tree. The cool air—she kept forgetting her damned jacket—took the edge off her temper. Instead of getting in her vehicle, she sat on the back bumper, hoping to smooth out the rest. What was wrong with her?

JJ had to confront a very ugly truth. Beth was right—she'd seen so many women in the ER over the years, victims of the men (and sometimes women) in their lives. And she'd cared for them and wanted so much to make them whole again. She'd often—especially in the early days, and with the most appalling cases—entertained fantasies of retribution while doing what she could to heal them. Her compassion was genuine, and yet—here was the ugly part—she always thought of them as different from her. Maybe even *less than* her. Because JJ would never let those things happen to her or her child.

She kept thinking that, even after Marcus threatened her, and even after he laid hands on her. JJ had all sorts of rationales for why she didn't want to file against Marcus, and some of them even made sense. But in the end, she didn't want to do so because she didn't want to be *one of them*.

JJ's epiphany was cut short when her cell phone rang. To her surprise, it was her mechanic, who seemed to have anticipated her call.

"Hey, Stan," she said. "I was going to drop by this morning—I had a little problem with one of my tires and wanted to see if you could track down a couple of retreads."

If she didn't replace her spare with two matched tires, she'd throw off the rest of them, but she couldn't afford to buy two brand new tires.

"No problem, JJ," Stan said. "I'll get right on it. Still driving the Bronco?"

"Until the zombie apocalypse."

"Cool," he said, but sounded uncomfortable. "Hey, this is kinda weird, but I got a call from my brother."

"Is he okay?" JJ asked. Stan's brother was one of the many overdoses who'd come through the ER. It'd been about six months ago, he'd thanked her profusely, and she hadn't seen him since.

"He's hanging in there. I don't know if you know, but Jamie's got a reputation."

For getting people what they want without asking questions. "I know," JJ said. "That's why it's called a reputation."

"Yeah. Well, he doesn't do that kind of stuff anymore, but he still gets calls. Yesterday, he got a call from Marcus."

JJ's mouth went dry. "Oh, yeah?"

"He wanted a gun."

JJ didn't know what to say. You could legally buy pretty much any kind of gun from pretty much anybody in the Mountain State, so JJ could only think of two reasons for her ex to seek out Stan's brother: because Marcus was a cheap bastard, and because he didn't want a record of the purchase.

Stan continued, "I just thought you should know. I'll get on those tires, give you a call when I find something. Take care of yourself, JJ."

"Thanks, Stan. I will."

Beth seemed surprised to see JJ back in the Sheriff's Department so soon. But not that surprised. She pulled a clipboard from her desk and slid it toward JJ. The printed pages swam, and JJ swiped a hand across her exhausted eyes.

"Where do I sign?"

55

———

Once Otto and Rachel had left Grant's office, D'Antonio and Luther settled into their chairs.

"What the hell are we supposed to do with the stuff about Adam being in her head?" D'Antonio asked. He covered his face with his hands and leaned back in the chair. "A traumatized kid trying to make sense of things that can't be made sense of, leaning on... what—the magical?"

"The paranormal," Grant corrected, but didn't elaborate.

Luther wasn't keen to jump in, either. He didn't know what the hell to believe when it came to Adam Rutledge. He didn't generally go in for superstitious mumbo jumbo, but he couldn't explain how Adam had found the girl, nor could he explain some of the things he'd *nearly* seen on the mountain with him that night, things slipping in and out of the shadows. Whatever it had been, he didn't care to repeat the experience.

"Do we have any evidence of Adam Rutledge having contact—actual, physical, corporeal contact—with the girl Rachel Nicholson before he and Ms. Tulley retrieved her?" D'Antonio asked.

"No," Grant answered.

"Do we have any indication of a recent relationship—or contact of any kind—between Adam Rutledge and his father Virgil?" D'Antonio continued.

"According to Adam, he didn't even know his father was alive until a couple of weeks ago," Grant said.

"I know he told us that in the hospital, but do we have any corroboration?" D'Antonio asked.

Grant spread his hands wide. "Something like that's kinda hard to prove, especially since Adam hasn't lived here in twenty years."

"And tell me again why Rutledge came back here when the Nicholson girl was kidnapped?" D'Antonio's tone of voice suggested he didn't expect a satisfactory answer.

"To visit his grandmother," Luther said, tired of being silent, but it didn't even sound convincing to his own ears.

"That Iris Rutledge is a piece of work," D'Antonio observed. "You think she knew her son was alive?"

"Probably, on some level," Grant said. "But do I think she knew what he was up to? At least so far as Rachel Nicholson is concerned, no."

"So let's recap. We've got two contemporary kidnapped children, safely recovered. We've got two... *historical* kidnapped children, dead and presumably dead."

"Any more on the second set of remains from up on the mountain?" Luther asked.

D'Antonio shook his head. "Young male, older than twelve but younger than twenty. We're going with the working theory Virgil Rutledge kept Danny Carpenter alive for a couple of years, but we're still waiting on forensic confirmation."

"That also assumes a working theory that Virgil Rutledge kidnapped Danny Carpenter," Grant added, "which is a good working theory, but one entirely without hard evidence."

"And what about Sarah Edmunds?" Luther asked. "Do we have a manner of death yet?"

"Her injuries were consistent with falling," Grant said, "and the preliminary examination found nothing to contradict accidental death."

"For what that's worth, with the condition of the remains," D'Antonio added. "So we've got Adam Rutledge connected to three of the four—"

"How do you figure?" Luther asked. He'd hoped they were past the Adam thing.

D'Antonio held up a finger for each in turn. "Danny Carpenter, Rachel Nicholson, and Aaron Schofield."

"What's his connection to Schofield? He has an alibi for the abduction."

"He ran," D'Antonio replied. "Innocent men don't run."

"Please!" Luther laughed. "That's not a connection. And innocent men do stupid shit all the time. You know they lie, usually poorly and usually about stupid things. Seems to me the same motivations that lead innocent men to lie could also lead them to run."

"I don't want to argue psychology with you—"

"Fine. Then how about math? Virgil Rutledge is connected to three of the four victims, and he happens to be in custody, which gives him bonus points." Luther put his head back and slid his hat over his face, appreciating the relative darkness if not the musky smell of head sweat. "Of course, Virgil is crazier than a shithouse rat."

The three men sat in silence for a minute or two, perhaps succumbing to exhaustion. Finally, Grant said, "All right, then. We'll interview the man again."

Luther started to rise, but Grant said, "Wait, Luther. There's one other thing." The Sheriff fiddled with a pen on his desk, a sure sign he was putting off something unpleasant.

"What's up, boss?" Luther asked. "Is it about Les? Esther's not changing her story, is she?" He couldn't imagine she would, but lately he was in a worst-case scenario kind of mood, and her backing out on Les's alibi for the kidnapping would qualify.

"No, Esther's holding firm. You brought everything to the

hospital you could find, right?" Grant asked. "I mean, drugs and drug paraphernalia from Les's trailer."

Luther did his best to ignore the sudden, sick feeling in the pit of his stomach. "So far as I know, but I was about one drugged body away from a total freak-out, so it's possible I missed something. Why?"

Grant set the pen aside and met Luther's questioning gaze. "I've been talking with Les's doctors about his symptoms and the preliminary tox screens, and we've had techs go over his place. There are some inconsistencies."

"What kind of inconsistencies?" Luther asked, sure he knew what Grant was about to tell him, and yet reluctant to hear it.

"Traces of chemicals in Les's system that aren't accounted for by what was recovered at the scene."

And there it is. In truth, Luther had known all along, but he refused to jump to that conclusion in front of the federal agent. "Could he have taken something elsewhere and made it home before it took effect?"

"Possible, but unlikely," Grant said. "These were all derivatives of something quite fast-acting. Les would have felt the effects within minutes. Do you believe Esther LaRue?"

Luther shrugged. "About everything that matters. I believe she wasn't there when Les took whatever he took, I believe she found him when she said she did and not before, and I believe she didn't see anyone else. So what do you think?"

Grant bowed his head, as if the commission of a crime were his fault because he was the Sheriff and he could imagine it. "That there's a good chance your brother didn't just overdose, that someone tried to murder him. I've been thinking about what connects Les and Aaron, other than both being found unconscious in Les's trailer."

"The drugs," Luther said. "Les apparently had a habit, and poor Aaron had one forced on him for a few days. He wasn't given the same thing as Les, was he?"

"No," Grant said. "Aaron Schofield was heavily sedated. There's some slight bruising around his mouth, suggesting that he was also suffocated."

Luther was momentarily overwhelmed by the image of the blue-lipped child he'd thought was dead, and by the urge to put it right. He cleared his throat. "I've been asking around, trying to put a name to Les's drug dealer."

Grant nodded, and D'Antonio cut in, "Probably someone local, but not Beecham County local."

"Don't shit where you eat," Luther said. "That's what I figured, too."

Grant attempted a smile. "Eloquent as always, Luther. I've put some feelers out, as have our federal friends. But really, until Les comes around and can tell us who his dealer is, it'll be hard to pin down an identity."

You mean, if Les comes around. Luther knew very well there were no guarantees on that account, or of his brother retaining the power of speech, or memory. He could damn well end up a vegetable for the rest of his life—

Luther suddenly realized his boss had been speaking to him, and he hadn't heard a damn word. "Sorry, Sheriff—what's that?"

"I was saying, in the meantime, we could still catch a break on the forensics, either on the van or from Les's place. For now, I'll give Virgil Rutledge's attorney a call and see when she can get over here. You want to set the rest in motion?"

The deputy nodded and rose. "Sure thing. But I need a minute to check in with Beth."

Luther casually headed toward the front desk, but watched to make sure Grant had shut his door before backtracking to look for Gerald Hayes, not Beth. He was starting to appreciate the new deputy's skills, especially around computers, but what Luther wanted could not be pulled off by Beth.

He found Gerald—thankfully alone—in the kitchen, pouring the dregs of a pot of coffee. Luther got straight to the point. "I could use some help with something, but it's one of those 'the less you know the better' kind of deals."

Gerald sipped and winced. "As my sister is so fond of reminding me, I can do stupid. What's the scheme?"

If he weren't so angry at the conniving bastard, Luther would have enjoyed finally having the opportunity to say the words he'd spent his whole law enforcement career yearning to say.

"I need you to go out to my dad's place and bring him in."

56

———

"Breakfast of champions," Harlan said, passing the baked beans to Adam. They'd found a couple of spoons and a can opener, but no bowls or plates, so they took turns eating from the can while sitting on the front steps.

"How did you do it?" Adam asked, scooping up the last bit of beans and dropping his spoon into the can with a clatter.

Harlan leaned back on his elbows. "And which *it* would you be referring to? The *it* where I managed to win your grandmother's heart, or the *it* where I stayed so goddamn handsome for so long?"

Adam squinted and wished he had a hat. "Tempting as the answer to the latter one is, I meant how you saved my life back at Teddy's."

Harlan shrugged. "I had help."

Adam waited, but apparently Harlan had said what he had to say on the subject. "Seriously? Now you're going to be humble?"

"That's something I've never been accused of before," Harlan said.

"Why don't you want to tell me?" The frustration that had been building, settling into Adam's bones and making them grind against each other, began to spill over. "For God's sake, it was my life! I'm the one who almost died, and I don't have a right to know? What if I need to help somebody—"

Harlan wheeled on Adam and stuck a finger in his face. "*That* is exactly why you don't need to know. This isn't like applying a goddamned Band-Aid."

"So I hear," Adam said, thinking of Rachel and how close he'd come there. He held Harlan's angry eyes (*but Harlan is also afraid*). Seeing his own state of mind reflected in the older man helped him let go of the sharpest, grating edges of his anger and fear.

Harlan sighed and rose slowly, perhaps painfully, from his seated position. "Come on then."

They'd found bottled water and paper towels in the kitchen before resorting to a fork-cleaning river hike, so Adam hadn't explored their surroundings. He followed Harlan, across brown grass kept patchy by intermittent trees. More trees congregated, gathering into a loose forest, as the murmuring of water grew louder. It was cool, and Adam shoved his hands into his pockets, just for something to do with them. He was watching the ground, attention caught by individual pebbles and dead blades of grass, when Harlan stopped, and Adam walked face-first into his back.

Harlan turned and gave him stink eye. "Sorry," Adam said.

The majority of the trees in the area were naked maples and other species that Adam once could have identified without their leaves, but no longer. Harlan stood next to one of the few pines, easily fifty feet tall, and gazed heavenward. Branches didn't appear on the trunk until twenty feet or so from the ground. Even then, they began as jutting stumps with no sign of life, before giving way to a sparse, green crown.

"This ought to do," Harlan said. He sat on the ground, and Adam sat next to him.

Adam had a vague recollection of a green canopy overhead while he lay on the ground at Teddy's. "Does it have to be pine trees?" he asked.

"No. As far as power is concerned, the kind of tree doesn't matter, so long as you're near one. I just think the needles on the ground make it more comfortable." He nodded toward the sound of the river. "Proximity to water helps, too."

Adam tucked in cross-legged, while Harlan sat back against the tree with raised knees. "You've probably heard tell of the granny women or granny witches that used to live in the hills."

"Not really," Adam admitted, somehow ashamed, as though he'd shunned his Appalachian heritage by not knowing.

"I shouldn't be surprised," Harlan said. "Iris doesn't much go in for that kind of stuff. Granny witches were mostly Scotch-Irish herbalists and midwives—healers, really, though some of them did divination here and there. Some people say they were on good terms with the local Indian tribes and learned from them. I don't know how much truth there is in that, but they did bring a lot of knowledge with them from the old country."

"Is that who taught Teddy how to make..." Adam paused, but he had no other word for it, "Ass tea?"

Harlan smiled. "No. But from what I've heard, we've got a fair amount in common with them. Many of the witches were Christians—as was your grandfather, in his own way—but that didn't interfere with them acknowledging the power of the earth and natural forces. And that's where power comes from for us—not from the divine, although I guess you could dress it up that way. But this—" Harlan set his palms on the ground, "This is the source of our strength."

"Okay," Adam said. He closed his eyes and smelled the damp earth, similar to the scent that had surrounded him at Teddy's, but overlaid with the aroma of the nearby river.

"This is where we got the power to heal you. Some of it came from me and Teddy, but most of it came from the earth. It's not limitless, but our human bodies and our capacity to... *conduct* it, for lack of a better word, are usually the limiting factors."

Adam had worked a lot of odd jobs over the years and once spent a few days helping an electrician rewire a portion of a building. He'd learned there are few things more unsettling than working with a drunk electrician, unless it's wondering if your house has been wired by one. He'd also learned the most basic principles of working with current, about the importance of choosing the right wire for the job to avoid a structure bursting into flames, about the relationship between run and—

"Resistance," Adam said.

"Exactly." Harlan smiled with satisfaction. "There are things we can do, with time and practice, to reduce that resistance, but there'll always be inefficiencies in the system."

"So how do I tap into the grid?" When the older man didn't answer, Adam asked, "Did I lose the metaphor?"

Harlan's eyes shut and his lips moved so imperceptibly Adam wondered if he'd imagined it. When he opened his eyes, Harlan asked, "Are you sure about this?"

"Yes."

"All right then. Place your palms on the ground."

Adam did. "Does it matter if my eyes are open or closed?"

"That's up to you. Might be easier closed, if you're self-conscious, or when you get to the point of visualizing."

Adam closed his eyes. Harlan instructed him in a slow, mindful way of breathing, something Adam imagined they might do in a yoga or meditation class. The occasional sounds of the forest, of his breathing and of Harlan's, became lost in the constant rushing of the river. Eventually even that became lost in a humming resonance that was neither outside Adam nor within him.

"What do you feel?" Harlan asked.

Adam concentrated on his hands, and a buzzing sensation tickled his skin. He didn't answer out loud, but Harlan continued, "Good. Now go deeper."

The buzzing traveled through Adam's hands, past his wrists and into his forearms, where his skin pricked as the hair stood on end beneath his shirt and coat. And the layers weren't enough. Adam grew suddenly cold, as though he'd dipped his arms into a frigid river. But it didn't stop there. His elbows, his biceps were like ice... Adam's chest grew tight and he gasped as the sensation crept toward his shoulders.

"Enough!" Harlan gripped Adam's wrist, sending a surge of raw energy through both men that knocked Adam backward. Adam opened his eyes.

"Enough," Harlan repeated more gently, his breath crystallizing in the air as though they sat on an Arctic tundra instead of in a temperate forest.

Adam's teeth chattered, and he couldn't stop shaking.

"Just relax. Here," Harlan said, shifting sideways. "Sit over here."

Adam kneed over and settled against the tree.

Harlan gave Adam's shoulders a quick, vigorous rub through his coat. "It's okay. You didn't do anything wrong. You're still recovering from yesterday, and we simply overdid it."

Adam said, "Like blowing a fuse." He shuddered one last time, but the cold was receding already. "You used that analogy in the hospital, about me seeing things through touch, and you said it might never come back. It hasn't exactly—at least, not like yours—but everything else I see and the way I see it... this is who I am, isn't it? Until I die."

The pine trunk wasn't broad enough for both of them, so Harlan scooted his butt across the ground to sit against its nearest neighbor. "It does look that way."

A band of morning sun broke through the thin boughs, trying to thaw the right side of Adam's chest. He closed his eyes and let it. He'd lost that earlier feeling of resonance, but a sensation of warmth had taken its place, spreading even from the cool ground beneath him.

"I said we had things in common with the old granny witches, but there's an important difference between us, too."

Adam didn't bother opening his eyes, but raised an eyebrow.

"Smartass," Harlan said. "I didn't mean because we've got different equipment. There were male water witches, too, and— never mind. It doesn't matter. My point is, supposedly granny witches were an accepted part of a lot of isolated mountain communities. It makes sense—sometimes they were the only doctors to be found for miles around. But people *like us* have never been accepted. We've always lived on the periphery."

"Otto knew about you," Adam said, opening his eyes to challenge Harlan. Rachel's father had been the one to introduce Adam to Harlan in the first place.

"Sure, he knew about me. He'd sought me out years ago because of his first wife. Let me repeat—*he sought me out*. That's the way it has to be. People seek us when they need help, because of all the times in between. All the times they don't want to have to think about what we do, and wonder whether they really want us living next door. Yes, some of the granny witches delved into things that couldn't be seen, whether it was affairs of the heart or spirits or the best places to build or plant. But they could do that because they spent the rest of their time dealing with the *seen* world, the fevers and wounds and warts that plagued people on a regular basis. We don't do that. We're just... scary."

Adam wriggled his fingers through the cool pine needles to the even cooler ground, releasing more scent from both. "Why are you telling me this?"

"I don't know," Harlan said, dismissively.

Adam didn't believe him. "Has something changed? Is something going to change?"

"The world is always changing, son."

Adam rolled his eyes.

"Sorry," Harlan said. "I guess I thought it was something you should know, something you should think about."

Adam stared at the ground, grabbed a handful of pine needles and squeezed them until their chill was gone. Releasing them back to the earth, he watched as they slowly sprang apart, but never quite regained their original shape. "Harlan, I've lived on the periphery my entire life. I just didn't know why. Until now."

57

"You know, I do have a life," Faith Callaway said.

"I'm glad somebody does." Luther could be here, or sitting with his brother at the hospital; he wasn't sure which was preferable.

"Ms. Callaway, I promise you I want to go home—home to Bethesda, that is—as much as you do," D'Antonio said. "But right now we've got a suspect in two kidnappings at large, and your client is the only one who may be able to identify him for us. Our prior agreement holds for this discussion as well, so he's got nothing to lose."

She raised an eyebrow. "Exigent circumstances aside, excuse me if I'm skeptical when a law enforcement officer tells me my client has nothing to lose. When are you transporting Mr. Rutledge to another facility, somewhere they're better able to monitor his mental condition?"

"We're a little short-staffed at the moment," D'Antonio admitted, "and we've had a lot of officers pulling overtime. But as soon as we can spare someone we'll transport him to the facility in Plattsville."

"Tomorrow at the latest," she said.

"Tomorrow at the latest," he agreed.

"Good," she said. "And that better not be contingent on what Mr. Rutledge shares with you today. The antipsychotics haven't had enough time to take hold, if they're even going to have an effect. I doubt you'll get any more—or anything more coherent—from Mr. Rutledge than you did the last time."

"Let's find out," D'Antonio said, the corner of his mouth inching up in a smile.

The man was charming to women, Luther had to give him that. Luther felt an unexpected twinge of jealousy.

Ms. Callaway had insisted on being present in the interview room this time, and Luther believed it would be helpful. She didn't have a lot of rapport with Virgil, but she certainly had more than anyone in law enforcement. Luther didn't voice his thoughts for fear of being smacked, but he also felt her gender was a plus. Unless the purpose was pure intimidation, he believed most interrogations benefitted from diluting the testosterone trapped in a small space. And having a woman present broadened an interrogation's tactical possibilities.

Virgil was already seated, with Deputy Kilbourne watching over him. (Gerald hadn't returned yet from Luther's errand.) Luther took Kilbourne's place, while Ms. Callaway, Grant, and D'Antonio squeezed next to each other to sit opposite Virgil. Callaway sat in the middle. The lawyer had asked to sit next to her client, but D'Antonio had overridden her, citing Virgil's instability as a security concern. Luther wouldn't necessarily say Virgil looked *less* crazy, but he would say he looked *different* crazy. Maybe Luther read too much into Virgil's expressions, but he appeared more calculating today, and less like he was about to make up nonsense nursery rhymes.

Ms. Callaway explained again about the cooperation agreement. Luther had the impression Virgil wasn't listening, but when she asked if he understood and was willing to speak with them, Virgil shifted his attention to her and said yes.

"You know the police—" she began.

"He's with the Sheriff's Department," Virgil interrupted, pointing at Luther. "And so is he," he continued, pointing at Grant.

"Yes, that's true," Callaway said. "And Mr. D'Antonio is a Special Agent with the FBI. I'm sorry if I misspoke—I meant the term police in a generic way."

Virgil nodded. "I just wanted to make sure you knew who they worked for. Because they might not have told you."

Definitely more calculating and less fruitcake.

"Okay. Thank you, Virgil. The authorities have been investigating a kidnapping, and they think you can help. But first, can you tell me why you decided to resume taking medication to treat your mental condition? What made you change your mind?" she asked.

"I could tell you, but you wouldn't believe me," Virgil said. He twisted his head to look at Luther. "You might."

Luther felt a jolt of fear, much as he had the last time Virgil had spoken to him. Except fear wasn't quite the right word. Perhaps he could put his finger on the precisely applicable word if the damned man would just stop staring at him.

"Virgil," Ms. Callaway said, "it's my job to help you, so I'd really like to know what's changed."

Virgil returned his gaze to her, and Luther felt like he could breathe again. Until the man spoke. "I knew I had to take the medication because my brain is bleeding where it shouldn't."

His attorney did a good job of not reacting, Luther thought, but maybe she heard crazy shit like that more often than he did. "Does it hurt?" she asked.

Luther tensed at the jangly sound of Virgil lifting his restrained hands. He raised them as high as his temple, as if to demonstrate.

"It's not bleeding into *my* head, it's bleeding into *someone else's* head," Virgil said. "But yes, it still hurts. And I think it hurts him, too. I don't like the medication, but it helps me control the bleeding."

Callaway glanced toward D'Antonio, which the agent seemed to take as his cue. "Mr. Rutledge, can you tell me if you know this man?"

Luther couldn't see the photograph D'Antonio showed to Virgil, but he didn't have to. He knew, from the careful way Grant avoided his eyes, that it was Les. Luther tried to breathe normally, torn between desperately wanting to see Virgil's expression and dreading the man's spooky eyes.

Virgil took the photo from D'Antonio and looked at it—even flipped it around to examine the back—before returning it and replying, "No."

Next D'Antonio showed Virgil the sketch of the man from the diner. Luther thought it wasn't a very good likeness, but it was the best they could do with the artist on hand. D'Antonio had someone he liked better, but she was caught up in another case in Pennsylvania and would be here as soon as she could get away.

"That's not him," Virgil said.

Again, Luther wished he could see the man's face; he could swear he heard amusement in Virgil's voice.

"That's not whom?" D'Antonio asked.

"That's not the man you're looking for," Virgil said. "The shape of his face is all wrong—it's too square."

Luther stepped forward without thinking and gazed down at the photo. "He's right. The cheeks should be leaner, and the brows lower."

"Mr. Rutledge," Grant said, "who is the man we're looking for? And where can we find him?"

Virgil glanced over his shoulder at Luther, who tried to back into position without stumbling. "*He* knows who you're searching for. That's why he'll be there. Eventually."

Luther's skin crawled, but—as was usually the case—he had no idea what the man was talking about. D'Antonio continued to push Virgil for more details, particularly about the man's identity, but Virgil refused to say more. He hunched forward, retreating into himself. Luther watched Ms. Callaway and Grant exchange a look—they were losing him.

Grant leaned forward, close to the table's surface so he could be sure he was in the man's field of vision. Luther hated when he did stupid shit like that. "Virgil," Grant said, "I want to ask you about something you told us the last time we spoke. You said your son is involved with taking children. Do you still think that's true?"

Luther watched the back of Virgil's head as it slowly tilted up, presumably to meet Grant's eyes. "Yes. Yes, I do."

Then he hunched even further, almost into a tuck, and began a low, humming sound, the kind of noise you weren't sure you were really hearing that made you look for an out-of-whack electronic device. Virgil held one arm close to his chest and the other out in front of him. The fingers on the latter hand moved in a pattern Luther couldn't make out, touching each other and springing apart, over and over and over. Luther couldn't decide if it was meant to communicate, or to keep something away. D'Antonio leaned behind the much shorter Ms. Callaway to look at Grant (his expression said, *we're done*), and both men stood.

"Thank you, Mr. Rutledge," Grant said. "We appreciate all your help."

Virgil continued rocking, and Grant motioned Ms. Callaway toward the exit. She said her goodbyes to Virgil (who gave no indication of having heard her) and waited to be let out. Kiss-Ass opened the door and entered the room in the attorney's place. D'Antonio exited next. Grant was about to depart when Virgil lifted his head and spoke again.

"Sheriff, my son did take those children, but not the first son who was resurrected. It was the other one. And he *will* be stopped by a righteous man."

58

hat's with the God thing? JJ wondered as she made her leisurely way through the woods back to her house from next door.

She was thankful the girls weren't traumatized by the morning's diner drama and subsequent interaction with the law, but it seemed strange to her that Evie would voluntarily go to a religious function this evening. Lately her daughter had been going with the Nicholsons to Rachel's Baptist children's group. They were rehearsing some kind of skit in Rachel's room right now.

It's not that JJ had anything against religion, but it was one of those things that had never clicked for her. Growing up, it seemed to JJ that her mother had all the talk about Christian values, while her father—who'd never set foot in a church if he could help it—had all of the practice, the actual Christian acts of helping people. That disconnect had bothered her, even more so when her parents' marriage ended in large part because her mother had an affair. (JJ strongly suspected so, anyway, but her father would never confirm it.)

Deep down, JJ had never quite forgiven her mother for betraying Max Tulley and breaking up their family. The two women did have a much better relationship now, and Evie went to church with her grandparents when she stayed with them. Still, as awful as it sounded, JJ would've felt more comfortable if the person drawing her daughter to church was a cute boy rather than the son of God. It was the kind of thing she'd like to talk to Grant about. He had a way of making JJ feel both more honest about her prejudices, and less guilty for having them.

JJ's cell phone rang in her pocket as she reached her yard. "Yeah, kid?" she said, assuming Evie had forgotten something, which happened approximately twenty-seven times a day.

"Is that how you taught our daughter to answer the phone?" Her ex-husband's voice slurred a little, and his now-nasal voice hardened his Ts to Ds.

JJ closed her eyes and leaned against the nearest tree. *I do not have the energy for this shit.* "What do you want, Marcus?"

There was a pause on the other end (was he sipping from a drink while talking to her?) before he said, "I want to speak to my daughter. Where is she?"

Apparently, the Sheriff's Department hadn't gotten around to serving Marcus with the TRO yet. As much as she'd love to see Otto deal with Marcus, the Nicholsons were under enough stress at the moment without adding Evie's father to the mix, so she wasn't about to tell him where to find Evie. "She can't come to the phone right now. If it's important, we can set something up, but—"

"I said I fucking want to talk to my daughter now," Marcus said.

"Yeah, well, you'll be lucky if I ever let you speak to her again, asshole." *Temper, JJ, Temper.* She hadn't meant to get into anything with him, not now. And yet, all she had to do was open her mouth and wait for the ill-considered recriminations to flow. "By the way, the dog lived."

She definitely hadn't meant to mention the dog. The thought of Trooper suffering at Marcus's hands filled JJ with rage at the impotent, pathetic man on the other end of the line. Not the best way to defuse a situation.

"JJ, what the hell are you talking about?"

"I got a restraining order." There, she'd said it. Come what may, it was done.

"You what?" His breath was heavy over the phone.

"You heard me," she said, rubbing the textured bark of the poplar tree next to her, harder and harder until her hand turned pink.

Despite the damage to his nose, Marcus's voice was low and deep when he replied, and it sounded as though his mouth was so close to the phone he was practically eating it. "You fucking bitch. You think a piece of paper will protect you?"

"It's not just a piece of paper."

He laughed. "Oh, so you think you're the only one with cop friends?"

"Of the two of us, I'm guessing I'm the only one with friends of any kind."

"I'm coming for you, and when I do, I won't be alone. By the time we're done, you'll be begging—"

JJ hung up. It wasn't very satisfying on a mobile phone. She didn't want to push a damned button, she wanted to slam a receiver in a cradle. Of course, if she'd been able to, her slamming probably wouldn't have stopped there, so better to rein in her temper while she still could. JJ tucked her phone in her pocket, wrapped her arms against the big poplar tree, and slowly tapped her forehead against its rough trunk. *You. Are. So. Stupid.*

Great. Now she had a raw forehead, too. And she had to work tonight—again—so hopefully it hadn't left a mark. She had enough time for a decent nap and a bite to eat before getting ready.

JJ smiled as she lifted her head. She'd been bludgeoning the tree just above the initials she and Adam and Danny had inscribed more than twenty years ago. She ran her fingers over the letters. First Danny's, then hers, then Adam's. It was hard to believe they—

No. That's too weird.

JJ took a step back, shook herself, then took a second look, tracing the lines with both eyes and fingers. But she still saw and felt it.

There were fresh marks on the tree where someone had gouged out Adam's initials.

Tiny hairs prickled on the back of her neck. Scanning through the gray trees, JJ could barely make out the shape of the Nicholson house in the distance. Her daughter was safe.

JJ went inside for her keys, so she could get her pistol from the car.

59

———

"You sneaky bastard," Luther's father said, with a hint of admiration. "I should have known you'd be behind this."

They hadn't gotten anything else out of Virgil Rutledge after he'd dropped his crazy-ass, unintelligible bombshell at the end of the interview. Rather than waiting for calls back on the drug dealer angle, Luther had gone straight to the source.

Pop sat across from Luther in the file room, wearing his usual white T-shirt and dark, crisp jeans, but his mini pompadour was slightly lopsided. He hadn't been officially booked, and the Sheriff didn't even know he'd been picked up. Luther was playing more than a little fast and loose with the rules, and he was doing his best to insulate everyone around him, to make sure if anyone went down for this, it would be Luther and Luther alone.

"You been to the hospital to see Les yet?" Luther asked.

Pop crossed his arms and his face twisted in an ugly sneer. "Is that what this is about? Me being a bad daddy to your dipshit brother?"

Luther's smile was so cold it made his teeth hurt. "Don't be silly, Pop. If being a shitty dad were a crime, you'd have been arrested forty years ago."

"Wanh, wanh, wanh!" Pop said, flapping the fingers of one hand in time with the baby crying sounds.

Luther dearly wanted to break every one of those fingers off his goddamn hand, shove them down his throat, and watch the man choke on them. He tried to push his temper down by promising to unleash it somewhere outside of an interview room. "I need to know who Les's dealer is," he said carefully.

"What makes you think I know?"

Luther waited him out. It didn't take long for Pop to answer his own question; the man did dearly love to hear himself talk.

"Because Les couldn't find his own ass to wipe it without a map. Fine. Why do you want to know who his dealer is? So you can punish him for your brother's own weak moral character?" Pop asked.

Luther shook his head. It was true that, whatever his role in the supply chain, Pop didn't sample the products that passed through. But for the man to mock someone else's moral character after introducing his son to a drug dealer, and presumably still taking his cut... well, that was just beyond wrong. Luther thanked the Good Lord he wasn't wearing his service weapon.

"The guy's not just a dealer. He's involved with the Schofield kidnapping."

Pop had never had the fine muscle control to raise his eyebrows, but his whole fat face crept up his skull in surprise. "Is he now? How about that? But I heard you found the Schofield boy."

"We did," Luther admitted. "But this piece of shit is still out there, and he was also involved with the Nicholson kidnapping."

Pop had seemed offended by the Nicholson kidnapping, so much so that he'd allowed Luther the use of his fancy UTV to find Rachel. But this time Luther had overestimated his father's moral outrage, and underestimated his resistance to harming his business interests.

"Sorry," Pop said. "I'm afraid I can't help you."

"You know, it's just a matter of time before he grabs another kid. And the next one might not be so lucky."

Pop smiled, the same icy smile Luther had turned on him moments earlier. "Then I guess y'all better be concentrating on protecting the kids, and leave the adults to take care of themselves."

Luther was so angry, he began to shake, a little vibration that he prayed wasn't visible to the man across the table from him. "You're quite the fucking philosopher, aren't you?"

Pop simply shrugged. "We done here, junior?"

Except Luther wasn't a Junior—thank God for small favors. And he bet his mom had gotten a beating over that when the old man saw Luther's birth certificate. Pop had strong ideas about legacy, and about being treated with the respect that was due him. With that thought, Luther grinned on the inside; he had one last shot.

"You know it's just you and me here, right? No cameras, no audio," Luther said.

"No shit," Pop said, smoothing his shirt over his protuberant belly. "The things I know about you, you'd be an idiot to open yourself up like that. And unlike your brother, *you* are not an idiot."

"This guy you introduced Les to, did he know Les was your son?" Luther asked.

Pop looked around the room, a predator's force of habit that had served him well over the years. "He mighta done. Doesn't mean I expected him to hold Les's goddamn hand while he took that shit."

"Maybe not," Luther said, and leaned across the table. "But I would think it'd be rude then, should the man decide to murder your son."

"Murder?" Pop's eyes narrowed. "What the hell are you talking about?"

"Les didn't overdose. He was poisoned, by this guy. On purpose."

Pop turned his head, so he was looking at Luther mostly through his left eye. When they were kids, Luther and Les used to call it his truth-telling eye. It was the one Rudy Beck stared you down with until you shit your pants in terror or told the truth.

"Why would he want to kill Les?"

"I'm not sure," Luther admitted. "Les probably saw something, knew something that was dangerous to him. But whatever the reason, he knew there wouldn't be any repercussions for killing your boy." Luther paused to let that sink in before adding, "He wasn't afraid of you."

"I got it!" Pop spat. "Remember, I'm not a fucking idiot, either."

Luther pulled a small notebook and pencil from his back pocket. "That mean you got a name for me?"

Pop squeezed his lips together and stared at the table. "I don't have a name. I mean, I have one—Mitch—but it's not worth writing down because it ain't real. But I can give you a name that can get you to Mitch." He reached for the notebook, printed a name and phone number in big block letters, and slid it back across the table.

"You know where Mitch lives?"

"I'm sure he moves around a lot, but so long as I've known of him, he's been based out of somewhere near Harbury."

"Like Loganville?" Luther asked, the site of their ill-fated raid.

Pop nodded. "Could be."

"What's he like?" Luther asked.

"We weren't exactly bosom pals," Pop said.

"I'll bet you weren't," Luther agreed, "but I know you've gotta be careful who you work with, even people on the periphery. You must have some impressions."

Pop leaned back and folded his hands over his belly. "I'd say he's smart. Devious, even. One of those guys that'll always come out on top, no matter what kinda shit hits the fan. Superior. He'd laugh at the people around him, but not so's they'd know it, just to himself. Didn't use his product that I could see, and didn't have a whole lot of philosophy built up around it, or around the lifestyle.

"So why'd he do it?"

Pop leaned forward, getting into his role as amateur psychologist. "Now that's the interesting bit. I'd say it was purely financial pragmatism—making money off the grid—except there was something else he got out of it. I could never quite make out what, but I think it was a power thing, power over his customers."

"Would you have pegged him for a kidnapper?"

Pop considered. "Something about him wasn't quite right, like sometimes he was imitating a person instead of being one. But no, I wouldn't have. Maybe if it was part of something else, but not kidnapping for the sake of kidnapping, or for—" His face twisted in distaste. "*You know.* Although I have to say, that boy was entirely too good-looking to always be alone."

When asked, Pop gave a description that matched the man Luther had seen in the diner, except with hair a little longer and wavier and the addition of a heavy brown beard.

"Okay," Luther said, rising.

"Finally," Pop said.

Luther motioned him to sit again. "Somebody'll come by to escort you out, get your stuff and everything."

"When?" Pop demanded.

Luther smiled. "When they get to it."

"You sneaky sonuva—"

Luther slammed the door on his father's protests.

60

"**D**eputy Beck!"

Luther only had a moment to wipe every trace of satisfaction from his face as D'Antonio approached from Grant's office. "Sir?"

"What's that about?" D'Antonio asked. He inclined his head toward the door Luther had shut.

"Nothing," Luther said. "Just a C.I. on another case, so I try to keep him out of sight. But I might have a lead on our drug dealer, and the description matches the man from the diner."

"Good," D'Antonio said. "Why don't we..." He scanned the hallway, then backtracked a few steps to peek into the kitchen, where he was pounced upon—verbally, at least—by Kilbourne.

"Special Agent D'Antonio, sir," Kiss-Ass said with so much pomp, Luther half expected a salute. "Deputy Marshall just buzzed for you. She seemed to think it was important."

His tone of voice indicated he doubted that was the case. D'Antonio nodded and said, "Thanks," but Kilbourne still hovered.

D'Antonio has a fan club, Luther thought, and almost smiled. Instead, he said, "You get the prisoner home again?"

"I'm afraid your department isn't big enough for everybody today," Kilbourne said, walking a fine line between openly being an asshole and demonstrating to a federal agent that he could play well with others. "Since he has to be kept separate, I've got Rutledge properly secured in place until your people get some of the new guys processed."

Luther refused to be baited and simply replied, "Okay."

"I'll meet you in the conference room," D'Antonio said.

Only slightly bigger than the interview room, the conference room felt claustrophobic to Luther. He twisted the blinds to let in a little afternoon light, then took a seat. Then he tried to concentrate on the task at hand, but his mind went completely blank. He'd hit the adrenaline wall and couldn't remember, *what am I supposed to be doing?* The third time he asked himself that, he decided what he was supposed to be doing was getting more coffee. Luther leaned on the table to rise, and his rolling chair nearly got away from him.

The door opened to admit D'Antonio, carrying two mugs of coffee, and Beth, with an armful of folded papers. D'Antonio handed Luther a mug. "You look like you can use it. I took the liberty of adding lots of cream and sugar, to try to preserve whatever remains of your stomach lining."

"D'Antonio, you're all right," Luther said.

"Uh-huh," D'Antonio said, obviously as aware as Luther was that their relationship was a work in progress. He waited while Beth unfolded several maps covering different regions of the state, some in more detail than others. Then he turned to Luther. "Sheriff's still tied up on a call. Did that lead of yours give you any indication as to location?"

Luther took a sip and shuddered—*damn, he wasn't kidding about the sugar!*—before poring over the appropriate map. "He thinks the same general area as where we found the van. Is Loganville still holding Vogler?"

D'Antonio nodded. "His alibi for the kidnapping checks out, but now he's saying when his friends dropped him off at the motel

Friday night, he noticed his van was missing but he was too shit-faced to care. By the time he started moving around the next day, it was back. He thought maybe he'd imagined it."

"Did y'all believe him?"

"Still holding him, aren't we?" D'Antonio said, running his hands through hair with pioneering streaks of gray. "And we didn't have the drug dealer angle before. I know it's not perfect, but let's get that sketch over to Loganville, see if they can scare Vogler into admitting he did a favor for a 'friend.' We've got something else, too. Marshall?"

Lost in studying the map, Beth startled when she heard her name. "Yes, sir. The Command Center got a tip on Jim Henderson's truck. Somebody driving a similar vehicle stopped at a filling station in Watkins County to put air in his tires. Guy remembered because their little coin-operated air machine was out of order, but he went ahead and got a compressor for him."

"Why did he bother?" Luther asked.

Beth shrugged. "He said he felt sorry for the guy. He was old, and his nose was messed up like he'd been beat up or in an accident."

"And the driver was alone?"

"Yes, he was alone. No camper on the back, and the truck was pretty well loaded up with firewood and crap, so nobody was hiding out."

Luther leaned on the table. The officer who'd let Harlan and Adam pass the checkpoint had mentioned firewood. He looked up and found D'Antonio watching him.

"I know you don't think Adam Rutledge is responsible for Aaron Schofield's kidnapping," D'Antonio began.

"But that doesn't mean he hasn't gotten himself wrapped up in the middle of it. And it's hard to swallow the truck showing up there as a coincidence," Luther admitted. Not that he was ready to hug D'Antonio and sing songs with the man. The agent had failed to remark that the arrest warrant for Adam was still active, and Luther doubted that was because he had no intention of serving it.

Beth cleared her throat. "I may have another unlikely coincidence for you."

The deputy shuffled through the stack of papers—apparently not all maps—that she'd brought in with her and finally pulled a paper-clipped portion free. She skimmed it, then glanced back and forth between it and one of the maps. "Yes," she said, allowing herself a mini fist pump. "Virgil's uncle, Theodore Rutledge, has a piece of property in Watkins County. So far as I can tell, it's not twenty miles from the filling station."

D'Antonio blew out his breath. "Okay. Good work. We have a current address on this Theodore Rutledge?"

"Yes, sir," Beth said. "But he lives in Virginia."

"I'll send someone from one of the local offices to interview him," D'Antonio said. "As for Watkins County—"

A harried-looking Grant pushed the door open and closed it carefully behind him, as if wary of pursuers. "What did I miss?"

Luther grinned. "Well, I hope you missed my excellent driving, because it looks like we're going on another road trip."

61

———

Standing on the front steps of the old house, Harlan handed Adam the last peanut butter sandwich.

"What am I supposed to do with this?" Adam asked.

"Eat it," Harlan said. "I imagine you'll work up an appetite, climbing that mountain."

Adam rolled his eyes. He'd meant, he didn't have a bag to carry it or the bottle of water he'd just refilled from the last jug. He mashed the sandwich, squeezing it into his coat pocket. "Are you sure up the mountain is the only way to reach someone?"

"Feeling lazy?" Harlan asked, grinning. Then he relented. "No, I'm not one hundred percent sure, but it seems our best bet. The river would lead us *somewhere* eventually, but there are also mountains between us and somewhere in that direction, and there's a good chance you'd have to climb at least one of them. Versus half a mountain this way. If you're able to reach somebody, our ride might even be waiting when you return."

"And what if I can't reach anybody?"

"Then we'll draw straws on who eats who first. Come on, son, hop to it. I don't want to have to worry about you making it back before dark."

If he got back late, it wouldn't be Adam's fault. Harlan was the one who'd let him doze by the trees for an hour. Adam looked around. He couldn't shake the feeling he was forgetting something, but there was nothing for him to forget. Except the cell phone (other coat pocket) and SIM card (pants pocket). He touched them both for reassurance.

"Okay," Adam said, having put off his departure as long as he could. "I expect a steak dinner when I get back."

"Then expect to be disappointed," Harlan said. "Be safe. I don't want to have to climb that damn mountain after you and carry your ass down."

Adam grinned and raised his water bottle in salutation. "Bring it, old man."

~

ADAM WISHED he had borrowed Harlan's watch.

They'd considered but dismissed the idea of him walking back up the road they'd driven down. It was a less challenging route, but it would only have taken him partway, and with all of its cutbacks and detours, it was easily four or five times farther than a straight shot. Now, Adam was rethinking their decision. It felt like he'd been hiking forever, and having tangible proof that he hadn't—by glancing incessantly at Harlan's watch—might have helped his state of mind.

Of course, Harlan's watch wouldn't have done anything to improve Adam's lung capacity. He paused for a moment, panting, and leaned against a tree to catch his breath. He unzipped his coat. Luckily he'd worn one with a snug waistband—good for keeping the cold out and a water bottle tucked in. Not long after he'd lost sight of the house, the terrain had gotten so steep he needed both hands free to keep his balance, grabbing at trees and rocks and catching himself when he slid on the leaf-covered ground.

Sipping at his water, Adam considered the rock outcrop just a few hundred yards above. It wasn't quite the highest point, but it was clear of vegetation and had the advantage of jutting out far enough—he hoped—for a decent view of the surrounding area. Adam tucked his water away and zipped up. He'd also reassemble his phone there and call Grant. Unless he saw something compelling from the granite perch, he was heading back down the mountain, whether he reached anyone or not. He and Harlan would figure something out. He'd hated to leave the stubborn old man alone for this long.

As he neared the outcrop, the terrain became less forested and more rock-strewn. The stones ranged from gravel to furniture-sized, and it reminded him of approaching the pinnacle where he'd found Rachel. He shivered at the thought, but blamed his chill on the water he'd just drunk. Still, even his rational, logical mind acknowledged it was reasonable to feel vulnerable approaching high ground that could be sheltering anyone.

Climbing atop the outcrop was easier than Adam had feared. He simply wandered around the closest side until he found the route with the best footing. It didn't require real mountaineering, but he did almost break his neck once hopping too confidently from boulder to boulder. The view wasn't as spectacular as he'd expected. Dense forest made it impossible to discern features nearby. Ridges rose all around, shielding most of the surrounding area from his line of sight, and a fuzzy white haze blanketed the distant low-lying areas that he estimated were associated with the river.

So much for reconnaissance. Now for communication. Adam sat on a hunk of rock that was large and flat enough to act as both seat and workbench. He placed his phone on the slab next to him, its surface a mix of whites and pale grays accented by darker, silver-green swirls of lichen. His fingers trembled; whether from exhaustion or anxiety, there was nothing he could do about it. He stood again to pry the SIM card from his pants. Grit crammed under his nails as he dug in his pocket's crevices after it, only to drop the card on the ground. Adam was too tired to swear, even if that had been his inclination. He simply picked up the piece of electronics and blew the dust from it as best he could, before painstakingly squeezing it back into his phone.

Then he pushed the button, and waited.

Thirty-seven percent battery. Not bad. But no bars. He stood and held the phone high above his head. Sometimes it just took a while to find the towers, right? *Still no bars.* Adam pirouetted, banging his shin against another rock and stumbling to one knee. He blinked back the tears, then blinked again to make sure he wasn't seeing things that weren't there. *Yes—half a bar.* Maybe the cell tower gods had required a pain sacrifice.

The phone buzzed in his hand, and a text message appeared. It was from JJ: *Call me. You need to turn yourself in NOW.* "Now" being— he squinted at the phone and did the math—Saturday night. Today was Tuesday. *I know it's a little past "now," but I'm trying, JJ. I swear,* he thought, scrolling through his contacts.

He didn't actually have Grant's phone number programmed in his phone, and if he dialed 9-1-1 out here, he doubted it would go anywhere. But there were a few numbers in his call log from recent weeks that must belong to the Sheriff—no one else had called him except JJ, and he'd put her in his Contacts. Adam dialed the first number and listened to it ring on the other end through the static.

"Hello," Grant said.

"Grant, this is—"

"You've reached Beecham County Sheriff Grant Mason's private line. If it's an emergency—"

Adam hung up. He had no idea what to say in a message to the man. He tried the number twice more, and reached voicemail both times. "Come on, I could use a break here. Please," Adam pleaded, to whatever force in the universe might be listening.

He went back to his call log and tried the second number. It took a few tries to get through—his phone kept dropping the connection—but eventually he reached Luther Beck's voicemail. Perhaps the two men were together right now, somewhere without cell phone coverage, which could be anywhere. He had one more number left to try... *Third time's the charm?*

An unfamiliar masculine voice answered on the second ring. "Beth, how the hell do I get a line out on this thing?"

Adam paused, mouth open, but his instincts told him to stay silent. The man continued, "I'm telling you, when I find that Rutledge sonuvabitch, we're not gonna have to worry about a trial. I—is there someone there? Who is this?"

Adam quickly hung up. Yes, he needed to tell somebody where he and Harlan were, but not *that guy*, whoever he was. *Frick*. He set the phone down and rubbed his face with his hands. His cheeks were cool, and slightly oily. Being on the run wasn't conducive to good hygiene, or good anything else. Iris would no doubt wrinkle her nose... *Iris*. Iris could drive to the Sheriff's Department or the Command Center or wherever the hell the people Adam trusted to not shoot him on sight had gone.

No answer. Maybe Iris was still at the hospital with Grant's dad. Which left only JJ, but he hated to involve her. She had her own problems—high-stress job, a daughter to raise alone, a violent ex to dodge... and then there was Grant. The Sheriff was a good man, and Adam thought she could be happy with him. Making her the go-between would strain their relationship, a strain he wasn't sure it could survive at this early stage. But he couldn't think of another option.

The phone rang and rang with no answer, save persistent bursts of static.

So I crippled my calves for nothing, Adam thought, trying to make light of the anxiety he'd felt since Harlan suggested this course of action last night. He stood, legs quivery, and took another swig of water before beginning his descent. If he was lucky, it'd take half the time.

But he'd be an idiot not to at least leave a message for Grant. He dialed the Sheriff's personal number and got his voicemail again.

"Grant, this is Adam Rutledge." He hesitated, stumped by the magnitude of everything he needed to say. "I know this'll sound crazy, but Danny Carpenter is still alive, and he kidnapped Aaron

Schofield. As of yesterday, I think he had the boy in a motel in Loganville. I don't know where they are now. Harlan and I are stranded at my Uncle Teddy's place in Watkins County, if you want to pick us up and arrest us or... I don't know. There's no cell reception—I had to hike up the mountain to call you—so I guess we'll just wait. Unless we come up with something better. Listen, Grant, I'm sorry—"

Sorry I ran, he wanted to say. And other things. But a beep cut in. He was out of time.

Adam tucked his phone into his pocket and headed back down the mountain, as quickly as his feet could manage. More than anything, he couldn't help but think that was the case: he was out of time.

62

An insistent sound cut through the fog in JJ's mind. She'd heard it earlier and ignored it, despite the fact the sound meant she was supposed to wake up. Alarm clock? Fire alarm? No, cell phone. She struggled to rise from the bed, a heavy weight upon her chest.

With dry eyes and an even drier mouth, JJ croaked, "Trooper, move." The words had no effect, but a forceful shove nudged the shepherd to the other side of the bed.

The phone stopped ringing in JJ's hand. *Dammit.* If it was important, they'd call back. She squinted at her phone, trying to make sense of the numbers that appeared there, particularly the hour. It was time to get ready for work. She set her phone on the nightstand, but it rang again before her feet even touched the floor. Recalling her earlier unwanted conversation with Marcus, this time she checked the caller ID before answering. *Iris.*

"Iris, what's up?" JJ asked.

She didn't waste time with pleasantries. "Have you heard from Adam?"

"No, why? Has something happened?"

"I don't know, but he called me about half an hour ago—didn't leave a message. I tried calling him back, but couldn't get an answer," Iris said.

JJ stood up and pushed her hair back from her face. Her pistol was still lying on the nightstand where she'd left it before her nap. She was lucky she hadn't picked it up instead of her phone. "Maybe he's turning himself in. Did you try calling the Sheriff's Department?"

"No, not yet. I thought I'd try you first. There's something else." Iris's voice trembled slightly. "I just got home, and someone's been here."

JJ jumped when Trooper chose that moment to lift his head, ears perked and angled forward, emitting a low growl. *Drama queen.* But she still switched her phone to the other hand, picked up her gun and walked toward the front of the house. Trooper landed heavily on the floor and padded after her. It wasn't quite dark. The pale, anemic light she associated with winter streamed in the windows. "What do you mean someone's been there?"

"I mean my driveway's torn up—not bad, but bad enough to see someone came and went in a hurry. The garden gate was open —although I can't imagine why, since the fence has fallen down— and when I went around back, I could tell someone had been in the dairy. The door sticks, and whoever it was, they didn't get it shut all the way."

JJ made a slow circuit through the living room, from window to window. Trooper's growl continued, barely loud enough to be audible, but it raised JJ's hackles as much as it did his. "It couldn't have been Adam?"

"No," Iris said, voice more firm now as she grew angry. "I could also tell someone had been tramping around, looking in my windows. They messed up my hostas."

There were no strange cars in JJ's driveway, but she couldn't help feeling she wasn't alone. Trooper crowded next to her at the front door, whining to go outside. JJ slipped on her sneakers and squeezed through. She told the dog to stay as she bumped the door shut behind her, hands occupied with phone and gun. "Iris, I think you should call it in."

JJ paced from one end of her porch to the other, straining to hear anything unusual with the ear that wasn't pressed to her phone. She cringed as a board protested beneath her feet.

"Are you okay, JJ?" Iris asked. "Is something going on there?"

"I got a restraining order against Marcus this morning," JJ said. "He wasn't too happy about it, and that's probably making me paranoid."

Iris's voice was low and grave when she spoke. "If you think you're not alone, lock yourself in the house and wait for the Sheriff. Now."

Says the woman who hasn't called the cops yet, either, JJ thought, inching down the front steps.

Trooper's deep barks resounded from the back of the house without warning. JJ stumbled and nearly dropped her phone, though her gun hand stayed firm. *Dad would never forgive me if I shot my foot off.*

"JJ?" Iris called out. "Are you okay?"

JJ replied in a soft voice. "I'm fine. I'm just going to have a quick peek first, before I make a big deal out of nothing. I gotta go —I'll call you back."

She'd been napping in sweatpants, so JJ had no pockets. She tucked her cell phone in the waistband, but the elastic wasn't snug enough and the phone fell through, catching in her pants leg at the bottom. *Sonuvabitch!* she thought, bending over to dig the phone free and reluctantly leaving it on the edge of the porch. *The damn thing doesn't work half the time anyway.*

Rounding the front corner to creep down the longest side of the house, JJ settled into the two-handed shooting stance her father had taught her—strong arm straight and support arm relaxed, cheek drifting toward her bicep. She strained to hear someone else—anyone else—among Trooper's increasingly frenzied barks.

As JJ reached the back corner, Trooper suddenly stopped barking, though the stillness resonated with canine echoes. A moment later, she heard the dog barrel through the house toward the front, skidding on slick spots and banging into the occasional wall. She paused and looked over her shoulder—paranoid—but saw no one behind her. Not yet anyway. And if Trooper had abandoned the rear of the house, that area was probably clear...

Clink!

Or maybe not. JJ recognized the sound of a brick being knocked from a small stack of them by the basement entrance. There was someone ahead of her on the back side of the house. Iris was right—JJ was out of her depth. It was time to call the professionals.

Just seconds after the clinking thump, Trooper took up barking again, at the front door. JJ crept back in that direction, staying as close to the house as possible without wading through the deep autumn leaves pooled against it, thankful Trooper's barking covered her crunching progress. She stopped at the front corner of the house and stood on tiptoes for a better view of her sloping driveway—still no other vehicles in sight. She'd be safest as Iris said, waiting inside the house. But she'd be exposed on her way to the front door.

Trooper paused in his barking. *That's a good sign, right?* JJ resolved to step into the yard, until an unfamiliar voice muttered, "I'm gonna kill that goddamned dog."

Following which, Trooper resumed snarling and foaming at the mouth.

Shit. A man at the front door and a man at the basement. For once Marcus hadn't lied—he'd brought backup. And if he hadn't lied about that part of his threat, with her luck the guy at the front probably was an off-duty cop. Maybe Iris had called the Sheriff's Department when she didn't hear back from JJ, but if she had, help wasn't going to magically appear anytime soon.

Thank God the girls are safe at church by now.

Even now, JJ believed locking herself inside was her best bet, but not in the main part of the house with all its windows. She could slip in the basement if Marcus wasn't still standing next to the basement door. (Presumably Marcus had knocked the brick over since the voice around front hadn't been his.) Once inside, she'd grab Trooper from the basement stairs and keep the dog down there with her. If, that is, the unidentified man hadn't breached the front door yet. *Too many ifs.*

JJ sneaked toward the back of the house as quickly as she dared, aware that Marcus's friend could be on her heels any second. Every subtle shush of the leaves vibrated through her hurrying feet, and she constantly fought the urge to turn and confirm she wasn't sensing the sounds of pursuit. Her breath was loud in her ears when she reached the end of the house and peeked around the corner.

No one was there, not in the quick glimpse, so a moment later, she risked a longer one. Still no one. JJ hustled to the basement entrance and squatted to retrieve the key. *Which one of these damned flowerpots...* It wasn't there. Evie must've used it sometime and forgotten—no, wait, there it was, in the cap of the watering can of all places. *What the hell was she thinking?* The next time—

Their firewood was stacked ahead of JJ at the far corner of the house. She froze at the sharp, crackling sound of someone lifting the tarp that covered it. Her head jerked up—*faster than her hands, they wouldn't move fast enough!*—and she dropped the basement key to place both hands on her gun. A man swung round the corner, elbows high in the same shooter's stance she'd been using.

"Stop!" JJ yelled.

The man pivoted toward her, adjusting for a target crouched on the ground. And a single gunshot reverberated across the mountain.

～

"Stay down!"

JJ's heart pounded, and her eyes swam. She ignored the pain in her arm, raising her gun again.

"I said, stay down! And drop the gun!"

The man on the ground fell onto his back, hand releasing his service weapon. Yes, service weapon. JJ had shot a cop. *Shit*. She advanced slowly, gun still pointed at him. She kicked his weapon away when she got close enough, thumbed the safety on her own and tucked it in the back of her elastic waistband, hoping for the best. *Goddamn sweats.*

Kneeling by the man, she said, "Just relax and let me take a look. You think Marcus ran off? He's generally a coward, but I'm not crazy about the idea of him shooting me in the back."

The man tried to sit—or maybe he was just writhing in pain—while JJ pushed at his coat to access his wound. Roughly speaking, she'd gotten him in the shoulder, but the exact location could be the difference between bleeding and bleeding out, or weeks of recovery versus months of rehabilitation. "I need to get your jacket off—"

There was a blur of movement—hands and metal—as he grabbed for JJ's wrists. She twisted and jerked away, felt his open handcuffs, and in a million-to-one move snapped them shut over the officer's own wrists.

"I'm trying to help you! Even if you're Marcus's goddamn flunky. Jesus! Now hold still." JJ again pushed his coat back, and the officer groaned in pain. She'd seen enough to know he wouldn't die of blood loss anytime soon, but she had to get that damned coat off. Which meant removing the handcuffs she'd just secured. "Where's the key to your cuffs?"

"Who's Marcus?" the man asked. "We're looking for Rutledge."

JJ stared at the man. Dark-haired, in his late twenties with a slim build, he didn't look familiar. Neither did his uniform, which was a different shade from the Beecham County Sheriff's Department. "Who are you?" she asked.

The man's face and lips grew pale, and he gave a shuddering shiver. He was going into shock. "Stupid fucking Kilbourne," he said.

"Is that your name?" JJ asked, trying to engage him while she searched for his handcuff key. The key ring attached to his belt on a heavy clip looked promising, but her fingers fumbled ineffectually.

She was so focused on the fiddly little mechanism, she never heard the man approaching her from behind.

"Hands behind your head, and face down on the ground—now!"

Shit. At least it wasn't Marcus. JJ raised her hands slowly as he had asked. "This officer has been shot," she said calmly. "I'm a nurse, and I—"

"Bullshit. I said, face down on the ground."

JJ kneeled, unsure how to comply with the rest without lowering her hands. "I just want to help," she said, twisting to look at the officer behind her.

"Shut up!" he said. "Where's Rutledge?"

JJ shook her head in frustration. "I have no fucking idea where Adam is. I can't believe you're still on about this."

"I'm not looking for Adam Rutledge," he said. "I'm looking for Virgil."

"What?" JJ gasped, her hands dropping with the shock.

JJ heard a clicking sound, and something moved in her peripheral vision. Intense pain blasted through her entire body, all at once, but also in sequential waves. She fell forward on her face, unable to move her arms to stop herself; everything had shut down. It seemed like the pain would never end. Until it did.

"If you wanted to help, you shouldn't have shot him," the man said, cuffing her hands behind her back.

63

Much of Danny's life had been spent tramping through wilderness. For the first time, he was feeling pretty goddamn sick of it. Not that he had any idea of where else to go, or what else to do. This was all he'd ever known.

He'd been hiking for about forty-five minutes, and the old house should be in sight soon. Danny and Virgil had worked on making the back access road passable, but they'd never made it as far as the house. Now they never would. *Sonuvabitch.* He couldn't believe the man who raised him had betrayed him that way. Danny had no earthly idea what those people had done to him—*inside my head*—but he knew Virgil was behind it. He'd like to blame Adam, but things hadn't been right between Danny and Virgil for a while.

Virgil was a strange one—no doubt about it—but Danny had always known there were things he needed to hide from him, things the man would not approve of. And he was right. Their relationship had begun to fray when Virgil discovered, not the drug dealing, but Danny's *little hobby*. The one that made the voices go away. Initially Danny denied what he'd done, but that hadn't lasted. Then he tried to rationalize it, and that had been a disaster. But Danny had always assumed their relationship would be restored, that Virgil would forgive him. Except, of course, forgiveness implied that Danny was done with it, and he wasn't. Not quite yet.

So Danny and Virgil had remained estranged, and whether Virgil forgave him or not, he never could have imagined that Virgil would punish him. *Try to kill him.* Because as much as Danny hated Adam, he knew the attack on his mind had Virgil written all over it.

Danny didn't know where else to go, so he'd gone home. Not for sentimental reasons, but because he knew he would—at least temporarily—be safe there, and because it had things he didn't want to leave behind, things that could help him in his new life.

And there it was—*be it ever so humble...* He and Virgil had spent a lot of happy years there. Well, maybe not happy. Danny wasn't entirely sure what that word meant. But they were simple times, and he was starting to think that's all he wanted anymore. That, and to kill Adam Rutledge.

He'd never quite believed in Virgil's crazy supernatural crap (although the past few days had him revising that position), but he did believe in instincts and intuition. You saw both at work in nature all the time. Right now, Danny's instincts were telling him that something was wrong, that his former home was no longer safe. He wasn't about to turn around and walk back to his car on a hunch, but he approached the house carefully. The back side of the structure had no windows, so staying on the path was an acceptable risk. As for weapons, Danny had never been a fan of handguns. They were only good at close range, where there were better lethal options, ones less clumsy and more amenable to the element of surprise. On the other hand, he'd grown up with long guns and had great respect for their utility over distance. Too bad he wasn't carrying one today.

He *was* carrying two knives, one strapped to his calf and a smaller one at his belt. As he approached the house, a fist-sized stone caught his eye, and he shoved that into his coat pocket as well. *Always good to be prepared.* He smiled. He found himself looking forward to the coming confrontation, certain there would be one.

Certain, that is, until he found no vehicle parked in front of the house. There had been recently, though—he could still see its tracks in the dry dust.

"Do you live here?"

Danny wheeled around to see who had spoken. An old man sat on the porch next to the front door, back against the weathered exterior and knees raised. No wonder Danny hadn't noticed him.

"I'm sorry. Did I startle you?" the man asked. "I didn't mean to."

But he was smiling, a secret kind of smile. Danny's temper flared, until he had a realization. He recognized that smile from the inside out, and now he knew why so many people got so pissed off at him. It made him laugh out loud. "You didn't, huh? Naw, I don't live here. I was supposed to meet a man to look at the property. But I take it you're not Mr. Rutledge."

The old man shook his head, still smiling. He stood with the help of a cane and lurched down the steps. Still, he'd risen more easily than Danny would've expected. Despite the silver hair, he doubted the man was as decrepit as he presented.

"You come in the back way?" the man asked.

Danny nodded. He didn't see any reason to lie. "Had to leave my car though. Turns out the road doesn't make it to the house. I was sure I'd be late, tramping in the rest of the way." He looked around, as though for the fictional Mr. Rutledge. "And you came in the main road? How the hell did you manage that, without a truck?"

Except Danny had seen tire tracks. The man didn't answer, just kept smiling and strode closer, slowly swinging from side to side as he leaned on the cane every other step. There was something familiar about him, something that made Danny flush cold with fear. That wouldn't do... "So who brought you here? And when are they coming back?"

The man shrugged both arms, lifting his cane as he did so. "As you can see, I'm alone now. What about you?"

Something was wrong. This was a trap. *No, it's not a trap...* Danny swung around, looking in all directions, this time without the casual pretense. No vehicles, no dust cloud, but what was that on the ridge? Was there a figure climbing down?

"Hey!" the old man barked. "I asked you a question. Are *you* alone?"

Danny looked at him, which was what he'd wanted. *Not a trap, a diversion.* Who was that up the ridge that he was trying to protect?

The man continued, "I imagine you feel alone, but are you really? I bet you'll never be alone again, that someone's voice will always be in your head no matter where you go... *Danny Carpenter.*"

Danny would've been less stunned if the man had hit him in the chest with a two-by-four. He hadn't been called that name by anyone other than Virgil for twenty years, and even the man who'd kidnapped him didn't always remember who he was. Danny couldn't breathe and he couldn't move. His brain tingled in his skull, whispering, *He's the one. He was there, in my head.* And somehow, that thought cut him free.

Danny took a step closer and slipped his hand into his pocket, hand tightening on the stone. "You may be right, old man. Maybe I'll never be alone. But you're about to be. Forever."

64

———

Adam tried his cell phone once on the way down, but, as he'd expected, there was no reception. He was making good time—too good, by the mud stains on the knees and seat of his pants—but he still felt he was losing a race against the clock. Had Harlan really expected him to get through to someone on the outside, or had he just sent Adam up the mountain on a quixotic mission to get him out of the way? And out of the way of what?

Teddy could be coming back. But why wouldn't Harlan want Adam there to meet Teddy? Unless it was because Teddy was successful in... whatever it was the man was trying to accomplish when he'd left them behind. Harlan had intimated it involved Virgil, but Adam hadn't felt a peep from his father since they'd tried to save Aaron Schofield.

And what about Aaron? Adam told himself that the silence he felt around the boy—and Virgil—was an indication that the child was out of danger. After all, Virgil might be crazy (scratch that— Virgil *was* crazy), but he obviously hadn't wanted the child to be harmed. If Aaron were in danger, wouldn't Virgil's mind still be agitated? Or maybe he was giving the man too much moral credit.

Adam thought it would be easier to come to terms with his—what, *gifts*? Harlan wouldn't choose that word—with his *special abilities* if they were more consistent. What was the point of having just enough insight to mess up your life without having enough to do any good? Just enough awareness to ensure you'd spend your life alone, without the satisfaction of looking back at the people you'd helped and saying it was worth it? It seemed cruel. And it made him even more determined to see Harlan and Iris back together, for whatever years remained to them.

Harlan... Adam experienced an unnatural lightness in his chest, like his heart had skipped a beat and wouldn't quite settle back down in his ribcage where it belonged. If Adam had worn the man's watch, could he have used it to home in on him? To reassure himself that Harlan was okay? The strangeness in Adam's chest wouldn't allow a satisfyingly full inhale. It didn't matter; the house was within sight now, and nothing seemed amiss.

Adam still held his hand absently to his chest as he stood at the forest edge and contemplated the last precipitous slope before the terrain plateaued into the floodplain the house sat upon. He'd practically dug a trench on the way uphill, digging his toes in and sliding back down. He'd even managed to uproot the single sapling perched precariously on the top edge. The bank was an almost-vertical drop of fifteen or twenty feet. The most sensible course would be to bypass it by hiking a tenth of a mile or so in either direction. He sighed, or tried to; he couldn't even stretch his lung capacity enough for a proper sigh. He turned, and...

"Aargh!" A primal roar raged through the leafless trees.

Not until the echo died away did Adam realize the sound had come from his own raw throat. He knelt on one knee, where he'd been knocked as if by a club. He put his hands to his head, his shoulders, his chest... nothing. He had no wounds. His eyes were drawn toward the house, where he could see a figure—Harlan. No, not Harlan. Or at least, *not just* Harlan. Someone else stood over him. Over his prone body.

Adam screamed again and scrambled down the slope. He lost

his footing immediately and fell, arms windmilling, until his heels caught the exposed soil. Pain shot through his thigh as it struck a stone and he pitched forward again, free falling to land at the bottom. *Hard,* on his chest. Initially, he thought he was fine, if a little stunned, and started to crawl to his feet.

But within seconds, Adam realized he wasn't breathing. He opened his eyes and mouth wide, trying desperately to inhale. A great vacuum had hollowed out his chest, like something from a science fiction movie. Surely his eyes would rupture with the pressure. His face burned and his eyes teared until finally, finally the weight lifted and his chest expanded. The first wheezing breath wasn't nearly enough.

Easy, Adam, don't panic... you've been here before. He forced himself to inhale slowly through his nose and out through his mouth until he was able to stand. And then to run.

He ran to Harlan, though everything in Adam wanted to chase after the man now running (*I'll kill him*)—albeit limping—from the scene, toward the river (*I'll fucking kill him*). Harlan lay face down in the front yard. A bloody wound on the back of his head (*Oh, Jesus; oh, sweet Jesus*) made Adam's knees give way.

"Harlan? Harlan, can you hear me?" Adam demanded, hand on his shoulder, but he would've been shocked if the man had answered. *JJ—oh, God—JJ, what do I do?* Adam pulled out his cell phone, hands shaking so badly he dropped it in the dirt. No signal. He tried calling her anyway, but nothing happened, not even a dial tone.

"Fuck!" he screamed, throwing the phone on the ground.

Adam paused to wipe the tears from his face—*when did I start crying?*—before gently placing his hand beneath the base of Harlan's head and neck and rolling him over. Harlan's face was so pale—the creases in his face looked blue—that he had to be dead already. No one could look like he did and live. Adam pressed his fingers against his carotid artery—nothing. He pushed harder, and decided he'd felt a pulse. Whether that was true or not didn't matter. He'd make it true.

He shucked off his coat and tucked it beneath Harlan's head. It still bled, but barely more than a trickle. Adam refused to consider what that might mean. Instead, he sat back on his heels and tried to remember what Harlan had taught him. He closed his eyes and placed one hand in the dirt. It was dry and gritty and mocked him with its indifference as it stuck to the blood (*Harlan's blood*) on his hand. *Relax,* he told himself. *Deep breath.*

And there was the familiar buzzing sensation, humming through the earth.

Good. Okay, now what? This morning, Harlan had said to go deeper, but they hadn't actually been healing anyone at the time. Adam was wary of letting the energy or whatever it was build up too much before connecting with the injured man. Could the shock do more harm than good? He rested his hand upon Harlan's chest and waited.

It wasn't working. Adam's grounded hand got colder, but nothing happened on the other end. There was no transference. Adam (*stay calm*) thought back to the night Harlan had healed him at Teddy's. He'd used direct skin contact, his hand to Adam's wrist. Adam hadn't triggered anything crazy while checking Harlan's pulse, but he told himself he'd lacked intent then, that he was still too burnt out for anything to happen organically. So he gripped Harlan's hand, and their connection went live as an electrical wire.

Images flooded over Adam, much as they had done with his father weeks earlier, but less violent, both in substance and in the way they passed to Adam. There was an older woman with kind, patient eyes (*Harlan's mother*), and a crying toddler who calmed in Harlan's arms. But most of the images were of Iris, from the time she was a beautiful, young married woman looking at him from the corner of her eye, until she was an elderly woman sitting impatiently in the dirt of a recently tilled garden, waiting for a hand up. Iris was his life. And as Adam witnessed Harlan's life, he tried to give it—give life— back to him.

But Adam's body grew colder and colder. His breath puffed out in frigid clouds, and the blood on his hands (*shaking hands*) no longer glistened, but was sticky. His chest grew tight with the sensation, as it had this morning, but this time Harlan couldn't make him stop. Adam's vision went dark, and he fell forward in a faint, coming to in time to catch himself as he hit the ground.

"Harlan, can you hear me?" Adam gasped.

His color was better, and Adam could see his chest rise and fall, but Harlan was still unconscious. He hadn't done enough. Adam gripped Harlan's hand with numb fingers and felt nothing, save more warmth than his own icy hands possessed. He put his hand to the earth and felt the same—no buzzing, just dirt. He had nothing left; he'd burned himself out again, and Harlan was still in danger.

Adam bent forward, arms tucked, forehead to the ground. To a stranger, it would have looked as though he were praying, so long as his eyes remained hidden.

Adam lifted his head, and his burning, furious eyes, and he heard the voice.

You know he's still out there. And he'll do it again. It's not too late. You can stop him.

Adam got up and ran toward the river.

65

Danny lurched through the trees, parallel to the path of the river. A stabbing, grating pain shot through his right leg with every step. *Shit!* It felt like the old man had broken his shin with his goddamned cane. He should've known better—he did know better! It was Adam's fault. Something about him overwhelmed Danny's good sense.

Except he could lay a lot of things at Adam's door, but this wasn't one of them. It wasn't Adam's fault; it was his own. He'd listened to his ego (*how many men have I killed, decades younger than this man?*) instead of his instincts (*he is not as he appears*). Danny's ego had gotten him in trouble from the start. All of the bad decisions he'd made over the past month could be traced to ego. He'd have to do better if he wanted to get out of this in one piece.

Danny paused, panting, to get his bearings. He hadn't been this way in years, and the forest landscape had changed too much to tell how much further he had to go. He'd wanted to avoid the potential exposure, but the best thing to do was head to the river and follow its shore. It wasn't far, and Adam was probably still hung up with the old man. Who the hell was he anyway?

Danny snorted as a deep section of the river came in sight.

Adam's fucking Obi Wan, that's who he was. As much as he tried to laugh it off (*How many times did we watch those movies together? Turn the piles of snow into our own Hoth cave?*), the idea made Danny nervous. He was pretty sure the old man wouldn't make it, but what had he been teaching Adam?

Danny still clutched the bloody stone, so he tossed it in the water before following the river downstream. The Adam he had known could be persistent—determined even—but he didn't have the edge Danny had, the hard edge you needed to do what had to be done. His Obi Wan had it—Danny had seen it in his eyes—but was that really something you could pass on to someone else? Something you could teach them?

He stopped in his tracks. It was something you could *inspire* in someone else. He may have just made a monumental mistake. But Danny hadn't had a choice; he'd worry about the consequences later.

Close to the house, the river was a deep pool, but now it narrowed to a hundred feet or so across and grew more shallow, speeding up a bit. It wasn't rushing, but there was a discernible current as the occasional branch floated past. The sky's reflection (white cloud cover from horizon to horizon) made the dark water surface impenetrable to the eye. The worn, wooden dock lay ahead. A few months ago, Virgil had invited Danny to visit—*Why don't you come down, and we'll go for a paddle like we used to? Before summer's gone.* At the time, Danny suspected Virgil was troubled by suspicions about him, but none so unremitting he couldn't pretend ignorance. And what if Danny had gone? Would they still be on speaking terms? *On speaking terms—that's an understated way to say someone isn't trying to kill you.* Maybe they would. But Virgil would have found out eventually, and they'd be right back where they were now. At an impasse.

The dock was tucked against a high spot where an eddy had eroded the shore to form a hollow, like a tiny bay. Of course, the earth hadn't stopped eroding just because someone had built there. The bank still technically met the dock, but now rested a few inches lower than the structure. Danny stepped awkwardly onto it, gripping a supporting post. *Damned shin.* With the exception of a spongy board or two, the dock seemed sturdy enough. It was short —maybe six feet long—and they'd only ever used it for launching and landing. Danny remembered the first summer his heels had hung over the edge while baking himself dry.

He stepped carefully off the dock. The aluminum canoe was where they always left it, upside down, well above the typical flood line. He swept off dead branches, and his groan was lost in the metallic rumbling as he flipped the canoe over. Two cheap paddles, aluminum shafts with black plastic blades, rested on the ground beneath it. One had a crimped bend near the handle—*useless*. He tossed the other one in the hull, then pushed the canoe down the bank. He'd forgotten how noisy the damn thing was—it rang like a percussion section with every pebble. He launched directly from the shore, not bothering with the dock, and got his uninjured leg wet to the shin. Still, he grinned.

Danny loved that moment of wobbling uncertainty, transitioning between the elements, so much as you could feel it in the stable, brute of a canoe. He still remembered the first time Virgil had taken him out. *You're not going to run, are you?* he'd said. *Or swim, I guess. You hit that water without my permission, boy, I'll see to it that you drown.*

He hefted a paddle to get used to the feel again, and noticed some damage to his hands—bruises and abrasions, mostly to his knuckles—from fighting the old man. *Tough old bastard.* His shin twinged as he settled on his knees. There were strange currents in this patch of water, carrying him to a gnarly, overgrown area he wanted to avoid. He needed to get the beast turned.

Just take your time; you're in no hurry.

Except, suddenly, he was. He glanced up and saw Adam Rutledge, running toward the dock like a wild man with murder in mind.

66

Adam knew he was drawing power from somewhere, from *someone* other than Harlan, to keep running as he was. But once he saw Harlan's attacker slipping away on the river, he didn't care where the power was coming from—only that he had it. And he would use it.

He kept his eyes on the uneven ground, watched it flash by beneath his feet. Adam's chest ached, his boots felt heavy, and the rushing in his ears was indistinguishable from the river next to him, but nothing could stop him. The dock was just ahead. He risked looking up and saw sunlight flash off a metal canoe as it drifted away from the shore. The distance between the canoe and the dock widened as a current took the vessel and a dark-haired man paddled to bring it around. *Come on.* Adam swung wide and slowed for his turn, wary of the gap between the ground and the weathered, wooden surface.

His lead foot skidded when it landed, sliding half the distance of the short dock. He had room for another running step or two before leaping from the end, kicking his legs like a track event. Adam was airborne, as he had been falling down the bank, but this time frigid water stole his breath away instead of hard ground. His splayed legs prevented his body from going deep and he surfaced quickly, gasping for air. But the cold was such a shock that his limbs were slow to respond. Combined with his heavy, water-filled boots, he found himself sinking beneath the water again. The world was darkness and light without features, with nothing but painful cold. Holding his breath, he struggled to peel off his boots, but the lacing was too complicated.

He's getting away, Adam.

He'd have to swim with his boots on.

Adam kicked off the soft bottom and surfaced, choking on gritty, turbid water. The canoe's stern line had caught in the branches of a submerged tree, and the man pushed with his paddle to get free. Adam swam toward the snagged boat, closing the gap stroke by stroke with the help of the current. He didn't look up, didn't even turn his head for a breath. Soon the shining object loomed ahead, and he reached out for the gunwale, lungs bursting.

Adam missed, lifted his head free of the water and sucked in air. River water poured over his face, blurring his vision, but the shape of a man moving toward him was unmistakable.

Pain shot through Adam's shoulder as the paddle stabbed at him, then pushed him underwater. Instead of resisting, wasting his strength, Adam grabbed the paddle and rode it back to the surface, then climbed it like a hanging rope, hand over hand.

The canoe lurched, and the man flattened in the hull, yelling, "Let go!" as he released the paddle.

Adam gripped his prize, falling back to the water, then shoved it away. His boots threatened to pull him under as he treaded water and watched a current catch the paddle and drag it downstream.

"Shit!" the man yelled.

Adam faced him. With broad cheekbones tapering to an almost delicate mouth, and dark brown eyes gleaming beneath low brow ridges, the man's identity was now undeniable.

"What's the matter, Danny?" Adam gasped. "Did you forget how to swim?"

Danny wiped splattered water from his face and grinned. The familiar expression pierced Adam's heart with guilt and regret and everything in between, until Danny said, "So you just left Obi Wan to die? Yeah, that sounds like your MO. Always leaving people behind."

Adam kicked hard, breaching the surface, and grabbed the gunwale. Danny had nothing left to strike Adam with except his fist. He landed a solid punch to Adam's cheek before Adam tucked his chin, shielding his face. Presented with a hard skull, Danny saved his knuckles and smacked Adam's ear with an openhanded slap instead. Adam winced and yanked on the gunwale, using it as a spring to grasp Danny's shoulders and flip him end over end as the canoe capsized.

Danny landed on top of Adam, taking them both under. The water was an icepick driving into Adam's slapped ear, and he couldn't see a thing. Danny kicked him in the side, purging some of his precious air, and Adam's head banged painfully against the metal canoe. Finally, Adam's feet touched the river bottom, harder and less silty here. He pushed off, chest squeezing and hands above his head for protection.

Surfacing, Adam coughed funky water from his lungs and spun around. He didn't see Danny. The canoe drifted slowly downstream, as Adam did, though their pace quickened as the river narrowed. Adam kicked awkwardly to the canoe, swam beneath it and came out the other side. *If he's not here...* Of course. Adam looked downstream and finally saw Danny, no more than ten yards away, searching for the paddle.

Are you going to let him get away? the voice asked.

Adam swam downstream, accelerating with the current. Danny had always been the daredevil, willing to jump in (or off) anything, but Adam was the stronger swimmer. He'd even worked as a lifeguard one teenaged summer in Pennsylvania. But this wasn't a pool. Adam lifted his head. Where the banks had once been malleable sand and soil, they now encroached, rocky and unyielding. Adam tested the current by trying to stand. He could barely drag a booted toe on the bottom, and the river built toward rapids, with rock-lumpy and white-flecked water ahead.

The passenger-less canoe bounced and bobbed erratically toward the far side of the river. Having retrieved the paddle, Danny swam for the canoe with an awkward, one-handed breast-stroke. Adam may have had the advantage of two arms, but those arms were tiring, his chest ached with the cold, and his legs were so damned heavy. Danny reached the canoe shortly before Adam and struggled to right it without losing the paddle. He succeeded, tossed the paddle inside, and stretched his arms over the gunwale. But Danny hesitated—no doubt anxious about capsizing the canoe —just long enough for Adam to seize his leg.

Adam yanked Danny under, but he slipped out of Adam's grip. The canoe swung around broadside in front of the men as they surfaced, stopping abruptly. Adam struck the vessel as the current pushed him onward, forcing him underwater. Sightless again, he clutched instinctively at the hull, tracing a raised seam with numb fingers until the vessel jerked free of whatever had snagged it. His flailing hand caught one of the canoe's lines and he followed it to the surface. Gasping for air, Adam couldn't get oriented. The world had been swallowed by a white haze.

No, he realized, *my brain has*. The cold was shutting his body down.

You can still stop Danny.

Adam wasn't sure he believed the voice anymore, but when Danny's body slammed unexpectedly against him, Adam figured it wasn't his choice to make. He let go of the line and clutched Danny instead. Adam's heel hit bottom, but he couldn't stand against the current and they both went under. Danny thrashed against him and got a hand around Adam's throat, thumb digging into his larynx. Adam felt himself choking, even while holding his breath, and coughed involuntarily. He grabbed Danny's wrists, as he'd been trained so many summers ago, and pushed him away. Then he spun Danny, secured him in a rear chokehold, and kicked to the surface, coughing and sputtering for air. They faced the wrong way around, the canoe out of sight. Adam peered over his shoulder at the oncoming rapids. What were the chances of getting them both through in one piece, Danny fighting him the whole way? Slim to none, he'd reckon.

You don't have to both *make it through. Kill Danny while you still can.*

Shocked by the words and the malevolent energy behind them, Adam relaxed his pressure. Danny reached back and clawed at him, grabbing his hair and then his ear. Adam reacted by doing exactly as the voice had suggested—choking Danny.

Adam squeezed the arm he'd looped around Danny's neck. His technique wasn't perfect, but it didn't have to be perfect to choke a drowning man. Danny released Adam's ear, tearing at his clothed arm instead, with no effect. Danny rotated his hands around until he found Adam's wrist. He gripped it and twisted, and Adam felt—

Another man fighting him for his life. They grappled in an apartment, sparsely furnished with walls all white. The unknown man—the man he was choking—had dark hair, a similar height and build, but was lankier and younger. He jerked the man backwards and dragged him across the living room toward a door with a cheap, full-length mirror. As he approached it, he saw his own hair was wavier, his face more narrow (I'm Danny; the man is fighting Danny). The younger man in his arms fell limp, and Danny lifted the beaten man so he could see the reflection of his end. So he could see...

Me. *The dying man, eyes closed and face flushed, looked like Adam.*

Adam's body slammed against a wall of rock, and Danny flew from his arms. Adam found himself tumbling and bouncing over smaller rocks. They'd entered the rapids.

The river surged toward a split ahead. Danny was gone. The canoe was gone. All that remained was the path in front of Adam. If he could see it. He rolled and spun until his head was well above the water and his feet pointed downstream. A submerged rock struck Adam's tailbone, pain shot up to his skull, and he adjusted his "seated" position to better protect himself. The boots that had nearly drowned him now took the brunt of the abuse, striking any obstacles first as Adam surrendered to the current.

On the other side of the fork, the river broadened again and slowed. Adam knew he had to get out of the water, but he was so tired. He leaned back and stretched his legs out straight. His feet sank, but the rest of his body floated. He let his head rest on the water, no longer bothered by the cold, and shut his eyes. Water lapped across his face, his mouth and nose, but he didn't react. His head sank lower, and one ear registered the roar of the fast-moving water behind him.

Except the roaring sound was alongside him, and it was transient.

It wasn't water.

Adam reluctantly opened his eyes and looked toward the shore. It was the road. A car had passed on the road, not thirty yards away. *Damn. I guess that means I can't stop now.*

He'd left his fine motor skills behind long ago, and his limbs weren't good for much, either. Adam kicked a little, flailed a little, and prayed a little. At least one of those things paid off. The river swung into a gentle bend ahead, where its now-mild current led him toward the shore. His feet caught on the sloping riverbed and he fell to his knees onto a mostly soft bottom, the water slowing his fall. Adam stood on shaking legs. They carried him as far as the edge of the water before he fell again. He shook uncontrollably, but the highway was only a few yards away. Adam crawled up the gentle bank, vision graying around the margins, until the biting sensation of gravel beneath his hands told him he'd made it to the shoulder. Then paved road was beneath him, retaining the slightest hint of the day's warmth. Adam stretched out upon it and tried to lay his palms flat, but they wouldn't respond. His body curled into a fetal position.

The sound of squealing breaks brought Adam to his senses, at least enough to inspire a moment of terror. *I'm lying in the highway.* He couldn't see very well—the world was an overexposed photograph—and his hearing was pretty well shot. He knew the person standing over him (*man—deep voice*) was speaking, but he couldn't make sense of the words. The man disappeared. When he returned, Adam had made it as far as his hands and knees. The man draped a blanket over his shoulders.

Adam lifted his dripping head and stuttered, "Ph-ph-ph-phone."

67

I*can't believe that fucker tased me,* JJ thought, massaging a sore spot on her arm.

She sat on a bench in a Beecham County Sheriff Department holding cell. By the time the ambulance had arrived at her house, she'd already been placed in the back of a cruiser, though she wasn't entirely sure how she'd gotten there. She did recall asking the arresting officer, when he'd returned to the car, about the man she'd shot. The asshole had threatened to tase her again if she didn't keep her mouth shut, so she did. He drove her to the BCSD, and she hadn't had a phone call or seen another human being since. A man and woman were arguing down the hall, but JJ couldn't make out the words until a door opened and they headed in her direction.

"—restraining order!" It was Beth, mid-sentence.

"How the hell was I supposed to know?" the man said. JJ recognized the voice as the officer she *hadn't* shot but *wished* she had.

"If you'd checked with someone who actually lives and works in this jurisdiction, you'd know. It's sitting right there—" Beth pointed back down the hallway, "just waiting for somebody—somebody like you—to serve it on her husband."

"I was kinda busy," he said, sarcastic.

"Yeah," she said, shaking her head. "And how the hell did that happen? We told you there wasn't a lock on the interview room—why do you think you had to stand guard?"

"I leaned a chair against the door when I left," he said. "And he was still cuffed!"

"With no leg restraints!" JJ had never seen Beth angry before, but the woman was boiling now. Beth put her hand to her forehead, smoothing her hair back with a shaking hand. Her breath hitched in her chest when she tried to inhale deeply. "Did you notify *anyone* about Virgil Rutledge before you ran off to find him, or did you wait until after you got a fellow officer shot to call it in?"

Virgil Rutledge? JJ had a vague recollection about him, but—like a lot of things associated with her arrest—she couldn't quite bring it to mind. JJ approached the bars of the holding cell. "What's going on with Virgil Rutledge?"

The male deputy, who wore the same type of uniform as the officer she'd shot, swung toward her. "You just keep your goddamn mouth shut."

Beth shot him a dirty look. "Officer Kilbourne here let Mr. Rutledge escape. He didn't find him at his mother's house, so then apparently he thought the man might've run to you."

JJ's mouth dropped open. "The only time I ever met the man, I almost blew his brains out, so it seems pretty damned unlikely that he'd come to me."

She realized her mistake as soon as her words left her mouth, but it was too late.

"Of course you almost shot him," Officer Kilbourne said. "You're a goddamn menace."

"You didn't announce yourselves—you didn't even park on my property! You showed up hours after my ex-husband threatened to kill me, after he said he'd do so with his cop friends."

"So you admit you knew we were law enforcement?" Kilbourne demanded, eyes triumphant.

JJ sighed and shook her head. It occurred to her that she

shouldn't be speaking with the man at all—had he advised her of her rights? Was she under arrest?—but it seemed a little late now. "I didn't know until after I'd fired the gun."

Disgusted, Kilbourne turned to Beth and said, "I can't believe you're buying this bullshit." Then he stormed from the room (*like a cranky five-year-old in his Big Boy boots*).

Beth clamped her jaw shut against whatever words tried to escape her mouth. Finally, she said, "Don't worry, we'll get this straightened out. I haven't been able to get through to the sheriff yet, but I will."

"So there's no word on Adam," JJ said. She wondered how Iris was holding up.

Beth grimaced. "There's no word on anything."

JJ sat on her bench, then changed her mind and lay down. She had a feeling she'd be here for a while.

68

———

The Watkins County Sheriff's Department was in sight when Luther heard D'Antonio's cell phone go off like a pinball machine in the backseat. A jackknifed tractor and trailer blocking the highway had slowed them down (no injuries, but damn scary to look at), and they were arriving at least forty minutes later than they'd expected.

"Shit," the agent said. "Four voicemail messages. Next time I'll remember to bring a sat phone. How do you people function out here?"

"Texts work better than phone calls," Grant said, looking down at his own phone as it chirped to life. "In theory."

The Sheriff's Department was supposed to be a staging area for everyone involved, so Luther was surprised there weren't more vehicles in the parking lot. He had a bad feeling... He looked in the rearview mirror at D'Antonio's face as the man listened to his messages, and the feeling got worse.

"Well, it seems we had the right idea coming over here, but we're late to the party," D'Antonio said. "Teddy Rutledge reported that Adam Rutledge and Harlan Miller are stuck at his property. There's already a team on the way."

Grant nodded, distracted, listening to one of his own messages. Suddenly, he yelled, "Fuck!" and stared at his phone in disbelief.

Luther wasn't sure he'd ever heard the Sheriff drop an F bomb. "What is it?" he asked, turning into the parking lot slowly, as if to drag out the inevitable.

"Rafael," Grant said, hesitating long enough for Luther to register, *so that's the agent's first name*. "Virgil Rutledge escaped from custody."

Luther was so shocked, he failed to hit the brakes as he eased into the parking spot. The front wheels struck the curb, but fell back to earth before rolling over it completely. He shut off the vehicle, then remembered he hadn't put it in park. "Are you fucking kidding me?"

Grant glared but didn't bother answering. Instead, he muttered at his phone while dialing and redialing numbers with fumbling fingers.

"You have any details?" D'Antonio asked. The federal agent seemed remarkably calm, considering.

"Not yet," Grant said. He held up a finger to forestall further details. "Beth, it's Sheriff Mason. What's the situation?"

He switched his phone hand so he could lean his arm against the window and rest his heavy head on his hand. "Uh-huh... copy that... I'll deal with the Kirby County Sheriff. In the meantime, tell Kilbourne I don't care who the *senior* officer is—he's attached to our department. He can either answer to you or go home. No, wait —he can either answer to you or sit in one of the holding cells until we get back to grill him about what the hell happened."

Luther should've known Kilbourne would be the one behind the fuck-up.

Grant lifted his head and sat up quickly, as if something had reached from his seat to goose his ass. "He did what! Jesus Christ... How is he? ... Well, thank God for that... No, it's probably best if she sticks around until Luther or I get there. But make sure she's comfortable... Thanks, Beth. I appreciate it. Things are moving here, too, so I'll try to keep in touch. Oh, and make sure Rutledge's lawyer knows, before it's all over the news."

Luther gave his boss a few moments to compose himself before asking, "Well, what did Kiss-Ass do this time?"

Grant's jaw jutted and swiveled slightly back and forth, until Luther feared for his dental work. The Sheriff may have gone unshaven and exhausted for more days than was fashionable, but at the moment he looked nothing but fierce. "Deputy Kilbourne noticed that Virgil Rutledge was gone approximately two hours ago. Instead of reporting it, he thought he'd try to find the man first."

"Sonuvabitch," Luther said. "Ass covering bastard—"

"He talked another Kirby County deputy into being his backup, and did a clandestine run at JJ's house," Grant continued. "Apparently, JJ just got a restraining order against her ex-husband—"

"Good," Luther said, relishing the role of interrupter for once, but not for long.

"Which I was not aware she needed," Grant said, heat in his voice as he leaned into Luther's space. Luther didn't react, and Grant's equanimity quickly reasserted itself. Which made his subsequent words even more surprising.

"JJ shot the other deputy. He's at the hospital in Plattsville. It's not serious, but Kilbourne put JJ in a holding cell." He pressed his hands against the dash and said, as though reassuring himself, "She'll be fine until one of us can get there."

The car fell silent. Luther thought what it must be costing Grant, to sit there with JJ miles away, sitting in one of his own cells. He nodded. "Yep, Beth will take care of her."

And I might just take care of that sonuvabitch Kilbourne when I get back. Luther and JJ didn't always see eye to eye, but he'd hells rather have her around than Kiss-Ass.

"Where did Teddy Rutledge call from?" Grant asked, shifting gears.

Luther turned in his seat as best he could with the steering wheel in the way, so he could see both men.

"Didn't say, but he wasn't with them. Details were sketchy in the message."

Grant squinted at his phone, then held it to his ear.

"You know if Teddy Rutledge has a record?" D'Antonio asked.

"Don't know a thing about the man," Luther admitted.

"We need to see if we can track down a picture of him, get it over to that filling station."

It took Luther's sluggish mind a moment to catch up. "You think he's driving Jim Henderson's truck. Alone." D'Antonio nodded. "Why would he leave Adam and Harlan behind? Too much heat?"

"Maybe. But it's interesting that Teddy called in around the same time Virgil escaped," D'Antonio noted.

Luther thought his caffeine must have run out about an hour ago, right about the time he was kicking glass to the side of the road, measuring with his eyes how far that big rig had gone over the edge of the mountain. "Wait a minute... are you telling me you think Teddy had something to do with Virgil's escape?"

D'Antonio shrugged his shoulders. "I don't see how they could've coordinated it, but it's hard to say until we get that damned deputy on the rack and figure out what really happened."

Luther glanced over at Grant. He'd finished listening to his remaining messages, and his phone rested against his bottom lip, as if he'd forgotten it was there. In fact, it seemed as if he'd forgotten the whole world. "Sheriff, you okay? Sheriff?"

Grant blinked, and a grunt escaped him before he achieved the power of speech. "Iris called, to let me know JJ was in trouble. Sounds like maybe Kilbourne checked her place first."

Luther snorted. "Then he's lucky Iris didn't shoot him."

Grant nodded, but his eyes were still focused somewhere in the distance. "And Adam called, from the top of a mountain."

"No shit? What'd he say?"

"That he and Harlan are stranded at Teddy's place, which we

already know. They'll be waiting for us. That the kidnapper had Aaron Schofield in a motel in Loganville yesterday. Apparently, we raided the wrong one."

"Assuming he's telling the truth," D'Antonio said. "And unless he was in on it, how the hell does he know where the kid was kept?"

Grant stared at Luther. There was something more, something bigger.

"What else did he say?" Luther asked.

"That the kidnapper is Danny Carpenter."

Danny Carpenter. Luther should have known, and on some level he probably had. Virgil Rutledge had as much as told them that's who it was; it had just seemed impossible. Grant still appeared stunned, and D'Antonio confused—it seemed Luther was the one whose mind was racing now.

"You think Danny helped Virgil escape?" Luther's mind turned over the possibilities, and the crazy things Virgil had said. "Or maybe didn't help him escape, but was *the reason* he escaped?"

"Hold on," D'Antonio said. "Danny Carpenter is the kid Virgil Rutledge kidnapped twenty years ago? The one whose remains we thought we just found?"

Luther nodded.

D'Antonio blew out his breath, slumped and leaned back. A tall man, his head fell over the headrest at an angle that made Luther's neck ache. "If Adam Rutledge is right, then we've got another body to identify." D'Antonio ran a hand across his forehead and sighed again before sitting up straight. "All right then, gentlemen. Let's get to it."

The parking lot may not have been full, but there was no shortage of activity inside the Sheriff's building. Of the half dozen or so people visible, all but one were on the phone. The outlier, a lanky woman in a brown uniform with her dark blonde hair in a low ponytail, strode toward them. "Sir," she said, then, looking from Grant to D'Antonio, amended that to, "Sirs."

Grant opened his mouth for introductions, but the woman

apparently knew who he was and didn't care to waste the time. "We've just had a call from a motorist about fourteen miles south of here. He came across a man, soaked from the river and half froze, asking specifically for Sheriff Grant Mason. Says his name is—"

"Adam Rutledge," the men said in unison.

69

Adam sat in the back of a Watkins County car, shivering, wrapped in a blanket and wearing a stranger's clothes. He didn't think he was under arrest, but at the moment he didn't care.

The clothes came from the person who'd nearly run him over. Adam didn't know the man's name—his hearing was half shot and he couldn't seem to keep the garbled words in his head—but his Good Samaritan was a Steelers fan, according to the towel and gym clothes he'd loaned Adam. He'd changed while leaning against the man's pickup by the side of the road, not bothered whether he put on a show for the passersby. Then he'd waited in the man's truck, heat blasting, until the first uniformed officers arrived on the scene. They weren't able to tell him anything about Harlan's status, but they did give him a blanket and a Clif Bar, so that was something.

Adam's eyes were open, but he persisted in a state somewhere between sleeping and waking. He had no sense of time, and kept discovering he'd been staring into space for an indeterminate period. Flashing lights approached from behind, rousing him from one such reverie. He tried to open the door (the officers had left him in the back seat), but it was locked. Panicking, he yanked futilely on the handle and yelled, "Hey!"

The officer who'd given him the Clif Bar opened the door and said something Adam didn't catch. He was already staggering toward the Beecham County Sheriff's Department vehicle as it pulled over ahead of them. Grant was the first one out of the car.

"Where's Harlan?" Adam called out.

Grant turned toward the sound of Adam's voice, but there wasn't enough road shoulder for him to pass; he had to wait for the man in back to close his door. The second man was the federal agent who had questioned Adam—how many days ago? It seemed a lifetime.

"Where's Harlan?" Adam repeated, stumbling over a rock and falling to one knee.

Hands pressed on Adam's shoulders through the blanket and helped him rise. It was Luther, looking worn out, with gray hairs in his mustache and lines on his face Adam didn't recall.

"Harlan," Adam croaked. His throat hurt as if he were screaming, but his voice sounded soft and echoey in his head, like a child speaking into a metal barrel. Luther released Adam, and he watched the man's lips for his answer.

"Easy, bud," Luther said, and lifted his eyes to the sky.

Adam heard nothing, or at least nothing he could identify. "What?" he demanded in frustration.

Luther turned Adam to face the river and pointed at the sky. A helicopter flew low over the mountains. So they were medevacking Harlan? If that was the case, his condition was serious, but at least he was still alive. Grant motioned Adam toward the car and ushered him into the back seat. He joined Adam while Luther and the agent sat in front. Luther started the engine, and soon dry heat blew against Adam's face.

"I can't hear very well," Adam said in warning. Luther made some kind of crack, which escaped Adam, and Grant gave the deputy a dirty look.

"We'll keep that in mind," Grant said, speaking slowly and

enunciating in an exaggerated way just short of cartoonish. "Have you been checked out yet?"

"No," Adam said, impatient. "Did you find the boy?"

Adam watched Grant's gaze flick toward Luther before he answered. "Yes. Aaron Schofield is safe, and he'll be okay."

Shivering spasms overtook Adam. Clutching the blanket tightly around his shoulders, he rocked back and forth, kneading his knuckles against his forehead, until he had his body under control. At some point, he realized Grant was talking to him. Adam interrupted, "What's that?"

Grant began again. "I said, the boy is safe, but we didn't get the man who took him."

"I know," he stuttered. "I told them, he's the one who attacked Harlan. I couldn't save Harlan, so I went after Danny, and—"

Grant squeezed Adam's forearm; he'd been rocking again. "Slow down, and start from the beginning."

Instead, Adam started from when he'd called Grant at the top of the mountain. His head bowed with fatigue as he spoke. Grant put his hand on the seat between them to draw Adam's attention when he needed clarification.

"You didn't see a vehicle when you got back to the house?"

"No. Not front or back."

"Would you have even noticed one?" Luther asked, voice soft and barely audible to Adam. "The shape Harlan was in?"

Adam nodded and felt an expected slosh of water in one ear. He tilted his head, gently jiggled his aching skull, and let gravity do its work for a moment before answering. "Yes, because I saw someone running, and I tried to figure out how he'd get away."

"And there were two roads going in?" D'Antonio asked.

Adam grimaced at a resurgent pain in his ear. "Not exactly. The front road we came in was pretty rough, and the trail around back didn't look fit for anything bigger than ATVs."

Adam felt more than heard a powerful knock on top of the car. Grant opened the rear door and a man in his early forties wearing a local sheriff department's uniform leaned against the frame. He said something to the Sheriff. Grant turned to Adam and said, "Tell him where you were on the river when you lost sight of Danny."

Adam described the area in detail, particularly the split, and watched the officer carefully to catch his response to Grant. "I know exactly where he means. There's a haul-out a little ways down the right fork that locals and the outfitters use in season, and a campground that might still have a handful of people. I'll send some uniforms over, see what they can see. It'll take a while. They've got to drive all the way down to the bridge and cross, then backtrack."

Grant said something else unintelligible (Adam felt as if he were dissolving in the seat as he ran through the last of his adrenaline) and the officer left. Adam started—his eyes had drifted shut —when Grant touched his forearm.

"Adam, why did you run?" he asked.

Adam looked away as answers ran through his head. *Because I panicked. Because Iris panicked, and things snowballed before we could see our way straight.*

Because that's what I do... I run.

"I'm sorry," was his only answer.

"Adam," D'Antonio said, loudly enough to get his attention. "You're not under arrest, but I want to ask you some more questions, and I do feel it's appropriate at this point to advise you of your rights."

Adam zoned out as he did so, unable to be bothered about what it meant for his future or whether he should cooperate. D'Antonio leaned over the seat (this vehicle lacked the mesh partition Adam remembered from the department SUV) and asked, "How did Harlan Miller become involved? Did your grandmother contact him?"

His indifference for himself did not extend to the people Adam cared about. He held his head up and lied. "Harlan just gave me a ride. He wasn't involved—he didn't know you were looking for me when we left, and I was careful to keep him away from the news."

"And your grandmother—"

"Didn't know anything, either. I panicked and ran. End of story."

D'Antonio's brows came together, and Adam noticed the slightest hint of scar on one brow that matched the pale scar on the man's lip. "Theodore Rutledge?"

"The man doesn't even own a TV," Adam said, as though that fact alone demonstrated a level of credulity that meant the man could be conned into anything.

D'Antonio looked to the other two law enforcement officers. Grant kept his usual calm expression, and Luther simply shrugged. "Fine," the agent said. "We'll revisit the details of your flight later. What led you to the property out here?"

Adam clued in that Luther's phone had rung when the deputy pulled it from his pocket, glanced at it, and excused himself from the car. Adam took advantage of the distraction, dropping his head again as he braced himself for more elaborate fabrication. Iris's voice spoke in his head, *Butter wouldn't melt in your mouth*, and he almost smiled. Once the impulse passed, he raised his head and said, "Now that my father is 'back from the dead,' I've been thinking about how I never knew anyone on his side of the family. Harlan took me to see great uncle Teddy, and Teddy thought it'd be nice for us to visit this property. He and my father spent a lot of time there together."

"But no one lives there?"

"Teddy was surprised to find that someone had been, although not for a long time." Adam bit his lips together, briefly and unexpectedly overcome by emotion. "My mother's photo was there, so it's a good chance it was Virgil."

"Just Virgil?"

"There were two beds, so there could have been someone else, but I didn't take the time to go through everything in the house."

"Danny Carpenter maybe?"

Adam clenched his jaw, then fought to relax it. It made his ear ache worse. "Could be."

"And what makes you think Danny Carpenter is alive?" D'Antonio demanded.

"I know he's alive because we almost killed each other in that river," Adam said, pointing at the blameless water.

"And that he took Aaron Schofield?"

The million-dollar question, the one Adam should have been preparing for. Not that it would have made a difference. "It just makes sense. It had to be him."

D'Antonio's eyes narrowed. "I've got news for you—nothing about this case makes sense. But you're telling me it's your *intuition* that Danny Carpenter is behind it."

"If you want to call it that."

"Bullshit."

Adam's lip curled involuntarily in an expression he knew would piss off the agent almost as much as his response. "Would you believe me if I told you I had a psychic vision?"

D'Antonio's face flushed, making his scar more visible. "Stop fucking around, Rutledge. Did your father tell you?"

Adam shook his head in frustration, and immediately regretted the motion. His ear was not right. "You can check your visitation records and answer that question yourself. I haven't been to see the man, so I don't know how he could've told me."

The car fell silent, except for the ringing echoes that persisted in Adam's head. D'Antonio sighed, looked to Grant, and nodded. The Sheriff's eyes softened, while D'Antonio watched Adam like a hawk. Adam couldn't guess *what* Grant would say, but it was obvious *who* it would be about. He braced himself, but could feel the nausea building already.

"Virgil escaped from custody a couple of hours ago. I'm sure we'll recover him quickly, but at the moment—"

Adam lunged toward the door. Grant opened it and backed out of his way just in time, as Adam fell to his knees outside and vomited. *It'll start all over, and this time Harlan can't help keep him out. He'll kill me.* He retched again, and what little he'd had in his stomach hit the edge of the blanket, now sliding from his shoulders. He glanced up and recognized Grant's shins.

"Tell the Watkins deputy I'm sorry about his Clif Bar. And his blanket."

Adam carefully placed his arm on a vomit-free section of asphalt and rested his head upon it. *It's already started. It was Virgil's voice I heard while chasing Danny. He's the one who kept me moving, past when I should have dropped. So maybe he won't kill me, but he'll make me kill someone else.*

He thought of Harlan, of the weight of his bloody, wobbling head beneath his hands. Of the helicopter rushing by on its way to God knows where.

And maybe I'll let him.

70

Luther leaned against the cruiser, half in the nearest lane of traffic. Only the uniforms slowing cars as they passed kept him from being a statistic. A ridge rose on the opposite side of the road, thick trees interrupted by a car-sized chunk of rock sunk into the earth. The rock was marked with two fuzzy white lines, the remnants of spray paint graffiti someone had tried to remove. Not that Luther could see it. All he could see was his brother, lying in a hospital bed, all tubes and monitors, alone.

He wasn't aware D'Antonio was standing next to him until the man began talking. "They found the canoe at the haul-out. It looks like Carpenter stole a car from the campground. The owner didn't even know it was missing. One of the fishermen gave us a half-ass description—a wet guy with dark hair and a limp. We've got an APB out on the car. If we get lucky... You okay?" he asked, giving Luther a gentle nudge as his legs strayed closer to traffic.

"The hospital called," Luther said. He paused, as the words struggled to find the path out of his chest. "Les didn't make it."

D'Antonio bowed his head, then turned and rested his arms on top of the cruiser and gazed out over the water. The shadow of the ridge now stretched across the entire river and had begun creeping up the bank on the far side. "I'm sorry."

"He's not—" Phrases jumbled in Luther's head, like someone had shaken up one of those word game things, with just about as much sense to be had from them. *Half-life* and *oxygen deprivation* and *pre-existing vulnerability*... "They said they've still got him on machines, but he's gone."

"Do you need someone to drive back with you?"

That's right; he needed to drive back. That's what he was supposed to do now. Except they had a suspect who... what did he do again? "What about..." Luther trailed off.

D'Antonio reached over and put a hand on his shoulder, leading Luther around the back of the cruiser. "Come on," he said. "I think we've got enough bodies to do what needs to be done. Don't take this the wrong way, but you're not irreplaceable."

His emotions—all kinds of emotions—seethed under a thin skin of numbness, and Luther desperately wanted to laugh. *Offering comfort with an insult must be one of those skills they teach at Quantico.* He hung back while Grant escorted Adam to the waiting EMTs, Rutledge arguing the whole way. Luther doubted Adam would be leaving in their ambulance. He watched as D'Antonio said something in Grant's ear, and the Sheriff's head swung around, looking for Luther.

Luther nearly broke down, seeing his own grief reflected on the Sheriff's face as he offered his condolences. "Are you sure you don't want someone to ride with you?" Grant asked.

"Thanks, Sheriff, but company's the last thing I need right now. What's gonna happen to him?" Luther asked, nodding toward Adam, who sat on a bumper while an EMT examined his ear.

"I'm not arresting him, if that's what you mean," Grant said.

Honestly, Luther wasn't sure.

He took the interstate back, in case the highway folks were still dealing with the earlier truck accident. It was a little farther, but he could drive faster, so time-wise it was the same either way.

Besides, he was looking forward to setting cruise control, to give his feet—if not his mind—a break.

To his surprise, they both went into standby. An hour and a half later, he reached his exit with his only conscious thought having been, *Time to turn on my headlights.*

At the outskirts of Plattsville, his blank mind was seized by anxiety. There were things he needed to be thinking about, but he couldn't rally enough to figure out what they were. His chest constricted as he pulled into a front row spot at the hospital. Luther rested his hand on his sternum, and the doubling sensation of the pulse in his wrist and the beating in his chest made him lightheaded. He took a deep breath, and it rattled a little on the inhale.

At least I'm in the right place to have a heart attack if I'm going to have one.

A thought finally solidified as he walked uncertainly through the glass front doors. *Who should I be calling? Who else needs to know?* The woman at the front desk gave him a sad smile as he passed. A few years younger than Les, Luther had helped her with a disorderly meth-head once when she was working in the ER, but he couldn't remember her name. He made it into the elevator, pushed the floor button, and left his hand resting against the metal panel, afraid the contact was the only thing keeping him standing.

The doors slid open with a ding, and Luther's stomach dropped as though the elevator were still moving. *Mom.* He didn't have to tell her, didn't have to face her, which he supposed was a bit of a blessing. *I'm sorry, Mom.* Luther reached out to stop the doors as they began to close, staggering across the threshold into the hallway. He was on the verge of tears, until he remembered, *Rudy.* That man could harden any emotion. He supposed he should contact his father before doing... whatever he had to do.

A doctor Luther vaguely recognized stood behind the nurses' desk and would have come out to meet him, but Luther waved him away. He needed a moment with Les first. And yet, he still paused outside his door. Because as long as he stood there, it wasn't real; it could still be a mistake.

Someone sat next to Les. Not his father—Esther. She placed Les's hand on the sheet and gently stroked his fingers before standing and rushing to Luther. Her head hit him on the chin as she flung her arms around him, and he bit his tongue, triggering a few waiting tears to fall.

"I'm so sorry, Luther," she sobbed.

Her hands gripped his shoulder blades as though she were falling, and he squeezed her back harder than he'd thought he would. He looked up at the ceiling, to protect his chin from her and keep the tears in check.

"I keep thinking, if I'd called sooner, or if I'd stayed—"

"Shh... It wouldn't have made a difference," he said, although he didn't know if that was true or not. "It's not your fault."

They held each other, until her breathing quieted and Luther decided she'd exhausted her sobs. "Esther," he said into her hair (*smells like apples*), "has my dad been by to see him?"

She stepped away, wiping her nose with her hand, and Luther wished he had a handkerchief to offer her. Then she cleared her throat. "No. I spoke with him, but he says he doesn't need to see him. He doesn't *want* to see him."

Luther heard the tension in her voice, and she couldn't meet his eyes. "It's okay," he said. "I think he's a bastard, too."

She laughed unexpectedly, then put her hand over her mouth to cut off the next bout of sobbing.

Luther said, "I haven't spoken with the doctor yet."

Hand still over her mouth, fingers pinching her lower lip, she said in a muffled voice, "They've just been waiting for you."

"Okay," he said, nodding. "Do you want to be here when they do it?"

Her face was pink and swollen, and he could see her red bottom lip trembling, even as she pinched it. "Would you mind?"

He smiled and felt a tear sneak down his cheek. "No, Esther,

I'd appreciate it. And I think Les would, too. But if you don't mind, I'd like a little time alone with him first."

"Of course," she said, suddenly embarrassed, and went back to the chair to retrieve her purse. "I'll just go freshen up."

Luther remained standing as she passed, waited for the door to click quietly shut, then waited as long as he could. He hadn't even looked at Les yet, not really. And Luther still couldn't, even as he sat in the chair, still warm from Esther's body. He started with Les's hand. He'd had such chubby hands when he was a kid—no knuckles at all until he was well into his teens. Now his fingers showed little patches of hair in the first joints next to his hand, a healed scar from an old sheet of metal roofing (Rudy had tarred Luther's ass over that one), and the odd unhealed scratch here and there. Luther examined those more closely, wondering, *Did you get these from him? From something he did to you?* Probably not. Probably just life.

His eyes crawled up and across the hospital gown toward Les's face. His brother was unshaven, and his beard was as patchy as Luther's own. A ghost of a laugh escaped Luther as he remembered one of Les's drunk friends saying, *Y'all can't grow proper beards. That looks like pubic hair!* He shook his head. That's one he probably wouldn't share, with Grant or anyone else. There were lots of things between him and Les that he'd never share with anyone else. Funny things that were too rude, secrets that were too shameful.

"They'll die with you, brother," he said, reaching out to touch Les's forehead.

It was still warm, his limbs were still pliable, and yet there was something missing in the slackness of his face. He knew his brother was already gone. But Luther continued speaking, not sure if it was for Les or for himself.

"I'm sorry," he said. "I'm sorry we didn't get a chance to pick morels together. Or go to a 'Skins game. You know, just stupid shit. I'm sorry I didn't get to see you get married. Esther's a good woman—better than I gave her credit for—and she might've straightened you out for good."

Luther's voice grew rough, but he dropped his head and pushed through. "I'm sorry I didn't do a better job, keeping you safe. This was my fault, things I set in motion a long time ago... And it meant we never got a chance to make things right. But I will. I will make things right."

He sniffed and wiped his forearm against his face. "I will kill the sonuvabitch that did this to you."

71

Danny's leg throbbed every time he shifted gears. Of course he'd have to steal a manual transmission. *Goddamn that old man and his fucking fake cane.* (Fake in the sense that there's no way he needed one; it sure as hell felt real.) That's okay—he'd switched out the plates in the far reaches of a Super Walmart parking lot, but he'd need to switch out cars soon, too.

He hadn't intended to start over yet, but fortunately he'd taken precautions. It was funny, though. He never thought this would be what took him down; he'd always assumed it would be his dealing day job, or that his other sideline (the one that made the voices quiet) would come back to bite him in the ass.

They'd come after him. Not just the law, but Rutledge—both Rutledges, for that matter. Maybe their desire to kill him would be what brought them together. Wouldn't that just be so sweet he could puke? There'd been four of them when they tried to kill him. Danny didn't know who the old guy was, but he'd been close to Adam, that much was obvious. Not family, but close. So who was the fourth guy? It also would've been someone close to them, and he didn't think either Adam or Virgil was exactly a social butterfly.

Left to their own devices, he figured the Rutledges were a bunch of goddamn hermits.

Rutledge hermits... Could it have been long-lost Uncle Teddy? He suspected Virgil had gone to see him a few times over the years, but Danny had only met the man once. It wasn't all that long after Virgil had taken him.

Danny massaged the outside of his thigh, now cramping from the calf pain in the same leg. Teddy had lived out in the middle of nowhere, some damn creepy place as befit a hermit. They hadn't stayed long, but Danny had gotten the impression Uncle Teddy didn't quite trust him. Maybe because Virgil didn't quite trust him. He probably thought Danny would tell Teddy who he really was. Danny grinned. No, that wasn't it. *Virgil didn't trust me because it was right after Sarah.* Well, then, he couldn't blame the man.

So with Adam's Obi Wan out of the way, that left the three Rutledges, with Virgil in jail, Adam off licking his wounds somewhere, and old Teddy being the wild card. Well, the Rutledges had a pretty volatile family history. Holding together for another assault wouldn't be easy without Obi Wan. They'd have to decide they weren't killing each other before they came after Danny.

What was the cliché their elementary gym teacher always trotted out? *The best defense is a good offense.* He'd get clear of this shitstorm first, but then that's exactly what he'd do. He'd hit them where it hurt. Danny smiled as he exited the interstate. *Hit them where they're vulnerable.*

72

———————

"I appreciate you giving me a ride," Adam said.

"Thank the deputy whose vehicle I commandeered. It'll take us a couple of hours to get to the hospital in Morgantown," Grant said. He straight-armed the wheel with one hand, the other resting next to the seat. The steering wheel seemed to be the only thing holding him up.

"Where's Luther?"

Grant glanced at him, then rubbed the scruff on the side of his face. "He had to go back to Beecham County. So what'd they tell you about that ear?"

"Perforated eardrum, but it should heal okay on its own so long as I'm careful. Gotta do a round of antibiotics, just in case. Apparently I wasn't supposed to be swimming."

"They'd prefer you drowned?" Grant asked.

The highway veered away from the river, settling into the familiarity of a tree-lined corridor. Although still cold enough to appreciate the car's robust heater, Adam was surprised to realize he'd miss the water. He'd felt like so long as the river was in sight, they were heading in the right direction, whatever their destination. Now, they could be anywhere.

"What do you think Danny will do?" Grant asked.

"I—" Adam's thoughts moved in sudden fits and starts, with gaps between. Making sense of them was like listening to Morse code with no key. "I have no idea."

"We found the car he stole from the campground," Grant admitted. "Owner left the keys in it because he was afraid to lose them in the water. Anyway, it was abandoned at a shopping mall seventy-five miles away. We're still trying to figure out where—and how—Danny went from there."

Adam rested his head against the seat and closed his eyes. There wasn't much light left in the day, but enough reached through the trees to flash red and orange against his eyelids from time to time.

"How'd you know where he was with the boy?" Grant asked.

Adam didn't realize he'd stopped breathing until he became aware of his own still chest. He started again, then said, "How do you think?"

"Was it just you?"

Adam took his time opening his eyes. "What's that?" he asked, and cupped a hand behind his bad ear.

Grant assessed the road, then faced Adam and enunciated very clearly, "Was it just you, or did Harlan help?"

"Does it matter?"

"If Danny figures out you needed Harlan's help to figure out what he was up to, I'd say that changes the cost-benefit analysis on trying to harm Harlan. Wouldn't you?"

"Jesus," Adam said, resting his head in his hands. Why hadn't he seen that? He inhaled deeply through his nose, trying to stay calm. "Yes, Harlan helped."

Although if he hadn't "helped" by stopping me, I might have killed Danny and we'd be done with all this.

"Was anyone else with you, anyone else who might be in danger from Danny?" Grant asked.

Adam opted for a partial truth. "Virgil was part of it, too. Don't ask me how. Harlan and—" Adam paused, almost slipping up. "—

Virgil figured it out between them. I was just the conduit, or the power source, or the... I don't know what I was."

"So Teddy didn't help?"

Adam considered. It didn't take a genius to connect Teddy leaving them behind and Virgil escaping from jail. If Teddy was with Virgil, he was probably safe from Danny. And if the authorities hadn't linked Teddy and Virgil, Adam didn't want to give them another reason to look at the man. "No. All Teddy did was drive us out to the property because we'd never been."

"Hunh," Grant said, as though he wasn't entirely convinced, but also didn't have the energy to call Adam on it.

That made two of them.

IT WAS dusk by the time they reached I-79, and full dark crossing the Monongahela River on the south side of Morgantown. Adam wished it was still daylight, and a month earlier. The sight of the river cutting through the mountains in their full red and orange fall regalia was... not *spectacular*, because that implied a distance he'd never felt. It was like the difference between randomly seeing a gorgeous actress on the street, and seeing someone you loved when they looked their best and knew it. The former was an anecdote you shared, but the latter was something you truly remembered.

Grant parked in a lot across from the massive red brick and glass hospital complex, and said, "Iris is probably already here. I called her as soon as I knew where they were flying him."

"Thank you," Adam said.

Grant nodded. "She's been good, helping out with my dad." Grant reached for his hat on the back seat. "How easy was it for you to recognize Danny when you saw him the first time?"

"Hard to say," Adam equivocated, wondering where Grant was headed with the question. "I was half-frozen, and he was trying to drown me with a canoe paddle."

"But you knew it was him? Immediately?"

"Yes. But I couldn't help but know it was him. I mean, I'd been *in his head* while he—"

"While he what?" Grant asked sharply.

Adam swallowed and looked out across the dark parking lot, staring at a car a few spaces away, trying to decide whether someone was sleeping in the back seat. "While he tried to suffocate Aaron Schofield." Grant made a sound, but Adam didn't turn. "Until we stopped him."

The wind picked up outside, whistling around the cars and bending the occasional landscaped tree. "So he is capable of murder," Grant said, rubbing his eyes.

"Yes." Adam recalled the images he'd seen while struggling in the river. He almost didn't share them, but had an intuition he should. "I also saw something from Danny's mind, when we were trying to drown each other. I think he killed someone else."

Grant's head jerked toward Adam. "How? When?"

"Choked him to death. I don't know when, but not that recently. Danny looked younger than he does now. I don't know who or where either, since I'm assuming that's what you'll ask next. I'd never seen the man before, but he, uh, he looked like me."

"Really? That's interesting," Grant said. "What did you mean, you stopped Danny from killing the boy?"

"It's hard to describe. I did something—with Virgil's help—that was painful."

"To Carpenter or to you?"

"Both," Adam admitted. "But I guess more so to him, because it made him stop suffocating Aaron."

"I didn't realize something like that was in your repertoire," Grant said, an edge of wariness creeping into his voice.

"Neither did I."

Another gust of wind buffeted the car. "Do you think someone else—someone like Leslie Beck—would have recognized Danny?" Grant asked.

"Not necessarily," Adam said. "There's a big difference between thirty-two and twelve, especially when you think the twelve-year-old is dead. And if he was wearing a beard when they met... You think he has some kind of relationship with Les?"

"In a manner of speaking," Grant said, hesitating.

Adam was so tired of dancing around the truth. "Just spit it out."

"Leslie Beck died from a drug overdose. We think Danny Carpenter killed him."

Adam recalled the sensation of being punched by Otto, weeks earlier. He hadn't quite regained his breath when Grant said, "We should go. Iris'll be waiting."

The wind took Adam's door from his hands and, with no car next to them, he surrendered it. His muscles had stiffened, and the air felt so cold it was hard to make himself move. Grant came around and slammed his door, then nudged Adam toward the entrance. But Adam's feet wouldn't move. He stood and watched as a helicopter flew low overhead, so low even his damaged ear felt overwhelmed by it, disappearing over the edge of the buildings. Presumably Harlan had come in that way as well.

"Come on," Grant yelled over the ambient noise.

Adam was rooted to the spot, even as his body began to shiver. When the next rush of sound had passed, he asked, "Why is it, I can almost kill a man, but I can't heal one? Tell me how that makes sense."

"Because you're not God," Grant said, as though the answer were the most self-evident truth in the world. "Now, come on. Iris needs you."

Of course, he was right. Adam followed Grant inside, past bleeding people and calm people, crying people and catatonic people (*which one will Iris be?*). Down one hallway and up another until finally, he saw her. White hair pulled back loosely at the base of her neck, wearing a roomy gray sweater (*Harlan's?*) over baggy jeans, she looked so small. She turned, as though she knew he was behind her, and held out her arms.

"I'm so sorry," he said, voice cracking, taking her hands. *I tried*, he wanted to say, but was circumspect in front of Grant.

Iris's eyes filled with tears, but her cheeks plumped as she smiled at him. *Those cheeks have been wasted on a lifetime of too little smiling*, Adam thought, his own eyes filling.

"Me, too. You know I love you," she said, then tugged him to her, burying her face in his chest. She stood on tiptoes to add, "You stupid child."

"Child?" he asked, smiling as a tear dripped on the crown of her wavy hair.

"Ridiculously tall child," she corrected.

"I love you, too, Gram."

73

———

"Ms. Tulley? Ms. Tulley?" A hand pressed her shoulder gently. "JJ?"

JJ sat up, inhaling deeply through her nose to cover a yawn. "Am I on?" she asked, the yawn escaping anyway as soon as she spoke. She rubbed her eyes and realized she wasn't in the break room at work. Beth stood over her, with a backdrop of bars. She was in jail. "Shit."

"That's a gift, being able to sleep like that," Beth said, sitting next to her.

"Hazard of the job. I can sleep anywhere, any time." *Except at home, thanks to ass-wipe Marcus.* JJ stretched her arms over her head and let out one last, jaw-popping yawn.

Beth handed JJ a paper sack. "Thought you might be hungry."

"Thanks." JJ pulled a thick sandwich free, then spread the bag on her lap for a table. "Oh, I live for the diner's egg salad."

"I spoke with Sheriff Mason," Beth said, handing JJ a can of iced tea. The deputy leaned against the cinderblock wall, raising one knee and folding her hands over her nonexistent belly.

"Oh, yeah," JJ said awkwardly, trying to neither spit egg salad on her lap nor look too hopeful.

Beth's smile was dark as the dirt under a mechanic's fingernails. "Pissed doesn't begin to cover it. And not at you. But he needs you to stick around until he gets back to straighten things out. Do you need to make any arrangements in the meantime?"

"What time is it?" JJ asked.

"Just after ten p.m."

JJ slugged some tea, then wiped her mouth. "I'm past due at the hospital, so if I could just call in and let them know someone needs to cover me..."

"No problem. We can do it as soon as you finish your sandwich."

The deputy was quiet while JJ ate, but it was a comfortable silence. It helped that JJ had no hang-ups about people watching her snarf down food—another hazard of the job. When she was done, she crumpled the bag around her soiled napkin and said, "Ready whenever you are."

Beth led JJ out of the cell to the nearest desk and punched a few buttons on the phone while JJ dropped into a chair. The desk was an old metal model, and someone—the child of a staff person? —had written initials on its edge with magic marker. *Initials...* JJ's mind went back to Adam's initials scratched out on the poplar tree. Marcus wouldn't have done that, not if he didn't know whose car was parked in her yard.

Beth stared at her, waiting for JJ's response to something she hadn't heard.

"I'm sorry—what did you say?"

"Just dial the number. But since it's Plattsville, you'll need the area code, too."

JJ got through quickly and explained the situation as best she could, promising to give her co-worker all the gory details later. As soon as she hung up, she asked, "Any word on the man I shot?"

"Why, you didn't want to out yourself to your colleagues on the phone?" Beth smiled. "The hospital already released him."

"Thank God." JJ sighed and slid lower in the chair. *Maybe this will work out after all.* She leaned the chair back. "I never shot anybody before."

"Me, neither," Beth admitted.

JJ nearly fell off the chair when a man's voice yelled, "What the hell are you doing here?"

"Sorely as I've been tempted," Beth muttered. She slid off the desk and straightened her frame to its full five feet of height. "I might ask you the same thing."

"Why is she out of her cell?" Deputy Kilbourne demanded.

"And why aren't you manning the front desk?" Beth asked, advancing on him. "How are we supposed to know who's coming and going?"

"I'd be more worried about who's already in here," Kilbourne said, staring pointedly at JJ.

"That's funny, because you weren't worried about it before," Beth said, arms folded.

JJ was surprised—Beth didn't strike her as the confrontational type, so she and Kilbourne must have been bumping heads for a while. Personally, JJ was content to avoid unnecessary drama for now. Her child was safe with the Nicholsons, she wasn't expected at work, and that bench hadn't been so uncomfortable after all. She stood and said, "No big deal, Deputy Marshall. Now that I've given the hospital a heads-up, I don't mind waiting in the cell until the Sheriff gets here."

Kilbourne stalked across the room after JJ as she went back to the cell, as if he didn't trust her not to climb the walls to escape, or maybe step through them. Beth intercepted him, widening her stance. She said in a low voice, "Deputy, this whole situation is bad enough already. Let's not go making it worse."

Suddenly something slammed from the direction of the unmanned reception desk. Kilbourne jogged toward the sound, just in time to walk into Luther as he entered.

"Who the hell's supposed to be out front?" Luther asked.

Kilbourne backpedaled, bumping against a filing cabinet and setting it to rock. Luther shook his head. He wasn't wearing his coat or hat, and his uniform shirt was rumpled. But the state of his clothes was nothing compared to his countenance. Eyes red and mouth tight, he looked ready to explode.

"Where's Sheriff Mason?" Kilbourne asked.

Luther aimed a look at him that could have melted steel. "He's still doing real lawman work, but he sent me to deal with this bull-shit." JJ flinched as he turned his gaze to her. "JJ, how you doing back there?"

She tried to keep her voice light as she approached the front of the cell. "I'm alright, Luther. You?"

"Don't ask," he replied. "Come on—I'll take you home."

"What do you mean, take her home?" Kilbourne asked.

Luther didn't bother looking at the other man. No one had closed the cell yet, and he motioned for JJ to exit the cramped area. "She's been here long enough, but you need to wait for the Sheriff."

"She shot a law enforcement officer," Kilbourne protested.

Luther turned to the deputy. "And that'll be investigated. As will the fact that you failed to report the escape of a suspect who posed a danger to the public, failed to follow pretty much *any* proper procedure—hell, I'd be surprised if you drove on the right side of the road—and that you attempted an illegal search without a warrant while pursuing an investigation without any kind of departmental authorization."

"She goes home and I have to wait, as if I did something wrong?" Kilbourne made a guttural sound of disbelief.

"*She* is a known quantity; you are anything but."

"Does that mean she's sleeping with you, too?" Kilbourne smirked.

JJ froze where she stood and watched Beth take a step to the side, so the desk was between the female deputy and the two men.

Luther blinked slowly and sighed. "We've all been under a lot of stress lately, so I'm gonna pretend like you didn't say that. So long as you don't open your goddamned fool mouth again."

JJ lingered, hesitant, and Luther put a hand on her arm to

escort her out of the cell. She winced involuntarily, and Luther turned sharp eyes on her. "What was that about?" he asked.

She opened her mouth but nothing came out because—and this surprised JJ—*Luther frightened her*. She glanced over at Beth, unsure what she wanted the woman to say, but wishing she'd say *something*. And Beth did.

"That's probably where he tased her," Beth volunteered.

That was *not* what JJ had wanted her to say.

Luther swung toward Kilbourne. "You *tased* her?"

"She was resisting arrest," the man said.

That made JJ angry enough to forget she'd been trying to de-escalate the situation. "I was trying to administer aid to the other officer—"

"Bullshit!" Kilbourne interrupted as he moved toward her, losing sight of the fact that Luther stood between them. "You were—"

Luther decked him. Laid the man out flat with one right hook to the jaw. JJ's mouth fell open. *Gathering flies, Mom*, Evie would have said. JJ closed her mouth, but it just wouldn't stay that way, as though the sight of Luther striking another officer had rendered the hinge in her jaw defective. It hadn't done a lot for Beth's either, JJ noticed.

Kilbourne groaned and began to move, arms beneath his chest, pushing off the floor until he was hunched on all fours.

Luther's expression hadn't changed, except maybe to relax a tiny bit. He shook his hand as he turned to JJ, ignoring Kilbourne on the floor. "Do you have any property here you need to take with you? Wallet or cell phone?"

"I, uh," JJ stammered. No wallet, but where was her cell phone? No pockets... she'd left it on the porch. "No. Nothing," she said.

Luther nodded. "Okay, then."

The only sign Luther knew Kilbourne still existed was a slight tensing in his shoulders, but JJ continued to watch the injured deputy as she stepped away from the cell. The man grabbed the corner of the desk and pulled himself to a standing position. He put his other hand to the red mark on the left side of his face and wiggled his jaw back and forth.

"You fucking coward," Kilbourne said.

Luther shook his head briefly before turning to face the other deputy. JJ raised questioning eyebrows at Beth, but the other woman simply shrugged. Deputy Kilbourne definitely was not popular among the Beecham County employees.

Kilbourne's eyes had filled with tears, but his mouth at least was still defiant. "You sneaky, sucker-punching fucking coward. I'd like to see you—"

Luther's left fist flashed forward in a short, explosive jab to Kilbourne's midsection. Kilbourne doubled over, face purple, then dropped to his knees as he gasped for breath. Luther bent over him, gently placing a hand on his back. "You got three choices moving forward: learn how to fight; learn how to keep your mouth shut; or learn how to stay down. If I were you, I'd focus on the last one."

Luther's face had pinkened, almost deeply enough to match his bloodshot eyes, and he was a little short of breath. Still, his voice was calm as he turned to JJ and motioned her around the heaving officer on the floor. "Shall we go?"

74

———

"Luther, are you okay?" JJ asked as they turned onto Main Street. It was dark now, and the periodic streetlights weren't kind to Cold Springs, making it appear more like a museum replica of a town than a place where people actually lived.

"Yeah," he replied offhandedly, mind obviously elsewhere.

The same streetlights that reminded JJ of a child's train set also acted as a slow-motion strobe, flashing across the vehicle's hood, illuminating the leading edge of the interior before disappearing as they hit the roof, only to repeat the process a few yards later. She stared at Luther's discolored knuckles as the light passed over them again, and again. "Are you sure you're okay?"

Luther swung his head around, as if he'd forgotten she was in the car. "I'm sure," he said. "But listen, I don't really feel much like talking right now if you don't mind."

"Okay." She wasn't sure she was capable of carrying on a conversation anyway. Her mind was overwhelmed by questions, but so dulled by mental exhaustion, she didn't know where to start. So she didn't.

Trooper must be crossing his legs and sniffing around the edges of the counters by now.

Several minutes later, Luther turned up her driveway, his high beams flashing against the treetops overhead as the vehicle bounced up the incline. He parked behind her Bronco and spoke in the dark. "JJ, there's something I need to tell you."

"Is it about Adam?" she asked.

"No. Well, not exactly." He scratched his scalp hard, back and forth along one side of his head. "There are things I can't say, because this is an open investigation, and things I'll leave for Grant to tell you when he comes by. But this one, this one I think you should know—I think you *need* to know—just in case."

"In case what?"

Luther laughed, a tired sound. "Hell, I don't know. Maybe I've spent too much time around Rutledges. Anyway, I'm not so sure about my job status after tonight, so what's one more black mark for running my mouth?"

"Luther, I'm sure—" JJ hoped Luther didn't see her flinch as his hand flew up in the dark.

"I don't want to talk about me right now," he said. "This is more important. JJ, Danny Carpenter is alive."

Just when I thought shit couldn't get stranger... "No, Luther, that's impossible. Virgil kidnapped him and killed him twenty years ago. You found his remains—"

He shook his head. "We don't know what we found yet. But it wasn't Danny Carpenter. Adam saw the man, after he bashed Harlan's head in."

"Harlan?" JJ gasped. "Is he—"

"I don't know, but it's bad. And Adam says it was Danny. Look, I imagine Grant'll tell you more, but in the meantime, I just thought you should know. You didn't shoot that Kirby Deputy with your daddy's shotgun, did you?"

"No, my pistol. How'd you know about daddy's shotgun?" she asked.

"Oh, I've heard tell stories..." There was something in his tone JJ couldn't put her finger on, a mixture of amusement and sadness. "I'm sure I'm being paranoid, but indulge me—keep the shotgun close. And keep Evie close, too. For that matter, tell Otto not to let Rachel out of his sight."

"You think the girls are in danger?" JJ asked, fighting the panic that flooded her chest. "Why?"

"Because it looks like Danny's the one that kidnapped Rachel. Among other things," he said. "Speak of the devil."

Stunned by everything he'd said, JJ smacked her head into the passenger window in her rush to see what he was referring to. Three flashlights approached through the woods from the Nicholson house. *Otto and the girls.* "You need to speak with Otto," she said, rubbing her temple.

"I can't, not right now. Please, JJ, I have to go." His voice was almost pleading.

"Oh, okay," she said uncertainly. He turned away from the dome light when she opened her door, so she couldn't see his face. "Thank you, Luther."

She closed the door behind her, then heard a whirring screech as the window rolled down.

"JJ," Luther said from the other side of the vehicle, "thank you. I do appreciate everything you did for Les."

"Sure," she said, but the window was already closing.

"Mom!" Evie called out.

JJ raised her hand in acknowledgment. But she couldn't let go of Luther's words as he put his vehicle in gear and backed up to turn in the driveway. He'd sounded as if Les were... *No.*

"Luther!" JJ yelled, waving her arms and running toward the driver's window. But he ignored her, rolling down the driveway.

"Mom!" JJ turned in time to be nearly bowled over by her daughter. Evie wrapped her arms around JJ and clung the way she hadn't for years, probably since she and Marcus divorced. "There were cops everywhere, and they wouldn't tell us what happened, and Trooper was going crazy, and we didn't know where you were—"

"Shh, baby, it's okay," JJ said, stroking her hair. "I'm right here, and everyone's fine."

"And then we found your phone..." Evie's voice disappeared in JJ's midsection.

"Good," JJ said. "I hope you kept it for me."

Otto and Rachel hung back, flashlights pointed at the ground, until most of Evie's energy was spent. Finally, Otto said, "The girls made molasses cookies with Dorothy to pass the time. Why don't you come over and have some, before Jacob eats them all?"

JJ was exhausted, but Otto's subtext was clear—*you need to come over and spend some time pretending like everything's normal*. "I'd love some. Let me get Trooper."

"He's already over there," Evie said, releasing her mother, but taking her hand with what felt like no intention of ever letting go.

"Really?" JJ said. That was quite a concession for both Dorothy, who didn't like animals in the house, and Otto, who'd had a difference of opinion with Trooper (and JJ, for that matter) a few weeks ago. "Thank you."

She could just make out his smiling nod in the glow from the flashlights. Rachel drifted from her father's side to JJ's free arm. JJ squeezed her, then took Rachel's hand as they walked together back through the woods. "I thought you ladies had a rehearsal tonight."

"We did," Evie said, "but we left early."

"Rachel had the pastor call us to pick them up," Otto said.

Again, his voice was thick with things he didn't want to say in front of the girls. That could mean a long night, waiting for the girls to go to sleep. Unless he didn't want to speak in front of Dorothy, either.

"Rachel thought something happened to you," Evie said.

JJ stopped involuntarily, jerking the girls' arms, and tried to pass it off as a stumble. "Did you?" she asked, striving for equanimity, for the same voice she used when they spoke about their social studies teacher or who got detention today.

"I was right," Rachel said, her voice soft but firm. Certain.

"Well, everyone's fine now," JJ said, pulling them both closer. "Especially my girls."

And if Luther was right, it was her job to make sure they stayed that way.

75

Adam waited in silence with Iris and Grant on uncomfortable chairs. Eventually, the Sheriff excused himself for a phone call. He hadn't been gone more than five minutes when a man in scrubs arrived to let Iris know Harlan was out of surgery. Dark-skinned and dark-haired, not much taller than Iris, the doctor had an earnest but no-nonsense way of speaking to her. Adam hovered at her elbow, but kept missing words. More likely, he was simply incapable of taking them in.

The doctor explained that the skull wasn't solid, but rather was made up of many fused bones. "Mr. Miller had a depressed fracture of one of the parietal bones—"

Adam's hands started to shake as the doctor pointed to that portion of his own skull, toward the back on one side.

"—meaning pieces of bone were pushed in." The doctor began demonstrating with his hands again. "We had to elevate the area."

"How do you do that?" Iris asked.

Adam couldn't listen, turning away as the man described drilling into Harlan's skull. He walked to the far end of the waiting room, rested his forehead against the wall, and closed his eyes. His skin crawled with sensation, and he hugged his arms to keep them from shaking as badly as his hands.

He wasn't sure how long he'd been standing that way when something brushed his arm. Adam swung around defensively.

"Easy," Grant said, stepping back and raising his hands in conciliation. "It's just me."

Adam felt like he'd forgotten to breathe for a very long time, that he couldn't remember the last time he'd ever breathed. He desperately sucked in air, again and again. He leaned forward, resting his tingling hands on his thighs...

"Hey," Grant said, taking his wrist firmly. "Slow down, and breathe through your nose."

His voice was reassuring (*how is he always so calm?*) and Adam did his best to comply.

"Good," Grant said. "I know this is a hospital, but let's try not to pass out. They tend to take it the wrong way."

Adam was still a little lightheaded, and his chest felt like interlocked fingers making a fist. No wonder, with everything he'd put it through today—jumping off a mountain, drowning in a freezing river, hyperventilating. At least he'd skipped the CPR this time. He thought of JJ and almost smiled. "I'm okay now," he said. "Thanks."

Grant nodded. "Your grandmother wants to talk to you. She went to find some coffee."

Adam followed Grant to the fourth floor, where they found Iris at the vending machines, sipping something that made her wince.

"Cafeteria opens again in a couple of hours," Grant said.

Iris raised an eyebrow. "Something to look forward to. Did you tell him?"

Grant shook his head.

"The Sheriff has to get back to Beecham County tonight," Iris said. It occurred to Adam that she was the only person he didn't have to strain to hear. "I think you should go with him."

"Iris, if this is about what happened in there—" Adam gestured vaguely, not entirely sure where the waiting room had been.

"Sweetie," Iris said, looking in vain for somewhere to set her coffee as she stepped toward him. Finally, she gave up and threw the nearly full cup in the trash.

"Lousy excuse for coffee," she said, then grabbed the sleeve of his sweatshirt. "Steelers, huh? You have a change of clothes?"

"No," Adam admitted. He didn't have anything except his damp wallet, and he was afraid to ask Grant about Teddy and the truck and the duffel bag that contained most of his earthly possessions, lest he get his great uncle into more trouble.

"Toothbrush? Comb? Razor?" she asked, patting his bearded cheek.

"No, none of that."

"Me either, though I could skip the razor." She took Adam by the arm and led the men toward the elevator.

"What did the doctor say, back there? When can we see Harlan?" Adam asked. He swallowed hard to force out the next question. "Will he make it?"

Iris's voice was cautious, stripped of other emotions, but her pressure on Adam's arm increased. "We can't see him yet. And he could go either way."

The doors opened, and the three of them stepped into an empty car. Adam avoided looking at their reflections on the shiny surface while Iris pushed the button for the lobby. Then she linked her fingers in his. "I intend to stay here until the end, whatever that may be. I'd appreciate it if you could pick up some things for me. JJ can help you pack."

Movement behind him—some reaction from Grant at the mention of JJ—distracted Adam. He turned his attention back to Iris. "I need to see Harlan, too."

"I know," she said, squeezing his hand. The doors opened, and she led him to the lobby. "But tonight, keep Grant awake while he's driving and spend the night in a decent bed at home. I'll call if there's any change."

Adam reached automatically for his cell phone, then shuddered at the memory of throwing it when he couldn't save Harlan. "I lost my phone."

"I'll call the house and leave a message," she said, and rubbed his hand between hers. "How did your hands get so cold?"

Adam treated the question as though it were rhetorical. "I don't have my car keys, either."

Iris set her purse down at a seating area near the entrance and pulled out an overstuffed key ring. "Good thing you gave me the spare," she said, unthreading a key with yellow tape from the rest of the ring.

Adam sighed. "Okay," he said, "but I'll be back here first thing tomorrow."

"Don't you dare leave Cold Springs before noon. Sheriff Mason, why don't you warm up the car while we say our goodbyes."

"Yes, ma'am." He nodded, placed his hat carefully on his head, then took her free hand in both of his. "Take care of yourself."

There was a burst of cold air as Grant passed through the wide front doors. Adam shivered. Iris reached up and, instead of putting his hood up as he'd expected, gently touched Adam's bruised cheek. "Did he do that?"

It was the first time she'd referred to Danny, or even indirectly to what had happened to Harlan.

"Yes," Adam said, swamped by a sudden, angry guilt because Harlan lay on the verge of death while he had a lousy shiner.

"The doctor told me with that degree of head trauma, it was a miracle Harlan was still alive. I said it was because the man's so stubborn, but it's more than that, isn't it? You did something to help him."

Adam turned away, but Iris took his chin in her hand and made him meet her intense, gray eyes. "Didn't you?"

"I didn't do enough."

She shook her head, then smiled, and he couldn't resist smiling back at her plumped cheeks. "You know that's your mother, right? She was the healer. And so long as you've got her in you, you'll be able to control the rest. I promise."

"HOW LONG'S it take to get to Cold Springs from here?" Adam asked.

"Couple of hours."

Adam massaged his head with his hand, only to find a sore spot, likely courtesy of the river rapids. "So what's going on with JJ?"

"You noticed that, huh?" Grant acknowledged. "She's been having a little trouble lately."

"With Marcus?"

Light from the instrument panel flashed off Grant's pale face as he turned to Adam in the dark. "Why am I the last one to know about this shit?"

So much for always being calm. "Is she okay?"

"*She* is." Grant let out a heavy breath, more like a fighter before a bout than a sigh, but had recovered his composure when he continued. "A couple of loaner deputies thought Virgil might've gone to JJ's, they showed up unannounced, and she shot one of them. He'll be okay. The other one took her into custody."

"Wait—she shot someone, and she's in jail? Your jail?"

"Not exactly," Grant said. "Luther punched the deputy and took her home. So I figured we'd kill two birds with one stone— see how she's doing and get you your car."

"Have you talked to her? Or Luther?"

"No. Both seemed like in-person conversations. Plus the Kirby County Sheriff was already breathing down my neck with the shooting. Now he'll want Luther's head, too. I'd like to have an hour or two of sleep before splitting that particular baby."

A pickup fell in behind them. Grant squinted and adjusted his rearview mirror, muttering, "Really? You want to ride up a Sheriff's ass?"

Adam struggled to process all the pieces he'd just gotten from Grant. "Evie and Rachel weren't around, were they? During the shooting?"

"I don't think so."

"Are you gonna prosecute JJ?"

"I don't make those decisions. I just investigate. The District Attorney's office makes that call," Grant said. It sounded practiced, like a sound bite he'd used before.

"So, you and JJ... will this make things weird for you?" Adam asked.

"It sure as hell won't make things simpler," Grant burst out, then turned to give Adam what he felt certain was a dirty look, even in the dark.

"You like how I did that? With the assumption of a relationship in the question?"

"Any assumption of a relationship would be wishful thinking on my part," Grant said.

"Maybe," Adam replied, unconvinced. "Either way, you have to admit that was classic interrogation technique. Maybe I could be a deputy, too."

Grant laughed. "Yeah, right. Between you and Luther, we'd be up to our eyeballs in lawsuits."

The idea tickled him so much, Grant laughed again. His laugh —not particularly loud or boisterous, but enriching—reminded Adam of Iris's smile. He suspected Grant didn't laugh enough, either. As its echo faded from the car, Adam imagined the sound filling the Tulley house, where he and JJ and Danny had laughed so much themselves.

"JJ and I are just getting reacquainted after twenty years," Adam said, "so I can't pretend to be an expert on the woman. And I imagine dealing with her ex-husband has done a number on her. But there is one thing I know that's fundamental to who she is. JJ is independent, but even more important to her is that she doesn't *become dependent*, if that makes sense."

"Okay," Grant mulled. "I think I see the distinction."

"It makes it hard for her to admit when she needs help, and it makes it hard for her to let people in. If you push before she's ready, she'll dig in and push back. But when she is ready, you gotta jump on it fast because if you don't she'll doubt herself and pull back, start putting up walls."

When Grant didn't respond, Adam wondered if he'd crossed a line. After all, the Sheriff hadn't asked for relationship advice. "Just my intuition, for what it's worth."

Finally, he heard the man sigh. "Why are you telling me this?"

"Man in my position, I figure it can't hurt to curry favor with law enforcement," Adam said, grinning as he pulled his hood up against the chill.

76

____

Heart pounding, Adam jerked awake, opened his eyes and gasped. The Dead Hollow curve stretched ahead, the still-intact guardrail reflecting headlights in the dark. The past and present were overlaid, and Adam was crushed between them. He waited for the sound of brakes, of snapping limbs, breaking glass and ripping metal. One ear ached with the effort of listening, but the car's engine and heater remained indistinct, white noise.

Adam drew breath again when the car emerged from the curve on the other side. His hands were gripping an unfamiliar seat, and his eyes skittered around in the dark until he recognized a blurry Grant sitting next to him. He opened his eyes wider, trying to focus.

"Sorry," he said. "I didn't—" *Scream, say crazy stuff, have a seizure...*

"No," Grant answered, as if he'd finished the question. "You're fine."

Adam's heart was almost beating normally again when they reached JJ's road. He stared as they passed the ditch he'd driven his car into a few weeks ago. Soon, Grant's headlights reflected off the hatchback, parked where Adam had left it before the trunk-or-treat—four days ago? Five? There was a light on low in one of the front rooms, and the motion-sensing porch light activated when their vehicle got close. Grant parked behind JJ's Bronco. Before he'd even shut off the engine, JJ came running out of the house in her socks, Trooper following slowly behind her.

"Go on," Adam said, grinning and slumping out of sight.

JJ slammed into Grant hard enough to knock the man's hat from his head. He didn't bother picking it up. The longer they held each other, the more Adam felt like a voyeur. He slipped out of the car, closed the door quietly behind him, and crept across the driveway toward his hatchback. The door handle felt funny. He squatted to examine it (*fingerprint powder?*), and a cold nose poked into his sweatshirt hood, touching his neck. Surprised, Adam toppled awkwardly onto his butt while Trooper stood over him, sniffing. Adam stroked the dog's neck and noticed a shaved area on one of his legs. "Looks like you've had a challenging week too, buddy."

And then JJ shoved the hood off Adam's head. "You know you're a dumbass, right?" she said, offering him a hand.

"Only because you keep telling me," Adam said, taking it.

She yanked him upright with a groan, then pulled him into an embrace. "I'm sorry," she said. Her whisper tickled his bad ear, but he got the gist.

Adam moved his head to her other shoulder. "For the record, I am, too, but I think it's time we all stopped apologizing for making the best choices we could in an unfortunate situation. Are you okay?"

"Of course," she said, and cold air sidled up to his chest as she released him. "You're the one that looks like you got the crap beat out of you. Again. You're coming in, aren't you?"

Adam shook his head. "Not tonight."

She leaned in and whispered something in his bad ear.

"I'm sorry—I can't hear," he said, pointing at his ear.

"What do you mean? Never mind." She raised her voice slightly, but stayed close. He almost expected her to use Pig Latin. "I said, you won't be interrupting anything. Evie's asleep inside, and Grant won't stay long."

"No, thanks. I really need to go to bed."

"My couch is probably more comfortable than anywhere you've slept for a while."

"It is," he admitted, "but I just need to be alone tonight."

"Okay," she said, tugging at the face of his sweatshirt to smooth the logo, then shook her head. "Iris called; I'll be over in the morning to help you pack. If you have time after, you want to ride over to Luther's with me? His brother—"

"I know," Adam said. "And I'll be glad to go with you."

"I was with him, when he found Les—Jesus, that was just last night. What a crazy fucking week. Anyway, we can talk about it tomorrow. I'll bring cheap muffins."

"And I'll make cheap coffee," Adam said, smiling.

His car started on the second try (*add getting a new battery to tomorrow's to-do list*). He let it run for a bit, until the engine settled into a regular rhythm. Grant and JJ still had their heads together when he turned in her driveway, but they hadn't moved inside, so she was probably right about Grant leaving early. Still, Adam hadn't lied about wanting to be alone. There's nothing he wanted more; he just wasn't certain it was possible anymore.

Iris's house looked strange, like a place that used to belong to him but didn't anymore. The color was indistinguishable in the dark, and he couldn't help feeling it was different, without being quite sure what it had been before. There were no lights on anywhere (*Iris should have a light outside, so she doesn't break her neck*), but a hint of moonlight bathed the clouds and made it appear as though the second story of the small, wooden house was leaning. Shadows clung so tenaciously to the chairs on the front porch, they could have been figures. He knew it was silly, but as cold as it was—as cold as *he* was—he couldn't go inside. He didn't want to sleep in his car, either. Knowing it had been searched somehow made it unfamiliar, too.

Adam took the blanket from the back of his car and made his

way to the nearest, largest tree. He couldn't remember what type it was and couldn't tell in the dark, but it didn't matter. Leaning against its trunk, wrapping the blanket around himself, he discovered he wasn't as cold as he thought he'd be. And it made him feel closer to Harlan. Adam looked at the stars—only a few of the brightest were visible, peeking past the scattered clouds—and felt as though he were looking at the night sky for him.

If there was a way to help Harlan, Teddy would know it. But right now, Teddy was likely in the company of a man who'd escaped from jail, and they'd be lying low. *That's okay. I found Virgil once; I can do it again.*

Adam let his chin sink against his chest...

Virgil stood before a stack of stones. The top one, at nearly chest height, had a slight incline and was large and flat enough to lie atop the rest. His father's altar. The boy in his arms had stopped crying—it was impossible for him not to think it was from a sense of reverence. He set the boy atop the stone. It had held heavier sacrifices before, but none so precious. The boy sat cross-legged, in that easy way of toddlers, and wiped the tears on his face with clumsy hands.

"I can't do this." The dead clearing swallowed Virgil's voice. "Not to my own son."

He reached for the boy—the boy mirrored, reaching for him in return—and the voice said, I thought you loved her.

"I do! I'd give my soul for her."

Exactly. You're giving up your soul for her. The child won't suffer, but will sit at the right hand of God in heaven, doubly blessed as an innocent and a sacrifice.

Virgil drew his hands back, and the boy waved his arms frantically and began to cry again. A knife, his father's favorite, still hung by its hilt from a couple of pegs on the side of the altar. It was rusty now—he hadn't cared for it as he should have; Lawrence would have beaten him for that in life—but the decay was superficial. He took the knife in his hand and felt the heft of it. It was lighter than he'd remembered, but then Virgil was a child when he'd wielded it last. He used his other hand to steady the boy.

"Adam, the first son of man," he began, but the boy cried harder, and he found himself crying again as well. "Shh, it's okay. He says you'll sit at the right hand of God. You'll be resurrected."

Virgil wiped the tears from his face with his knife arm, nearly stabbing himself in the shoulder. He snuffled up snot and blood, then picked the boy up again with his free arm. "Shh," he said, bouncing him lightly. "It's okay."

If she does die, it won't just be for this life. It will be for eternity.

"No, that's not true!" he sobbed into the air. "She was a good woman."

She's going to hell. Unless you offer him to a merciful God.

"No," he blubbered, but he raised the knife anyway. The child went suddenly quiet, and stared at him with the same compassion that lived in his mother's eyes. As if he knew, and had already forgiven him. Virgil set the boy awkwardly back on the altar, as was proper, and gripped him by his hair. The wavy hair he'd said was too long, but Charlotte had adored and refused to cut. He took a deep breath, and the knife arced through the air—

Slicing off a lock of his hair.

But he wasn't done yet.

He ran the rusty blade across his own hand, until blood flowed freely from his palm. Then he muttered a few words (Lawrence had said they were Latin, but in his dark moments, Virgil had his doubts), and smeared the blood across the stone next to the boy. Virgil tossed the knife on the altar and said, "I'm sorry, Charlotte."

And he walked away.

~

ADAM WOKE, shivering, still sitting with his back against the tree in front of Iris's house. He couldn't say a burden had been lifted, but he did feel he had the understanding to help bear it.

He stood, retrieved the spare key from beneath the edge of the house, and went inside. The phone rang before he reached the stairs, and he picked his way carefully through the dark house to the kitchen, both hoping it was and praying it wasn't about Harlan.

"Hello?" he said, grabbing Iris's ancient landline from its cradle. "Hello?"

"I'm glad you know I couldn't do it," a deep, rough man's voice said. "Not even with him whispering in my ear, and not even to save her. Your mother meant everything to me."

"Where are you? Is Teddy with you?"

"Don't worry; I'll stay away now. You won't be seeing me, inside or out," he said. And he hung up.

Adam stared at the buzzing receiver. *That's what you think.*

He climbed the stairs and crawled into bed in his borrowed clothes, sparing a look at his empty nightstand before turning out the light. If he didn't get his duffel back, maybe he could get the photo of his mother from the old house by the river. Tomorrow was soon enough to worry about that, and everything else.

Adam's breathing grew slow and even, and soon a light snore from his waterlogged sinuses joined the soft sounds of the house. He slipped back into the dream, the one that had haunted him his entire life, but this time it was his; it came from *his* memory.

The child watched as his father disappeared into the dead woods, leaving him alone in the darkness. The stone beneath him was cold and hard, and the smell of blood frightened him. He was so tired; he just wanted the reassuring smell and soft feel of his mother next to him.

And suddenly she appeared.

He couldn't smell her or touch her, but she was there in front of him. His mother smiled, and he smiled back at her. Her mouth moved, and he didn't understand the words, but they made him laugh simply because she said them. She reached toward him, and his cheek tingled where she touched his face.

Adam stirred, hand brushing the key at his throat, and smiled before sinking into a deeper, dreamless sleep. But the dream continued, in a hospital bed more than a hundred miles away where...

He pulled his car to the shoulder as far as he could before shutting it off.

It was a damned bad accident—sounded like they'd have to cut the woman out. She was already dead. No one would admit it, but he knew. He could feel it. And yet, when he saw the figure of a woman down in the hollow, he thought, maybe she's confused and wandered off. He didn't tell anyone (he was probably wrong, and didn't need it to get around that he was following ghosts again), just left his keys in the ignition in case someone needed to move his car, stepped off the shoulder and climbed down the ridge.

He didn't think to take his flashlight, but somehow he didn't need it; there was enough light for him to see where he was going. He couldn't get close enough to make out her face—the distance between them never became more or less—but there was something familiar about the woman. He must have known her before... He realized he was thinking in the past tense now. He'd gone too deep into the forest to have any illusions that she was still living. But where was she leading him?

And then he heard the cries of a child. He stumbled for the first time as he ran—that was a voice of the living! How in God's name could a child wander this far?

His skin began to crawl—how had he not realized where he was? Because it was dark and he hadn't been there in years, and, perhaps most powerfully of all, because he didn't want to remember. The trees thinned ahead, and in the small clearing that old bastard's sacrificial altar still stood. A bloody child sat upon it.

"Sweet Jesus, no!" he begged, stumbling toward its cries.

He shuddered when he saw the bloody knife next to the boy. But there was nothing wrong with his lungs, that was certain. Maybe the blood had come from someone else.

He tucked his hands gently beneath the boy's arms, picked him up, and the cries stopped instantly. It was as if the child knew him.

"Have you been waiting for me?" he asked, holding the child away, turning him to check for injuries. The boy reached for his mustache, his thumb at an odd angle, and Harlan laughed. Pulling the boy close again, he saw a flash of metal. A key hung from a chain around his neck. He touched the key, and that's when he saw the woman smiling at the edge of the trees, just long enough to recognize her.

"Oh, Charlotte," he sighed, gently rocking the boy who now seemed *content to tuck his head against the big man's shoulder. "I knew it wouldn't end well for you. I'm so sorry I was right."*

And he began the long hike, back toward the road and the Sheriff and all the emergency personnel. The child slept in his arms, and he glimpsed the narrowest sliver of the possibilities.

"The truth is, you weren't waiting for me, little man," he said. "I've been waiting for you, maybe my whole life. We won't have much time together now, and later, you'll make me wait again, for years and years and years. But you'll come back and I'll be waiting. Because our fates are linked together, you and I. I can't say how exactly, but I bet it'll be exciting."

The bandaged body didn't stir in the hospital bed, but the man inside the body did, the slightest flutter of the soul. And somewhere, somehow, deep within his buried mind, a woman's voice whispered, *Patience, Harlan. You're not done with him yet.*

ACKNOWLEDGMENTS

Thank you to the usual suspects: my editors Alida and Calee, my beta reader/everythings Sandy and Paul, and my readers who email and comment and write reviews and just generally remind me that there really are people I cannot see who share this amazing experience with me.

An extra special thanks to my husband for becoming more of a sounding board and co-conspirator (willing or otherwise) while I write this series. If you like the characters in *Founder*, you should thank him, too—without Paul's lobbying, it's very likely the body count would have been higher.

If you'd told me a year ago that I'd be writing a supernatural thriller trilogy set in West Virginia, I'm not sure if I would have laughed or given you stink eye. And yet here I am, delighted to see the result. (I can't wait to find out what happens in Book Three.) But this has not been an easy series to write. I'm grateful to everyone around me who kept a brave face, even while wondering, *What if this doesn't work?* It also has not been an easy series to market. I'm grateful to the readers who took a chance, even while thinking, *Wait, there's a psychic?* I'll continue to do my best to make sure your journey is worthwhile.

ABOUT THE AUTHOR

A recovering criminal attorney, Judy K. Walker writes from her home in Hawaii, where she is surrounded by husband, dogs, cat, and assorted geckos. Her life's journey may have taken her thousands of miles from her West Virginia origins, but she's thrilled to return to her roots in the *Dead Hollow Trilogy*. She also writes the Sydney Brennan Mysteries, a private investigator series set in Tallahassee, Florida, another of her stops along the way.

Many readers need an extra nudge to take a chance on an Indie Author, because—let's face it—they're afraid one of my dogs barfed on the keyboard and I hit "Publish." If you enjoyed *Founder*, please consider leaving a quick review on your retailer or book review site of choice—just a few lines will do. Thank you!

You can learn more about Dead Hollow and connect with me online at:
www.judykwalker.com